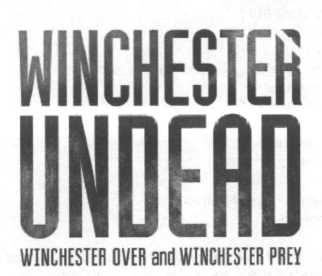

WINCHESTER UNDEAD

WINCHESTER OVER and WINCHESTER PREY

« DAVE LUND »

A PERMUTED PRESS BOOK

ISBN: 978-1-61868-670-1

WINCHESTER UNDEAD
Winchester Over (Book One) and Winchester Prey (Book Two)
© 2016 by Dave Lund
All Rights Reserved

Cover art by Dave Lund
f8industries.net

Edited by Monique Happy Editorial Services
moniquehappy.com

PERMUTED
PRESS WINLOCK PRESS

275 Madison Avenue, 14th Floor
New York, NY 10016
permutedpress.com

WINCHESTER OVER

Book One

PROLOGUE

February 13th

Bexar stopped near the creek. Using the increasing density of the trees for cover, he tried to catch his breath.

The go-bag and extra ammo bag weighed down his already-heavy load of pistol belt and chest rig. He could hear javalina on the trail, snorting in annoyance at his presence. He turned, facing the ground he had covered, scanning for threats with his rifle in the SUL, or "ready" position.

It was amazing how good life had become in Big Bend, and how quickly and drastically that had changed. His best friend and friend's son lay dead, bullet holes in their heads, fired from his own pistol. His best friend's wife was also dead, and all Bexar could do was hope that his own wife and daughter were still alive.

There hadn't been any more gunfire echoing in the mountains, but that didn't mean they were safe. His family's only hope was to get to their backup camp, their small cache site, and then hide or run.

Still breathing heavily, Bexar looked back and scanned his six once more before continuing down the trail, hopefully into the waiting arms of his wife and child.

Bexar had always planned for the end, had made extensive preparations for all sorts of eventualities, but nothing like this had ever crossed his mind. If he had only known seven weeks ago what lay ahead for his friends and family, he could have saved them. But now, he had to save himself first.

CHAPTER 1

December 26th
NORAD, Peterson Air Force Base, Colorado

There were so many new protocols, new communication requirements, and new layers of oversight that he wasn't sure information could actually get out and be useful at all. Why he couldn't just send a signal up the chain of command, get it approved, and have it shotgunned out was beyond him.

After 9/11, the U.S. Government had pushed through changes, using the Department of Homeland Security (DHS) and the Federal Emergency Management agency (FEMA), to make the timely dissemination of critical information to all the agencies and entities involved faster and more accurate. But Major Wright was frustrated with the bureaucracy. Even after all this time, he found there was a stifling of the flow of information, which put his country in danger and made his job of protecting it that much more difficult.

It was much easier as a lowly fish in the Corps of Cadets at Texas A&M. You had a fish-phone-tree, you got information, and within five minutes all thirty fish in the outfit had the information. It always seemed like a disaster drill as an eighteen-year-old fish, a freshman in the Corps of Cadets. There were countless pushups in the hallway, getting "smoked" by your sophomore Pissheads—looking back, it was quite possibly the happiest time of his life, even though at the time it was exceptionally hard.

Having attended Texas A&M University on a Reserve Officer Training Corps, or "ROTC" scholarship, Major Wright was happy that his former squadron in the Corps of Cadets was standing high in the rankings to win the General Moore Award this year. Wright decided at that moment he would put in to take some vacation for once, and go back and sit in The Chicken, drink cold Shiner, and play bones until "Rose Colored Glasses" played over the bar's speakers. Maybe he could make some calls and actually get tickets to the usually sold-out home football games.

As Wright sat staring past the glass wall of his office into the "bullpen," the group of consoles and computers manned by the airmen, he noticed Airman Jones suddenly become very animated. The young enlisted man waved over Technical Sergeant Arcuni to look at his screen, and whatever Arcuni saw on the screen caused the blood to drain from his face. Arcuni locked eyes with Wright, abruptly snapping him out of his daydreams. Arcuni rarely got excited about much of anything—a former skydiving instructor for the Wings of Blue at the U.S. Air Force Academy, he had developed a steel constitution when it came to high stress and deadly surprises.

Wright stepped out of his office to see what could possibly have made Arcuni and Jones so agitated. Arcuni quickly tapped through a series of keystrokes on his computer, and the console's imagery appeared on the main screen on the bullpen wall. The screen showed a large flight of heavy aircraft flying over the polar cap towards North America. The aircraft were not using transponders, but the advanced computer identification software used by NORAD for just such an event identified the flight as possibly Chinese Xian H-6Ks.

Recent intelligence reports put the total Chinese inventory of all the variations of the H-6 bomber at one hundred fifty aircraft. Looking at the display, it was apparent that if those numbers were accurate, every one of those aircraft was now inbound towards the continental United States. Wright reached for the handset at Jones' workstation, dialed five numbers, and waited for Colonel Garnett to answer.

"Colonel, we have a problem."

Brazos County, Texas

After the fifth traffic stop that morning during which the driver had simply yelled at him, Bexar regretted not using some vacation time to stay at home with his family the day after Christmas.

Officer Bexar Reed was what is referred to in the police world as a "motor," a motorcycle officer tasked with the primary focus of enforcing traffic law. The last driver who had yelled at him prior to speeding off had been traveling fifteen miles per hour over the posted speed limit, yet he had blamed Bexar for everything from entrapment to ruining Christmas.

While Bexar was getting yelled at for trying to keep drivers safe, his young daughter and wife were at home enjoying a lazy day around the house. Jessica Reed, who everyone called Jessie, was a math teacher at one of the local high schools, so she had the privilege of enjoying a lengthy Christmas break.

Starting his motorcycle, Bexar decided to drop off his tickets at the station and go home. The only people at work today were the required patrol officers and their sergeants; not even the patrol lieutenant had come to work, simply telling the sergeants to call him if something came up.

Bexar checked back in service with Dispatch, then rolled on the throttle for the short ride back to the station. This was the best part of the job—getting paid to ride a motorcycle every day. The weather was cold and sometimes wet, and the summers were beyond brutal with all the required equipment and uniform he wore, but still the ride was worth it. Bexar put up his mental "blinders," doing his best to ignore any traffic violations around him with the intent of heading home.

In short order, Bexar pulled his motorcycle into the sally port at the police station, retrieved the few citations he had written that morning out of his saddle bag, and walked into the building to drop them in the lockbox for court. Before leaving, he wanted to check in with the patrol sergeants but found their offices empty. The report writing area was empty as well, although the patrol parking area was full of patrol cars.

Checking the patrol briefing room, Bexar found nearly the entire shift of officers and both patrol sergeants watching a movie on the projection screen typically used for training. Sergeant House, the officer in charge, looked at Bexar and said, "Be-X-aR, why're you still here? Why don't you head to the house for the rest of the day?" Like the county in Texas, Bexar's name was pronounced "Bear," but the sergeant liked to poke fun at him.

"Thanks, exactly what I was thinking, Sergeant. Hizzouse," Bexar replied. He could hear House laughing as he walked out of the room and back towards his motorcycle.

Bexar shrugged on his heavy leather riding jacket, pulled on his helmet and gloves, started his bike, and pulled out of the parking lot. He had gone just three blocks when the warbling alert tone coming across the radio filled the speakers in his helmet with a screeching sound. It was the tone used by dispatch for felonies in progress such as burglaries, assault with a deadly weapon, or for other serious situations like an active shooter.

Bexar pulled into a side street and stopped, waiting to hear the call details so he could respond. These were the times he missed a patrol car, just for the

Mobile Data Computer. The MDC in patrol vehicles displayed the call information so officers didn't have to wait for Dispatch's description. Better yet, officers could tap the screen of the computer and it displayed a map showing the exact location of the call. Bexar had no MDC on his motorcycle, so he had to rely on his memory and his knowledge of the city. Every tool he needed to be the best traffic cop he could be was wired into the motorcycle, pushing the weight of his motor to over nine hundred pounds, but when it came to the tools needed to do routine patrol work, there was simply no room on the bike.

When the alert tone finally ended, the dispatcher, sounding very keyed up, came across the radio and announced, "All units be advised, reports of imminent attack on the United States, warplanes en route and expected to cross the border within the hour, authority NAWAS EOC!"

It took Bexar a second to remember that NAWAS was the National Warning System. Moments later he heard his patrol lieutenant, who had obviously been contacted at home, direct all units to 10-19 PD, order Sergeant House, the OIC, to call his cellphone, and advise that he was en route to the EOC.

The EOC, or Emergency Operations Center, had been built to endure a variety of natural and manmade disasters, unlike the police department headquarters, which was constructed of glass and was built to look good for the city. It had been some time since Bexar had heard a 10-19 used over the radio; it meant return immediately to a specified location. After 9/11, all but a small handful of police and emergency 10-codes had been outlawed for local law enforcement by DHS. Each police department had their own variation of the 10-codes, so the idea was that by eliminating most of the codes and using plain language to communicate with each other, it would simplify inter-agency communication.

Bexar hadn't moved. He sat on his idling motorcycle and stared at his radio, not sure what his next move should be. Finally, he looked up from his radio, took his cellphone out of his uniform shirt pocket, and sent a text message to Malachi Laing, his best friend, and Jack Snyder. The text simply read: "WINCHESTER."

Tucking the phone back in his pocket, Bexar put his bike in gear and turned on the emergency lights and siren before speeding off. But instead of turning left towards the EOC, he rolled on the throttle and turned right.

Grayson County, Texas

Malachi Laing, still in his underwear, sat in front of his computer in the home office he had built. He always found the holidays tiring, but this year he was also the on-call IT administrator for a large web-based business outside the Dallas area, so he found himself even more tired and annoyed than usual.

Frustrated, Malachi was actively fighting off, and trying to fix, the damage from a series of DOS attacks against his company's enterprise servers. If he couldn't get this situation handled, he would have to make the drive into the physical office, ninety minutes away.

Fully engrossed in his task, Malachi nearly didn't hear the ding from his cellphone telling him he had a new text message. He assumed it was yet another executive telling him there was something wrong with their e-mail, but was surprised to see it was from Bexar.

Stunned, he read the one-word text over and over again, his mind not fully accepting what he saw. Picking up the remote, he turned up the volume on the big LCD TV mounted on the wall, which was as usual tuned to Fox News. He was just able to catch the end of a report from the lawn of the White House, "... officials recommend sheltering in place, stay indoors ..."

Malachi didn't hear the rest of the report. The remote fell out of his hand as he quickly stood, yelling, "Amber, get The Bags, it's time to go, fucking WINCHESTER!"

Arlington, Texas

Jack Snyder was tending to his winter garden with his wife Sandra while their seven-year-old son Will played in the yard with the new toys he had unwrapped the previous morning for Christmas. A few years earlier, Jack and Sandra had begun learning what many in the Dallas/Fort Worth Metroplex considered "old-world" skills, with the idea that the modern conveniences enjoyed now would someday be gone. Their first project was to start a simple garden, which had grown to take over most of their backyard. From the back porch, Jack could hear the chime of a new message on his cellphone, but decided to ignore it; the office could wait until tomorrow. But Will jumped up and ran over to retrieve the phone for his dad; since he was too young to be allowed to touch the phone without supervision, Will looked for any opportunity to play with the phone without getting in trouble.

"Dad!" called Will. "It's from Bexar and it says 'Winchester' like the gun. What does that mean?"

Jack dropped his trowel and ran inside to turn the TV to Fox News. He knew that if Bexar called "Winchester," something big was going down.

CHAPTER 2

NORAD

In quick order, Colonel Garnett had sounded the alarm up the chain of command, and the two Air National Guard F-15C aircraft patrolling the northwestern corner of the Continental United States had been rerouted to intercept the new threat just identified by Major Wright.

16,000 ft. above Wyoming

Lieutenant Colonel Dorsey had retired from active duty in the Air Force four years ago, but had since joined the Air National Guard and was assigned to the 186th Fighter Squadron, which flew out of Great Falls International Airport in Montana. Although it was a long drive from his home in Kalispell, Dorsey didn't mind so much, because he was still able to strap into his high performance fighter aircraft and enjoy his first love, flying. Today he was on station with his wingman Major Futch, making lazy laps around the northwestern region of CONUS, the CONtinental United States.

Dorsey and Futch weren't just colleagues. Out in the real world they were also good friends, often spending hours hiking together around Glacier National Park. For Dorsey, after thousands of hours in the cockpit of an F-15, it was easy to let his mind wander, and he found himself wishing for the thaw after the long winter that would see the reopening of Montana's beautiful Going-To-The-Sun Road.

Dorsey was brought crashing back to reality when the controller's voice abruptly broke through the silence in his helmet, directing them to fly north immediately, over the Canadian border, to intercept a large flight of possible Chinese heavy bombers. Snapping the wings to the left, pulling back on the control stick, and pushing the throttle all the way forward, Dorsey and his wingman were now rocketing straight towards a possible threat to their country.

Dread began building in the pit of Dorsey's stomach. Usually, if they were sent to intercept another aircraft while on patrol, it was typically a private pilot who had violated a Notice to Airmen, restricting an area of flight privileges. Today, Dorsey was sure he would be intercepting enemy aircraft. Not only were he and Futch about to see their first air combat since serving in the first Gulf War, it would be the first time either of them had to engage an enemy so close to home.

The White House

The President sat at his desk in the Oval Office, reading over a bill he was hoping to introduce soon, one that was rumored within the political circles of Washington, D.C. to grant amnesty to any and all persons who were currently in the country illegally.

Chris McFarland had heard the bill being planned and discussed long before this day, and it really bothered him. The consequences of such a bill being passed into law seriously jeopardized the security and sanctity of the United States. However, as an agent of the Secret Service, and as the head of the Presidential Protection Detail, not only could he not talk about what he knew was coming, there was also nothing he could do about it.

Listening as a series of standard check-ins were conducted with all the agents currently on duty, McFarland began walking towards the Security Command Room to get a cup of coffee when a single word was heard firmly and clearly over the radio, and any thoughts of coffee instantly disappeared.

He pushed into the Oval Office with four other agents, practically picking up the President and hustling him out a secret exit to the right of the desk. As the President began to protest, McFarland said, "Mr. President, we are under attack. You must evacuate!"

In less than thirty seconds, McFarland and the other agents had emerged with the President onto the White House lawn, where they were met by one of the Secret Service Quick Response Teams. The QRT did not look like the other agents, who were wearing specially tailored suits—the QRT were dressed all in black with a full tactical load-out, looking to the casual observer like a police SWAT team. In reality, they were much more highly trained than most police department SWAT, even the fabled LAPD teams.

Forming a protective formation around the President, the group moved quickly towards the Marine helicopter just landing on the lawn, and as they placed the President inside sans salutes and ceremony, the rest of the First Family were also escorted onto the helicopter. McFarland followed the President inside, buckling the seatbelt of the POTUS while talking into his radio to coordinate with the Secret Service team standing by with Air Force One, which was starting its engines on the tarmac at Andrews Air Force Base. Less than twenty minutes after the code word had been spoken, McFarland smiled as the wheels of Air Force One left the runway. He had successfully evacuated the President.

Northern Montana

Lieutenant Colonel Dorsey scanned the sky ahead of the nose of his F-15C while pushing the fighter as fast as it would fly towards the incoming flight of heavy bombers. Before making the Canadian border, Dorsey was told by one of the controllers that the bombers had split into three groups: one headed for the West Coast, one flying towards the center of the country, and the last group flying towards the East Coast. Dorsey and his wingman, Major Futch, changed their flight path to intercept the group of bombers headed towards the West Coast.

Twenty minutes after the change in direction, Dorsey looked at the display and the data from the AN/APG-70 radar, confirmed a lock, and was given clearance to engage the bombers. The plane shuddered as, one by one, he launched the entire complement of AMRAAM (Advanced Medium-Range Air-to-Air Missiles) loaded onto his plane that morning. He heard Futch over the radio informing Control that they were Winchester, having spent their complement of missiles, but to Dorsey's surprise, Control ordered them to continue to engage with the plane's mounted 20mm Gatling gun until other air assets could reach the threat.

Surprised but willing, Dorsey and Futch continued towards the bomber threat. Approaching the flight, Dorsey pushed his fighter high above the large formation of bombers, and dove the plane with the sun at his back. Pulling up and away from their first engagement with the 20mm Gatling, Dorsey keyed his mic. "Did you see any windows?"

"No, not a one," replied Futch. "Couldn't tell what it was, but there's something under their wings. Looks like the spray unit under a crop duster. Also, those pilots either have balls of steel, or there aren't any pilots at all; not a single plane moved position, course, or speed."

"Okay Major," Dorsey responded, "I'm coming back around. I'm going to come in slow and from behind the flight. If they're drones, let's take our time and make each round count."

Over the next few minutes, Dorsey and Futch were able to down twenty aircraft, but another forty bombers remained in flight, never changing speed or direction as they continued south towards the major population centers of the West Coast. Out of ammo and dangerously low on fuel, the two pilots changed course towards the refueling waypoint, where a Boeing KC-135 Stratotanker was on station and waiting to give them enough fuel to get home and re-arm.

What neither of them saw was that, as they pulled away to refuel, the modified H-6 bombers began releasing a chemical spray from the apparatus under their wings, leaving a deadly trail in the sky to fall to the ground and onto the people below.

NORAD

Major Wright was monitoring the three flights of Chinese bombers over the country. Each flight had been engaged by various fighters and all had reported the same thing. The H-6 bombers appeared to have been modified to fly as drones, and they all appeared to have some type of spray apparatus under their wings.

One fighter pilot on the East Coast had just reported that the bombers had begun spraying some sort of substance into the air, when Technical Sergeant Arcuni yelled across the room, "Major, missile launch detected off the coast of California!"

Twenty miles off the Southern California coast

Lieutenant Commander Boyd moved the collective of the Eurocopter HH-65 Dolphin he was piloting towards the projected path of a speedboat headed towards the coast. A fishing vessel had radioed a sighting on the Coast Guard frequency, and his Dolphin helicopter had been sent to intercept. The technology war between the Coast Guard and drug smugglers was at a fevered pitch, with drug smugglers now using high-powered speedboats to run drugs, boats that could outpace the ships currently in the Coast Guard inventory. But his Dolphin could keep up with the speedboat, and once they found the boat, could disable it with the mounted 50-cal machine gun.

Boyd smiled, but wasn't overly excited. This was the third intercept this month, and he could only expect more with the new year.

A large missile suddenly erupted from the blue ocean directly in front of his flight path. Boyd pulled hard aft on the cyclic and yanked the collective into his armpit, over-torqueing the engines, but it was too late. With too much speed and too little altitude to avoid the impending impact, Boyd's copilot never even had a chance to transmit what they had seen before the forty-three-foot-long JL-2 missile slammed into the speeding Dolphin helicopter.

The helicopter exploded in a large fireball, in turn piercing the fuel tank of the nuclear ballistic missile and creating an even larger explosion. The other three missiles had cleared the explosion made by the helicopter and were quickly gaining altitude, but pieces of the first missile, and what was left of the helicopter, fell to the surface of the water.

Fifty feet below, the captain of the Jin-Class ballistic Chinese submarine wasn't exactly sure why one of the missiles he had launched had failed and then exploded, but the tremendous shockwave created by the explosion had caused significant damage to his boat. The captain would never learn the fate of the new world he was helping to create, for his submarine was fatally damaged, taking on large amounts of water and descending quickly towards the ocean floor.

CHAPTER 3

NORAD

"Major, missile launch detected, approximately twenty miles off the coast of Southern California!" Major Wright looked up at the main screen on the large wall of displays as Technical Sergeant Arcuni typed the command to put his display on the screen.

"Major, three inbound, computer projections put one traveling towards the East Coast, possible target New York City. Second is projected for Little Rock, and the third is ... DETONATION! We have a high altitude detonation! Possible EMP attack over the West Coast, approximately ten miles above Las Vegas!"

Major Wright engaged his handset and grimly informed Colonel Garnett that the Midwest, as well as the East Coast, had been targeted for an electromagnetic pulse, or EMP, attack from the sea-launched intercontinental ballistic missiles (ICBMs).

Lake Elsinore, California

Just landing from an Accelerated Free Fall instruction skydive, Bill pulled the Motorola handheld radio out of his jumpsuit pocket to start talking his student down under canopy. After trying to key the radio three times, switching it off and back on, he realized it wasn't functioning about the same time he heard a pop and felt his parachute container shift.

Looking over his shoulder, he could see that his reserve pilot chute had deployed, and realized that the pop he heard was probably the Automatic Actuation Device firing and cutting the closing loop for his reserve parachute.

Bill looked back at his student and saw that the student's reserve parachute was beginning to deploy behind the first student jumper, giving the first jump student a two-canopy-out malfunction. From inside the drop zone office, someone was yelling that they had lost power, and as he looked to the runway approach he saw that the Twin Otter that was landing had lost power to its engines.

Within seconds, everything had simply stopped working.

In the meantime, Bill's student had not reacted to the two-out scenario as he had been taught in the First Jump Course, but had let the canopies pull apart and rotate into a down plane. He was plummeting straight down towards the ground at seventy miles per hour.

Shrugging out of his parachute harness, Bill began running to where his student had impacted the ground. The student was still alive, but barely so, with obviously broken bones in his legs and arms. Bill began trying to stabilize the student's neck, yelling to Steven, the drop zone manager, for the trauma bag and to call 911.

Bill looked back up at the other tandem pairs still in the air and saw that they were fighting their own two-out malfunctions. He then noticed three large, high-flying aircraft passing overhead in formation, each trailing a thick, dark cloud that looked nothing like a contrail.

Steven came running with the trauma bag and began stabilizing the student, but they were suddenly covered by a thick, oily substance raining down from the sky.

Distracted, they paused for a moment, then looked back at the student only to see his body shudder with a dying breath. Steven checked for a pulse, checked for breathing, and, finding neither, closed the dead skydiver's eyes.

Bill cursed, and Steven began gathering the medical supplies he had dumped out of the trauma bag. As they both stood to walk back to the hangar, the dead student suddenly sat upright and grabbed Bill's jumpsuit, pulling him off his feet and onto the ground.

Steven could only scream as the dead student, moaning loudly, grabbed Bill and bit violently into his throat, spraying blood across the three of them. Now covered in oil and blood, Steven dropped the medic bag and ran for the hangar.

Brazos County, Texas

Bexar leaned forward over the tank of his motorcycle, rolling the throttle back as far as it would go. The LED emergency lights were flashing, the siren was blaring, and Bexar had his motorcycle accelerating well over one hundred miles per hour as he rounded the curve leading to the entrance to his neighborhood.

Bexar brought the motorcycle upright and stood on the brakes hard enough that the ABS caused the tires to chirp and the bike to shudder. Scrubbing enough speed, he pushed the handlebars and, as he let the bike lean over to make the turn into his neighborhood, the motorcycle suddenly lost power, the siren quit blaring, and the LED lights stopped flashing.

The LCD display for his radio and video recording system were also blank, and Bexar was surrounded by silence as he rounded the corner and let the motorcycle coast into the corner gas station. Bexar noticed that all the station lights were out, and the clerk was walking out the front door, looking bewildered.

Bexar stopped the bike. As he looked back at the intersection he saw that the traffic signal was dark, and the cars on the road were rolling to a stop. He needed to get home, but he still had another mile to go.

Pulling off his helmet, Bexar opened both saddle bags and retrieved the medical trauma pouch containing a CPR mask, two tourniquets, Israeli bandages, and a Quick Clot pouch. He also grabbed the box of spare CR123A batteries that powered his weapon light and tactical light. The last thing he retrieved was the most important item in a motorcop's saddle bag next to his ticket book—his water jug.

Starting off in a slow jog towards his house, made difficult by his knee-high leather motor boots, Bexar heard a low rumble coming from the west. Glancing over, he saw a plume of smoke rising from the direction of Texas A&M University. The smoke wasn't unusual, since the Brayton Fire Training Field was over in the same direction, next to the Easterwood Field airport, but the rolling sound of an explosion, followed by a second and a third, was.

Grayson County, Texas

After receiving Bexar's text message, Malachi changed into a pair of tactical pants, with a rigger's belt holding up his XD .40 caliber pistol in a Blade Tech holster. Malachi's long beard completed the look of a mall-ninja with his tactical gear, but the gear actually had purpose.

Malachi and his wife Amber were quickly loading their old International Scout with their Get Out Of Dodge bags, their bug-out food, some spare MREs, water, and all the ammo they could load. Most of their GOOD load was already packed in their AT Chaser off-road camping trailer, since they had planned to leave in a hurry to make the rendezvous with the other two families.

Amber put the last of the Meals, Ready-to-Eat (MREs) and the last case of .223 ammo in the Scout before making a final sweep of the house with her GOOD checklist. She had to make sure they weren't leaving anything essential; they had a long trip ahead of them.

Malachi cursed himself that they hadn't completed a practice load-out like Jack had told them to; he was quickly running out of room in the little Scout and trailer. Luckily, he had installed overload springs on the old 4X4, and had upgraded the axles to DANA 60s the year before, but hadn't had the chance to change out the old straight-six for a 350 V8 as he had planned. At least the old motor had been rebuilt a couple of years ago and ran reliably.

Amber came back out to the driveway after finishing her GOOD checklist, and was pushing the button on the garage door opener to close the garage door, but it was not responding. Malachi looked across the street and noticed that the neighbor's Christmas lights had gone off. He then realized the whole neighborhood had lost power.

"Pull the cord and drop the garage door by hand, I'll get the truck started. We need to get out of here." Malachi took his cellphone out of his pocket to pull up the GPS route to the rendezvous point, but the phone wouldn't turn on. The new Pioneer stereo he had installed in the Scout last month also wouldn't turn on, nor would the iPod in the center console.

At least the truck had started, Malachi thought, before it dawned on him. "Amber, I think we just had an EMP event. No wonder Bexar called 'Winchester.' Pull out one of the ARs and get some spare mags loaded; this trip might get interesting." After a few moments, Amber was in the passenger seat of the Scout, the rifle in her lap, and Malachi was pulling out of their driveway, thankful that his old Scout still ran a vacuum-advanced distributor with points, and that he hadn't upgraded to an electronic ignition.

Arlington, Texas

Jack and Sandra finished their GOOD load-out in about the time they had expected. Over the past two years, Jack had insisted that they practice loading the

Toyota Land Cruiser FJ45V with their gear so they'd know if the gear would fit. He had purchased the old FJ about six years ago and started restoring it. The birth of their son Will had slowed the project due to money and time, but Jack had at least rebuilt the old straight-six to be tough and reliable.

He had also sprayed the truck with Line-X inside and out, instead of using a traditional paint job. The roof had a full length roof rack, and Jack had fabricated a rack across the back bumper that held their full-sized spare tire and six, five-gallon "jerry cans" of gas. The axles and suspension had been beefed up from stock, and Jack was happy with what he had built, especially when he and Sandra had gotten interested in prepping with their friend Bexar.

It had been two hours since Jack had received Bexar's text, and in that time the power in the house had gone out and both of their cellphones had stopped working. But now with their GOOD load-out complete, Will was strapped into his seatbelt in the back seat, and the family was heading out towards the rendezvous cache site to meet Bexar and Malachi.

From what Jack had seen on the news before the power went out, there was widespread looting at area Wal-Marts and grocery stores, civil unrest, and a police force that was overwhelmed—they needed to stay off the Interstates and try to take a much-less-traveled route, even if it took longer.

Jack planned to take surface roads until he could get to State Highway 287 that traveled to Mansfield. They were trying to reach a piece of land just outside of Maypearl, Texas, home of the old Assembly of God Royal Ranger's campgrounds. The group had chosen the location two years ago as a central rally point and the site of their survival cache.

Jack, Malachi, and Bexar had grown up there, in the semi-obscure, church-based scouting organization, learning how to become woodsmen and men of moral character. They had spent many a summer on the side of the lake, camping on one side and attending the church youth camp on the other.

Two years ago, without permission and under complete secrecy, the group had found a remote location on those campgrounds and built up a large cache of supplies they might need for long-term survival in the case of a social and economic collapse in the U.S. It would also be a rally point in case of invasion or other major disaster that would leave society and the government in upheaval. Jack knew that, in the worst case, he and Sandra had enough supplies in their GOOD load-out to survive for at least three weeks.

Living so close to the Dallas/Fort Worth International Airport, the constant drone of overhead commercial aircraft had become background noise to Jack and

Sandra. It was the silence in the sky above him that drew Jack's attention now. There were no planes in the air.

He could hear gunfire in the distance. Looking back in the direction of the airport, he could see several plumes of thick, black smoke rising into the air. "Damn," said Jack, "must've been an EMP; it's the only way that all of this would stop working and cause the aircraft to fail."

Sandra looked at him in horror. "There were hundreds of people on those planes."

Nodding his head, Jack replied, "If it happened here, let's hope it didn't happen everywhere. There's something like ten thousand aircraft in the air above the U.S. at any given time during the day." Dreading the trip ahead of them, Jack put the FJ in gear and pulled out onto the street behind his house.

Brazos County, Texas

It took thirty minutes, but Bexar finally made it home to his wife, Jessie, who had become increasingly anxious. After the power went out at the house, Jessie had begun to worry because her cellphone also didn't work, and she was now in near hysterics with the sound of the rolling explosions in the distance.

"Dammit Bexar, you could have called me or sent me a text or something! I'm your wife!"

"I'm sorry baby," he replied. "I didn't expect the motorcycle to die on me, and I would have been home a half-hour ago if that didn't happen. Once I knew something was wrong, I was running Code-3 to the house."

"Can you do that, won't you be in trouble?" asked Jessie.

"At this point, I really don't care. Besides, they were calling us back to the department when I fled for the house. I'm reasonably sure if this isn't what I think it is, I'll probably get fired."

Bexar changed out of his uniform while Jessie began loading up their old Jeep Wagoneer. Their two-year-old daughter Keeley was still napping, which made loading the Jeep with their GOOD bags much easier. Jessie hated the old 1965 Jeep Wagoneer, but Bexar had owned it since high school and couldn't bring himself to get rid of it. That old Jeep was like his first love, and it would have broken his heart to sell it. Bexar was happy to have it after he and Jack had started prepping; the old reliable truck with no electronics other than a new CD player had its advantages for a prepper.

Bexar took off his Kevlar vest and put it aside, along with his heavy police duty belt. Even though neither was part of his planned GOOD load-out, he felt they might be needed. He changed into a pair of green tactical pants with a rigger's belt that held his well-worn Kimber TLE/RL II Pro with a TLR-1 tactical light in a Raven Systems holster. Two spare Wilson Combat 8-round magazines slid into a mag pouch on his left side, and his trusted Emerson CQC-7 clipped to the inside of his back pocket. Bexar slid his custom-made C-M Forge knife into the sheath on his belt, and went back outside to help Jessie finish loading the Jeep.

Three hours after the massive power failure had hit, Bexar Reed's family pulled out of their driveway and turned north on State Highway 6 towards the group cache site in Maypearl.

CHAPTER 4

Virginia Beach, Virginia

Eric had just finished patrolling the beachfront on his police bicycle and begun riding back to the station when his supervisor's voice came across the radio, instructing all units to return to their designated patrol zones—NAWAS had issued a warning that an attack on the U.S. was imminent. Not sure what sort of attack that could mean, Eric downshifted and peddled back towards his area of responsibility on the beachfront.

Stopping at the traffic light, Eric saw some people pointing towards the sky. Looking up, he saw a large formation of aircraft overhead. The planes did not look familiar to him; even though he wasn't an aviation buff, he was used to seeing large military aircraft in the Virginia Beach sky, but these looked different.

The contrails trailing the aircraft also looked different, less like contrails and more like what you would see coming from beneath a crop duster. Still watching the aircraft, Eric pulled out his phone to call his wife, but it was dead. "Figures," he grumbled, angry that his brand new smart phone was already failing. He had given up his trusted "dumb" flip phone for this new phone two weeks ago because his daughter was about to have her first baby, and he wanted to get photos when it happened.

Then he heard the sound of tires skidding on pavement and the unmistakable sound of a motorcycle sliding on pavement. The traffic lights were all dark, and a motorcyclist was sliding headfirst towards the intersection where a truck had already come to a stop in the middle. A dark, oily mist was falling from the sky, and Eric knew this was going to be a bad wreck.

Pedaling towards the collision, Eric tried to call Dispatch on his radio and was surprised to find that his radio wasn't working either. The accident was bad. The motorcyclist was wearing a half-shell helmet but it was obvious that his neck had been broken when he slid headfirst into the stalled truck. Eric knew the rider was DRT—dead right there—by looking at the rider's neck, which was bent at an impossible angle, but he pulled on a latex glove and checked for a pulse anyway. There was none.

Looking at the motorcyclist's lifeless brown eyes, Eric pulled the glove off and tossed it on the ground. "Sorry buddy, what a shitty way to go." As he began to stand up, he saw the rider's head move slightly in his direction. Eric had seen enough freshly dead to know that sometimes the body will spasm slightly as it shuts down, but he was startled by the gargling moan that rattled from the rider's chest. Pausing, he looked more closely at the rider; the head and eyes had moved and locked onto his, but the eyes still looked dim and lifeless. Without warning, the motorcyclist's gloved hand shot up, and, with incredible strength, latched onto the lapel of Eric's police shirt, pulling him down to an impossibly wide mouth.

Bystanders who had seen the accident screamed as the downed motorcyclist savagely bit into the police officer's throat, tearing away chunks of flesh as the officer writhed and screamed in pain. They remained rooted in fear as the motorcyclist stood, head flopping awkwardly to one side, and began stumbling towards them.

U.S. Highway 287, Texas

Jack and Sandra and their son Will were making fairly decent time on the highway in their old FJ. So far the traffic wasn't too heavy, and the only cars they saw were a couple of older vehicles; everything else had stopped dead in the road. Occasionally Jack had to drive on the shoulder around people who had given up and started walking away from their abandoned cars.

Pulling onto the inside shoulder to drive around another group, he saw that they were pointing up to the sky. Slowing to a stop, Jack got out of his truck and stood next to it, looking up at the sky. Traveling from the north was a formation of large aircraft that he didn't recognize, and didn't look like anything he had ever seen at an air show either. He assumed this was probably the reason Bexar had called "Winchester." Climbing back into his truck, he saw an oily film suddenly cover his truck and windshield.

"What's that, honey?" Sandra said.

"I don't know," replied Jack, "but I think it fell from those planes that just flew over." Once again climbing out of the old truck, he poured water out of his bottle onto the windshield and wiped it clean. Everything around him was covered in the oil. Jack started the truck, drove around another group of stalled cars, and continued south.

Approaching the city of Mansfield, the Snyder family came upon a group of people gathered around a man lying in the middle of the highway. They were kneeling around the body, a large pool of blood spreading out around them. "Sandra, get behind the wheel. If something happens, come get me," Jack said as he exited the truck. Sandra slid over to the driver's seat, put the truck in gear, and waited.

As Jack walked up to the group, he immediately knew something was very wrong. There were five of them, and they weren't administering first aid, they were eating the entrails out of the still-steaming body on the ground. Choking back the bile that rose in his throat, Jack drew the Kimber Pro-Carry he carried in a custom leather holster on his right hip and instinctively pulled the pistol into the SUL position on his chest. "What is wrong with ya'll, stop what you're doing!" he shouted.

One of the group turned his head towards Jack and rose shakily to his feet. He was wearing an Army uniform with a name tag that read Jones, and the insignia on his short-sleeved shirt showed he was a staff sergeant. He also had a horrific gash on his neck. The front of his shirt was covered in blood, and pieces of flesh hung from his teeth, his gaping mouth still dripping blood from the victim on the ground.

As Jones began stumbling towards Jack, a deep gurgling moan came from the large hole in his neck. Jack's hands were shaking, but he pointed the muzzle of his 1911 at Jones and shouted, "What the fuck? Stop! Stop or I will shoot you. STOP!"

The thing that used to be Jones did not seem fazed by Jack or his pistol; Jack fired twice center mass with no effect. Taking a deep breath, Jack raised the muzzle a fraction of an inch higher and fired a single round into Jones' forehead. Jones dropped to the ground and was still, but the other four that had ignored the exchange while they feasted on the entrails of their victim all stood and turned towards Jack.

"Holy shit, SANDRA!" Without bothering to holster his pistol, Jack turned and sprinted towards his FJ as Sandra began rolling forward, trying to close the twenty-five-yard distance between them, and slammed on the brakes as she neared. Jack never broke stride in his sprint, placed his foot on the big steel bumper, and jumped onto the hood of his truck. Grabbing the roof rack with his left hand, his adrenaline racing, he screamed "GO! DRIVE, DAMNIT, GO!" Sandra dropped the clutch, pushed her right foot to the floor, and drove through two of the creatures shambling towards them.

With Jack on the hood of the FJ, hanging onto the roof rack, Sandra drove until they were out of the small town of Mansfield. Pulling to the side of the highway, he climbed down, still shaking, pulled the magazine out of his pistol, and traded it for the one on his belt. Tactical reload complete, Jack looked at the dents on the front of his truck and turned to Sandra.

"I don't know what the fuck that was, but that guy shouldn't have been alive. He shouldn't have been able to get up, he shouldn't have been able to absorb two rounds to the chest, and he sure as shit shouldn't have been eating the other guy. What the shit?"

Eyes wide, Sandra replied, her voice trembling, "I don't know babe, but the sooner we get to the cache site, the sooner we can talk to Bexar. Maybe he has an idea of what's going on."

State Highway 6, Central Texas

Highway 6 was rarely all that busy since it had been expanded from a two-lane highway back when he was attending Texas A&M, but even with most of the cars stopped in the road Bexar was making good time in the Wagoneer.

The original Get Out Of Dodge plan had the family traveling Highway 6 to I-35 in Waco, where they could make their way to Maypearl in quick and easy time. However, during the drive to the little town of Hearne, Jessie had come up with a good point—if everything with electronics, including newer cars, was dead, Waco might be dangerous, and the I-35 would probably be a parking lot.

Over the years, Bexar had learned many things about his wife, one of which being that she was usually right. Agreeing with her, Bexar decided to take Texas Highway 14 to Mexia, a small Texas town famous for being the birthplace of Anna Nicole Smith.

In Hearne, people walked in the streets, around cars that had stopped in the road. Bexar heard gunfire in the not-too-far distance and wasn't surprised. Hearne, Texas was the only place in the world where Wal-Mart had to shutter their store due to rampant employee theft.

Scanning the road and side streets for threats, he pushed his Jeep a little faster than he would have liked through the maze of parked cars. Just as they drove past the big new gas station on the north end of town, their front right tire went flat.

"Well ain't that just our luck? Jess, we're really exposed, grab my rifle and pull guard for us while I change this damned thing." Bexar climbed out of the Jeep, pulled the highlift jack down from the side of the roof rack, grabbed the four-way lug wrench out of the box on the rear bumper, and unbolted the spare tire from the back of the truck.

Jessie climbed out of the truck with Bexar's favorite rifle. Last year he had splurged and built it off a Noveske Lower Receiver and a LaRue Tactical Upper with a full length quadrail. A bunch of Magpul furniture was used, and the flat top rifle had a mounted ACOG red-dot sight. It cost Bexar a lot of money to build that rifle, but he was happy to have it and, as a cop, he could write the rifle off on his taxes as a "work" expense.

As Bexar put the highlift back in its place on the roof rack and began bolting the flat tire and rim to the back of the Jeep, he heard Jessie call, "Stop or you will be shot." Bexar threw the four-way into the back of the Jeep and turned to see where Jessie was pointing the rifle's muzzle. In the blink of an eye, Bexar drew his pistol and pointed it at the man stumbling towards them from across the highway.

"Sir, stop where you are or you will be shot," she shouted again. "Sir, stop!" The man stumbled closer, his clothes covered in blood, his head flopped to the side at an impossible angle, and bite marks covering his face. His left eye was missing, along with some of the flesh on the left side of his face.

Bexar joined in. "Dude, fucking stop or you'll be shot!" The man continued to stagger towards the Jeep, crossing the yellow line on the road. The AR-15 Jessie held cracked once, and a single round tore through the blood-covered chest of the man. Bexar whispered "Jesus" as he put two .45 hollow point slugs into the man's chest, and then one in the middle of the man's forehead. The back of the man's head exploded and the body fell to the ground.

Bexar pulled his pistol into the SUL position and, as he scanned the surroundings for more threats, he told Jessie, "Get in the Jeep, keep the rifle out, something is really wrong, go!" Jessie climbed into the passenger seat, leaving her seatbelt off, and turned around to calm Keeley, who was screaming in the back seat. Bexar started the truck and drove north towards TX-14 as fast as he could. They had to get to Maypearl, to the safety of the group cache and the safety of their friends.

CHAPTER 5

South of Gunter, Texas

Malachi had always known that his route to the cache site was the worst out of the three, because he had to drive through or around D/FW, but he also knew there really wasn't a better site for all the members in the group. He drove south on TX-289 and through Gunter, Texas, trying to avoid the bigger towns in the Metroplex, although he wasn't sure if it would work. Getting to Gunter was relatively painless; the traffic was light to begin with, so when the EMP hit there weren't all that many cars to drive around. They passed a number of people on foot and pushing shopping carts. Some had their carts loaded with beer, others had televisions and Playstations and such. *If they knew the truth, they would've stuck with the beer*, he thought.

"NMP," he said aloud.

"What?" said Amber, turning to look at him.

"Not my problem. All these people, Amber, I have to remember that it's not my problem. We can't stop to help, and they won't listen to us if we try to help them make better choices, all of them. I just have to remember they're not my problem."

"Do you think those are our planes?" Amber asked, pointing up through the windshield. A number of large aircraft were traveling in formation to the south from the north.

"The contrails look wrong, like they're spraying something, like they're actual chemtrails," he responded. Malachi didn't buy into most conspiracy theories, such as stories of a secret base under Denver International Airport, or that shapeshifting alien reptiles secretly ruled the earth, but he did find them entertaining enough to read about them on occasion. Overall, it was staggering what some people believed, and how large of a following their beliefs could generate on the Internet.

"Okay, what's a chemtrail?" Amber asked, interrupting Malachi's musings.

"It's a conspiracy theory; some folks believe that the government is spraying the population with some sort of mind-altering chemical from high altitude aircraft. To most people the clouds look like contrails, but to the conspiracy kooks, they say they're 'chemtrails' from the government. They've been blamed for everything from the spread of cancer, to boron to promote mind control, and those aren't even the craziest ideas."

"So people actually believe that?" asked Amber.

"Yup, tinfoil hats and all."

Their conversation was interrupted when, all of a sudden, the Scout's windshield was covered in an oily mist falling from the sky. Malachi pulled over and used water from his gallon jug to rinse the windshield off. He was surprised to find that the substance smelled slightly like sulfur.

Dodging more cars stopped in the roadway, Malachi started to reconsider his decision to try to split the route between Dallas and Fort Worth. Arlington and the surrounding area were in the way, never mind Coppell, Frisco, and a goodly number of other cities stacked one on top of another. Looking to the south, it was obvious there were a lot of things on fire, a lot of danger. Turning to Amber, he said, "Babe, this isn't going to work, we're going to have to go around. I say we go east, less to go through and less to come back through to get to Maypearl."

"Sure, east sounds good," she replied.

Malachi and Amber approached the intersection for FM 121, drove around a bad accident in the intersection, and turned east towards McKinney, Texas. The detour was uneventful; they saw a few people riding down the Farm-to-Market road on everything from an old Ford tractor to a small John Deere lawn mower. But as they got closer to McKinney, they were quickly put on high alert. Peering at the looming column of thick black smoke ahead, Amber said, "It's like the whole town is on fire."

Entering the city on Highway 75 and getting close to their exit, Malachi had to drive through the grass on the side of the highway to get around an accident that had the entire road blocked, while up above on the overpass, people milled around a tanker truck that was on fire. *How they could stand the heat?* Then one of them fell over the edge of the overpass to the pavement below, and he slammed on the brakes. "Holy shit!"

Amber anxiously peered out the window. "At least those other people are running to help him."

Three people had run towards the fallen man from where they had been standing next to a darkened convenience store on the corner. They stopped abruptly when the man suddenly stood up, his right ankle shattered, the bones protruding from his lower leg. The three would-be rescuers stood paralyzed with fear as the crippled man stumbled in their direction with an otherworldly moan. Grabbing the shoulder of one, the man with the shattered leg took a big bite of flesh out of his rescuer-turned-victim's neck. Blood sprayed from the large open wound, covering the pair in the warm crimson fluid. The good Samaritan collapsed to the pavement with a wet gurgle, as he could no longer scream with his neck severed, while his two friends ran away.

Malachi stepped out of his truck. Running towards the attacker, who now had ribbons of his victim's flesh dangling from his wet bloody mouth, Malachi drew the XD .45 holstered on his right hip and fired two shots center mass. The man moaned and staggered towards Malachi, who fired two more rounds center mass before firing a fifth round aimed at his attacker's head. The back of the man's head exploded in a rainbow of blood and gore.

Malachi reached for the spare magazine on his belt with his left hand and deftly executed a tactical reload, all the while scanning for more threats. Amber screamed, and Malachi saw that the man who had had his throat ripped out had begun shuffling in his direction. Malachi raised his pistol and, taking no chances this time, fired a single head shot, felling the second man.

"Malachi, we've got to go, NOW!" screamed Amber.

Malachi ran towards the Scout, pistol still in hand. Amber was standing on the hood of the still-running truck, pistol out, firing rounds at an approaching group of about twenty people, all with grotesque wounds similar to the two that Malachi had just killed. Malachi closed the distance much faster than the shambling not-so-dead could, and Amber barely made it in the door before he shifted the truck in gear.

Malachi pounded the steering wheel. "Shit, shit, shit, shit, what the shit is going on?"

"I don't know," said Amber, "but that first guy should never have gotten up, and the second guy was dead from that huge bite wound, and, oh, I just don't know."

"Amber, we've got to haul ass, I can only hope that Bexar or Jack know something we don't."

They finally made it through the chaos that was McKinney, Texas, and out into the countryside, but with having to drive around abandoned vehicles in the road, and the general slow-going of an old Scout pulling a trailer, the sun soon loomed low on the horizon and it was apparent they wouldn't make it to Maypearl that day.

Amber held her hand up to the horizon. "Three fingers left 'til the sun drops, so about forty-five minutes of daylight."

"I don't know about you," said Malachi, "but I don't want to pop up the AT tent; I'd feel better if we drove through the night or found someplace more secure." Amber nodded in agreement.

Just outside of Farmersville, Malachi found what they needed. A squat metal building with large overhead doors, it appeared to have belonged to some sort of earth-moving company, though he couldn't tell what company because the small sign by the fence had been painted over to say, "Closed for the end of the world." The paint was still wet. Malachi didn't care, just as long as they found a safe place to hole up.

He stopped the Scout on the side of the road and extinguished the lights, but left the truck running. "I'm going over the fence to toss the emergency lever for the gate," he said. "Pull the truck through and I'll secure the gate behind us. And Amber, while I'm going over, cover me with the AR."

Malachi jogged to the chain-link fence and climbed over. Amber stood on the driver's side of the Scout, AR braced on the door frame, muzzle pointed towards the dark metal building. Malachi opened the metal cover for the electric gate, flipped the lever that clutched the electric motor, and slid open the gate. Amber drove the Scout and trailer into the yard and Malachi closed the gate, re-engaging the lever to secure it.

The sun had set, and with dusk the temperature started to fall as well. Amber exited the Scout and formed up with Malachi to clear the building and area so they could figure a way into the building.

It was eerily quiet, just like the days following 9/11 when there had been no air traffic in the sky, and it seemed that the whole world had stopped. Relying on their training, the couple used good tactics to cut the pie around the building's corners—Amber with the long gun in front for immediate threats, Malachi holding onto her belt with his left hand, walking mostly backwards to give rear security. The southeast side of the building had an employee door that was propped slightly open with a brick. There was a butt can and a bench next to the door.

"Smoker's door," whispered Malachi. "Looks like they forgot to lock it up when they painted their new business sign."

Malachi and Amber stacked on the door, Amber pulling on the end of the adjustable sling to tighten it, and they waited, breathing quietly through their mouths. Listening for threats, listening so hard he began to hear his own heartbeat in his ears, Malachi whispered, "I love you," in Amber's ear, squeezing her shoulder with his left hand as they exploded forward and leapt through the door.

Last year Malachi and Amber had spent a week with Jim Smith at Spartan Tactical on his compound in Jacksboro. They had learned an incredible amount from the former Delta Operator, including the value of accuracy and smooth movement, but Jim also taught them how to clear rooms precisely and with lightning speed.

Amber pushed straight through the door, running the wall to the right; Malachi planted his foot in the doorframe and crossed over to the left, running the wall to the corner while sweeping back towards the middle.

"SHOW ME YOUR HANDS; SHOW ME YOUR HANDS NOW!" Amber had found someone, but Malachi had to finish clearing his area of responsibility, trusting his wife to be okay and to trust in her training. Three rapid shots erupted, echoing loudly in the metal building, followed by Amber yelling, "Clear!"

Malachi responded "Clear," and walked over to Amber with his pistol in the SUL position. Fifteen feet in front of Amber on the floor was a man in blue Dickies coveralls. A name tag identified him as "Flea." Flea looked dead, but he also looked like he'd been that way long before being shot by Amber. There were two neat holes in the center of his chest, and a single hole just above the bridge of his nose. Black gunk spilled onto the floor from the hole in the back of his head.

Amber was still staring at the corpse in front of her. "It's like he was a fucking zombie or something."

"This is some crazy fucking day," Malachi said, shaking his head.

He released the chains of the large overhead door and pulled it up. Amber went to get the Scout while Malachi grabbed Flea's pant legs and dragged his body out the "smoker's" door.

Less than five minutes later, the Scout and trailer were safely inside the large workshop, and Amber had lit their old trusty Coleman lantern. The lantern had belonged to Malachi's father and had to be at least forty years old, but it still worked using white fuel and glowing mantles.

They tried to enjoy their light meal, but the carnage of the day had extinguished most of their appetite. Malachi cleaned up their dinner, and Amber took a multi-tool to the taillights of the Scout and removed the bulbs. The brake lights were a tactical liability, broadcasting their location to the world where electric light appeared to be a thing of the past.

WINCHESTER OVER

Malachi looked at the black smudge on the floor where Flea had been killed for the second time, and took off his hat, remembering the morale patch velcroed on the front. He had found it on the Internet; it had a body in crosshairs and the words "Zombie Killer." He removed the Velcro-backed patch and threw it onto the black stain. The patch wasn't as funny anymore.

CHAPTER 8

South of Mexia, Texas

The sun was low on the horizon, and the drive was slow-going for Bexar and his family. A surprisingly large number of semi-trailer trucks were on Texas-14 when the EMP hit, leaving the southbound highway clogged with trucks. Bexar drove into the ditch around yet another accident blocking the small two-lane highway. He wasn't sure why there were so many trucks on SH14; maybe some sort of advanced warning had come across the CB channels before his police dispatch had gotten the teletype? What Bexar wouldn't give to be able to turn on the radio and get some updated news.

"Are you even listening to me?" Jessie asked loudly.

"Uh, yeah honey, go get a mani-pedi, you deserve one."

"You dick, that's not what I was talking about, but if you see a little Vietnamese guy with a nail file out here in Bumfuck Egypt during the end of the world, pull over so I can get one."

Bexar laughed. "Okay, seriously, what were you saying?"

"I don't think it would be smart to drive through the night, but I don't want to pitch the tent; I don't think it would be safe out here," Jessie repeated.

"Well, I don't think I'll be able to find anywhere that will honor my Hilton Honors points, so where were you thinking?"

"I don't know," she sighed, "but we need to find somewhere safe."

"Okay, we have about thirty minutes until sunset; let me figure out where we can circle the wagons."

Bexar scanned the area around the highway, but in central Texas ranch country, there wasn't much shelter to choose from—just a lot of open land, deer, cattle, single wide trailers, and probably a few meth labs. Slowing the truck, Bexar turned to Jessie. "What about that airport?"

"Babe, there's a plane on fire at the end of the runway, I'm not so sure that would be a good place."

"No," he replied, "the other end, with the hangars. What if we break into one of the hangars, push the plane out, and pull the truck in. We would at least be hidden and have shelter. Besides, if a plane's burning at the south end of the airport and no one cares, then surely no one will notice if we're there for a night. And look at all that junk piled up next to the hangars. I seriously doubt anyone would notice us." When Amber shrugged, Bexar made his decision.

He turned into the airport and took a right away from the FBO, driving past the large hangars and tie-downs to the open-ended T-hangars. One was empty, so he backed the truck into it.

Walking around the hangar, Bexar found a large blue tarp covering a partially disassembled aircraft in the tie-downs. He cut the tarp loose and brought it back to the hangar. Using some 550 parachute cord, he hung the tarp in front of the truck in the hangar, blocking the truck from view. The tarp wasn't quite long enough to cover the entire opening, but he figured that the gap left between the top of the tarp and the hangar gave him a good vantage point from the gear rack of the truck to see out into the airport without being seen.

Jessie walked around the hangar to make sure the Jeep wasn't visible and, satisfied with their safety for the night, took two large rocks and weighted the bottom of the tarp to keep it in place.

Surveying her work, she said "This will do honey, but I think we should keep a watch tonight. If you sleep first, I'll trade out after a few hours."

Bexar looked at the watch on his wrist. "Fine, you take first watch. Give me four hours and I'll take the rest of the night. We can leave at sunrise ... goddamnit!" he exclaimed.

"What?"

"My watch is dead. I really liked this watch." Jessie had given Bexar the watch, a G-Shock Riseman, for his last birthday, and he loved it; he had wanted one for some time. Holding his hand up to the western sky, Bexar squinted and said, "Two fingers, only about thirty minutes left until sunset."

Jessie gave Keeley a cereal bar while she warmed up some canned chili on their Coleman stove. After eating, Bexar took one of the big red jerry cans of gas down from the back of the Jeep and poured the whole can into the Jeep's tank. They were going to have to find more fuel if they didn't get to Maypearl soon. After laying Keeley down to sleep in the back seat of the Jeep, Bexar curled up on the ground with a woolen surplus Army blanket, and Jessie climbed on top of the roof rack with the AR for first watch.

"I love you Bexar, sleep fast," she whispered.

CHAPTER 7

Air Force One

Agent McFarland knocked on the door to the President's in-air office.

"Mr. President," he announced, "we have lost communication with command at Denver. Current satellite imagery shows that most of Washington, D.C. is on fire, and there are swarms of reanimates moving throughout the destruction. Colonel Olive has informed us that we have approximately four hours of fuel remaining and then we will be forced to land."

The strain showing in his face, the President replied, "Why can't we refuel in-air again?"

"Sir, the last KC-135 over CONUS had to land to refuel, but Colonel Olive said that after the pilot advised that the approach for MacDill was overrun with reanimates, he hasn't been able to raise the crew nor any of the other ground assets in the Air Mobility Command. He is suggesting we land at Groom Lake. We still have some communication with them, and we think it would be the best choice for your safety."

"No!" The President was adamant. "We will not hide in the desert; tell the colonel that we're going to Denver so we can reestablish contact with the VP, and try to take back control of my country."

"Sir, I strongly suggest—"

"I don't care what you suggest, tell Olive those are my orders," the President said, dismissing him.

Outside of Mansfield, Texas

Jack and Sandra's trip on TX-287 was taking much longer than they had possibly imagined. The roadway was a nearly impassible nightmare, and Jack was spending a lot of time driving around disabled vehicles and wrecks. He gave up staying in the southbound lanes, traversing the median if he needed to clear an impasse. The only living people they had seen in the past two hours were a handful of people fleeing on bicycles to the north; the other dozen or so they had seen were dead in the road. All of them had bite marks and head wounds, and all were being picked apart by large turkey vultures.

They passed a burning gas station, and Jack looked down at the gas gauge on his FJ. "We've burned about half a tank, after using the gas in our jerry cans, and I'm not sure what we'll be able to find for gas." Gunfire rang out in the near distance. "I think we'd better find a safe spot to hole up for the night. We're not going to make it 'til tomorrow, and I don't want to drive through the night, it just wouldn't be safe."

Their son Will sat quietly in the back seat, staring out the window at all the death and destruction. Although he wasn't able to fully comprehend what was going on, he knew that something was really wrong, and that his parents were scared.

Jack drove for another half-hour, finally reaching the first turn towards Maypearl. As they passed an RV park, a naked man ran by a large fifth-wheel RV, three undead shambling after him.

Soon Jack saw a row of industrial buildings on his left, with no cars in the parking lot. "Let's see if we can get any of those overhead doors open, then we can park and hide in the building for the night. I think it would be a lot safer that way."

All of the rollup doors were locked, but Jack found an unlocked door at the back of the building beside a picnic table and a butt-can for cigarettes. Walking into the building, Jack reached out and flipped the light switch next to the door by habit; when nothing happened, he looked around sheepishly, glad no one had seen him trying the light switch. He pulled open the first overhead door and Sandra backed the FJ into the space.

"Too bad we don't need a new countertop," she said, "those granite pieces would look real nice."

"Yeah they would, but I don't know when we'll get to go back to even enjoy our kitchen, if ever," Jack mused.

Sandra took out the family's trusty old Coleman lantern and stove, while Jack shut and secured the doors in the building. The family ate boiled deer sausage in silence, then, wrapping themselves in woolen Hudson Bay blankets, lay down on the hard concrete floor to sleep as best they could in their frightening new world.

CHAPTER 8

December 27th
Denver International Airport (DIA), Colorado

Shortly after midnight, Air Force One began a hard fast combat approach to DIA. Instead of the usual gentle gliding approach like an airliner, Colonel Olive pushed the nose of the big modified 747 forward while applying some rudder input to drop altitude quickly, making a large spiral towards Runway 34-L. No lights were visible on the airport grounds, and the runway lights were dark as well, although there were some smoldering aircraft wrecks near some of the other runways. In fact, the only light that Colonel Olive had seen while approaching DIA was from Denver, and it was all from fires.

Colonel Olive hadn't had to land a plane wearing night vision goggles in some time, but after the many years he'd spent in the Air Force, he was confident just the same; an extraordinary level of skill and confidence had marked his rise through the Air Force ranks, and had paved the way for being given flight command of Air Force One. Olive was confident that the landing would be easy, but he was worried about taxiing across the airport to Concourse C, where the President would exit the aircraft and enter the tunnel leading to the secure structure six stories beneath The Great Hall.

Landing roughly, Colonel Olive pushed the reverse thrusters as far as they would go while giving some rudder input to move past some debris on the runway he hadn't been able to see on approach. The input was too late, and two of the tires on the right main were ruptured by the bent aluminum, causing the large aircraft to yaw violently to the right towards a large lump that had just appeared out of the shallow depth of his night vision goggles. That lump was, in fact, an overturned fire apparatus, but in the last few seconds of Olive's life, he wouldn't know what happened—that the rightmost CF6 engine had struck the fire apparatus, setting off a chain reaction of disaster.

The engine was ripped from under the wing and the aircraft spun violently to the right, still traveling over one hundred miles per hour, and the plane began to roll, digging the left wingtip into the tarmac. The wing succumbed to the force of the strike and broke, causing the fuselage to roll while spraying fuel from the wing tanks. The fuel ignited on the still-running large General Electric turbofans, and as it continued rolling down the runway, Air Force One erupted in a large ball of fire.

Mexia, Texas

Bexar was exhausted. Jessie had woken him to switch places, and as he climbed on top of the Jeep's roof, he cursed silently. Jessie quickly fell asleep, leaving Bexar to stare out into the darkness.

He couldn't see anything past the tie-down aircraft outside of their hangar, although there was a glow from the still-burning aircraft at the other end of the runway. Staring into the darkness, his eyes began playing tricks on him, seeing movement in the shadows where there was none.

Climbing off the roof, Bexar found his small backpacking stove and pulled his worn Zippo lighter out of his pocket to light the stove. He'd quit smoking years ago, but had kept the lighter for sentimental reasons. Jessie had given him the custom-engraved lighter for their first anniversary. With the fuel tab lit, he poured some water into an old blue enamel camping cup and waited for the water to boil. Instant coffee tasted like instant coffee, but it was better than no coffee. Seeing movement out of the corner of his eye, Bexar quickly turned, his rifle coming up instinctively towards the threat, safety thumbed off, only to find Keeley standing next to the Jeep, clutching her blanket.

"Hey baby girl, go get some sleep so we can enjoy our camping trip and our drive tomorrow. You might even get to see Will tomorrow afternoon."

Without a word, Keeley climbed back into the back seat of the Jeep and lay down. "I'm sorry the world is ending, we were just trying to build a nice life for you," Bexar thought to himself. Climbing back onto the roof of the Jeep to continue watch, Bexar drank his burnt-tasting coffee, all the while fighting the fear of the dark and the pull of sleep.

"WHAT THE FUCK WAS THAT?"

Bexar jerked awake, knocking over his blue coffee cup and sending it clattering to the hangar floor. Looking over the top of the tarp, he could see the sun coming up, and about a dozen people slowly shuffling from around the tied-down aircraft towards his hangar. *How long was I asleep?* he thought over and over. He was puzzled by the group of people until one of them moaned—it was a guttural animal moan, a call to feed, and Bexar shivered at the sound.

"Shit shit shit shit, Jess, damnit, toss everything in the Jeep, we've got to go! Give me a second and then drive off." Stepping onto the hood of the Jeep, Bexar pulled the C-M Forge knife from his belt and cut the tarp down. Now with a clear view, he sat back on the roof rack, feet still on the hood of his truck, and raised his rifle, lining up his sight and squeezing the trigger. Left hand out on the end of his rifle, pulling against the LaRue FUG, Bexar stabilized the rifle and quickly drove the muzzle to the next threat as the back of the first undead's head exploded outward from the energy of the Black Hills 55-grain bullet.

Breathe, red-dot, squeeze, drive, breathe, Bexar continued his rhythm while Jessie started the Jeep and put it in gear. *Breathe, red-dot, squeeze* ... nothing. Nothing happened. Bexar slapped the bottom of the magazine and brought his left hand up to pull the big Badger Latch to cycle his AR, but the bolt wouldn't move. Bexar rolled the rifle to the left as he stood up on the hood and brought the rifle down to his side. *Fuck, bolt over*, ran through Bexar's head as his right hand found the grip of the Kimber on his right hip. Well-practiced, he let the rifle hang on the sling to his left side and brought up his left hand to support the grip of his pistol. Taking aim at the next threat, there was suddenly only blackness.

Dazed, Bexar woke up at the other end of the airport. He could see the blue sky, and could hear noises off in the distance, but everything felt like it was a thousand miles away, like in a dream. Sitting up, he saw he was next to the Jeep, Jessie about twenty feet in front of him, pistol up, shooting.

Crashing back to reality, he heard Keeley screaming and crying from inside the Jeep. The jammed AR was still slung across his torso, so Bexar mortared the rifle to force the bolt over to clear and discarded the damaged round. Swapping in a fresh Pmag from his belt, he stood up, but the world spun and forced him to his knees.

"Jess, what the fuck ...?" he called.

"Babe, you hit your head on the hangar as we drove out; you've been out cold for about five minutes. We're about to be overrun, about fifteen more coming our way!" she called back, her voice shrill with tension.

Bexar laid flat on his belly, taking a prone firing position so he wouldn't get dizzy and could fire his rifle accurately. Trying to slow his breathing, he took aim.

Squeeze, breathe, and drive to the next target, he chanted silently. In less than a minute the rest of the shambling threats were down, and Jessie helped Bexar into the passenger seat before pointing the Jeep at the entry gate and quickly driving away from the airport where they had nearly died.

Bexar dug in the glove box and found two packets of BC Powder. Although he knew it wouldn't help with a concussion, he hoped it would maybe dull some of the pain throbbing between his ears.

CHAPTER 9

Farmersville, Texas

In the small, north Texas town of Farmersville, Malachi found the morning of December 27th bitterly cold, and the lightly insulated metal building didn't help. He and Amber huddled together, quietly discussing what their next steps should be; specifically, what their plan should be to exit the building safely. They decided on a plan that would see Malachi sneaking through the building to the outside, checking that the coast was clear, and then signaling Amber to roll up the big door.

Amber took her station at the roll up door and waited for Malachi. Two light taps on the door was her cue, and as she pulled on the chain the door began its noisy ascent. Malachi ran in a combat crouch towards the gate at the front of the property that they needed to open to drive off. Nearing the gate, Malachi heard the Scout's motor turn over, followed by a loud moan to his right. Turning and driving the muzzle of his rifle towards the threat, Malachi saw a dead person shuffling towards him, arms up, mouth open, and uttering a deep moan that shook Malachi to his core.

With a little bit of distance comes a little bit of time, so he was able to flip the level from the gate and pull it open before raising the muzzle of his rifle. Amber pulled up just as Malachi pulled the trigger to the rear and ended the dead man's shambling afterlife.

Mexia, Texas

Bexar and his family made the short drive from the airport into the center of the little central Texas town in very little time. They found the town burning and overrun by the undead. It was amazing how quickly the dead had taken over the living. The drive through town took longer than Bexar had wanted, spending much of his time in second gear, dodging the shuffling hordes. Each gaping mouth they passed would turn and stumble in the direction of their vehicle, blindly looking to feed. Bexar didn't know how far or how long they could follow his Jeep, but he hoped they gave up soon.

Mansfield, Texas

Cold MREs with instant coffee was the breakfast of choice for Jack, Sandra, and Will. After breakfast, they reloaded the FJ and prepped to leave.

Jack walked out of the "smoker's door" and into the cold north Texas morning to scout their exit route. He brought his AR up and slid along the side of the metal building towards the roadway, stopping short of the building's corner, then slowly sidestepping while slicing the pie to check the blind spots behind the building's corner. Seeing movement, Jack stopped and dropped to a kneeling shooter's position.

Across the road, aimlessly milling about, were twenty or so undead. If he began engaging the threats, he knew Sandra would burst through the door and assist, but he felt their best bet would be to get the truck out, take care of the immediate threats, and flee in the vehicle. Slowly sliding back the way he came, Jack went inside and outlined a quick operational plan to Sandra.

Pulling on the chain and opening the large overhead door seemed to take forever; it also made an incredible amount of noise. Will was in the back seat of the truck with his seatbelt on and both doors were locked. Jack knelt next to the open driver's door, rifle up, ready to engage any immediate threats. Sandra worked the chains, pulling the door up. Once the door was high enough to clear their vehicle, she ran to the passenger door, climbed in, and slammed the door shut, locking it. Jack waited until his wife was secure before he broke cover and climbed into the driver's seat of the running truck.

Pulling out of the bay and around the front of the building, he saw that, predictably, the undead had been drawn towards the sound of the opening door and the running vehicle, and were lurching towards them in the hopes of a fresh meal. He was able to miss most of them, but struck the last straggler with the front right corner of the brush guard on the FJ. Jack didn't slow down, didn't even look back, he just kept driving.

Driving from Mansfield to Maypearl would normally take just under an hour, but today Jack wasn't sure how long the trip would take. Luckily, the small Texas back roads provided them with some security. There were very few disabled cars on the roads, and since their encounter that morning, he hadn't seen another undead. In fact, they hadn't seen anyone living or dead since leaving their temporary shelter. Jack kept the speedometer at forty miles per hour the entire way until they came to the outskirts of Venus.

The old downtown of Venus looked like every small town in north Texas: a couple of open shops and a few abandoned buildings. It was easy to forget that the world had drastically changed the day before. When Sandra suddenly yelled "STOP!" Jack slammed on the brakes, nearly catching another undead in the brush guard on his truck.

Moaning loudly, the creature began clawing at the passenger window, making Sandra scream. The lost soul pounded on the side of the FJ, slowly following the truck as it pulled forward. Neither Jack nor Sandra saw the forty or so undead that came stumbling out from the side streets, crossing into the center of Main Street and directly into the FJ's path. Their attention was quickly brought forward again when the first of the undead swarm collided with the center of the brush guard and landed on the hood of the truck.

Jack slammed his right foot back down on the brake while his left foot pushed the clutch to the floor. Shifting into reverse, he backed up as fast as he could, swerving around the first undead he had missed, then stopping and turning onto a small side street to carve a path around the swarm. After three more blocks, the living dead man on the hood, who looked to be about twenty, was still beating on the windshield, trying to get at fresh prey. Jack stopped the FJ, leaned out of the driver's door to get the right angle, and fired a single shot into its head. He then grabbed the man by his blood-soaked jeans and pulled him off the hood of the truck, leaving a sticky blood smear.

They were getting close to the cache site and the safety of like-minded friends. Jack feverishly hoped they all made it to the rendezvous.

CHAPTER 10

South of Farmersville, Texas

After turning onto Highway 78, Malachi decided they were going to be in a lot of trouble, pretty much screwed, whichever route they took. They should just make a run for it with the fastest and most direct route. The biggest problem would be traffic, he figured, but he also felt that as long as they didn't stop for too long, they should be able to outpace any zombies they came across.

After all of the bad movies, the books, and the jokes, it had actually happened—the dead had risen to hunt the living. He couldn't believe it. He even had a couple of boxes of the zombie killer Hornady ammo that had come out a while back, but now the joke just wasn't funny anymore.

The trip to Rockwall was quick and effortless, but he was feeling nauseous from the stress. The handful of small towns they drove through were eerily quiet, with no signs of anyone living, dead, or undead. They finally made it to the I-30; the westbound lanes appeared to be relatively clear, but the eastbound side was a parking lot of disabled cars. So many new cars laid to waste, left to forever rot on the asphalt in Texas. The only vehicles Malachi had seen on the road that were still running were at least thirty years old, mainly old CJ Jeeps and K-series Blazers. Someone might have taken steps to protect the electronics on their more modern vehicle with some sort of large Faraday cage, but he knew that was absurd. If you were willing to take the steps to EMP-proof a modern vehicle, you might as well just build and maintain an older vehicle that would be more robust after an EMP event anyway.

Maypearl, Texas

Jack pulled off the small highway into the ditch where he, Malachi, and Bexar had constructed a semi-hidden gate onto the property. They had split a cedar fence post, lashing the two together but leaving one side unsecured so it could be moved like a gate, but wouldn't be obvious. Jack opened the gate and stood over watch with his AR while Sandra pulled the FJ through. After securing the gate behind them, they drove the quarter mile through the property to their big blue water tank. The tank held no water and had hopefully remained unmolested; it held the group's cached supplies.

State Highway 171, Texas

Bexar and Jessie encountered few problems in the back country of central Texas after making it out of Mexia, but their luck changed as they approached the south side of Hubbard, Texas. It was obvious that several large fires burned uncontrolled in the town. Bexar needed to get to a Farm-to-Market road on the other side of the town, but before driving into a potential threat, he grabbed the binoculars and climbed onto the roof of the Jeep. In his magnified view he could see a jackknifed semi-truck across the center of the roadway, and it looked like someone had been in one hell of a firefight. The truck was riddled with bullet holes, and shell casings littered the roadway. Then Bexar finally realized what he was looking at—an ambush point.

With his family in the vehicle and no backup available, the last thing he wanted to do was engage in some sort of prolonged gun battle, but after watching the roadblock for nearly fifteen minutes and not being able to think of an alternate route, Bexar decided to chance it.

Keeley lay down on the floorboards of the back seat with Bexar's Kevlar vest spread over her. Although it wouldn't stop a direct hit from a rifle round, it would hopefully be enough to protect her from rounds slowed down by coming through the truck. Jessie hung out of the passenger window with the AR as Bexar inched the Jeep forward. Getting closer, Bexar saw that he could drive into the ditch to the left of the roadblock, turn right, and hopefully make it across the road to the other side of the ambush point. He saw no one; it was possible that the roadblock was abandoned, that they had been overrun, or that the undead had triumphed.

Abruptly the Jeep's windshield shattered with a pop; the rifle report was heard immediately after. Keeley began screaming and Bexar put his right foot to the floor, shifting through third gear. Jessie was yelling something, but he was too focused on evading the threat to hear what she was saying.

They cleared downtown at sixty miles per hour and didn't stop until a couple of miles north of the town.

"Holy shit, everyone okay?" he finally managed.

Jessie said, "Bexar, you're bleeding, but I'm okay, and Keeley's just scared."

Touching his head, looking in the rearview mirror, Bexar realized that glass from the windshield had cut his face. He could also see daylight filtering through the small hole left by the bullet's path through the roof of the Jeep.

"Damn, that was close." He dabbed at the blood with his shirt sleeve. "We've got to get to Maypearl and hope the others make it safely. I'm not sure we can do this on our own, and we really can't keep traveling much longer."

CHAPTER 11

Denver International Airport (DIA), Colorado

Ever since they'd started building the airport, so many conspiracy theorists had made so many different claims about it that most of America had written off the conspiracies as crazy, but Cliff was amazed at how right some had been. The simple fact was, the facility actually existed.

Some theorized that the facility was the size of a ten-story building but built underground. Others claimed that "the grays" were housed in the facility: the little gray aliens that made contact in New Mexico in 1947 after their craft had malfunctioned.

Some said it was "the greens," a race of shapeshifting reptilian aliens, and even that the Bush family were a part of that race of otherworldly people. From there the claims grew even wilder, but what really set off the first round of theories was one of the murals painted in the airport right before it first opened. The infamous "Children of the World Dream of Peace" mural had an imperialistic-looking soldier with a sword, machine gun, and gas mask; to the conspiracy theorists this alluded to what really lay beneath DIA, except that it wasn't a New World Order launching pad with aliens, it was simply a facility to replace the Greenbrier bunker in West Virginia that had been exposed by the media in 1992. Regardless, Cliff still found it ironic that he was currently one hundred feet below the Great Hall at DIA, on the run, and hiding in the super-secret facility from a super-secret government experiment that had gone wrong.

Cliff crawled through a service corridor between the isolated interior walls of the facility and the cut-rock face underground. This was not the fight that Cliff had trained for when he had been recruited as a college athlete in ROTC at St. Olaf University. After graduating with a degree in Business Administration and a minor in German Studies, Cliff was whisked away to the secret training facility in Virginia known simply as "The Farm."

After two years of intense training that rivaled what Tier-1 military special forces operators endured, Cliff then spent another two years learning specific spy tradecraft to operate sans diplomatic cover in foreign lands. Cliff was a seasoned tactical operator, but he was primarily a spy who had spent the last two years undercover as a Canadian-based clothing manufacturer in mainland China.

During his two years in China, Cliff had been trying to gather information about a possible secret Chinese facility that housed ancient artifacts from Tibet. The intelligence that his department had received was that the Chinese military had taken possession of an ancient technology, possibly alien in origin, from the Soviet Union during the collapse of the communist government. The Soviet Union had stolen the technology from Nazi Germany in 1945, who had found the artifacts during the Himmler and Hess expeditions to Tibet. The Nazi plan for a super-human army had hinged on the mythology surrounding the Tibetan artifacts, which to Himmler were sacred to his occult beliefs.

The artifacts contained spores that could bring dead primates back to life, but nothing over twenty pounds. They weren't sure if this was due to the actual weight of the monkey, or the species of monkey. During the fall of Nazi Germany, the Russians had learned about the expedition and the experiments on the Jews, and feared that Hitler had gone through treatments so as to be unkillable. Therefore, when the Russians found Hitler's bunker, they had taken him alive and kept him imprisoned for five years outside of Leningrad. Eventually, the Soviets realized that the Nazi scientists had not been able to solve the weight barrier.

Regardless, not wanting to take chances, they had shot Hitler in the head and burned his body before dumping his ashes into the sea. For the next forty years, the Soviets decoded the spores, learning that they contained a complex virus, but they too were unable to successfully pass the weight barrier. They did discover that other mammals were not affected by the virus, only primates.

In the thirty years since, the Chinese had gotten it right and solved the weight barrier. This much Cliff had been able to learn, but the location of the facility was still a mystery, although he had begun to believe it may be in the caves and caverns of North Korea.

Having confirmed the existence of the virus, Cliff's organization had arranged for a group of scientists contracted with the Defense Intelligence Agency to work on this new threat. Cliff had been able to secure a reanimated dead chimpanzee for the group, who believed they were only about six months away from being able to counteract the ancient virus that had been modified to reanimate the dead. If there was any chance for the future, it lay with this group of scientists at their facility in Groom Lake, Nevada. Cliff hoped they were still safe. He needed to get to them, but first he had to get out of Denver, and to do that, he had to make it out of the damned airport.

CHAPTER 12

Maypearl, Texas

Jack drove across a small section of grass before getting to the dirt road leading to the Royal Rangers campground. The camp was built at a Soil Conversation Service Site Reservoir, which was a decent-sized lake that stocked fish. The water could be made to drink with a little filtration and chlorine treatment, and there were plenty of wooded areas that gave limited trapping for food. However, the most important part of the site was the group's cache.

Their original idea for the cache was to have some sealed containers buried far away from the parade grounds the campers used to hold their church services, but they were afraid that some camper might dig up the cache by accident. They had ultimately decided on buying two large blue plastic water containers, nearly six feet tall and six feet in diameter, but instead of holding water, they modified them to form a single tank.

The modified tank had a top section that slid upwards, but would sit flush on the ground to prevent showing a seam. The bottom of the tank was buried, and created a watertight enclosure for the group's supplies. By the end of that three-day long weekend trip, Jack, Malachi, and Bexar had built, filled, and buried their modified tank.

Bexar had a friend at the City's road and sign department make a sign that looked official and read: "Property of the U.S. Government Water Conservation Program. Report Problems (888) 895-5553." That phone number went to a call service voicemail that simply asked the caller to leave a message describing the problem. Malachi had found the number; he wasn't sure who owned the phone number or the voicemail, but it didn't matter since the chances of someone calling the number due to a single sign on a secluded property in Maypearl, Texas was pretty remote.

Jack was glad there hadn't been a Royal Rangers camping trip this week, since it may have been hard to explain why they were there; then again, would the campers have stayed on site two days into The End Of The World As We Know It, or would they have fled for their homes. In reality, he figured most of them would probably still be here, albeit undead.

After about ten minutes of slow driving, Jack stopped his FJ by the blue tank. It looked just like they had left it, and he hoped the cache was still intact. Will stayed in the FJ and Sandra held watch with the AR while Jack opened the tank. First, he had to dig out the seam that was just below the surface of the ground, revealing the combination padlock. After entering the combination, Jack slid the lip of his Hi-Lift jack under the hook of the latch and began cranking. It took about a minute to raise the top section of the tank on its tracks, and it took both he and Sandra to push the top over on the hinged track to fully open the tank.

Jack jumped into the tank and inspected the cache—everything looked like it should. Unfolding the step stool left in the tank, he began lifting out his family's cached items, followed by the group's items. The personal items of the other families would stay in the tank in case Jack had to leave before the others arrived.

Malone, Texas, FM 308

Farm-to-Market Road 308—Bexar wondered how many signs the Texas Department of Transportation had to replace each year because someone stole it, or fired a bunch of .308 holes in it. Malone was a ghost town, and Bexar couldn't tell if it was because anyone left had hunkered down, or if they had fled to some other location, or if they were all infected. Either way, he really didn't care since it was still better than what they had encountered in Hubbard.

Wary of another ambush, undead or otherwise, Bexar lay on the roof of his Jeep with the binoculars for nearly an hour for reconnaissance after reaching the outskirts of the town. Not seeing any activity, they moved ahead, keeping the Jeep's speed at around fifty miles per hour, weapons drawn and ready to go. For safety, they had Keeley lay on the floorboards again covered by his Kevlar vest; Jessie was ready to go with the AR. Malone flew by the windshield, and quickly the Reed family arrived in Mertens, Texas. Ahead of them stood a small group of grain silos, all of which were on fire. Several people stood by the silos, watching them burn.

Bexar slowed by the edge of the group. "Hey buddy, is everyone okay? You shouldn't be near those things if they're burning; they've been known to explode." The man turned, but instead of answering, moaned and lurched towards Bexar and his Jeep.

"Ah SHIT!" Bexar pulled the 1911 up from his lap, fired once into the face of the dangerously close undead, and let the clutch out on the Jeep too fast, stalling the engine. The loud report of the .45 had caused the other undead to turn and begin towards the stalled Jeep. Jessie opened the passenger door, stood in the door frame, and began taking shots over the windshield with the AR as best she could. Bexar pushed in the clutch, turning the ignition key back and forth to engage the starter while pumping the gas pedal. The motor roared to life, and Bexar took one more shot at an undead through his open window.

"GET IN!" he shouted.

Jessie sat back in the passenger seat, and hadn't even closed her door when Bexar began pulling forward as fast as he could. Two miles down the road, he pulled the spare pistol magazine from his belt and switched the magazine in the well of the pistol. Being down two rounds in an eight-round magazine wasn't a way to stay, so another tactical reload was in order.

CHAPTER 13

Lake Ray Hubbard, Texas

The scariest part about driving on a highway that crosses a lake and is semi-clogged with cars disabled by an EMP is not that there's nowhere else to go and you might get stuck. No, the scariest part is that you might get stuck and eaten by a zombie. Malachi was overwhelmed by the constant stress of the past two days, and found himself driving on autopilot as he crept the Scout and trailer through the disabled vehicles. On his right, towards the heart of DFW, numerous large fires were burning out of control. To his left there wasn't much to see, just the cold winter sky and the lake. *Where did all the people from those abandoned vehicles go?* thought Malachi. *What happened to all the people?*

As he neared the end of the bridge, he came upon a smoldering fire in the opposite lane. A semi-truck hauling a trailer full of hogs had run into the K-barrier and overturned. Dead hogs scattered the roadway around the truck, many of them savaged with large chunks of flesh missing from their throats, necks, and bodies.

As they inched forward past the front of the wrecked semi-truck, they could see a massive pile-up behind the truck, with at least thirty cars involved in the horrific accident. In his detached state, Malachi observed that major traffic accidents were practically a given after an EMP, because most cars now on the road had power brakes and power steering, all of which would fail when the motor stopped.

Movement on the other side of the barricade brought Malachi back to the present. Someone in the cab of a lifted F-250 quad-cab pickup truck was waving at them. As he drove closer and began to slow, it became apparent that the person wasn't waving at them, the person was dead and clawing at the window trying to get to them.

"Damn," he muttered, "where there's one there's two and two there's more."

"What?" said Amber, still staring open-mouthed at the carnage on the highway.

"Something Bexar used to say about State Troopers on the highway. If you see one, there's another nearby. If you see two, there's going to be a lot more. There's a zombie in that truck and those pigs were eaten by something. I think we might have trouble."

Slowing for a moment to plan a route through the wreckage on his side of the highway, Malachi saw more undead than he could count coming towards the center barrier, and towards his intended escape route. Glancing in the side mirror of his Scout, he saw about another dozen undead shambling towards the back of his trailer.

"Fuck! Okay Amber, looks like we're trapped. I'm going to charge ahead and hope to clear the horde."

Malachi downshifted and let out the clutch. The K-barrier wall was between his truck and the approaching zombie horde to his front; as long as he kept moving he could outpace the zombies coming from the rear. If he'd bought an older-bodied Scout with the flip-forward windshield, Amber could have engaged the undead to the front as he drove, but he hadn't, so he could only press on and hope for the best. As he gained speed, the lumbering undead on the other side of the highway began tumbling over the concrete divider. Even though they weren't very coordinated, they were persistent, and they all got back up and continued their chase.

Malachi cleared the last wreck. Taking advantage of the section of open road, he pushed the old six-cylinder motor with everything he had. Changing gears as they passed the last of the undead falling over the barrier, he knew he couldn't stop or all would be lost.

Looking back, Amber said, "I wonder how long they'll keep following us?"

"I don't know Amber, but I'll let someone else figure that one out. FIDO, let's just go to 635."

"Say what?" said Amber.

"FIDO—Fuck It, Drive On. I say we go for broke and push on to 635, take the loop and see how I-45 looks. The bottom end of the city isn't as populated; we might get lucky and have a clear run to the cache."

For the first time that morning, Malachi was able to cruise at fifty miles per hour, slowing only to dodge an occasional stalled vehicle. He realized he hadn't seen any other moving vehicles on the road since this morning, and a dark feeling of isolation descended on the cab of the Scout as hope began to wane.

CHAPTER 14

Denver International Airport, Colorado

After two hours of feeling his way in the pitch-black darkness of the unfinished spaces between the rock face and the "exterior" walls of the underground complex, Cliff had finally found what he was looking for: one of the thirteen escape passages. He wasn't exactly sure where this vertical shaft led, but he was sure it went to the ground level and freedom from the super-secret-base-turned-undead-tomb. Cliff hoped it wasn't the one passage that led to an opening near the symbolic Masonic cornerstone in the Great Hall—the conspiracy theorists had gotten that one right, even if there weren't any aliens.

Two hundred and twenty-one rungs later and Cliff was at the hatch, spinning the latch handle to release the door. Once the latch was engaged in the open position, the hatch pushed open with a hiss of hydraulic pistons and locked. Although Cliff was never really sure how deep the facility was beneath ground level, he calculated that if the rungs were twelve inches apart, he had started the climb twenty-two stories below the surface.

He had spent the climb with his FNP90 slung across his back and out of the way so it wouldn't catch on the rungs of the ladder, but now the hatch was open to the outside world and since he wasn't sure what awaited him, the rifle came back around to the front of his body. Leaning back against the wall of the shaft, Cliff checked the face of his Suunto Core watch and saw it was nearly 1500 hours local time. It occurred to him that his electronic watch had survived the EMP event because he had been in a shielded facility.

Reaching into the cargo pocket of his battered TAD operator pants, he pulled out a pair of Oakley sunglasses and put them on before entering the harsh afternoon sunlight. Easing upwards, Cliff pointed the barrel of his rifle towards the threat of the unknown and scanned the grounds before climbing all the way out of the rescue shaft. Looking through his ACOG, Cliff could see the white and blue tail of the most famous 747 in the world; he also saw that the aircraft lay broken across the ground, parts of it still burning. A pack of undead milled about near the aircraft, and Cliff assumed that the Commander-in-Chief was dead, but it was still his duty to go check.

LBJ Freeway, south of Dallas, Texas

Malachi was surprised to have found the I-635 relatively clear of vehicles and had made good time getting to the I-20. His plan was to try to make it to the I-45 and if that was clear, to push on to the I-35 to get a straight shot at Maypearl. If their luck held, they would be at the cache site in less than two hours. Malachi held his hand to the horizon. "Looks like we have about three hours of daylight left. If we can keep this pace up, we should make it to the group site in about two hours."

"What if we don't make it before dark?" asked Amber.

"We'll have to find another safe place to spend the night out in Indian country," he replied.

He knew Amber was worried; she did not want to spend another night outside of their group site. If the others were already there, they had safety in numbers. Regardless, they had still gained a little safety getting away from Dallas and all the undead people.

Cache Site near Maypearl, Texas

Jack passed Sandra the last of their personal survival stores and some of the group's provisions out of the bottom of the tank, but left Malachi and Bexar's stores in place. The last piece of gear he passed up was in a large, off-brand Pelican-style case. This was Jack and Sandra's Sunforger heavy canvas wall tent, made from material purchased from Panther Primitives. Malachi and Bexar had purchased similar tents; the group had fallen in love with the tents when they had been a part of the Royal Rangers frontiersman reenactment group, Frontiersman Camping Fellowship. The tents were well-made, and were cool in the summer and warm in the winter. Not only that, they could run a wood-burning stove in the tent to heat and to cook on. Instead of the traditional wooden frame, the group had all opted for the galvanized steel poles that were much more lightweight, and took less time to set up than the wooden poles. They had even taken the time to dye the bright white canvas earth tone colors so they didn't stand out.

The only thing that Jack missed was the handmade cots they used to have. With the ground cloth down and the tent set up, Jack and Sandra quietly and quickly put their night's supplies in the tent, but readied their truck for departure if they needed to flee. They would both feel safer once the others made it.

Sandra took Will inside the tent, setting up their small camping table and cranking up the old green Coleman stove. After all the stress and exertion of the day, they needed a good meal tonight, especially since she wasn't sure when they might have another chance to cook a good meal.

Jack gathered up the group's homemade proximity alarms. This was a device that held a ten-gauge shotgun round that they loaded without any shot, only with the powder. A length of high-tension fishing filament and a small spring were used to create a trip wire that set off the shotgun cartridge noisemaker. It was simple, required no batteries or high technology, and worked well. The group had loaded one hundred shells for the trip alarms and sealed them in an ammo can in the cache. Jack set out six of the devices in a loose circle about two hundred feet from their camp, on the more obvious approach routes. For each device, he took a stick of camo face paint and ran the end of the stick down the fishing line for camouflage, making it look more like a small vine than a trip wire.

Milford, Texas

After escaping the zombie horde in Mertens, Bexar hadn't slowed down much until they'd nearly reached the Milford city limits. The town was empty and on fire; it appeared that only ghosts remained. He didn't know why it seemed like everything caught fire after the end of the world, but he did know that clearly there weren't enough living people left to fight the fires.

It was with no small relief that Bexar found that FM 308 crossed over the I-35 and not under it. The Interstate was littered with stalled vehicles, accidents, and hundreds of people milling about between the cars and accidents. At a second glance, they realized that none of those people were alive—I-35 was a tomb of the undead.

"Holy shit!" cried Jessie, "look at that, honey, we need to get out of here."

"Couldn't agree with you more, Jess," said Bexar as he let out the clutch and started across the bridge. He guessed they were only about forty-five minutes away from Maypearl with only about two hours of daylight left. They had to make it to the group tonight. He hoped the group was there.

CHAPTER 15

Interstate 20, south of Dallas, Texas

Malachi and Amber made good time, but just before reaching I-45 Malachi stopped the Scout so he could put more gas in the tank. This would be the third jerry can of gas Malachi had used for the trip. As he got out of the truck, he noticed a sign notifying the public that this was a prison area and not to pick up hitchhikers. *In this day and age, who actually picks up hitchhikers anymore?* Malachi thought to himself as he pulled the gas can off the rack. *Only two cans of gas left and then we'll be in trouble,* he thought, but then he realized they had passed thousands of cars abandoned on the road, all with gas in their tanks. It wasn't looting if it was for survival.

While fueling the Scout, Malachi scanned the area around him for a suitable candidate to steal gas from. As luck would have it, across the median was a full-ton Ford truck with a long trailer full of lawn equipment. Most of that equipment ran on regular gas and not two-cycle anymore, especially the professional-grade gear. There were even four large red plastic gas cans on the trailer, held down by a bungee cord.

"Hey, I'm going across the median to get the gas cans from that lawn crew trailer," he called to Amber.

"Ok babe, I'll hold cover here."

Malachi ran across the median and found two of the four gas cans full. Two ten-gallon gas cans were better than no gas, so unfastening the bungee cord, he pulled each can out of the trailer and began the walk back to his Scout. The farmer's walk with a gas can in each hand was laborious, but completely worth it. He was about twenty feet away from the Scout when he heard Amber scream, followed by the loud crack of a rifle shot. Amber fell to the ground, her AR-15 clattering to the concrete.

Malachi ran the rest of the distance, the gas cans still in hand.

"Babe, can you hear me? Amber? FUCK!"

Amber was unconscious and bleeding badly. She had been ambushed by an unseen sniper; who and why he didn't know, and quite frankly didn't care at this point. He needed to get his wife out of here and to safety.

Malachi scooped Amber up and put her on the bench seat, sliding her across to the passenger side. Another rifle round punched through the windshield of the Scout and into the empty driver's seat. Malachi pushed the gas cans into the back of the Scout, picked up the AR Amber had dropped, and jumped into the driver's seat just as another round punched through the shattered windshield, barely missing his head. He had felt the bullet pass right by his ear. Putting the Scout in gear and accelerating as fast as the old truck would go, Malachi swerved back and forth, hoping to avoid any more shots.

No more shots hit the truck and after about five miles of fast driving, he stopped the truck to check on Amber. She was still unconscious and bleeding, but she was breathing and had a pulse. Her breathing was shallow and her pulse weak. Malachi grabbed the trauma kit out of the back seat of the Scout, found the EMS shears and cut off Amber's blood-drenched shirt. The rifle round had entered just above her left breast and exited out her back, shattering her left shoulder blade. The entry wound was large, nearly the size of his pinky finger. Malachi placed a QuikClot sponge in the larger exit wound and a tampon in the entry wound. He then positioned a large amount of gauze on both wounds and wrapped Amber's chest in medical tape.

He had to get to the group for help, although he wasn't sure what sort of help they would be able to provide— without a surgeon and a hospital, there really wasn't much anyone could do. His wife would somehow either live, or she would die.

"Stay with me baby," he pleaded, "I need you to hang with me. I can't lose you."

CHAPTER 18

Maypearl, Texas

About an hour after sunset, the Reed family turned onto Main Street in the little town of Maypearl. They were almost at the cache site, but first they had to get through their last obstacle, the town.

The town's cafe was fully engulfed in flames. A crowd of about fifty people stood shuffling to and fro in front of it, except it was obvious that these people were no longer alive—they were the undead; their only purpose was to hunt the living. Bexar had quickly learned his first lesson of the new world order, and took the first road to the left. As he drove away from the burning building and the throng of undead, he hoped that the fire would be enough of a distraction so they wouldn't follow him.

Bexar drove through the small town, taking the side streets to meet back up with FM 66, the Farm-to-Market road that became Main Street once you entered Maypearl. They were so close to the cache site that he couldn't risk having the terrifying, undead mob follow them. Although the group's survival location was secluded, it wasn't fortified and wasn't easily defended. They had bet their safety on being hidden and out of the way, not even considering that the dead would rise and walk the earth.

Less than ten minutes later, anxiously watching for any sign of trailing undead, Bexar pulled the truck up to the hidden gate at the entrance of the group cache site.

Cache Site near Maypearl, Texas

Jack heard a vehicle out on the main road stop briefly, then continue up the dirt road towards him and his family. Drawing his pistol, he took a concealed position near some brush. Hopefully Sandra had also heard the approaching vehicle and would practice good noise discipline. It was too late to warn her, but Jack was confident she would react correctly. They had discussed situations and tactics like these before, but Jack was never really sure how much of it his wife took seriously. Now that TEOTWAWKI—The End Of The World As We Know It—was here, they needed those skills to stay alive.

Relief washed over Jack as he saw the old familiar Jeep Wagoneer approach the camp; Bexar had made it to the cache. Not wanting to startle Bexar and risk being shot, Jack stood slowly, holding his hands above his head while moving out from his cover. The Jeep was dark, with the lights off, but the hazard lights flashed once to acknowledge Jack. Leading the way, Jack walked with the Jeep and the Reed family back to the camp.

After hugs all around, and comments about how each other's kids were getting so big, Bexar and Jack set out retrieving the Reed family's items out of the water tank cache.

"Dude, am I glad to see you," said Bexar. "I wasn't sure if you and Sandra got my text since everything went dark right after that. Was the drive from Arlington hard?"

"We just got here a few hours ago, and the drive was surprisingly hard for how close we were," replied Jack. "We had to overnight it out in the wild. Have you seen them? Have you seen the dead walking?"

"Fuck dude, I don't know what that's about!" exclaimed Bexar. "I don't know how it happened, but Dispatch broadcast an alert, and Command wanted everyone to respond back to the station, but it felt wrong, it felt really wrong, so I sent the text and hauled ass back home."

"Good thing you did," said Jack. "Have you heard from Malachi?"

"No, I got no reply from either of you. How about you?"

"Nope, nothing. DFW is pretty much on fire; we saw a lot of aircraft that had fallen out of the sky between Love Field and Dallas Fort Worth International; that's a lot of destruction. Malachi would have had to go through it, but maybe he was able to get around it. What do you think, an EMP event?"

Bexar grimly nodded his head. "Looks like it, my phone, everything, even my watch died. Did you see those planes go over after everything went dark?"

"Yeah, sort of looks like the chemtrail nutters were right on those."

Bexar climbed down into the base of the cache site tank and in short order had lifted his family's gear up to Jack, including a canvas wall tent nearly identical to Jack's. The tent was erected and positioned such that, along with the vehicles, it would provide a blind for their cooking fire. It was like a family camping trip, but the games and happiness were replaced with worry and dread.

Wilmar, Texas

Malachi was driving as fast as he could without crashing the Scout and trailer. Amber's breathing had become even more shallow, her skin clammy and pale. She was slowly dying, and Malachi knew it. He had to get to the cache site and hope the others would be able to help him.

In just a few short hours the world had changed drastically; any emergency help he could have depended on had vanished from existence. Malachi figured if he could keep this pace up, he should arrive at the cache site in about ninety minutes.

"Hang on baby, I'm getting us there, I'm getting help, but you've got to stay with me."

Malachi reached over and patted her hand. It felt very cold, but it moved a little, so he knew there was still hope. He continued holding her hand while speeding down the dirt road, thankful there weren't any disabled cars on this road. Amber moved her hand again, and Malachi looked at his wife. To his shock her eyes were dim and milky, her skin already turning greenish-gray. A moan erupted from the very core of the woman that had once been his wife, and as it escalated into a bloodcurdling scream, Amber lunged at him, tearing a large chunk of flesh from his forearm with her teeth.

"WHAT THE FUCK AMBER!? AMBER—WHAT THE FUCK!?" screamed Malachi in pain and disbelief.

He slammed on the brakes, nearly causing the trailer to come around the rig. By now his brain had absorbed the realization that Amber was obviously not alive. Opening the driver's door, Malachi fell out of the Scout to the asphalt below. Amber thrashed through the interior, following her husband onto the roadway.

He tried to draw the pistol on his right hip, but couldn't get his right hand to work—Amber had severed the tendons and muscles in his forearm. Grabbing his belt with his left hand, he jerked it hard to the left, bringing the holster and pistol within reach of his left hand. Awkwardly drawing the pistol and having to rotate the grip by squeezing the pistol with his left hand, Malachi raised the XD Compact, focused on the front sight, and squeezed the trigger. Amber's skull exploded backward, spraying the side of the Scout with bone and brain matter. Malachi collapsed onto the road and sobbed.

CHAPTER 17

Cache Site near Maypearl, Texas

As the sun's edge disappeared below the western horizon, Jack and Bexar had finished the night watch rotation, each sitting watch for four hours. Sandra would start tonight's watch, ending in the morning with Bexar, who was also responsible for stoking the fire's coals and starting the morning's coffee.

Because of the added security, the group decided to use a fire and conserve the Coleman white gas. With the children put to bed and sleeping, the four friends wanted to stay up and chat, but the incredible stress of their cross-Texas trip and the strain of the night watch rotation took their toll, and all but Sandra went to their tents for the night.

About two hours after the last blue light of dusk had slipped past the horizon, Sandra heard a vehicle approaching. It stopped out of sight in the distance, and then resumed driving towards their camp. Just before the headlights appeared around the trees, Sandra quickly and quietly woke the others. Wearing only what they had worn to bed, the group quickly dispersed into a hasty L-shaped ambush and waited for the approaching threat.

The vehicle drove over one of the trip-wire alarms, firing a blank shotgun shell, the sound echoing into the night. Immediately the vehicle stopped, and extinguished the headlights. A door opened and closed in the darkness.

Jack and Bexar, holding the front line, shone their rifle-mounted Surefire lights on the vehicle; it was Malachi driving the Scout. He was very pale and covered in blood, his right arm was bandaged, and blood could be seen seeping through the bandage.

Extinguishing the weapon lights and lowering the muzzles, Bexar and Jack called out to Malachi and walked up to him. Bexar tried to give Malachi a hug, but before he could Malachi fell to the ground, crying.

Jessie and Sandra had come out of the woods on the passenger side of the Scout to find the vehicle empty, but there was a body wrapped in a camouflage poncho on top of the AT Chase trailer.

Choking, Malachi sobbed, "She got shot. There was a sniper where we had stopped on the south side of Dallas. It was something big, hit her in the shoulder and blew out the entire back of her shoulder blade. I tried to help her, but it was too much. Just too much blood, I was trying to hold her hand and talk to her, but it was too much." Then, holding up his right arm, bandage soaked through with blood, his right hand dangling lifeless, he said "She bit me!"

"Wait," said Bexar, "your wound is from where she bit you?"

"Yeah, I can't fucking believe it. She tried to come after me so I had to kill her."

"Was Amber bit?"

"No, just shot. Fuck! Does that mean I'm going to die? I'm going to be one of them?"

"I don't know," said Bexar. "Let's hope not, but we need to get your wound cleaned up and some water in you, you look like shit. In the morning we'll dig a grave for Amber."

Jessie helped Malachi over to the dwindling fire between the tents. Sandra retrieved the group's trauma bag from the cache and began tending to Malachi's grotesque wound.

CHAPTER 18

Denver International Airport, Colorado

Approaching the first pieces of wreckage scattered over the runway, Cliff soon encountered several of the undead wandering about out in the open. Attached to the end of his short barrel FN-P90 was a Gemtech suppressor; although it wouldn't make his rifle a silent whisper like in the movies, under cover of the loud popping sounds from the burning wreckage, the rifle report shouldn't be noticed. The sun was starting to set, and he needed to secure shelter if he was going to survive a Colorado winter night.

It was peculiar to Cliff, not moving from cover to cover with quick movements. Although the threat he faced was from the undead, not armed enemy combatants, he still walked in a tactical crouch out of habit, rolling his feet heel-to-toe to keep the muzzle of his rifle level while moving. Ten years ago, during his training at The Farm, Cliff had smiled to himself when his instructors were teaching them that technique—Cliff had mastered the movement as a freshman member of the marching band at John Marshall High in Rochester, Minnesota.

Rifle up, eyes open, controlled breathing through his nose, Cliff was within thirty yards of the first undead. The reticle of his Trijicon ACOG in line with his first target, steadily breathing out, Cliff gently squeezed the trigger and was satisfied to see the undead's head explode away from his shot. Driving his rifle to the right, the next shot was lined up and fired. Moving closer to the dozen or so undead remaining, Cliff saw he had been wrong; they had noticed the rifle's report, their heads snapping towards Cliff.

"Well shit, that didn't work like I planned," Cliff said aloud. Staying in his combat crouch with his rifle pointed up, he began to move at a much quicker pace to the right of the group. Like a quarterback flushed out of the pocket, Cliff kept his eyes downfield and continued to pick off undead targets while on the move. Having made a large semi-circle around the group while shooting on the quick-walk, the remaining undead were sent back to the grave with a single shot. Cliff quickly made a tactical reload, placing the magazine from the rifle in the deep back pocket of his pants. The magazine still had unspent rounds that could come in handy later.

Rifle up, Cliff made a slow circle to scan for threats in all directions. Satisfied that he was for now alone on the desolate runway, Cliff took off at a trot towards the wreckage of the President's aircraft.

The front half of the fuselage had come apart at the wing root, and had rolled to a sliding stop in a drainage culvert near the fire station located on the taxiway. Although lying on the aircraft's port side, the cylindrical structure of the front section of the aircraft appeared to be mostly intact. There was a chance that someone had survived the crash. Regardless, he would have to verify the President's status.

Maypearl, Texas

Jessie checked on the children still sleeping in the tents before coming back to the group sitting around the fire. Bexar had given Malachi one of his "spare" flasks of Jack Daniels whiskey, which Malachi had quickly consumed while recounting everything that had happened since he'd received Bexar's text message. Between the stress of his journey, the horror of losing his wife, his bad injury, and the effects of the whiskey, Malachi eventually succumbed to it all and fell into a drunken slumber. Bexar and Jack were prepared for this, and wrapped him in a blanket covered with a poncho, then handcuffed his left hand to a chain wrapped around the rear bumper of the Scout.

"Well Bexar," said Jack, "if you're right and he's infected, this will give us a chance."

"Jack, I'm sure he's infected. I think he's pretty much fucked and there's nothing we can do about it."

CHAPTER 19

The sun peered over the edge of the eastern horizon and the twenty-eighth of December had begun for the new world.

In Maypearl, Bexar stoked the fire to shake the winter's cold and prepare the coffee for the group. The blue enamel coffee pot was placed on a couple of rocks over one edge of the coals. Rather than wait for the water to boil, Bexar went to his Yeti cooler. *These perishables won't last much longer*, he thought, *especially with the wide-flung temperatures of a central Texas winter.* Out of the cooler came a dozen eggs, a bag of shrodded cheddar cheese, a Tupperware of salsa from his favorite taqueria back home, a twenty-pack of handmade flour tortillas from the same taqueria, and a package of Slovacek sausage. Looking at the breakfast in the making, he thought he would probably be able to find eggs again, but the rest of it would be gone forever after this morning.

Thankfully, Will and Keeley had slept through the night, but young children know no snooze button and both were now happily awake with the early morning energy found only in children. Jessie and Sandra awoke with the children and began tending to their immediate needs. Jack soon followed out of his tent and, after stopping in the woods to relieve himself, walked up to Bexar.

"That looks great," he said. "Have you checked on Malachi yet?"

"No, I was waiting for you to get up if I didn't hear anything from him before then."

"Okay, let's go over there."

Bexar picked up his AR which had been propped against the camping table and slung it over his shoulder. Jack wore his pistol but let Bexar give cover with the long gun while peeling back the poncho and blanket from Malachi's face.

Cold lifeless eyes stared back at them, and Malachi's skin was cold to the touch. As Jack reached to check for a pulse, Malachi's head suddenly turned and his teeth snapped at Jack's hand.

Jack jumped back. "Shit, that was close!"

"Well doesn't this just suck? Sorry Malachi, I love you and will always remember you." Bexar fired a single shot and gave his friend final rest. Malachi was dead.

CHAPTER 20

NORAD

Major Wright had not been able to contact his wife since the attack. The facility he was in was hardened against the effects of an EMP, even if it wasn't physically hardened like the former facility in "the mountain." He knew that the EMP events had disabled most of the electronic devices in the U.S., but that hadn't stopped him from repeatedly trying his wife's cellphone using a SAT-phone that was on site.

They were on Day Three of the attack, and he didn't see how they would be allowed to leave any time soon. Using data from hardened radar installations, he had reviewed the tracks showing that nearly every aircraft had fallen from the sky. He had examined the communications from the National Command Authority and had seen that the nation was in its death throes. Satellite Intelligence (SATINT) showed that just about every major city was nearly engulfed in raging, unchecked fires. The dead roamed the streets, and the living were quickly becoming an endangered species.

Over the past twelve hours, Wright had regained communication with five other government facilities. Some of them were physically hardened against attack, others had some preventative measures in place. As much as he had hated Cheyenne Mountain when he was a young officer, Wright desperately wished he was there now. On hand, in the new facility—away from the mountain and back on base—there were some provisions, but they wouldn't be able to survive a direct assault by the undead.

The National Military Command Center Reservation at the Raven Rock Mountain Complex, known simply as Site R, was still online. Camp David appeared to be a complete loss to fire, and had been overrun by the undead. Mount Weather Emergency Operations Center went dark with the EMP event, which it should have survived but satellite imagery showed that a large commercial aircraft had crashed through the middle of the command complex.

United States Strategic Command (USSTRATCOM) had been responsive for the first eighteen hours after the attack, but had since failed to respond. One of the enlisted men had been able to patch into their systems and gain access to the video feeds for the security systems—the lights were on, but they were completely overrun by the undead. No living survivors could be found, and the same appeared to be the case with the facility under Denver International.

Wright could only assume that Air Force One had suffered a fatal incident while attempting to land at DIA, after losing the aircraft's transponder and judging by the complete lack of radio traffic. The other VC-25 never made it off the ramp, the Vice President presumed dead with all others onboard.

It was staggering how quickly the virus had propagated and spread. There was still a lot of data to review, but at first glance it appeared to Wright that nearly every city in the lower forty-eight states had suffered a major system failure, compounded by additional major damage from crashing aircraft, uncontrolled fires, and the rapid spread of the undead.

Besides the handful of secured facilities still operating in the U.S., three carrier strike groups (CSGs) were returning as fast as their support ships could sail. Three CSGs had been in port in the U.S. when the attack happened, and the other three had gone dark shortly after the attack and were presumed to be lost to the undead.

CHAPTER 21

Cache Site near Maypearl, Texas

To Bexar and Jack it was obvious that they were in trouble. After burying Malachi next to his wife Amber, the group sat in the still winter air, trying to keep warm near the dwindling fire. Even the children were subdued while they played together.

"Malachi said that Amber hadn't been bitten, though I'm assuming they were covered in whatever fell from those chemtrails," Jack said.

"Yeah Jack, that's a problem," replied Bexar. "We've seen that the dead rise again to feed on the living. The living are then killed by the dead, and reanimated by whatever the dead are carrying, but if someone dies any other way they rise from the grave as well. That's fucked up."

"Bexar, what do we do? How do you make it through something like this? We always planned on riding out the storm and then rejoining society as it clawed up from the ashes, but how does the human race even survive something like this?"

"Jack, all we can do is stay here and do what we planned. Ride out the initial storm, then try to find other survivors."

"Okay, well, we better go through Malachi's stuff and figure out what he has that we can use." Jack stood and walked to Malachi's Scout and trailer. Bexar joined him, and soon the contents of Malachi's vehicle were laid out on the ground.

In the Scout were Malachi's rifle, pistols, and some ammo, along with his med-kit, two full five-gallon jerry cans of gas, ten cans of Coleman fuel, two Coleman lanterns with twenty extra mantels, three cases of MREs, and ten gallons of water in two blue water jugs. In the back of the truck were two plastic ten-gallon gas cans full of fuel. The clothing that Malachi and Amber had packed didn't fit anyone else in the group, but they kept useful items such as shoelaces, belts, and a few cotton shirts.

Bexar was amazed at how much stuff Malachi had stuffed in his little Scout and trailer, but the really interesting items were found in the cache site. Besides more MREs, water, and batteries, buried underneath some of the other gear were a handful of homebuilt Faraday boxes, which were designed to shield electronics from an EMP event. They were amazed Malachi had thought to construct them.

The group had generally believed that society would fall due to a global economic collapse resulting in rapid inflation, followed by mass starvation and civil unrest. Ever the geek, Malachi had prepared for an EMP. The first Faraday box contained a Yaesu mobile ham radio with microphone and speaker. The antenna was found outside the box. The second box contained a high end Garmin Global Positioning System unit, not the typical small GPS for daily travel, but one used for expeditions. The last Faraday box contained a Voyager shortwave radio that could be hand-cranked. The radio also had an attached solar panel.

Assuming that the Faraday boxes worked as they had been designed, the group now had a way to navigate. Hopefully, there were still others in the world able to broadcast on shortwave radio, and maybe still some HAM operators with working gear who had survived. Besides the electronic gear, Malachi had also stashed another four thousand rounds of Black Hills .223 ammo, along with another two dozen Magpul thirty-round Pmags.

By the time they had finished pulling all the cached items out of the bottom of the modified water tank, the sun was high overhead. The kids went to the tents for their afternoon nap, which gave the adults more time to play with the newfound gear.

Bexar loaded each of Malachi's Pmags, while Jack wired the Yaesu radio into his FJ and mounted the antenna on the roof rack. Sandra put the shortwave with the solar panel out to charge, while she and Jessie broke down the MREs from their boxes to save weight and space before packing half of them in the FJ and the other half in the Jeep. The task complete, Jessie grabbed the shortwave and climbed on top of the Jeep's roof rack, Sandra following behind her. They began scanning through the shortwave channels.

"Wait Jessie, go back, I heard voices on that channel," Sandra suddenly said excitedly.

Jessie went back to Channel 15,260 and called, "Bexar, Jack, come here quick!"

"... *with that news I am sorry to inform you that it would appear the first cases of the virus have been found in the U.K., and the efforts to contain the outbreak to the continent have failed. We at the BBC have been instructed to inform all citizens that they should not leave their homes. If any family members take ill with the virus or are bitten, quarantine them immediately and notify local authorities. Do not try to aid them, you will be exposed. Globally, we have reports of mass outbreaks across every continent save Australia and the Antarctic. We have lost all contact with the North American continent, and it is now assumed that the United States, Canada, and Mexico are completely overrun. South America reports widespread panic, riots, and looting.*

On the continent, most of Eastern Europe has gone dark after the nuclear exchange and the Ministry of Defense is still monitoring the nuclear fallout and radiation as it drifts to the west. We are told that we are not in danger of receiving any direct radiation, but we will continue to update as we can.

Ministry satellites continue to track the risen dead as they spread out from the major metropolitan locations in the infected areas. If you are listening to this broadcast from Western Europe, northern Africa, or even the United States ..." The station turned to static.

"Jack, what happened?" said Jessie.

"Jessie, shortwave can be weird, but anyway, it looks like we lost the reception we had." Jack turned to Bexar. "We might be in more trouble than we thought, and we're still really close to D/FW."

CHAPTER 22

Denver International Airport, Colorado

Cliff was not having a good day. Being forced to navigate the interior of an aircraft hull that is lying on its side is harder than it would seem. The plastic trim used throughout the aircraft was slippery, and Cliff had a hard time keeping his footing. More often than not, he had to crawl on his hands and knees. Thankfully, he didn't have to crawl through a commercial 747 with hundreds onboard who were now undead and would now be trying to eat him, he thought. At least he was crawling through the destroyed hulk of Air Force One.

After what seemed like an eternity, Cliff found what he was looking for. The First Lady was dead and would not reanimate; an unsecured drink cart had crushed her skull. The Speaker of the House was also onboard; Cliff thought he had already been evacuated to one of the other secure locations.

The Speaker was also dead, well, undead actually, straining against his seatbelt trying to reach Cliff. A single round from his suppressed P90 put the Speaker in his grave for good.

The President's body took longer to locate, but he was also undead. Someone had bitten a large chunk of flesh from his torso, and his intestines spilled from the large hole in his midsection. Another single shot from his P90, and Cliff became the only living person to have killed a sitting President. *Not guilty*, thought Cliff, *the President was already dead, I just put down his walking corpse.*

Done with the gruesome task on Air Force One, Cliff tried to quickly exit the wreckage. The President was dead. The Vice President was presumed dead, and the Speaker was dead. There was a long road ahead; he hoped there was still someone alive in the chain of succession to lead the country.

To complete his mission, Cliff had to reach one of the secure facilities that hopefully hadn't been overrun with the undead. To do that he needed food, water, and shelter, but what he really needed was transportation. He had to find a vehicle that would have survived the EMP, one that was old enough to be free from having an electronic ignition and a computer. Luckily, he had an entire airport parking lot full of cars to search.

Cache Site near Maypearl, Texas

Sandra cranked the generator handle on the shortwave radio while walking around the cache site, trying to catch any more transmissions from the BBC, but she was having no luck. Jessie maintained watch at the camp over the sleeping children, while Bexar and Jack took their rifles and patrolled through the church campgrounds. They hadn't cleared the campgrounds yet to ensure the fence was intact and there were no other people. Speaking in hushed whispers as they walked, Bexar said, "Honestly, Jack, I don't know that we're safe here. We're not far from Dallas, we're very close to Waxahachie, and I don't know if this barbed wire fence would hold off more than a few undead."

"If we have the time and could scare up the equipment, we could get shipping containers and build a wall around the camp."

"Yeah, but we'd need a crane and a truck. I don't think we have that sort of time right now. I think we're too close."

"Okay Bexar, then what, what's the answer? Do we wait and hope, or do we leave; do we plan and be ready to leave, what?"

"I think we should plan to leave. We might have warning, or we might have to flee immediately, but we should plan for both."

"Yeah, but where to, Bexar? What would be safe? Everything in this part of Texas is near something else, even in the Panhandle there are cities everywhere. East Texas is full of pine trees and meth heads. Hell, we probably wouldn't be able to tell the difference between the undead and the meth heads."

"What about west?" Bexar replied. "Not the Panhandle and not all the way to El Paso, but maybe a bit off the Interstate somewhere outside of Junction or Marfa. Wide-open nothing out there."

"It's wide-open nothing because there *is* nothing. What would we do for resources once our stores run dry? Besides, what if the undead keep walking, what would keep them from walking right over us out there?"

"What about the Davis Mountains, Jack?"

"No. But what about the Chisos Mountains? Get up in the basin, there's wells in that area, fresh springs, plenty of mule deer, and even javelina to eat. There's one road into the basin and we could block that easily enough. The couple of trails that lead into the basin would also be really easy to block, if a Zed could even walk up those trails."

"Zed!" Bexar stopped and looked at him. "Really Jack, we're calling them 'Zeds' now?"

"Hey!" said Jack, laughing, "what would you call them, 'tangos,' 'food-pyramid challenged,' or what?"

"Anyways," Bexar said, "Big Bend National Park, that's a good idea, but even before the end of the world it was a smooth twelve-hour drive from here. We're going to have to get through the Hill Country before we can get out on the Interstate. This'll take some work, we can't let any more of us die."

Back at the camp, Jessie was digging into the cooler for the last of the cheese sticks for the kids' after-nap snack, when Sandra called to her, "Come here Jess, I'm getting the BBC again!"

Jessie trotted over to Sandra and hushed the children so they could listen.

"... *encounter an infected person, they will die from the infection and reanimate shortly after death. Current reports have death from an infected bite coming as quickly as fifteen minutes, and as long as four hours. Prior to death, the newly infected experience high fever and hallucinations. After succumbing to the infection, the dead reanimate anywhere from almost immediately to ten minutes later. Children are reported to reanimate quicker. Persons who die without being bitten by an infected are also reanimating. Thus far, authorities have not found anyone who is immune to the Yama Strain. Upon death, immediate trauma to the person's brain and/or brain stem will prevent reanimation. Persons who have already reanimated will not stop until the brain and/or brain stem is destroyed. Further reports ...*"

"Damnit, lost the signal again."

Sandra and Jessie heard a low whistle come from the tree line. Pistols up towards the sound, Bexar and Jack walked slowly into the open. Sandra and Jessie told their husbands about the BBC broadcast, and in turn, Bexar outlined their plan to relocate.

Denver International Airport, Colorado

Cliff made his way along the runway and taxiways back towards the terminals. He didn't plan on going into the terminals, but he had to get past them to get to the large parking lots. In the darkened windows of the terminal he could see a lot of movement. He paused to look up at the glass and saw an undead child, a little girl, pressed against the glass, clawing with her dead hands to get to the living prey. The little girl was followed by an undead adult, then another and another, until, in the blink of an eye, the entire glass wall of the terminal was full of undead, hungry for Cliff.

In hindsight, Cliff realized he really should have walked out on the runway towards the other side of the airport, away from the terminal, but a lot of good that lesson did him now. He broke into a light jog in an attempt to gain some distance from the growing mob of undead. He wasn't sure how strong the glass was, but however strong it may be, he was sure it would eventually give way.

Rounding a baggage cart on the jog, Cliff ran chest first into a reanimated line worker still wearing his cold weather gear, orange vest, and ear protection. Cliff palm-heel struck the undead man in the chest as he was trained to do, his reaction instinctual from training, but it didn't work against someone who felt no pain, no surprise, and was not alive.

Too close to bring his rifle up, Cliff's hand fell to the Safariland holster on his right thigh. Pushing the hood forward and depressing the ALS button automatically, he brought his Sig Sauer pistol up and was only able to fire a single shot before the undead had pushed him backwards. It was enough; the reanimated line worker's skull exploded out from the blast, covering Cliff with brain matter, blood, and pieces of bone.

Cliff's ears were ringing. He hadn't thought about his pistol not being suppressed, which made him wonder how many other workers were on the flight line in the working level of the airport. The answer was not long in coming, as a chorus of moans erupted from the darkness under the terminal.

"Well, shit on me," muttered Cliff while holstering his Sig. He was only a few thousand feet from the fence line, and almost a mile to the little bit of safety the fence offered from the hordes of undead coming up from the depths of the airport. He knew he didn't have to run fast, he just couldn't stop running. With a deep sigh, Cliff started his run for the fence, running for his life.

CHAPTER 23

Denver International Airport, Colorado

Like a running back making a dash for the sideline to gain speed and distance from a defender, Cliff ran at an angle, away from the terminal and towards the fence line. Former flight line workers, now part of the legion of undead, continued to spill out of the dark underbelly of the airport's terminal at an alarming rate. Their speed wasn't an issue, as they lumbered forward at roughly the speed of an elderly power-walker at the mall; the problem was the sheer number of them.

Cliff didn't have the ammo or the time to put every one of those things down for good. He knew he had to make the fence to get more time to escape. Getting closer to the fence, he broke right, towards a large gate chained closed with a padlock.

Unlike in the movies, shooting a lock off a chain is fairly hard. If he was on a mission that would require breaching, he would use his modified Remington 870 shotgun, but Cliff only had his pistol and rifle.

As he reached the gate, the nearest threat was closing in from about forty yards away. Cliff took an angle to the padlock and quickly put six rounds into the top of the lock with his rifle. It broke open just in time for him to spin around and put down the four closest threats with head shots.

Now with a little more time, he was able to twist the lock, breaking it loose, and pull the chain out of the gate. He pushed the gate open and stepped through. Retrieving a pair of flex cuffs from his back pocket, he then secured the gate. It wouldn't hold the approaching horde forever, but it should slow them down, or at least he hoped it would.

Taking a moment to catch his breath, Cliff scanned the large parking lots before him. There was some movement, but nothing that looked like it was alive or undead. Instead of using typical movements from cover-to-cover close to the vehicles, he gave the parked cars a wide berth as he proceeded down the aisles.

The threat he faced didn't lay in wait to ambush you at a choke point, no, they grabbed you if they could and would bite to kill. The added space didn't give him any cover from a gunman, but it gave Cliff the reaction time he needed from a surprise undead reaching for a kill.

He needed a vehicle that would run well, but old enough that it wouldn't have been affected by the EMP. The Colorado concrete field was full of a seemingly endless supply of new Subarus and Toyotas. Walking at a fast pace across the ends of the aisles, he saw a vehicle outline that gave him some hope. The roofline was unmistakable, and happened to be a type of vehicle he had experience with.

Walking to the vehicle, Cliff found an old Volkswagen bus, an air-cooled, Type 2 VW Transporter. The van was a bay-window, and should have originally had a 1600cc motor from the factory in Wolfsburg, Germany. It looked to be in good shape, so the owner either maintained it well, or had spent time and money making it right.

Lifting the rear deck lid to look at the motor, Cliff found a clean engine bay with an upright motor that sported dual Weber carburetors. It looked like he'd found another VW fan who had built up a nice van. The old-style vent windows on the passenger side made for easy entry, and in less than ten minutes Cliff had hotwired the van. The old VDO gauge on the dash indicated that there was three-quarters of a tank of gas left, which he hoped was accurate; regardless, he would have to stop for gas a few times to make the long drive to Nevada.

CHAPTER 24

December 29th
Cache Site near Maypearl, Texas

Jack sat through the last night watch, stoking the fire's coals to start a kettle for coffee. The rest of the group would be waking up soon. He hoped today would start better than the day before. Yesterday Jack and Bexar had had to kill their longtime friend. He knew that Malachi had already technically been dead, but it still hurt to have to put your friend down. Still, he hoped someone would do the same for him if he ended up like that.

The last four hours sitting and listening in the dark winter night gave Jack plenty of time to think of a plan with a schedule to leave, and how to make it happen. Clearly, they would need to use the bulk of Malachi's gear and cached items, although they would leave some of the duplicates here at the cache site due to weight and room constraints in their caravan of vehicles. Between their three vehicles and the supplies they carried, Jack calculated they had right about ninety gallons of gasoline. Guessing that each of the trucks could average about fifteen miles per gallon if they kept their speed around fifty miles per hour on the open road, and that it was about six hundred miles from Maypearl to Big Bend, they only had half the amount of gasoline they needed to make the trip.

They would have to scavenge gas en route, unless they only took two of the trucks. Then they could make the trip with barely enough gas, but they would lose a lot of their newly gained supplies in the trade. They would also need to restock their gas stores before getting into the park because there were only two gas stations in the park, assuming that they hadn't already been drained dry. Besides losing the ability to carry more gear, if they took two trucks and one failed, they would be in a lot of trouble. *No*, he thought, *better to take all three trucks*.

Dawn was beginning to break over the horizon when Bexar walked up to the fire pit, stamping his feet to try to warm up. "Jessie's still sleeping and has Keeley in her sleeping bag to keep her warm. We really should have bought the wood stoves for the tents; that would have made for easy cooking and a comfortable tent at night."

"Yeah Bexar, if it wasn't for the dead walking, we could have bartered for something over the summer, or bought it with our silver coins, but we missed the planning meeting for the end of the world—who would've guessed zombies?" Jack replied sarcastically. "Well, I've been thinking about our trip, and before we do anything else, we have to decide if we're taking all three trucks or just our two."

Bexar thought for a moment. "I'd say we at least try to start with all of them, then at least we have a backup, and could bring more of our gear."

"I agree," replied Jack, "but gas supplies are going to be a bitch. Also, I think we should bring as much of Malachi's gear as we can even though I'm figuring the trip to be roughly six hundred miles, and we only have enough gas to get about halfway there. How are we going to siphon more fuel, don't modern cars have a screen or something to prevent that?"

"Yeah they do," said Bexar, "but it isn't too big of a deal. With a truck we can get under and puncture the tank to drain it into our cans. With a car you just pull the back seat bottom out, the fuel pump access is there and easy to get off. It's popular with drug runners who pack gas tanks with dope."

"Really? Guess I didn't realize that, makes sense though. That'd be pretty funny if we found a car full of dope while trying to source gas," Jack laughed.

Bexar and Jack spent the next three hours laying out all their gear, packing and sorting it for the trip. Jack would lead the convoy in his FJ, Sandra and Jessie and the kids would be in the middle driving the Wagoneer, and Bexar would be in the Scout in the rear position. Like a diplomatic escort, the wives and children would be in the protected position of the convoy.

The sun was low in the western sky when the group finally thought to check the GPS unit Malachi had packed in a Faraday box in the cache. Yesterday it wouldn't turn on and they initially thought it hadn't survived, but while planning the route it occurred to them to try plugging it into one of the trucks to see if the batteries were merely empty.

Jack retrieved the Garmin GPS, plugged it into the cigarette lighter on his dash, and the device turned on. After booting and calibrating it, Jack entered their destination as the main Ranger's Station in Big Bend National Park. The calculated route showed a drive time of eleven hours.

"Dude, it works, I can't believe it. Also, it says the time is 4:30 p.m., so it's nice to know what time it is again."

"Good job, Jack. I think it's too late to leave today, but we should plan for first light tomorrow or the next day."

Outside of Denver, Colorado

Cliff was happy with how well the VW's owner had rebuilt the van. The motor sounded great, and even the steering was tight. He drove the van through the airport exit and turned onto E-470 to try to stay away from the heart of Denver, driving on the wrong side of the highway because of the blocked traffic.

A plane had crashed onto the highway near I-75, and part of the road was completely impassable. As much as he would have enjoyed driving to Longmont to get a beer from the Left Hand Brewery, it just wasn't going to happen. Nearing I-25, it looked like much of Denver was burning; he guessed a lot of the fires had started when all the commercial aircraft began falling out of the sky. They weren't shielded from an EMP like Air Force One had been.

The traveling was slow going, taking Cliff the better part of the day to make the trip around the outside of the city and onto Colorado State Highway 128. He had come across many undead, but had yet to see another living person. He was convinced that if anyone else was still alive in Denver, they weren't long for this world. The Yama Strain had definitely taken hold.

Soon the sun would be low against the mountains to the west, so Cliff needed to find shelter. He needed food and water, but more so he really needed more gas. The upgraded motor the van's owner had installed worked great, pushing the old German steel over the mountains, but the added power came with a hefty fuel price. For almost the past three days, Cliff had been running on no sleep and little more than a couple of protein PowerBars and some water. To his right was a sign for Wal-Mart, but he hadn't been too excited about going to Wal-Mart before the dead had started walking, much less now that it was probably full of undead. Finally he saw a sign for Walgreens. He hoped it would have less people than a big-box store, and that there would be some food and water left on the shelves.

Cliff circled the parking lot to check for any signs of undead before backing onto the sidewalk in front of the main doors. Exiting the van, he left the motor running; he was sure it would attract the undead, but at least he wouldn't be left trying to get the van started while under attack.

Although the storefront windows faced the waning afternoon sun, the interior of the store was surprisingly dark. Cliff pushed the momentary switch on the Surefire light on his FN; it helped but things weren't as good as they could have been. The reanimated cashier stood near her post, a large piece of flesh missing from her left shoulder. As she moaned and reached for Cliff, he quickly dispatched her with a suppressed round to the forehead. The sound of the rifle, even though suppressed, brought forth a chorus of moans from the darkened back of the store.

Patience is a virtue, he thought, and was rewarded by the sound of shuffling feet coming towards him. There weren't any real surprises, and by the time the last moan had been silenced, a dozen bodies lay near the cash register, released from their fate as a walking corpse.

Grabbing a shopping cart, Cliff held his pistol in one hand while dragging the cart behind him with the other. Every can of soup and chili on the shelf went in the cart, as did the beef jerky and protein bars. Opening the cooler, he was greeted by the horrid smell of rotting meat and sour milk. The bottles of Gatorade and water went in the cart, but then a cold, gray hand shot out through the drink racks, grabbing him by the wrist and trying to pull him into the cooler.

"Fuck!" He shot three times before the undead's grip went slack. After taking a few moments to catch his breath from the scare, Cliff loaded the van with his new supplies and left.

Making an illegal U-turn, he pointed the van towards the Rocky Mountain Municipal Airport. If he was lucky he might find a hangar to park the van in and take shelter. If he was lucky, he might find some cars to siphon gas from in the morning, but worst case scenario, he thought the van might run on Avgas, or aviation fuel.

CHAPTER 25

Broomfield, Colorado

Reaching the Rocky Mountain Municipal Airport in Broomfield, Cliff continued out onto the ramp to see where the smaller General Aviation aircraft were parked. Parked on the ramp to his left were a handful of small aircraft. That there weren't many wasn't too surprising since it was the dead of winter, but at least it gave him a direction to drive.

He was thankful that this airport was much smaller than DIA, but it was still larger than most small municipal airports around the U.S. From what he could see, there weren't any undead out in the field or on the runway, which made sense since most pilots wouldn't have been at the airport in the middle of the Colorado winter when the attack came. Luckily, the airport also had a fence wrapping around most of the perimeter, so there was a little protection gained from that.

A few moments later he located the old T-style hangars with sliding doors. He didn't want to use a hangar with a door that rose upwards, because although he could hand-crank the door up, it would take forever, and could put him in a bad position if he was trying to leave in a hurry. Faded blue paint and a padlock were all that kept him from gaining access to the second hangar from the end. Removing this padlock would be quieter than the last; he'd had the time to make a shim for the lock.

Emptying a Dr. Pepper soda can he had taken from Walgreens, Cliff took out his SOG multipliers and began cutting the can. Making a modified "T" shape with a point, he bent it slightly; now it would only take a little effort to shift the Master Lock padlock open.

In short order Cliff had opened the faded blue doors and found an old Beechcraft Bonanza sitting in the hangar. Further investigation of the hangar found it clear of persons, dead or otherwise, and a pull bar, which he used to pull the plane out of the hangar, letting it roll towards the tie-downs. It was a nice, well-maintained airplane, but he really didn't care where it ended up or if it was damaged in the process, he just needed it out of the way.

Once the hangar was emptied of its aircraft, Cliff backed his procured VW van into the hangar and turned off the motor. It was time to close up shop and scavenge for the supplies he needed out of the airport.

Checking the cabinets in the hangar, Cliff found a few cans of Plexus, some cleaning rags, a garden hose, and three gallons of distilled water. The hose and water were the big find. Distilled water did him no good since he needed electrolytes, but he could pour out the water and the jugs would get him started on his task. A section cut out of the garden hose would be the other piece to the puzzle; with these tools he could siphon gas and bring it back to the hangar. Also in the hangar was a basic set of tools, a socket set, some vice grips, and a variety of screwdrivers. All the tools went in a plastic tote in the van; when you're driving an old air-cooled Volkswagen, you never know when it might break down and leave you stranded if you don't have some tools.

Cliff left the hangar and pulled the door closed, leaving the lock off but tying a small piece of 550 cord through the lock hole. That would keep the undead out, and also let him know if anyone else went into the hangar while he was gone.

The sun was getting low on the horizon when Cliff set off at a trot towards the fly-in restaurant he had passed earlier near the ramp. It would have been faster to drive around the airport, but that could bring a lot of attention, undead or otherwise. He had a mission to complete, and he had to be alive to complete it.

First, he needed to find gas. In the small airport parking lot he found a couple of beat-up old Subarus and an old Chevy K1500 Blazer. The Blazer was his first choice, so after quickly scanning the area for threats, he slid under the back of the old truck. Using his Emerson knife, he cut out a section of the hose between the gas tank and fuel filler opening. Lying on his back, he slid the section of garden hose he had brought with him into the tank and began sucking on the other end. The gas flowed quickly, and some got into his mouth. Coughing, he filled the three water jugs with gas, left the hose in the gas tank, and ran back to the hangar. Three trips later, he had completely filled the VW's fuel tank and had three extra gallons of gas for his trip.

It was now dark. Cliff shut the hangar doors, set the door pin, and tied the doors together from the inside. He was exhausted. He needed to get some sleep, but he still had some work to do first. Setting the alarm on his watch for five o'clock in the morning so he could start out before the sun came up, he pulled out a Phillips screwdriver and removed the bulbs from the turn signals, the dome light in the van, and the taillights. If he was driving at night, he wanted to be completely blacked out, and not accidently illuminate his position by bumping a turn signal. He also disconnected the horn.

Maypearl, Texas

The trucks were packed with all but the essentials the group needed for the night and one of the tents, which everyone was now sharing. The roof racks of both the FJ and Wagoneer were nearly overloaded, and all three trucks sat low on their rear springs. The group's plan was to wait to review the full route the GPS suggested. Much like everyone who wished Google Maps had a "not-through-the-ghetto" option for directions, they did not want to be routed through a big city like Austin en route to Big Bend. They had to get this right.

Bexar took the first watch, followed by Jessie, then Sandra and Jack. The trucks were repositioned to face the camp's exit, through their secret gate, so they could make a hasty exit if they needed to.

Dinner was beans, rice, and Gatorade, the last cooked meal at their cache site. The fire dwindled and twilight gave way to darkness, and everyone but Bexar went to bed. The dark winter sky was aglow to the north from the fires. Dallas was on fire, and Bexar knew that their time at the cache site was up; it would be nearly suicidal to stay. Even if the fire didn't continue to spread that far south, the undead hordes would be pushed this way, like rats fleeing a sinking ship. In a few short days Bexar had decided that if there was still a God left in heaven, he was the angry and spiteful God of the Old Testament.

CHAPTER 20

December 30th
Maypearl, Texas

The orange glow on the horizon persisted throughout the night. Jack said that during his watch he was sure it had actually become brighter.

Sandra had stayed up with Jack during his watch, enjoying the alone time with her husband. It had only been three days since the world ended, but it felt like a lifetime ago. Speaking in hushed whispers so as not to wake the kids, they discussed what their future was, and what sort of future Will would have in this new condemned world. There were no easy answers.

They'd also talked about whether Maypearl had been the best choice for their cache site. Malachi had wanted to use their favorite camping spot at Paw Paw Creek on Lake Texoma, but that would have meant Bexar had a much longer drive, never mind that the fluctuating water levels and the popularity of the campsite would have put their cached supplies in jeopardy.

The orange glow of the night sky blended with the crimson of the rising sun. Sandra longed for the heat of the sun. The night had been bitterly cold, and even if it wasn't much above freezing during the day, it was still warmer than it had been.

A sudden shotgun blast from within the campgrounds roused Bexar from his tent, and sent Jack flying to his feet, both with their ARs in hand.

"Was that one of the trip wires?" Bexar asked.

"Jesus, Bexar, go put pants on, I'll check it out," Jack replied.

Bexar went back in his tent and came out a few seconds later dressed in loose pants, untied boots, and a hooded sweatshirt. Sandra took Will, still groggy, to the

Jeep, where they were quickly joined by Jessie, with Keeley in her arms crying at the top of her lungs. The sound of the crying toddler was soon drowned out by the gurgling moans of the undead. More shotgun blasts went off.

"Shit!" exclaimed Jack, "there's got to be two dozen of them—Bexar, grab our shit, I'll cover." The sound of the undead trampling through the brush wasn't nearly as loud as the chorus of moans coming from the dark woods. Bexar threw his rifle over his back and dove inside the tent to gather the last of the gear. He worked as fast as he could, accompanied by the sound of Jack firing his AR and cursing loudly.

Outside the tent, Sandra started the jeep and turned on the headlights. With the wood line illuminated, they could see another two dozen or so undead making their way through the brush. The lead zombie looked horrible, wearing only a pair of soiled and torn jeans, with a large gaping hole where his belly button had been. Only the remnants of intestines that had spilled out of his body remained, dragging on the ground behind him. Bexar exited the tent just in time to see Jack squeeze the trigger of his AR and explode the undead's head backwards.

Bexar took what he had gathered up from the tent and threw it in the back seat of the Scout. They didn't have time to take down the tent; luckily, they had packed the other two.

"Jack, wheels up man, we've got to go!"

"Right, Bexar, what about the gate?"

"Fuck it, we'll get to it when we get to it—let's roll!"

Jack sprinted for his FJ and started the engine. Bexar dropped to a kneeling firing position and began taking out the closest undead threats. "Breathe, sight, and press," he repeated quietly to himself. The Magpul CTR stock pulling into his shoulder, he systematically drove the rifle to the next target and repeated the process. Having brought down the four closest undead, Bexar stood and moved fast to the Scout.

Jack was leaning out of his open door to cover Bexar's retreat, and only began to drive once Bexar had started his truck. The three of them started towards the gate. Slowing, Jessie got out of the Wagoneer and ran to the gate; there she stood ready, pistol in hand, waiting for Sandra to pull the Wagoneer through. With her focus on the vehicles pulling through the gate, she didn't see the old undead woman shamble up behind her from the woods. As the cold, dead hands grasped her shoulders and began to pull her over backwards for the kill, Jessie began screaming loudly.

Bexar had stopped the Scout when he saw the zombie approaching his wife, but didn't have time to warn her. Instead, he opened the driver's door and stood in the doorframe, steadying the rifle on the top of the windshield. As the old woman pulled Jessie off balance, he had the one minute of angle—1MOA—to get the point of his red dot lined up with the bridge of her nose. Before the zombie could bite and kill his wife, the old woman's head exploded, showering Jessie with skull and brain matter. Jessie ran as fast as she could to the Wagoneer now clear of the gate, and jumped in.

Like it or not, the group was back on the road, and would be until they reached the safety of the Chisos Mountains.

Rocky Mountain Metropolitan Airport, Colorado

Although this all seemed like some sort of bastard training exercise thought up for the Survival, Evasion, Resistance and Escape (SERE) school Cliff had attended ten years prior, Cliff knew that it wasn't; he was completely on his own, and the enemy gave no quarter. The few hours of sleep that was afforded in the cold aircraft hangar outside of Denver was the best thing Cliff had experienced in the past seventy-two hours.

At least the undead won't water board you if you're caught, Cliff chuckled to himself. He lit a chafing dish after bending a wire coat hanger he'd found in the back of the van to make a little cooking stand for his procured can of vegetable stew from Walgreens. He had another long day ahead of him, so he took a little extra time to pack things just right in the van after breakfast, and to relieve himself in the corner of the hangar. Once he was set, he pulled the locking pin for the hangar doors and untied the 550 cord he had used to secure them through the night. Before pushing the door open slightly, Cliff drew his pistol and held it close to his chest in the SUL position. About three to four inches of fresh snow had fallen during the night. Although a curse for the drive, it was a blessing for Cliff's security. He could instantly recognize that no one, dead or alive, had been near his hangar during the night. This was the first good break he'd had since the facility under Denver International had gone dark.

Cliff pushed the hangar doors open far enough for the van to clear, climbed into the old VW, and started the motor. In a few moments he turned onto Airport Way and continued on his route towards I-70. As he drove, he occasionally thought he could see movement in the dark windows of businesses along the road, but saw only a handful of undead moving out in the open. He had still seen no sign of any living people. He knew the Yama Strain was exceptionally virulent, but surely someone else had also survived.

CHAPTER 27

Maypearl, Texas

Jack led the three-vehicle convoy out of the old Royal Rangers campground and away from their compromised cache site. As they approached the town of Maypearl, Bexar saw that the fire had done considerable damage, but had mostly died out. There was no movement in the town at all; it seemed as if death had swept through the town, laying all living things to waste.

In the lead vehicle, Jack booted the GPS that Malachi had protected from the EMP and selected their destination. The GPS advised the group to turn north back up to I-20, but that would lead them back into the very area they were trying to escape. No, they needed to move south and point west as soon as possible, putting as much distance between them and the undead horde behind them as possible.

On the south side of Maypearl, Jack stopped the convoy for a quick pow-wow and planning session. Walking over to Bexar, who was standing next to Jessie by the Wagoneer, he said, "Bexar, I don't think there was anything alive in that town."

"Yeah," Bexar agreed, "I didn't even hear any dogs barking."

Jack continued, "The GPS says to go up to I-20 and head west, but I think we'd be better off hitting I-35, and heading south to get to I-10 somewhere west of Boerne."

Bexar thought for a moment. "I agree, except that I-35 was a parking lot of death when we crossed it heading up here. We can hit it for a little ways, but we need to get off before we get anywhere near Waco. Then we can see if we can find a highway heading west. I don't want to get any closer to San Antonio than Boerne, and even that seems a little close."

Colorado

Cliff reached I-70 without any issues. The number of abandoned cars was surprisingly small, and he found the drive fairly easy even with the fresh snow, but was still concerned that he hadn't seen any signs of life since climbing out of the underground facility. He really didn't want to be the last man standing in this hellish new world.

He turned onto the Interstate and headed west towards Groom Lake, Nevada, keeping his speed around forty miles per hour in an effort to conserve gas, and also to drive safely around the abandoned vehicles on the roadway. *It would be nice*, he thought, *if all the people that had been in those cars and were now nowhere to be seen had fled to safety*, but he was a realist, and thought those people had probably all been killed and were now wandering the countryside, looking for their next victim.

The drive took Cliff through the heart of Colorado skiing country, and as he passed through Breckenridge and Vail, the thought of a bunch of rich, undead skiers lurching through the resorts in their expensive sweaters and North Face jackets made Cliff smirk. Even though the thought was funny, the threat was real, so he stopped the van in the middle of the highway, clear of any other vehicles, and filled up the tank with the three gallons of gas he had stored in the water jugs.

Scanning for threats, he chose another truck to steal gas from about two hundred feet further up the highway. This time he drove his van close to the fuel source and left it running while he slid under the Dodge Ram to repeat the same fuel siphoning process he had done the night before. He wanted a full tank and a backup, since he didn't want to stop again until he was on the other side of Vail.

Hillsboro, Texas

Hillsboro was a sad town long before the dead rose from the grave to hunt the living. The once well-stocked outlet mall had withered away years ago, with much of the retail space sitting vacant. For Bexar, the best part of Hillsboro was that it was the last stop for a Braum's hamburger and shake. There weren't any more Braum's south of here in Texas. Not that it mattered now; any Braum's food or ice cream in the store would have gone bad by now.

The convoy stayed on the Interstate through the town, passing several clusters of undead. Each turned to follow their new prey, stumbling down the road behind their vehicles. Although the group quickly outpaced them, Bexar worried that the undead might not ever stop the chase; that he and his family and friends would never be able to stop and rest, or they would be forced to fight for their lives. *Won't they get distracted after they can't see us anymore and wander off somewhere else?* thought Bexar.

His mind continued to wander as they drove. The convoy was keeping pace between forty and fifty miles per hour, driving around undead and abandoned vehicles, but even those obstacles weren't enough to keep him from becoming sleepy and distracted. He wished the group had some sort of two-way radios so they could talk to each other, and he really wished the radio in his truck would still play music, not that there was probably anyone left in the radio stations to broadcast it.

When the group reached the outskirts of Whitney, they stopped to survey the area. Jack could see movement across the roadway, but from that distance he couldn't tell if the person was dead or alive.

CHAPTER 28

Glenwood Springs, Colorado

Cliff made good time, considering his situation, but once he reached Glenwood Springs he had to slow down because there were a lot of abandoned cars in the road. He had expected to find some sort of signs of life as he came into civilization, but there was a complete lack of people. If anyone was still alive, there should be some signs of their survival, cooking fires or something, yet there was nothing.

If they were all dead, truly dead, he would have seen bodies. There was nothing, not even the undead. Glenwood had burned, and although it didn't look like any large fires were still burning, much of the typical urban sprawl—shopping centers, restaurants, stores, and apartments—had obvious and significant fire damage.

As he neared the Highway 82 turnoff, it was apparent that a massive battle had preceded his arrival by a couple of days. He couldn't tell if the fight had been between factions of the living, or between survivors and the undead, but for all the damage and all the carnage, there was a distinct lack of bodies. Further down the road though, there were at least one hundred bodies strewn about on both sides of the river, obvious battle casualties that also appeared to be covered in bite marks.

Cliff had downshifted and slowed the van even more to survey the carnage when out of the corner of his eye a movement caught his attention. With a loud curse, he slammed both feet down onto the clutch and the brake pedals while jerking the wheel of the old van to the right. He was able to miss the first two undead, but hit the next three while skidding on the snow, front wheels still turned to the right.

In his mind, time slowed, and he chastised himself both for being distracted and for reacting incorrectly. He knew a driver can either evade or brake, but can't do both and expect to retain control of a vehicle. Striking the three walking undead, physics once again proved master and the van lurched hard onto its left side. Cliff's head bounced off the side of the van and hit the windshield hard.

Central Texas

Children do not trouble themselves with the worries of the adult world. They simply have no concern for what time a parent went to bed; they will still wake up at a ridiculously early hour. Children don't care if you're hungover or sick, they will awake with the need for attention, love, and breakfast. Young children especially will have no thoughts about the total collapse of society, or that the dead have risen to hunt the living.

Will and Keeley slept through the encounter with the handful of undead in Whitney. The convoy managing to drive away from the threat with no problem. They napped as they passed through the small towns of Meridian and Hico. As the group approached the east side of Dublin, Texas, however, their good fortune lapsed, and both children awoke and demanded to be let out.

Sandra flashed the headlights of the Wagoneer to signal Jack to pull over. Jack was now on station to find a safe place to let the kids out for a good half-hour, someplace they could run and play, someplace safe in a world overrun by the dead.

While in college, Jack had dabbled in skydiving, making a handful of training jumps at a little drop zone at the airport in Dublin. Ten years ago the airport had been small, with only a handful of hangars and buildings, and it had been wide open and surrounded by a fence. The idea of finding a schoolyard playground scared Jack, but he figured the group could circle the wagons to create a safety buffer out in the field next to the runway.

He led the convoy into the airport, past the old weathered hangars, and drove across the runway to the open area between the runway and the fence line. Once the kids were out and happy to be playing, Bexar and Jack began to come up with a plan for a side trip.

"Dublin, as in Dublin Dr. Pepper," Bexar said, "made with the original cane sugar formula. Come on, everyone sells it here, how hard would it be to sneak into a gas station and take a case of it?"

"Bexar, do you know how crazy that sounds? What about the kids and our wives?"

"They'll be fine, Jack, we'll just be gone for ten minutes, besides we need some snack food for the kids and we really need a bunch more Gatorade if we're going to the desert."

"Okay, but we better move fast," Jack said, "and we're taking the FJ so we don't have to dick with that trailer on the Scout."

Bexar told the girls what they were doing and before much protest could be raised, he and Jack climbed into the FJ and took off across the airport as quickly as they could.

Leaving the airport, they turned towards town in search of a convenience store. They passed a nursing home and could see roughly three dozen elderly undead shuffling around the property.

"That's so fucked up!" exclaimed Jack. "Those poor bastards were lying in wait for death, and when it finally came it was taken away from them!"

"Jack, let's just hope that none of them head this way until we get back to the airport and get out of here."

The first store they came to looked like it hadn't been updated since the mid-sixties, and the fuel pumps were about as old but looked like they'd still been operating when the end came. A couple of oilfield trucks were parked in the parking lot, as well as a sheriff's patrol car.

Bexar parked the FJ by the fuel pumps and left the motor running as they climbed out and walked to the front of the store. The windows were dark and they couldn't see inside the store. Bexar pulled open the door and held it open with his foot while Jack made entry, switching on the light on his AR. Both were overwhelmed by the stench of death, and they hoped that whatever it was, it was really good and dead.

Sensing movement behind the counter, Bexar moved the muzzle of his rifle left to light up the possible threat with his weapon light. Behind the counter stood Flo the cashier, ready to help any new customers, white apron and name tag still on her body. The milky white orbs of her eyes flashed in the light as she raised her undead arms towards the fresh meal. Bexar thumbed the safety down and pressed the trigger to the rear, and Flo's head exploded backwards, covering the lottery scratch-off display.

The single shot brought a handful of moans from the dark towards the back of the store. Sweeping left, Bexar found another zombie just as Jack's AR barked through the dark store, engaging his own threats. They shot another four undead in the store before being able to call clear.

"Jesus, Jack," said Bexar, "maybe we should throw something into the darkness next time to see if there's a reaction. Flo scared the crap out of me!"

"Who the fuck is Flo?" asked Jack.

"The clerk. She was standing behind the counter, name tag and all."

They searched through the store, finding the Dublin Dr. Pepper they had come for, as well as three cases of Gatorade, two cases of water, some lighters, and a few candy bars. Ten minutes later, they were back on the road and headed back towards the airport, Jack at the wheel. Bexar hunched over the dashboard in the passenger seat, scratching at a lottery ticket.

Jack looked at him incredulously. "Seriously, a scratch-off?"

"Bash all you want," said Bexar, "but I just won twenty bucks! Let's go back and get Flo to cash it for me."

"Fuck you," replied Jack, and Bexar started laughing.

Jack looked back at the road just in time to see one of the nursing home undead bounce under the bumper of the FJ before the truck lurched to the left.

"Shit, blew the front left tire, but I don't think we should stop with those other old-guy undead headed this way."

"I'm with you, Jack," said Bexar. "Airport first, and the girls can give cover while we fix it."

Now driving with a flat tire, it took them twenty more minutes to make it to the middle of the airport, where they found the Scout with the trailer abandoned, their wives and children nowhere to be seen.

CHAPTER 20

Glenwood Springs, Colorado

Cliff's first thought was that someone was knocking on the door of his walkup outside of Alexandria, Virginia. Consciousness began to wash over him like waves, and he slowly began to remember where he was and how he got there. The van was lying on its side, and Cliff was crumpled against the driver's door between the bench seat and the metal dashboard.

The smell of gasoline was overwhelming as he began wiggling his toes, working his way up his body to make sure he didn't have any serious injuries. With more consciousness came more pain. He was sure he had a concussion, but at least nothing seemed to be broken.

The fuel he had stored in the distilled water jugs had spilled out, covering much of his gear, including the food. He still had three more MREs in his go-bag with the extra ammo and a few other items, but the newly acquired supplies were tossed about in the van. Pulling himself out from under the dash to look out the cracked windshield, he was greeted by a blackened face that had no lips and only one eye, and was clawing at the windshield. His immediate reaction was to draw his pistol, but checked himself—if he shot through the windshield he risked breaking open the only protection he had.

Cliff gathered his rifle and his go-bag and pushed open the side doors of the van, which were now at the top of the van, climbing out on top of his stolen wreck. Scanning the area, he saw about a dozen undead shambling towards the van from the rear, and another six from the left. And then there was the one-eyed, no-lipped one at the front, clawing at the top of the van to reach him.

Closest threat first. Cliff knelt on top of the van and put down "no-lips" with a single round from his FN rifle. Spinning on his knee, Cliff took another eight shots and put down the six coming from the left. Turning again, he was about the engage the dozen coming from the rear when he saw a trail of smoke coming from the engine bay in the back of the bus. He didn't know if the glass EMPI fuel filter had broken in the wreck, spraying the hot motor with gas, or if oil had burped out onto the muffler, and frankly he didn't care. All he knew was that with all the gas-covered cargo in the van, this was going to be bad.

Cliff shouldered his go-bag and leapt from the van, running across the highway and diving behind the large concrete K-barrier. Peeking over the top of the concrete barrier, he heard a deep *foomp* from the gas in the cabin catching and erupting into a fireball. *The good news*, Cliff thought, *is that I still have my rifle and go-bag. The bad news is that if there's any more undead in the area, the moths have their flame.*

Trying to stand, his world began to spin and he had to sit down again. The concussion must be a bad one. Taking another peek over the concrete barrier, he saw what looked like at least fifty more undead stumbling out of the shadows of the burned town towards the burning van. Weighing his options, he glanced at the river behind him, but with temperatures in the high twenties, crossing the river would be a death sentence.

Cliff worked his way west, staying behind the cover of the concrete divider, moving as quickly as he could without succumbing to the nausea and dizziness. He needed a vehicle, and although the highway was littered with vehicles, all of them were too new to have survived the EMP. If a car had been able to survive the event, it wouldn't have been abandoned on the highway. Cliff didn't know where he would find transportation, but he knew he couldn't stay near the burning van and hope to live.

Dublin, Texas

Jack and Bexar found the Scout and trailer abandoned when they limped the FJ with its flat tire back onto the airport. Their wives and children, and the old Jeep, were nowhere to be found. They parked by the Scout, and found no note or indication of where their families had gone. Scanning the airport, Jack saw eight or nine undead who seemed very interested in the last hangar of the row.

"Check it out Bexar," he said, "my guess is they're in that hangar."

"We can't engage the Zeds," said Bexar. "If they're in the hangar, the rounds might punch through the walls."

"What if I get in the Scout and drive by slowly, drawing them off the hangar, and you flank to get the right angle and put them down?"

"Sounds like a plan, Jack," said Bexar, walking at a brisk pace with his rifle towards the undead.

Jack started the Scout and drove out across the runway past the undead, then turned and started driving back towards the FJ, away from the last hangar. Eight pairs of undead eyes snapped around towards the movement and locked onto the slowly driving Scout. He continued to drive slow enough to keep the walking dead interested in a hot meal, but just fast enough to be out of their reach, and out of range when Bexar started shooting them.

Bexar lay prone in the grass next to the runway and began lining up his first shot. Slowly letting out a deep breath, he squeezed the trigger of his AR. Twelve shots later all eight undead lay on the ground, released from their doomed fate.

Jack turned and drove quickly towards the hangar, and Bexar leapt to his feet and jogged towards the hangar as well. The side door to the hangar was unlocked, but Jack stopped short of opening the door, instead calling out, "Are you guys in there?"

"Yeah, is it clear?" was the reply.

"Yes, we're here, and we put down the zombies."

Jessie opened the door and came out carrying Keeley; Sandra followed, holding Will's hand. Jessie began talking quickly. "While you guys were out, that group of undead surprised us. We started to drive towards the front but an old truck pulled up and some guys started taking shots at us with a rifle. We left the Scout and drove over here, found the hangar unlocked, and hid. Did you guys see the truck or those people?"

"No, we haven't seen anyone alive in the whole damned town."

Jessie was crying into Bexar's chest now, the stress bleeding off quickly. "Let's get the fuck out of here."

CHAPTER 30

Dublin, Texas

The GPS routed the group back into Dublin proper, but with Jessie's report of other survivors in the area with unknown, but seemingly ill intentions, the group left the airport and turned away from the town. They were going to have to find another tire for the FJ. They had prepared for flat tires of course; they had a spare, plugs, patches, and the ability to fill a tire on the trucks, but they hadn't counted on completely destroying a tire by being forced to drive on the flat. Before leaving the airport, Jack and Bexar stripped the shredded tire from the wheel, but kept the wheel.

Reaching Highway 36, they turned right but detoured around the town. After the near miss in Dublin, they wouldn't stop except to find shelter for the night and scavenge for fuel. They had enough food to make it to Big Bend, but fuel was still a problem. If this had been a vacation with a nice open Interstate route, they probably would have had to stop three times to refuel on their way to the park, but driving the meandering country highways, Jack figured they would need four or five fueling stops.

Bexar's mind wandered, almost drifting into sleep as they drove down Highway 377 nearing Comanche, Texas. As the last vehicle in the caravan, it was easy to let your mind and body forget about driving, so he didn't notice at first that the Jeep in front of him hadn't just slowed down, but had slammed on the brakes. Swerving abruptly left, he slammed on his own brakes, just missing the Jeep, the heavy trailer bucking against the trailer hitch of the Scout. There was a roadblock about a mile up the road, and it didn't look like an accident, it looked like an ambush.

Bexar left the Scout running, grabbed his rifle, and walked up to Jack's truck. Jack was standing on the side of the FJ with his binoculars up to his eyes.

"Looks like someone set that up on purpose," he said, "but it also looks like they placed the wrecked vehicles so other vehicles can snake through the middle to pass."

"That's if no one is there," said Bexar. "If people are there that sounds like a kill zone. Doesn't sound too friendly, and so far we haven't exactly found too many friendly people who aren't already dead."

"Bexar, I don't know, I wouldn't count on it ... WAIT!" Jack said suddenly. "I just saw a glint on top of the semi-trailer on the left. I think there's someone up there looking at us through a scope! Any ideas?"

"Well, I don't know," replied Bexar. "I think going straight up there is a really bad idea. I don't think we could really get around the town and back on the road too easily, and I have no idea where to drive to go around this town."

"If we wait here too long do you think they'll just come after us?" asked Jack.

"Definitely," said Bexar. "Tell you what, let's circle the vehicles, put the kids in the middle, hold perimeter, and let me sneak around the back of their ambush. Give me about an hour. I'll go down to the railroad we crossed back there, get into town, and flank them. Then you can try walking up and talking to them from a couple hundred yards out."

"That would probably work," Jack said. "Let me have your Kevlar vest, too."

"Okay, let's circle the vehicles, let me get some gear together, and I'll head out." After discussing their plan with their wives, the group moved their vehicles into a circle and fanned out in a protective circle in case someone tried to attack their group.

Bexar topped off his AR mags, put his Camelbak Mule on, stuffed some beef jerky in the pockets, and set off. He wore his Eagle chest rig, and carried four AR magazines, four magazines for his 1911, his med kit, and his SOG multi-tool. He really hoped he wouldn't need all that gear, but rarely has anyone ever complained they had too much ammo when in battle.

"Tell you what Jack, instead of an hour, how about you give me about ninety minutes? I don't want to risk moving too fast and being detected, or getting injured."

"Got it. God speed, my friend," replied Jack.

Glenwood Springs, Colorado

Cliff made it about a mile to the west before having to stop and rest. It would be a couple of days before he felt close to normal after that crash. All he had was his bug-out bag, the suppressed FNP90, about two hundred rounds of ammo, his pistol, and an absolute need to make it to Groom Lake in Nevada.

As he was resting he noticed a work yard and an oddly built office building surrounded by a fence, inside which were some police vehicles. Those Crown Victorias would have been rendered useless by the EMP but maybe there were still some cops alive, or if not, maybe one of them had a worthwhile personal vehicle Cliff could steal.

Walking cautiously down the embankment and towards the building, he scanned for threats. So far it appeared that the surrounding zombie population was only interested in his still-burning van, but he knew it paid to be cautious.

Nearing the building, Cliff found a patrol car with the driver's door open. The state police officer's duty belt was caught in the seatbelt, and that officer was very much undead. This was why so many police officers didn't wear their seatbelts, for fear of being caught in the seatbelt and shot. In fact, many of them called the driver's seat the "death chair," since that's where angry gunfire was usually directed when shooting at a police car. The officer's duty pistol was on the ground near his body, the slide locked back, and run empty of ammunition. Cliff stopped about ten yards from the undead cop trying to get at his fresh meal and fired a single round through his skull.

The pistol was a Glock 22, and on the now properly dead police officer's duty belt were two full magazines of .40 caliber ammo for the Glock. The pistol and ammo went into Cliff's bag, but he left the Taser, ASP, and OC pepper spray in place. He seriously doubted a zombie would react to OC spray, seeing as it barely worked on aggressive people. It might be funny to Taser the undead, but there wasn't any room for funny right now.

The trunk of the patrol car turned up even more useful items. The cop had a "bail-out" bag with more pistol ammo and magazines. There was also an AR-15, with an ACOG, five Pmags full of .223, a medical kit with some QuikClot, a couple of Israeli bandages, a small package of BC Powder, and three tampons. The BC Powder was a godsend, and he quickly downed two doses in an attempt to quash some of the pain in his head. The tampons were also a good find, since they did a good job of plugging bullet wounds. "Good kit there, sheepdog," Cliff said to the dead police officer. The AR and the ammo were left behind because of the added weight, but the pistol ammo and medical kit went into his bag.

Cliff left the patrol car and jumped over the fence into the secure parking area around the department. There were a few modern pickup trucks and a couple of other all-terrain vehicles, but the only vehicle that interested him was an old Chevy K1500. It appeared to have a suspension lift and oversized tires, which could be handy. He just hoped that it had an old ignition system, and that the former owner hadn't done something like an LT engine swap.

After breaking into the truck, he opened the hood and found a dusty old 350 sitting between the fenders. It was carbureted and appeared to have an old points ignition. It only took a few minutes to hotwire the truck, and although he was greatly relieved to have a running vehicle, he was annoyed to see it only had about a quarter of a tank of gas. Assuming a twenty-five gallon tank and that the truck *might* get ten miles per gallon, he calculated that he would have just enough gas to get stranded again.

A half-hour later he had finished siphoning gas from patrol cars into the newly stolen truck, and now, with a full tank of gas, he was ready to get back on the road. Unfortunately, he couldn't find anything to fill up with extra gas, so he would have to scavenge for gas sooner than later.

During all the noise and commotion of getting the truck ready to leave, Cliff saw movement in the windows of the dark police station, and none of it looked good. It was quite obvious that the building was a tomb for the undead. Using the electric gate's manual override, he turned back onto I-70 and pointed west.

CHAPTER 31

Glenwood Springs, Colorado

Driving west on a dirt road away from the police station where Cliff had procured his "new" truck, he had a nagging feeling that he had missed something, which finally materialized into a solid thought: *If that troop had been attacked by a zombie, then killed by the same, where was that zombie?*

After he had crashed the Volkswagen van, he had seen a number of zombies, but not in nearly enough numbers. In fact, since running for his life at Denver International Airport, he hadn't seen nearly *enough* zombies. The thought was interrupted by the end of the dirt road. To his left was the river, and to his right was a low chain-link fence, put in place to keep animals off the highway. Without thinking, he had driven north instead of backtracking the way he had come. After some quick work with his SOG multi-tool, the fence was cut away from its poles and Cliff drove out over it.

Finally back on the road with a working vehicle, he stuck to the wrong side of the road since there were fewer abandoned cars on this side of the center barrier. He kept the speedometer hovering near fifty-five miles per hour so he could conserve fuel. His focus was on survival, not shaving a few hours off his arrival time.

The worst possible scenario would be that he found Groom Lake in the same condition as the base at DIA, dark and overrun by the undead. It would be easier if he could set up some communication links; if Groom Lake was down, there were only a few other locations he could retreat to. He knew he could take an excursion to one of the secret supply caches that the U.S. military had set up throughout the country, but there weren't any close by; most were spread out near the coast to supply a military resistance in case of invasion, or for the more likely scenario of civil uprising.

If Groom Lake turned out to be a complete loss he'd have to make a new plan, but hopefully he could still get some supplies from the underground facility. There were other similar secret bases throughout the U.S., about a dozen of them, but Groom Lake was a known rendezvous point for key leadership in the military, separate from the civilian bunker at DIA. It was also where most of the Yama Strain research was being conducted. If a vaccine existed, that's where it would be.

Comanche, Texas

Bexar walked for nearly an hour before reaching a point on the railroad tracks where he felt he was far enough into town to safely flank the roadblock. He made his way through the brush on his belly, low crawling slowly out of the rail bed and into a slightly overgrown pasture.

He was an avid reader of military history, including his all-time favorite, "Force Recon Diary, 1969," but he was no military man. He hadn't had the field training of those Marines in Vietnam, and he didn't really know how to move stealthily through an open field. His training was good, but it was all very specialized in the tradecraft of being a police officer. The majority of his training time was spent in the saddle of his police motorcycle, making his way through endless mazes of orange cones to hone his technical motorcycle riding skills. Now he wished he would have spent more time seeking out training in field craft.

His plan was to get about one hundred yards from the roadblock, if possible. If he was close enough, he might be able to see who he was dealing with, and hear what was being said. He knew he could accurately engage the threats with his rifle if he needed to.

The route looked clear, so Bexar began picking his way through the pasture, which was full of scrap and trash, as well as brush. There was a very fine line between ending up on American Pickers and Extreme Hoarders, and whoever owned this land had well-crossed the line, but the junk was useful because it gave him some cover as he moved methodically from scrap pile to scrap pile.

Climbing quickly and quietly over a fence, he sprinted to the back of a building that abutted the hoarder field. It looked like the back of a gas station, and there was a work truck parked on the side of the building. In the bed of the truck was a ladder, and he crouch-walked to the truck to retrieve the ladder. He wanted to get on the roof of the gas station to recon the roadblock. Unfortunately, the ladder turned out to be an eight-foot step ladder, and the roof was about twelve feet high, but with a little extra effort he was able to pull himself onto the roof top and low crawl to a large air conditioning unit. He had no illusion that the sheet metal construction of the AC unit would stop a bullet, but it would give him some cover while he got his bearings.

Peering over the edge of the AC unit, Bexar realized he was a little closer to the roadblock than he had wanted. He was only about seventy-five yards away, but he had a little elevation on the roadblock, and could actually see over the semi-truck and the other vehicles down the road to where Jack and the caravan were located. The roadblock was slightly to his left, and he could see three men lying in ambush. He hadn't brought a mirror or something shiny to flash towards Jack to let him know he was in position, so he would have to wait for Jack to make the first move.

Twenty minutes later, Jack slowly drove the FJ towards the roadblock, stopping about fifty yards from the semi-truck. Using the vehicle for cover, Jack called out to the men at the roadblock, "I'm representing my group and want to speak with you. All we want from you is to be allowed to safely pass so we can continue our journey. None of us are infected. We mean you no harm; we won't stop, we only want to pass through your town."

The reply came quickly. "You can go, but there's a toll—your vehicles, your food, and your ammo for safe passage. You can keep whatever else you can carry."

"No!" exclaimed Jack. "That's a death sentence! We're not giving you our vehicles or anything else, we just want to move past!"

"You don't get it, asshole," Jack heard from the roadblock. "That's not a request; we're taking your food, your ammo, your vehicles, and anything else we want. If you're lucky, we'll give you the women back when we're done with them!"

From Bexar's perch he saw two more townsmen emerge from the house across the street. One of the men was armed with a large rifle, the other a short shotgun. The man with the rifle lay prone, taking position behind the rifle aimed at Jack.

Bexar and Jack's original plan had been that Bexar was supposed to signal with a single shot if something was wrong, but if he did that Jack would be killed when the rifleman opened fire, so instead he took a deep breath, let it out slowly, and squeezed the trigger on his AR. The reticle of his site rested comfortably just over the top of the rifleman's head as his trigger broke to the rear. The rifleman's head in his site exploded in a red mist. Shifting slightly, Bexar lined up the shot to the man with the shotgun, firing a round through the bottom of his jaw. A follow-up shot finished the kill, and the two men lay dead in the street of Comanche.

Jack dove behind the FJ when the firing started, eventually pointing his AR towards the threat. Bexar continued breathing steadily, driving his muzzle towards each new threat. Seconds after the firing had started, all of the men at the roadblock lay dead in the street of their town. Bexar had fired a total of ten rounds, Jack fifteen.

Bexar moved quickly to the back side of the gas station, climbed down the ladder, and continued his run towards Jack. This time he didn't run back through the hoarder field, but straight towards the roadblock and Jack. Jack was in the FJ, rifle pointed forward through the open window to engage any threats during Bexar's retreat. Diving inside, Bexar yelled "GO," and they were off to collect their families in the other vehicles.

"Holy shit balls, that was intense," said Jack. "Were you on the gas station roof?"

"Yeah, on the left," replied Bexar. "The first guy was laid out behind a big rifle, the second guy was the sweeper. Damn, that was nuts."

"What now?" asked Jack. "Do you think we should try to drive through the town?"

"No," said Bexar, shaking his head. "Damnit, I think we need to find a spot to hunker down for a bit, see if they have any vehicles and try to chase after us."

"Okay fine," said Jack, "but where do we do that?"

"I don't know. I say we turn back and haul ass; we can hide or set an ambush for anyone after us. We have about three hours 'til sunset, if we can get hidden and safe, then maybe we can figure out if we can go through the town, or maybe there's a reasonable detour that doesn't take us through anything big, or burn too much fuel."

The group retreated, backtracking on Highway 36. A few miles from the shootout, Bexar slowed and turned his truck into an open cattle pasture gate, and the group followed him into the field. Bexar climbed out of his truck and closed the gate, securing it with a small length of 550 cord. Once behind the closed gate, which provided a little safety from the wandering undead assuming the fence was intact, the group drove across the pasture to a small stock pond. The pond was surrounded by some trees, which should help to conceal them from the road.

After their hasty retreat from the group cache site in Maypearl, Jack decided it would be best to leave the tent packed for the night, and once again a watch schedule was agreed upon. As Jack took the first security watch, Bexar unpacked his old Coleman stove to cook a few cans of chili for their dinner.

Jessie struggled to get Keeley to eat so she would sleep for the night, but being a toddler, she absolutely refused to eat any of the rations from their go-bags. Will, on the other hand, found his place in the trees, and climbed the one closest to their home for the night while waiting for the chili.

Much like the wagon trains that crossed the west before them, the group pulled their vehicles in a loose circle with the bedrolls placed between them. The children were in the middle of the adults, who were in the middle of the vehicles. If someone, living or undead, attacked, their circled "wagons" would hopefully give them some protection. After dinner, Jessie relieved Jack from security watch, while Bexar and Sandra cleaned all their rifles before going to bed. Jack sat in his truck, looking through the GPS. He had to find a route around that damned little town.

Interstate 70, Colorado

Cliff made good time. In two hours he had made it through Parachute and was just outside of Grand Junction. The abandoned vehicles on the Interstate had been sparser than he'd expected, which made the driving not too difficult except for the blanket of fresh snow from the previous night. No society meant no road crews, which meant no snow plows and no salt on the bridges.

The truck's gas tank was down by half, and he needed to stop and find fuel and shelter. The sun was starting to get low on the horizon. If he could also find some food and water, that would be a nice bonus, but he knew at least he had two stripped-down MREs in his bug-out bag. If he could find another small airport like the one he'd stayed at the night before, he'd be happy.

Driving closer to Grand Junction, he came upon a small blue sign indicating an airport located off the exit. It took very little time to follow the signs to the airport, but unlike the previous night, this was no small airport. It must have been quite busy before the EMPs hit, and busy meant people, people who were probably undead now. That wasn't going to work.

Scanning the area for other options, he saw a small Shell gas station and a Holiday Inn. As much fun as a night in a Holiday Inn might be, a hotel full of undead sounded like a horrible way to die. The gas station would have to be his choice for the night; most gas stations have a front and back door, as well as roof access from a back room. Maybe he'd be lucky and the gas station wouldn't have been ransacked, leaving him some gas cans, food, and water.

Road trip food always upset his stomach, but he had an undying love for an unnaturally produced, beet-stick-with-cheese food product sold by the pair in a vacuum formed package. Next, the Holiday Inn—he needed some blankets and a pillow.

Cliff parked the big Chevy truck at the side of the building so he could maintain some sort of tactics. He wouldn't be surprised if everyone in the hotel was dead, but he didn't want to be surprised by someone who wasn't.

Approaching the hotel with his rifle up, he took a quick peek around the corner, checked the area around the convenience store, and scanned the glass front. The store was in extreme disarray, but it looked like there was still some stock on the shelves. The windows and glass doors were intact, which was a good sign. Moving quickly in a tactical crouch, he reached the front doors and found them unlocked. Pulling one open, he was struck by the pungent and overwhelming smell of rotting death. He took a deep breath before stepping into the gas station.

The front aisles were clear of bodies, dead or otherwise. Behind the counter he found the source of the smell—a blonde woman who appeared to have been dead for a couple of days lay crumpled on the floor. She had a small semi-auto pistol in her hand, the slide locked back over an empty chamber, and there were bite marks visible all over her body. She had shot herself in the head. She must have known what she would become. The bite marks were bloody, so he knew she'd been bitten before she killed herself. Once the heart stops, blood stops pumping, except to drain out of a low spot. He hoped that whoever bit the clerk had left, but he knew it was probably in the gas station somewhere.

Cliff cleared the rest of the store, including the storeroom and back office. Finding no one else, he let out a deep sigh and pulled open the front of the beer cooler. Just as he grabbed a six-pack of Sawtooth Ale, a hand reached through the beer bottles from the back of the cooler and latched onto his hand, sending the beer crashing to the floor. The hand was half-rotten and blackened, with bone showing through chunks of missing flesh.

Cliff's free hand dropped to his pistol, and he thumbed on the X300 light as he brought it up. He could see the dead orbs of a zombie's eyes looking back at him through the cooler. The undead creature moaned while trying to pull him into the cooler. Cliff fired three times and the zombie's grip fell free.

He couldn't believe he hadn't checked the walk-in cooler. Checking his arm and hand, he didn't see any scratches that had broken his skin, so he grabbed another six-pack of Left Hand beer and shut the door. With an arm full of bags from the stockroom, he began "shopping." Placing the bags by the store's front door, he took the beer, a windshield scraper, a jug of freeze-rated windshield wiper fluid, and four three-gallon red plastic gas cans. Packages of Pop-Tarts, Slim Jims,

Combos, and beef jerky also went into the bags. In the storeroom he found a garden hose the clerk had probably used to spray off the parking lot, and cut off two four-foot long sections of hose. He was going to need them to siphon gas.

Storing his scavenged items in the truck, he started looking for cars to siphon gas from. To the north he saw a sign for a car rental agency; that would be his destination. Most rental companies didn't keep their own fuel tanks, but rentals were rented out with a full tank of gas, so maybe his luck would continue.

A quick drive to the rental car company's lot where, as he'd suspected, he found a handful of small and midsized vehicles. Hose section and gas cans in hand, Cliff first approached a red Dodge Avenger. He broke the driver's window, reached through to unlock the back door, pulled out the bottom of the back seat of the car, and unscrewed the fuel pump from the gas tank. The Dodge held just enough fuel to fill three of his gas cans, which he used to top off the truck's gas tank. He repeated the process on another car in the lot before driving back to the gas station, happy he had a full tank of gas and four full gas cans for tomorrow's drive.

Again parking the truck at the side of the gas station, he walked over to the Holiday Inn to begin his quest for blankets and a pillow. He had no intention of going in the front door, so he walked along the outside of the hotel looking for a room with open curtains so he'd be able to see if the room was devoid of undead. The sixth window he passed had the curtains open, and it didn't look like anyone was inside. He tapped the barrel of his rifle against the glass to see if there would be a reaction in the room; hearing none, he broke the window and climbed into the hotel room. This time he made sure it was actually empty; that had been a close call in the gas station.

He pulled the blanket off the queen bed and found a spare blanket in the closet, along with a spare pillow stored in a zipped up bag. He was about to crawl back out the window when he had a moment of clarity, the kind that could change the world, and he quickly darted back into the bathroom to take two unopened rolls of toilet paper and three large bath towels.

He had intended to sleep in the gas station, but the smell was so bad he couldn't bring himself to do it. Instead, he hung his new towels up on the inside of the windows of his truck to keep himself out of view, opened a beer, and tried to enjoy his dinner of Pop-Tarts and beef jerky as the sun set.

CHAPTER 32

December 31st
Outside of Comanche, Texas

Bexar took the binoculars out of his bag and made his way down the hill towards the road leading from the group's campsite. It was the last watch, and already the horizon was glowing orange to the east. He was about two hundred yards south of the camp, which was blocked from view of the road by a cluster of trees near a stock pond.

In the distance, the distinct rumbling pop of a group of motorcycles with straight pipes emerged from the east. A few minutes later the sound grew louder, and a single rider appeared, riding past the entrance of the cow pasture at about fifty miles per hour, joined a short time later by a group of seven riders rolling up the roadway from the same direction. They were traveling slowly, about twenty miles per hour, revving their motors, and stopping and looking behind them. The first rider returned to the slower group, discussed something with someone who appeared to be the leader, then continued on in a westerly direction.

Bexar could see that the group had on cuts—leather vests with the group's club logo in yellow and black—identifying them as the "Pistoleros," a one-percenter group that Bexar had had run-ins with as a peace officer. There were always rumors that they were heavily involved in major crime, but it seemed like their hangers-on were the ones getting caught with meth, stolen property, and illegal guns, never a club member. The group continued on their western trek, and about thirty seconds after the last motorcycles had roared off, the moaning sound of the undead reached his ears at his look-out post. Zombies, hundreds of them, were shambling up the road, following the motorcycles.

Bexar stuffed the binoculars in his cargo pocket and began low crawling up the hill back to the camp, praying he wouldn't be noticed by the lurching stream of undead passing on the road below. By the time he had reached camp, Sandra was boiling water for coffee on the Coleman stove, Jessie was feeding the kids, and Jack was already loading the trucks.

"Guys, we've got a problem, we need to leave, and soon," he reported. "A pack of Pistoleros just passed on the way towards Comanche, but they had a large group of undead following them. It was like they were deliberately leading the zombies towards the town."

Jack shut the door on his FJ and turned towards Bexar. "How're we supposed to leave soon if there's a pack of zombies on the road?"

"I don't know, we could cut some fence and cross fields to get some room, but nothing good can come from this," Bexar replied. "If they stop in town for any amount of time, those walking corpses will eventually spread out. We can wait, but I don't think we should wait long; we need to get out and away from that damned town."

Jessie picked up Keeley, then turning to Bexar said, "Babe, we're in the middle of cow country. I bet most of the dirt roads around here end up back on that same highway. Those guys might keep riding; why don't we prep to bug-out and then wait and see what happens?"

"Well okay," Bexar said. "Jack, what if we cut the fence behind us, I'll move forward and try to see what happens from a safe distance. We can always stay here another night, but if those one-percenters or the zombies start this way, we'll have to move fast or we might get overrun."

Grand Junction, Colorado

Cliff woke up slowly. Those few beers had been a jolt to his body, and his head was a little fuzzy as the sun rose outside of his blanket-covered truck cab. Trying to make as little movement as possible to keep the truck from shaking, Cliff reached up and gently pulled back a corner of the towel to look out the windshield. Nothing appeared to be moving, so he unlocked the door and climbed out to relieve himself on the side of the building. Today was a big travel day. He knew he had to gain more ground and gain it faster than the previous day, but he absolutely couldn't afford another wreck with a walking corpse.

At least once the mountains were in his rearview mirror he knew the drive would open up—there wasn't much of anything on the highway until he was well into Utah. He hoped the road would be reasonably clear so he could maintain something resembling highway speed for most of the day.

The road was fairly clear of abandoned vehicles and debris, and he was able to push the speedometer past fifty miles per hour a few times before he had to slow and drive on the shoulder to dodge vehicles. It also hadn't snowed again last night, so all in all it was an uneventful drive, which he was grateful for. It took ninety minutes, but he made it to Green River, Utah. He wasn't sure the people who lived in the area had even noticed that the world had ended; tough to notice that all electronics had ceased to work when you're a modern day mountain man living a rough life in the woods.

Five hours later, Cliff stopped outside of Beaver, Utah to fuel up the truck from his gas cans. The truck's tank was full but now his red plastic gas cans were empty. Everything seemed quiet on the highway so he grabbed the empty gas cans and began searching for a suitable candidate from a number of vehicles abandoned haphazardly across the highway. Between his truck and a couple of semi-trucks sat an old Ford Ranger pickup, from the days when the Ranger was a full-sized truck. He knew it would have easy access to the gas tanks, so he got to work, leaving his rifle in his Chevy because it would get in the way trying to climb under vehicles. In short order the fuel filler hose of the Ranger was cut free, the garden hose inserted, and the first gas can filled. Switching gas cans, he began to fill the second one, not noticing that he had attracted the attention of a high school marching band that had been driving back from a Christmas parade when the EMP hit, and whose charter bus was hidden from view on the other side of the semi.

Cliff squeezed the garden hose together to stop the flow of fuel so he could switch containers again. Without the noise of the fueling, he could now hear what sounded like shoes dragging across the cold pavement. Lying flat on his back under the old Ford, he tilted his head back and saw dozens of feet shuffling in his direction from around the front of the semi-truck ahead.

Quickly pulling the garden hose out of the gas tank, he screwed the cap back on the gas can and shimmied out from underneath the truck. Turning to pick up the gas cans, he came face-to-face with a large, fat teenager, his left eye missing and skin hanging from his left cheekbone. His blackened fat hands grabbed the garden hose that Cliff held out in front of him.

People often believe they will rise to the occasion when danger confronts them, but Cliff had learned from his years in combat working for an Other Government Agency that, when placed in a high-stress situation, people will only fall to their level of training. His training had been exceptionally good, as were his skills, but he had only been trained to fight living people.

His first instinct was to give a strong palm heel strike to the band member's solar plexus, because that maneuver gave you time and distance to fight your way to your primary weapon and to safety. But then he remembered that it had not worked very well on the undead maintenance worker at DIA, and was therefore unlikely to be any more effective against an already dead teenager whose grip strength would rival a power lifter.

The teenage zombie pushed Cliff onto his back. Cliff's left hand shot up and grabbed the zombie's stiff neck, while with his right hand he grasped the knife in his back right pocket. The Emerson CQC-7 opened up as it was pulled from his pocket, as it had been designed to do, and Cliff drove it into the left temple of the band member. The knife stuck firmly in the kid's skull and Cliff pushed the dead weight off of him.

Bounding to his feet, he drew his pistol. He didn't have enough rounds to engage the thirty or so remaining members of the undead marching band. Moving in a quick combat crouch, rolling his feet heel-to-toe to keep the muzzle of his pistol level, he quickly shot the four closest to him before reaching his Chevy truck and his primary weapon. The FNP90 in hand, Cliff jumped into the bed of his truck and stepped onto the roof. Kneeling for stability, he began to slow his breathing—*just like my training at the Farm*, he thought, *breathe in through the nose, aim, breathe out slowly and press the trigger to the rear.* The breathing helped to slow his heart rate so he could focus and regain the fine motor control in his fingers. The fight-or-flight reflex affects everyone, even the highest trained Tier-1 operators, and like them, Cliff focused on his breathing and relied on his training to overcome the situation. It took slightly longer than five minutes, but once he was done the marching band had permanently left the field.

He climbed down from the roof of his truck, and this time he properly cleared the vehicles in the area. All he found was the band's bus driver, who had been mostly eaten by the teenagers.

A cool breeze blew up the highway from the town below, carrying the faint moans of more undead. Trouble was coming; he needed to un-ass this spot, get moving and fast. But first things first—Emerson wasn't going to make another knife again and Cliff loved his CQC-7, so he jogged over to the fat teenager to retrieve it. Then he loaded the fuel cans in his truck, hoping the three full cans would give him enough fuel to elude the approaching horde. This was an unacceptable situation, but he had to evade before he could regroup.

CHAPTER 33

Outside of Comanche, Texas

Judging by the position of the sun, Jack guessed it was nearly noon when Bexar walked back into the camp. Although the temperature was in the low forties, Bexar was soaked with sweat.

"After a bit I thought I'd try to keep count of the passing undead, but after about four hundred of them shambled past, I couldn't keep up," he reported. "They're all headed towards the town, and I haven't heard anything more than some sporadic gunfire since the first outbreak. My guess is, that was the rest of the living in the town trying to fight the bikers and their zombies off. They probably lost, or are hunkered down. I haven't seen a single zombie come back from the town. I also haven't seen any stragglers or others passing in about the last half-hour. I say we load up and haul ass while we can!"

Jessie gently shut the door on the Jeep and joined the group. "Keeley's down for her nap in her seat in the Jeep, so now would be just as good a time as any to leave."

Jack nodded. "No good can come from those bikers running a pack of zombies like that; we don't need to be anywhere near those guys."

Heading back to their vehicles, the group, with Jack in the lead, started down the dirt trail running along the fence towards the highway. Turning left, they drove away from the bikers' zombie horde. The road was reasonably clear and they were able to settle into a fifty-miles-per-hour cruising speed. They needed to get far away from Comanche, but fuel was still a precious commodity, and driving any faster would only burn their gas up faster.

The night before, Jack had used Malachi's GPS to plot a route around Comanche. Crisscrossing the countryside on small Farm-to-Market roads, his plan would take them to Highway 183. The sooner they could get out of the Texas back country and to Big Bend National Park, the better their chances were of surviving.

Their gas supplies had already been low when they were nearly ambushed in Comanche. Now that they had some distance between them and the bikers, Jack started looking for a safe place to siphon gas. Reaching the tiny town of Zephyr, Jack pulled the convoy into the parking lot of a surprisingly nice new high school football stadium. Parked in the stadium parking lot was a big Ford work truck, which was of no use to them since it burned diesel, but what was useful was the lawn equipment and the big red gas cans on the large trailer. Between the commercial lawn equipment and the gas cans, they gained nearly forty gallons of gas. Their vehicles were topped off and the newly acquired gas cans strapped down to the roof racks.

Bexar held his hand up to the horizon; he had only four fingers of sunlight left. "Less than two hours until sunset," he said. "We need to get hidden and set up for the night."

Jack nodded. "Yeah, but if we keep this pace up, it'll take us a week to make Big Bend."

Outside of Parowan, Utah

As indicated by the sharp increase in billboards, Cliff was getting close to a town named Parowan. Following the same plan as the previous nights, the hunt for the local small airport was on. Just on the outskirts of town, the familiar blue and white airport sign appeared at the side of the highway, and Cliff took the exit to see if his luck would continue to hold.

The airport was small, as he'd assumed it would be, so he drove past the fixed-base operators (FBO), then past the hangars out onto the taxiway and to the far end of the field. There should be at least some fencing to help give him a little protection, but he wished it was summer rather than the middle of winter so he could sleep on the roof of a hangar without the fear of being killed by the cold temperatures.

He also needed more gas. A couple of cars were parked at the FBO he'd passed on the way, but it would have to wait until morning; the sun was low on the horizon and he didn't want to be stuck under a car siphoning gas at night. While he watched the sky turn from orange to a deep blue, he enjoyed another dinner of

Pop-Tarts, beef jerky, and a cold beer. As the stars came out, Cliff cleaned his FN and then his pistol. He also changed his socks. Even while in-country in some third world shit hole he'd had access to antibiotics, but now if he let his health slip and got an infection, it could very well kill him. With that thought, Cliff threw his empty beer bottle out of the open window of his truck, rolled the window up and hung his towel blinds, wrapped himself up in his hotel blankets, and tried to get some sleep.

CHAPTER 34

Zephyr, Texas

Bexar looked around at the brand new high school football stadium. He wasn't the least bit surprised that such a nice facility didn't even have paved parking. In small-town Texas, football is king.

After their need for a quick exit from the group cache site in Maypearl, Bexar didn't want to set up the wall tent. It was more of a permanent living quarter that they could use in Big Bend. No, tonight they needed a building they could break into, defend if needed, and leave in a hurry without any loss. The field house on the north end of the stadium looked to be just about as good of a place as any. Although there wouldn't be any running water and they couldn't flush, it would be nice to sit on an actual toilet again, sort of like a single use port-a-potty.

Jessie and Sandra stood rear guard next to the vehicles, which they had pre-positioned facing outwards for a quick getaway if needed, while Jack and Bexar reconnoitered the building for an easy way in. After a few minutes, Jack went to his truck and returned with his old Mossberg 500 Special 12-gauge pump shotgun. He pushed five shells into the shotgun's magazine tube and walked up to the metal exterior door. Three shots later he had shot the door free using the same technique that the military and police forces the nation over used for door breaching.

Bexar pulled his rifle tight and took position next to the door as Jack pulled aside the broken door. The two stood quietly for about twenty seconds, waiting for a reaction from inside the dark building. If there were any undead inside or nearby, the shotgun would bring them out. As if on cue, deep inside the recesses of the dark field house they heard the sound of metal clanking, then a moan followed by some banging.

They waited, but no zombie appeared out of the darkness of the interior. They were going to have to go in and find it if the group was going to stay for the night. The long-practiced tactics for clearing buildings were changing with the new world order. Adapting, Jack and Bexar didn't breach the doorway with quickness of action; they calmly walked through the darkened doorway, weapon lights on, shining deep into the dark corners.

They found themselves behind the counter of the closed concession stand, which had no undead but plenty of candy bars, a great find that they would enjoy later. Creeping slowly and carefully, Bexar cleared the locker rooms while Jack cleared the showers. They finally found the noisy ghoul in the dark and dusty weight room. He had probably been the football coach, wearing khaki pants that were too small around the waist and a faded polo shirt with the school's mascot embroidered on the right breast. The zombie was pinned to a flat bench under the bar of a Smith machine, loaded with three, forty-five-pound plates on each side.

"Guess he slipped and got stuck under the bar," Jack said, lifting his rifle and firing a single shot into the dead coach's skull.

Rather than dragging the body through the building, Bexar shut the door to the weight room. The girls brought the kids into the building to one of the locker rooms, while Bexar and Jack brought in the bedrolls and secured the trucks. Night fell to the quiet sounds of Snickers bars being opened and eaten.

CHAPTER 35

December 31st
Parowan, Utah

Cliff woke with the rising sun lighting the cab of the truck. As he had done yesterday, he slowly lifted the edges of the towels one at a time to peek outside for threats. The passenger side was clear, the windshield was clear, but then he nearly shot through the glass at a dead face almost touching the glass on the driver's side window. Milky white dead eyes peered at the window, but once Cliff was able to get his breathing under control and his heart rate to settle down, he realized that the zombie hadn't appeared to see the movement.

He just wanted to get out of the truck to piss, siphon some gas, and get back on the road, but first he'd have to dispatch the undead man. Inching over to the passenger door, he opened it and slid out of the truck as quietly and smoothly as he could. With the suppressor still on his rifle, as it had been since climbing out of that damned hole in the ground in Denver, he made his way around the back of the truck.

Taking three big steps, Cliff moved away from the truck, and with a single shot coughed out of the barrel of his rifle put the zombie down for good. Rifle up, Cliff made a 360-degree check of the area for further threats, then took care of his most urgent step of the morning with a long piss.

Back in the truck, the instant coffee packet from one of the MREs was poured into a water bottle and shaken to mix. It tasted slightly more horrible than usual because it was made with cold water, but he wanted the caffeine. Another round of Pop-Tarts and beef jerky finished out his breakfast

Cliff started the truck and drove towards the FBO. After a quick security walk of the area, he crawled under an old Dodge truck with his gas cans and his garden hose. Thirty minutes later the Chevy's gas tank was full, and the four small gas cans were full as well. He guessed that he now had enough gas to make Groom Lake, but with the base being in the middle of absofuckinglutely nowhere, he thought it would be smart to stop one more time, to be safe.

Zephyr, Texas

Jessie sat the last watch for the night, which worked out well because Keeley woke up early and was hungry. She was down to only a few cans of condensed milk; after that they would be on to the powdered milk. Thankfully, Keeley wasn't an infant or the need for baby formula would have been overwhelming.

Off in the distance she heard motorcycles rumbling, but she couldn't get a fix on the direction or how far away they were. But if she could hear them, she was sure they were too close for their safety. The group's vehicles were obvious beacons of survivors, what with all the gear strapped onto the roof racks. She needed to get the others up and on the road before their vehicles were spotted.

With Keeley holding her hand, Jessie let her AR rest on the sling across her chest and stepped inside to wake up Bexar. "Babe, we've got a problem."

"Huh?"

"Wake up," she said, "I heard some motorcycles in the distance; I think we need to get the hell out of here."

Jessie sat Keeley down as Bexar began to wake up the others. Going to the darkened doorway, she stood back in the shadow of the building to hold security while the bedrolls were gathered. In less than ten minutes the group was awake, bathroom breaks were taken, and they were packing the bedrolls in the vehicles. Just then the motorcycle roared by.

At first the rider didn't seem to notice the group, but then his head snapped to the side to look over his shoulder, and he slammed on his brakes. While the biker was making a U-turn in the road, Jack stepped forward, shouldered his rifle, and fired ten rounds towards the biker. The bike swerved to the side but the rider stayed upright and rode off as fast as he could, although it appeared the motorcycle now had a flat tire and might have been leaking gas.

"Well shit on us Jack, we've gotta get; I bet he was a scout with the group from yesterday."

"Right Bexar, let's get the fuck out of here."

The group was on high alert as they quickly left the gravel parking lot. Bexar figured the bikers would give chase. Of course he hoped they wouldn't, but in his experience with biker gangs, he knew they would come and it would turn violent. Bikers fueled on meth could ride all day and all night without stopping to rest. Bexar spent more time gazing into his rearview mirror than at the road ahead.

CHAPTER 36

Near Brownwood, Texas

Bexar flashed the headlights on his vehicle, and Jessie waved back and flashed her headlights at Jack, who waved and slowed to stop the convoy in the road. They didn't bother to pull off the highway—there was no traffic, and the only other moving vehicles they had seen in the last two days were the bikers. Jack, Sandra, Jessie, and Bexar all met in the middle of the road for a quick pow-wow.

Bexar started. "Jack, I really think we should get off this highway and head south towards Junction. I'm worried that the bikers will follow the highway and catch up. If we can go a different direction on a different road, we could maybe shake them."

"Sure," said Jack, "but what if they take that road as well?"

"Well yeah, they could," replied Bexar, "but how would they guess which road to take? The sooner we can move off course the better, I think."

Their wives agreed, so the convoy drove into Brownwood and turned south. In the town of Brownwood, the only movement they saw were undead trapped in some of the gas stations, clawing at the windows to get at the vehicles driving by. They saw a few houses with smoke coming from the chimneys, which seemed like a good sign, but would be disastrous for those people if the bikers followed them into the town. There wasn't anything Bexar could do to help them; he could only hope that the people in those houses would keep safe.

It seemed like days of driving, but it was really only a few hours. The continually high stress of driving around abandoned vehicles and reanimated dead bodies in the road made the trip to Junction, Texas seem exceptionally long. By now they needed to gas up their convoy, so they had to stop. The closer they got to town, the more gas stations and fuel stops appeared, but unfortunately they had no way to get the fuel out of the underground tanks at the gas stations, so they were still scavenging and siphoning gas when needed.

If we'd chosen diesel-driven vehicles we would've had a near endless supply of fuel, with all the abandoned semi-trucks on the highway and their large saddlebag fuel tanks, Jack thought. He brought the convoy to a stop on the side of a Valero station, hoping to find fuel in some of the vehicles abandoned near the gas station.

Everyone got out of their vehicles except for Sandra, who elected to stay with the kids in the Jeep. Keeley was napping, and even though Will was awake, it wouldn't be safe to bring him out in an unknown area unless they had to. Over the past few days a new group SOP—standard operating procedure—had been developed, that they were always armed whenever they got out of their vehicles.

Jack called over to Bexar, "Hey Bexar, how much ammo do you think we have between us for the ARs?"

"Quite a bit Jack, why?"

"I'm guessing it'll be some time 'til someone makes any more ammo, and we might run into an issue in the future. I want to try something new. I'm going to try using a hatchet."

"Heh, well okay, but keep your AR on you," Bexar said.

Jack's AR hung across his back by the sling. After retrieving his hatchet from a container on the roof of his truck, he gestured for Jessie to join him in sweeping the area to find suitable vehicles to siphon gas from. Bexar climbed on the roof of the Jeep and stood watch over the kids and Sandra.

Jessie took point with her pistol up, Jack pulling rear guard with his hatchet, and they moved around the corner of the store. The glass front doors of the store were wide open, which was good in that there shouldn't be anything trapped in the store, but it was bad in that anything that had been in there was now out here with them. The area around the pumps and the parking lot was nearly empty of cars, and the few vehicles near the pumps were diesel pickup trucks.

"Maybe there's some more over by the McDonalds?" Jessie whispered to Jack over her shoulder.

She led the pair across the front of the store and around the far corner to the McDonalds. Protruding from the front of the restaurant was a large tour bus that appeared to have traveled out of Mexico. It had wrecked and driven right into the front of the McDonalds, into the PlayPlace.

"Oh shit, this is bad, Jack, we need to fall back," Jessie said.

Gunfire erupted from the other side of the gas station.

"Fuck, come on Jessie!"

Jessie and Jack broke tactics and sprinted back across the front of the store, coming around the corner of the station to see their vehicles surrounded by a wall of zombies. Sandra was trapped in the Jeep with the kids, and undead were clawing and banging at the windows trying to get at them. Bexar was still on the roof of the Jeep, pulling the trigger on his AR as quickly as he could aim. By a quick count Jack estimated there were still sixty undead standing.

"Jessie, hold your fire," yelled Jack. "If you miss you'll hit Sandra and the kids! Run forward and try to get a safe angle on some of the zombies on the edges, I'll go around the other side!"

Before Jessie could respond, Jack sprinted away to the right, trying to get around the horde for another angle to engage. On the far side of the convoy he ran into three undead who were slow getting to the party. One had a badly broken ankle that he was attempting to walk on, another had a very badly broken leg, and the third was missing part of his right leg below the knee.

Jack still had his hatchet in his hand, so he ran up to the one with the broken ankle and planted the hatchet firmly in its skull. The zombie dropped with a wet thud, but the hatchet stuck and pulled out of Jack's sweaty hand. Jack reached over his shoulder and pulled his AR around from his back, ducked his head out of the sling and brought the rifle to bear just as the next crippled zombie got close. A trigger pull and it was out of its misery, the third killed moments later.

Looking back at the Jeep, he saw that Bexar was still firing as fast as he could, but one of the undead had broken the back glass of the Jeep and was trying to claw his way inside the cabin. Jack put the reticle of his optic on the back of the zombie's head, took a deep breath, and fired.

The interior of the Jeep exploded with blackened undead brain matter, but the threat had been stopped, and the body blocked the broken window. Jessie continued to pick off the edges of the swarm, and Bexar worked as hard as he could, leaving about twenty still to kill. With carefully placed shots Jessie created a gap in the mass of undead, leaving a path to the Jeep. Sprinting towards it, she called out to Bexar as she jumped up and extended her left hand. Bexar quickly caught her hand and pulled her onto the roof.

"If those bastards are going to get my daughter, I'm taking as many as I can with me!" she said determinedly.

Another five minutes of sharp shooting and the horde was all finally down, the barrels of the ARs were smoking, and both kids were screaming.

"Holy Christ balls, Jack," said Bexar.

"Yeah, help me get this bastard out of the back of the Jeep," Jack said, pulling on the rotting corpse.

Nobody was sure if the splattered brain tissue on the inside of the Jeep could cause any issues, but to be safe, the tarp covering the gear was pulled out and discarded as well.

"Hey Bexar," called Jack. "Over by the McDonalds I think I saw an old CJ with some jerry cans in the back."

"Cool," said Bexar. "Give me a minute and I'll head over there, but we need to be quick. All that noise would've attracted some attention."

"Roger that," Jack called over his shoulder as he trotted off towards the Jeep.

Not only did the old CJ have four five-gallon jerry cans in the back, they were full of gas. On the floor in the back of the old Jeep they found a length of garden hose and a heavy hand-cranked pump, like what they used on farms to fuel up tractors out of fifty-five-gallon drums of fuel, as well as a set of large bolt cutters. This was like finding the Holy Grail.

With these tools they could break into the underground tanks of gas stations and hand-pump the gas out. The tires on the CJ looked like they would fit his rig, which was down a tire from their quest for Dr. Pepper.

Running back to the group, Jack excitedly told them of his find, then led the group in their vehicles back to the CJ. Twenty minutes later all three vehicles had full gas tanks, all their gas cans were full, and Jack had taken the four wheels and the spare off the CJ. The tires, still on their rims, wouldn't fit on the FJ's roof rack, so they were spread out over the three vehicles and also lashed to the top of the Scout's trailer.

Without further delay, the group turned southbound to try and make it to Fort Stockton before dark. It would be impossible to make it all the way to Big Bend that day, and Jack believed that Fort Stockton might be a little far with the daylight they had left. Darkness was once again a curse; if the zombie horde from the gas station had attacked them at night, he wasn't so sure they would've won that fight.

Outside of Groom Lake, Nevada

Shortly after noon, Cliff turned off the "Extraterrestrial Highway" and onto Groom Road, which would take him over the mountains and into the Groom Lake dry lakebed area. This was the infamous "Area 51."

Cliff laughed out loud; he'd been here a few times over the course of his career, and believed that the public would be amazed at what really went on. Area 51 was known to be a secret government facility with exceptionally long runways carved into the dry lakebed. Throughout its history, it had hosted testing for numerous top-secret aircraft, including the A-12 and the F-117A. However, its biggest secret was the underground facility that housed bunkers, storerooms, and other facilities with the express purpose of providing for the continuity of government, much like the facility at Denver International, or the publicly outed, obsolete Greenbrier facility in West Virginia.

Some incredible projects had launched and landed at Groom Lake, but contrary to popular belief, none of them involved aliens. One of those projects included the Air Force space program vehicles. If NASA had been able to openly use the technology developed at Groom Lake, the Space Shuttle would have been retired years before it finally was, and if civilians could use it, space tourism would cost about as much as a Southwest flight from Dallas to Denver.

"Holy shit!" Cliff suddenly remembered there were about three dozen Air Force personnel currently in orbit. "Guess those guys are on their own."

The drive down Groom Road was slower than usual due to the snowfall that was starting to accumulate, but eventually he reached the first gate to the property. He was worried about the status of the facility because the gate was unmanned; in fact, he hadn't seen any of the standard roving security teams either. These were not good signs. Luckily, the mountains were still between the gate and the facility, so he would have ample cover to recon the site before blazing into the unknown.

CHAPTER 37

South of Fort Stockton, Texas

Jack looked at the GPS on his dash. It displayed a local time of just after 3:00 p.m. Glancing at the western sky, he figured there might be about three hours until the sun dipped below the horizon. The GPS also showed it should take just over three hours to arrive at Panther Junction in the park, so assuming nothing else went wrong on their drive, they would need to find another spot on the road to secure sleep tonight.

Part of the problem on this lonely two-lane Texas highway was that in this part of Texas people had to drive two hours just to go grocery shopping; there really wasn't much of anything but large swaths of ranch land. On the upside, there weren't a lot of people living in the area, so the population of undead should be lower as well.

The unending high desert ranch land made it easy for Jack's mind to wander. Miles of old telegraph wire ran along the top of some of the fences in the area, long since disused but left in place for no other reason than that it would take work to remove them. Jack couldn't fathom why someone would choose this part of Texas to run a ranch; there was better land to ranch, and better areas to live. The only action he could think of in the area was the illegals and drug runners cutting across the ranches.

Nearly two hours south of Fort Stockton, the group drove up to a tall green and white building and covered inspection area surrounded by concrete barriers. It was the Border Patrol checkpoint; Jack had been stopped there before when he had been coming back from a backpacking trip at Big Bend. Today the station appeared deserted. Gone were the familiar green and white trucks that should have been parked next to the building. Jack slowed and pulled across the highway to park under the covered area, the group following close behind.

They paused to stretch as they climbed out of their vehicles, but unlike a normal road trip, each of them had a weapon in hand, and faced in different directions to give safety coverage. Bexar walked up to the building and found the door unlocked.

"Hey Jessie, let's clear this real quick and see if they have a chemical toilet."

"Got it," said Jessie, following him into the building. It only took about five minutes before they returned outside and declared the building free from the undead. This would be their home for the night. Unfortunately, there were no low-water or chemical toilets in the building, but there were some Porta-Johns outside, which was better than nothing. Someone would need to stand guard outside of the Porta-John while another member of the group took the opportunity to relieve themselves.

They could hear the javelinas roaming in the brush as night fell and the group broke out their dinner. They discussed their situation in hushed voices, including their worries about the biker gang. Jack was optimistic they had eluded them, and Jessie and Sandra agreed, but Bexar couldn't shake his worries that they had not.

Groom Lake, Nevada

Cliff set out on foot, leaving his truck hidden off the road just past the abandoned guard shack. The guard shack was unlocked but the power was still on, which gave Cliff some hope, although it was also to be expected since the facilities at Groom Lake ran on nuclear power. This had started in the 1950s with a first-generation reactor under development for the Navy. The last Cliff had heard, there were currently twelve reactors powering the facility, which sounded ludicrous if you didn't understand how large the facility actually was, and how much power some of the systems inside, especially the computers and labs, required.

None of this was visible to the public because the majority of the facility was built underground, except for a small cluster of buildings and the obvious runways. The facility was built deeper and was more secure than the fabled Cheyenne Mountain nuclear bunker, although their missions were drastically different.

Cheyenne Mountain accommodated a communications, radar monitoring, and command structure for the U.S. military, whereas Groom Lake contained the "black" scientific research projects, and also a large bunker designed to house most of the necessary members of the government and their families. The research and continuity-of-government bunkers were for the most part separate, but there were some underground access points between the two facilities. Most of the government officials who would be whisked to safety underground here knew that Area 51 existed, and had been instrumental in black projects such as the Lockheed SR-71 Blackbird and A-12 reconnaissance aircraft, the latter developed in the CIA's Oxcart program; but only a few knew about the current big project.

The primary research at Area 51 now was code-named the Kali Project, and its mission was to study the Yama Suain. In the mid 1950s one of the double agents run out of Station Moscow told her handlers an incredible tale.

At the end of The Second World War (WWII), the Soviets had found a drug in Adolf Hitler's bunker that he had intended to use to be able to return after death as a kind of super-soldier, unable to be killed by conventional means. Earlier in the war, Heinrich Himmler had located the substance used to make the drug, a virus, derived from spores and mined from a meteorite found in a temple near Tibet. He was known to have made several expeditions to Tibet to confirm his occult beliefs about a superior race. There he discovered stories of Tibetan priests who were able to raise people from the dead. Himmler located the meteorite, which had been kept as a sacred artifact in a remote temple, and took it back to Germany.

The Germans tried for several years to produce results that mirrored the legends of the Tibetan priests, but were unsuccessful. Upon the collapse of the Nazi regime, the meteorite and the research was discovered by the Soviets, who spent considerable resources trying to do the same thing the Germans had attempted. The Soviet scientists were able to reanimate small primates, but did not have any success with humans or other animals.

When the Soviet Union fell, factions within the KGB—the Soviet security agency who knew of the project—smuggled the data and some of the scientists out of the chaos that was Russia at the time, and into North Korea. Kim Il-Sung did not have the technology to host the research, so he ordered the former KGB officers executed, along with the Russian scientists. The North Korean leader then traded the meteorite and the research data to China in return for the raw nuclear material he needed to start his country's nuclear program.

In 1964, a single spore sample from the meteorite was smuggled out of the USSR and into the U.S. The research started immediately, which gave way to the Kali Project. Through primate research, American scientists found that reanimates lacked most of their higher brain functions, and also turned cannibalistic. The only way to destroy a reanimate was to destroy the brain.

At the time, the Kali Project found that infection was not transferred through a scratch or bite, but only via blood contact with infected brain tissue. The final update that Cliff had read on the Kali Project revealed that the research team was approximately twenty-four months away from finding an antidote that would neutralize a reanimate and inoculate the living. Cliff hoped he would find the science team alive and well, and working in the underground facility. If not, he assumed the data would still be there, but had no idea who would be able to use it.

CHAPTER 38

January 1st
Groom Lake, Nevada

Cliff spent that entire evening, and most of the night, concealed in the mountains above the lakebed, observing the aboveground portions of Area 51. He saw no movement at all. Although society as they knew it had ended, he still expected there to be some movement at the base.

The lights were on all around the base, which he considered a positive sign, even though with the redundant systems the lights and other services at the base would continue to function long into the future without intervention. In the early morning hours he finally left his post, hiking back to his truck for a quick combat nap.

After a breakfast of cold Vienna sausages and a protein bar that he had stolen from the gas station, he decided to simply drive onto the base. No amount of surface observation would tell him what he really needed to know about the underground facilities, but if the facility was overrun, he would need to retrieve the hard drives from the Kali Project's lab.

There were a few other similar secret facilities around the country, not counting the overrun facility at Denver, but if he was going to trek to Texas he needed to raid the military storage facility here. More ammo, more MREs, and better clothing topped the needs list; a cold weather sleeping system followed close behind. The hotel blankets helped, but it was still damned cold in the old truck.

He hoped for breezy access but expected the worst, so he took the time to clean his rifle and pistol, adjust his combat load out on his carrier, and check his magazines. It took an extra thirty minutes of prep time before Cliff finally pointed the truck down the mountain road towards the base.

Near Marathon, Texas

The group woke at sunrise, which was now the norm since the dead had risen and started hunting the living. Bexar was on the last security watch for the night and surprised the group by having a kettle of instant coffee hot and ready for them. It was a cold morning in the Texas high desert, but barring any sort of disaster, they should be in the National Park in a few hours. If they were lucky, they might find other, peaceful, survivors; if not, they'd find the Park overrun by the undead. It was a toss-up since winter was historically Big Bend's busiest season.

If it was overrun, it would most likely be in the busier sections such as The Basin or near the Rio Grande, but there were a lot of areas the undead could still be hiding. They could even have set up at one of the old homesteading sites, also popular because they were usually near a natural spring or well.

One week earlier most of the group would have groaned at the thought of being forced to use a Porta-John, but this morning they were all thankful for the luxury. Morning rituals complete, coffee consumed, and cold breakfast eaten, the group was back on the road without any other delays.

Within forty-five minutes they had reached Marathon. They hadn't seen a single vehicle, person, or undead creature on the road. Entering the town, Bexar flashed his headlights to signal a stop, and the convoy slowed to a halt in the middle of the highway.

Jack met Bexar at the girls' Jeep. "What's up Bexar, something break?"

"No," Bexar said, "but I remembered there's a little bookstore about a half-mile into town. We should raid it. Some reading material would be nice for a change, since it might get boring, and some park guides for wildlife, trails, and fauna could come in handy."

"Okay, not a bad idea, but only if the town isn't overrun," Jack replied. "I don't think it's worth the fight since we could raid the ranger stations; they usually have some park guides. The selection would probably be small, but it'd be better than someone getting bit for a book raid."

"Right, Jack," Bexar replied. They all returned to their trucks, and the convoy drove into town.

Marathon looked like a ghost town, but to be frank, it had looked like that even before the zombies had come. The small bookstore was in the squat row of shops on the right side of the main road, but it was past the turnoff to drive south towards the Park. Planning for a quick exit, Jack made a wide U-turn in the street so that they were pointed in the direction they wanted to go.

The kids were awake and watching out of the windows of the Jeep. Jessie climbed on the roof of the Jeep to provide security for the kids, and Sandra and Jack decided they would be the ones to go into the bookstore, with Bexar holding rear security outside. So far they had seen no movement and no people, alive, dead, or undead, but that didn't mean they were alone. The power was out, which was no surprise to anyone in the group, but it did show that even in the remote wilds of Texas, there was trouble.

Jack checked the front door and found it locked. Sandra and Bexar gave rear security watching from the door for any undead or other threats approaching while they were in the store. Jack knocked loudly on the door and pressed his face to the glass. There was no response, so he walked a few feet down the sidewalk and picked up a potted cactus, then walked back to the storefront and threw the cactus through the large plate glass window at the front of the store. The window exploded inward with a loud crash, startling Sandra and Bexar.

Bexar looked at Jack, who just shrugged and crawled through the broken window into the store. Sandra followed Jack into the store; their first priority was to clear the store of any threats. Declaring the bookstore clear, they began filling shopping bags with various books. There was no time to browse, so large portions of the fiction section went into the bags, as did a large stack of newspapers, which could be useful for toilet paper or fire-starting material. Sandra took more time to select informative books and maps of the Park, while Jack began carrying out the loaded shopping bags. When they had more time they could sort through what they'd stolen, but for now speed was their friend.

They worked quickly and quietly, but the quiet was shattered by a single rifle shot. All heads turned towards Jessie standing on the roof of the Jeep.

"Guys," she shouted, "we've got to get the fuck outta here! There's a whole shit-ton of zombies that just turned the corner and they're headed this way!"

As if on cue, the stillness of the mid-morning desert filled with a chorus of moans from the approaching horde. Jessie began taking more shots, putting down the faster-moving zombies, and Bexar ran out into the street to start giving cover and help Jessie put down the first of the approaching undead. Jack and Sandra ran behind Bexar to their trucks. By the time the group was in their vehicles, the horde, which looked to be about one hundred strong, had almost reached the convoy.

Jack and the girls had left their vehicles running during the raid, but Bexar had turned his off. Jack began to pull forward and Sandra followed, but all Bexar heard from the Scout was the click of a starter that wouldn't turn over. Three more times he tried, and three more times the starter clicked but wouldn't turn over. He had only a few more moments before he would have to abandon the Scout and try to evade the undead on foot, hoping that the group would notice and come to his rescue.

With one last try the starter turned over and the Scout roared to life. The tires chirped as Bexar dropped the clutch, and he felt something hit the back of the trailer. Working through the gears, he took the turnoff towards the Park and began catching up to the group. As he did so, he felt the trailer move against the Scout. Checking the side mirror, he saw he had picked up a passenger. The bump he'd felt as he was leaving must have been this undead falling onto the trailer. Amazingly, it hadn't fallen off yet.

Bexar sped up and pulled alongside Sandra and Jessie, waving and pointing to the back of his trailer. Sandra was behind the wheel, so Jessie climbed into the back seat, rolled down the window, and drew her pistol. It took three shots, but Jessie put the zombie stowaway down for good, which luckily fell off the trailer after being re-killed. *Problem solved*, Bexar thought. He slowed the Scout and fell back into the rear position of the convoy.

Once again the road was quiet, and the group passed no other vehicles and saw no signs of life or the undead along the lonesome Texas highway. About an hour after taking care of the undead hitchhiker, they passed the entry gate to Big Bend National Park. There were no vehicles at the ranger's station, and the entry booth was abandoned. Driving a bit faster than the forty-five-mile-per-hour speed limit, they reached the main visitor center about thirty minutes after passing the abandoned ticket booth. This was one of the busier spots in the Park, but they had to pass it to get anywhere else. Before cresting the hill and driving into the parking lot, Jack stopped the convoy to hold a quick conference.

"Bexar, what do you think about checking the visitor center before driving right up to it?"

"That would be smart," agreed Bexar. "Who knows, maybe we'll find survivors, but regardless, they have a potable tap outside the building so we can top off our water supply."

Bexar elected to stay with the vehicles to hold security, and Sandra decided to stay with the kids for their snack time. Jessie and Jack set off into the desert about a hundred yards away from the road to sneak up to the visitor center. Bexar stood on the roof of the Jeep, as had become the typical security arrangement, and scanned the visitor center's building with his binoculars. If anyone was looking they could see him, but he was also confident that he was far enough away to not be shot.

Watching Jack and Jessie approach through the desert, Bexar was amazed at how quiet the world was around him. Even in the middle of the National Park, he could always hear passing motorcycles or vehicles during past visits. Not now. There was no sound but the wind blowing across the desert.

Jack walked in a crouch through the desert brush towards the visitor's center, his rifle tucked into the SUL position. His hatchet was back in his belt, retrieved from the undead fight the previous day. They might need to kill a zombie quietly, and sound attracted more of the undead. Where there was one there were two, if there were two there were six, and if there were six they would quickly have a horde. Jessie followed about twenty yards behind Jack, also crouching, which was good tactics for an ambush. Jack really hoped that the undead weren't capable of staging an ambush.

He neared a break in the brush next to the road in front of the building and took a kneeling position. He really should lay prone, but he wasn't too keen on lying on the desert floor with all the scorpions and snakes that were often out. Jack smirked to himself, thinking that was yet another on the list of why he wasn't a Navy SEAL.

Jessie took a kneeling position about twenty yards to Jack's right as he took his binoculars out of his cargo pocket to survey the building and area. There were a few vehicles in the parking lot, but no movement around them. The front doors to the visitor's center were closed, and a thin piece of rebar was bent through the handles. That seemed odd, since it looked like anyone could take it off and walk inside, unless there was something inside they were trying to keep from getting out.

Jack continued watching the dark windows of the visitor's center. After a few minutes he thought he could see shadows moving behind the glass, but it was hard to tell because the windows were tinted and the building was dark. He guessed that there were undead locked inside the building—hard to tell how many. On the upside, he couldn't think of anything of value that they would need in the visitor's center. The potable water tap was outside the building near the parking lot, and the restrooms were accessed from the outside as well, so there would be a chance to use a normal toilet again. Well, semi-normal, they were super-low-flow biodegradable chemical-based toilets, but that still beat everything else they'd used over the past week.

Jack and Jessie watched the area for about thirty minutes, and when they felt comfortable with it, returned to the rest of the group.

"So, what's up Jack?" Bexar asked when he walked up.

"Well," Jack said, "looks like there isn't any activity around the building. There's a few cars in the parking lot, and it looks like there's probably undead in the building, and someone locked the doors from the outside using a piece of rebar."

"Do we actually need anything out of there?" Bexar asked.

"No, I can't think of anything of value," replied Jack. "It's mostly an information desk and a gift shop, but it does look like we'll be able to get to the water point, and we might be able to use the restrooms since they have a separate entrance."

The weary travelers climbed back into their vehicles and drove towards the visitor's center. Jack led the convoy into the parking lot, and they left the vehicles pointed towards the other parking lot entrance in case they had to leave quickly. After his experience in Marathon, Bexar also left his vehicle running.

Their first priority was to see if the water still worked out of the water access point. Bexar guessed that it was gravity-fed from tanks further up the mountain, but he wasn't sure. Jack tested the tap and found water flowing easily, so they were in luck. It only took about ten minutes to fill all the water jugs, and now they had enough to last them a few more days. They would continue using this water source as long as it lasted, but there was no guarantee it would last at all.

As the last water jug was lifted into the FJ, something hit the front doors of the visitor's center from the inside, causing the doors to flex outward against the rebar lock. Even from a few yards away in the parking lot, they could hear the moans coming from inside the building. There was no doubt what was locked in the building, and it sounded like there were more than a few. The bathroom breaks would have to wait—they needed to move on from the parking lot rather than risk that the improvised door lock would hold.

Quickly the group was back in their vehicles and on the road headed towards the Chisos Basin. The beautiful scenery took a backseat to their fears for their future, and the troubles behind them.

CHAPTER 38

Groom Lake, Nevada

The cars parked in the small parking lots outside the various topside buildings on the base were mostly government vehicles, since the majority of the workforce commuted by airline from Las Vegas every day. One of the most reliable and consistent airlines in the United States was operated by the U.S. government with the sole purpose of ferrying their employees back and forth from home to work every day. Cliff guessed it would beat sitting in Denver traffic.

One of the Boeing 737s used for the "commute" was named Janet, and Janet was sitting on the ramp. He was fairly sure it wouldn't have flown since the EMP event. For a fleeting moment he toyed with the idea of entering the compound through the primary access points in one of the old hangars near the north end of the flight line, but with no above-surface security, he had to assume that something had happened to the personnel here.

He hoped the base was just trying to keep a low profile by appearing to be shut down, but if that was the case, they would have cut the external lighting and power around the guard shack. In a world without electricity, the guard shack stood out like a lighthouse in the Nevada desert.

Cliff decided to access the facility through one of the escape exits, similar to what he had used to flee from the facility in Denver. In this case, the access point was an unassuming manhole cover on the base road to the west. If the electricity was still on in the underground portions, it would hopefully be lit and his card access would still work. That would make his journey much, much easier than his escape from Denver had been.

With no need to maintain any sort of stealth, Cliff simply drove his truck across the base, across the flight line, and out onto the road, stopping at the manhole cover that led into the facility nearly one hundred fifty feet below ground. Leaving most of his supplies in the truck, he grabbed his go-bag and his bump helmet, to which he attached a PVS-14 night-vision scope. Even though he assumed the facility would be illuminated, he couldn't take any chances.

Chisos Basin Campground, Big Bend National Park, Texas

Pulling into the basin camping area, Bexar and the others were faced with a few surprises. A handful of tents were standing, but there were no vehicles parked in the areas they could see from the road. The restaurant and gift shop had burned to the ground, but that fire hadn't triggered any other fires. The Civilian Conservation Corps, or CCC-built cabins, were still standing, as were the two small motels, the little rangers' station, and the convenience store, but again there were no vehicles to be seen.

Bexar couldn't explain it. As the group pulled to a stop in the main parking lot, he began to get the same feeling he got while sneaking up on drug dealers when he worked nights as a beat cop. His sixth sense was setting off alarms in his head, and that usually meant something was wrong.

"Guys, something isn't right," he called out. "It's really strange that there's no cars around, and I'm worried about the buildings, the cabins, and the motels. That there are a few tents in the camping area isn't too big of a deal and we can deal with them later, but the rest of it is a problem. We can circle the wagons here, feed the kids, and then start clearing cabins, or maybe we should clear the ranger station and use that building as our base of operations. What do you think?"

Jessie looked around at the motels and cabins, then back down towards the tents. She knew her husband, and if he felt something was off, it probably was. "Babe, let's clear the ranger station and set up in there; at least the glass is tinted and it'll let us hide."

Jack and Sandra nodded in agreement.

"Okay Jack, you're with me," said Bexar. "Girls, hold tight for a couple of minutes so we can clear this thing."

Sandra took station on top of the Jeep while Jack and Bexar jogged to the squat brown ranger station. Bexar gently pulled on the front door and found it unlocked. Jack grabbed a rock from the landscaping and threw it through the open door into the dark building. It clattered loudly as it bounced off the walls and rolled across the floor. They waited for a long ten seconds to pass. With no response from inside, they slowly made entry. About five minutes later, they exited and waved the girls over.

Will walked to the ranger station holding Sandra's hand, and Jessie carried Keeley. Jack held the door open. "Don't take the kids into the back office, looks like one of the rangers was bit and he killed himself. It's pretty bad so we just shut the door to the office for now. The rest of the building is cleared, and we left all of those doors open."

"Great, now what do you want to do?" asked Jessie. "You want Sandra and I to babysit while you and Bexar clear the rest of the camp? That's bullshit, it'll take all day and maybe some of the next!"

"Okay honey, let's break for lunch and we'll come up with a plan together," Bexar replied.

Jack retrieved his Yeti cooler and passed out the last of the hotdogs, a few slices of cheese, and the last of the Shiner Bock beers. Everything was still fairly cold and they all knew that this would probably be the last of food like this for a very long time, if not forever. Will and Keeley drank the last of the condensed milk. From here on out, they would be on powdered milk until that was gone as well.

The lunch topic of discussion was the plan for the afternoon. Eventually they agreed that Jack and Bexar would go to the top of the cabins and start working their way back down the mountain towards the ranger station. There weren't as many cabins as rooms in the motels, so it would be the easiest start. After two hours, or earlier if they were finished, they would come back and check in with their wives. If the girls got into trouble, one of them would fire a shot out the door as a help signal and the boys would come running down the mountain to them. If the kids cooperated and went down for a nap after lunch, the girls were going to take the binoculars and start scanning the tent area, the Window Trail, and the trail up to Emory Peak for any signs of survivors or the undead.

Finishing lunch, Bexar and Jack began gearing up for the expedition. Jack took a small pack with some food and his Camelbak hydration pack, as well as his AR, pistol, and hatchet; he also stuffed his short-barrel Mossberg shotgun into the Camelbak straps. Bexar shrugged on his Kevlar vest, followed by his Eagle chest rig, then his Camelbak. A broken-down MRE was also stuffed into his Camelbak. He press-checked his pistol and holstered it, then gave his AR a press check followed by bumping the forward assist twice and shutting the dust cover.

Neither of them could remember exactly how many cabins there were, but they knew there were quite a few, some of them designed to house close to a dozen people. Hopefully their expedition wouldn't take too long, and if they were truly lucky, they would find nothing but friendly survivors. Geared up and strapped on, they took some time to look out the tinted windows towards their destination, scanning for any threats before opening the door.

The walk to the first cabin was short, and they decided to start low and work up instead of the other way around as planned. That way they started out closer to the girls, if something happened. Bexar held rear security while Jack looked in the windows, followed by tapping on the glass. Nothing inside the cabin responded to the window tapping so Bexar pulled the screen open, which creaked loudly in protest, while Jack opened the unlocked door and entered. The cabin was too small for two people to clear, so Bexar stood outside by the door, continuing his duty with rear security.

"Holy shit!" yelled Jack.

"Jack, you okay?"

"Yeah," he replied, "but it looks like someone fucking exploded in the bathroom, there's blood everywhere, and ... shit, there's a small foot in here. No leg, nothing but a foot!"

"Damn!" said Bexar. "Well, I guess we're in for some undead love. Maybe there's only one, and that was the one who bit the ranger."

"Doubt it, coming out!"

Bexar expected Jack to exit, but instead his ears were suddenly ringing from the three shots Jack had fired in the cabin.

"FUCK!" yelled Jack.

"WHAT HAPPENED?" screamed Bexar back, his ears still ringing.

"Found the owner of the foot, little bastard was under the bed, damned near shot my foot off when it tried to bite me!"

"Jeez Jack, are you bit?"

"No, but fuck'n A, I'm going to stand on the bed and pull up the covers, you clear under the bed."

Bexar drew his pistol, crouching low, and flipped on the TLR light attached to the pistol as Jack pulled up the blanket.

"Clear!"

The undead kid was now truly dead, so they stepped out of the cabin and shut the door behind them. A series of rapid-fire pistol shots rang out below them.

Jack and Bexar turned and begun sprinting down the blacktop road towards the ranger station. As they rounded the corner they saw Jessie on the roof, firing her pistol at a group of about fifteen undead by the front door. Bexar raised his rifle but Jack swatted the barrel down. "Dude, check your backstop, you'll shoot through the glass and into the building. We've got to get a safe angle."

Bexar peeled off to the right and kept running. Jack stopped, shooting at a safe angle to distract the undead and pull them away from the front of the ranger station, which worked well enough on a few of the zombies. Bexar stopped and knelt, trying to control his breathing so he could shoot accurately. Jessie yelled at Bexar, "I'm out, and my rifle is inside the building."

"Okay, get to the middle of the roof and lay flat," he replied.

Jessie disappeared from view, and the undead turned their full attention to the two rifles firing at them from the parking lot. The horde thinned from the directed rifle fire, and as the undead continued to fall it became apparent that the glass front door was shattered. It took a mag change, but Bexar finally dropped the last undead, which had literally fallen at his feet.

"Jessie, where's Sandra and the kids?"

"They're still inside!"

"Shit Jack, form up, let's go in fast."

Bexar stood next to the door. Jack ran up behind him, got set, and squeezed his shoulder.

"Go!"

Bexar stepped forward. Planting his boot against the doorframe to keep his balance on the shattered glass, he pushed off and made entry into the building, rifle up and weapon light on. Three undead stood in view in Bexar's field of fire. Bexar continued to run his wall, firing three shots at each zombie; he heard Jack do the same from his side of the room.

"Clear!"

"Clear," Jack answered.

"Sandra, where are you? Are you okay?" Bexar called, but no one answered.

Both of their ears were still ringing from the rifle fire, but they could hear crying coming from the dead ranger's office. The door was still closed, so Jack knocked. "Hey honey, it's us, it's safe, we're going to open the door."

There was no response from the other side of the door and the crying continued. Jack turned the doorknob and slowly opened the door. The dead ranger was still on the floor behind the desk. Sandra was crouched in the corner, holding both kids in one arm, pointing the dead ranger's pistol towards the door.

"Whoa Sandra, put it down, it's us." Sandra didn't move, so Jack slowly walked into the room and gently pulled the pistol from his wife's shaking hands. Both of the kids were crying, and Sandra started crying when Jack hugged her.

"Coming in," Jessie called from the front.

"Enter," was Bexar's terse reply. The adrenaline was already starting to fade, replaced by shaking hands and an overwhelming feeling of exhaustion. Jessie retrieved her rifle and came to the office door.

"Hey guys, I don't know how many there are, but there are probably a dozen or so more undead shuffling out from around the motels. We need to get clear."

Bexar took Keeley from Sandra's grasp and handed her to Jessie. "Right, we need someplace for the night, but first we need to decide whether we stay and fight, or flee for now."

Looking at Sandra, Jack replied, "I say we flee for now, regroup, and try again tomorrow."

"Okay, how about Hot Springs or Cattail Falls?" Bexar asked.

"Let's do Cattail Falls, I think that'd be a safer spot for now."

Everyone nodded. Bexar gathered Jack's cooler and the rest of the gear in the ranger station and carried it out to the vehicles in two trips. Jessie took the kids to the Jeep, and Jack helped Sandra to the Jeep. The convoy left as quickly as they could, driving the winding mountain road with Bexar in the lead.

About thirty minutes later, Bexar turned onto the unmarked road that led to the Cattail Falls trailhead. The service road gate was locked, but Jack defeated the padlock with his shotgun. The small creek and trees at the trailhead would be their camp spot for the night, maybe longer. They were safely out of the way now; for any of the undead to make it to the camp, they would have to traverse The Window and the open desert.

Within the hour, the wall tent was up and the sun was setting across the desert mountains. Their dinner was warming on the Coleman stoves. Bexar opened a bottle of whiskey and, for the first time in nearly a week, allowed himself to relax slightly. They couldn't live in this spot forever, but it would do well for right now.

CHAPTER 40

January 2nd
Groom Lake, Nevada

It was two o'clock in the morning and Cliff was soaked with sweat, hanging from a pipe in the ceiling above the drop-ceiling tiles. The last four hours had been an utter disaster. Cliff had run out of ammo for his FNP90 and resorted to using his pistol, which wasn't suppressed. Then he ran out of ammo for his pistol, and was running for his life with nothing but his Emerson folder in his sweaty hands. He had missed the stairs, and was now hiding in the ceiling above a janitor's closet on the second level below ground—the levels were numbered in descending order.

After opening the manhole above ground it took Cliff about ten minutes to climb down to the first level. In the first few minutes in the facility he had seen no signs of life, dead or alive. The facility had electricity and the lights were on, but it looked deserted. How wrong he had been.

On the first floor he had encountered only two undead security personnel. The security guards' pistols and ammo were still on them; Cliff hadn't taken them in order to save weight, but now he wished he had. Another bad choice in this series of fuckups.

He had to either make it to the fifth level to the storage area, or back up to the first level to the re-killed security guards to get their pistols and ammo. Regardless, he had to first get past the hurdle of the undead below him, on the other side of the ceiling he was hiding in.

Immediately after running his rifle dry of ammo, Cliff had transitioned to his pistol, letting the rifle hang by the sling. He lost count but estimated that he had taken down around seventy undead so far in the facility, and he was still in the primary underground facility. After he reached the fifth level to resupply, he had to make it to the seventh level to pull the hard drives from the labs used in the Kali Project. From there he could reach one of the tunnels that connected the primary facility to the hardened bunker.

He hoped that some of the people involved with the project had fled to the bunker when everything had started to go wrong, and that some of the people needed for the continuity of government were still alive and well in the bunker. However, at this point, he had his doubts that he would find anything other than what he had found so far—a large underground tomb of undeath.

The shuffling and moans below the ceiling were getting quieter, which was a good sign. He was confident he could take a single undead with his knife, even two, but the eight that had chased him into hiding would have taken him down without a doubt.

Still grasping the hanging pipe, Cliff reached down to the ceiling below and gently pulled up on a dislodged tile. A sliver of light broke the darkness, and he could see only a single zombie, facing away from him and beginning to shamble away from the janitor's closet he was hiding above.

Too bad the building had correctly built firebreaks between the rooms, or he could have simply worked his way to his destination while above the ceiling tiles. Cliff pushed the dislodged tile out of the way and, hanging from his hands before dropping to the floor, landed quietly on the balls of his feet. He quickly pulled the Emerson knife and drove it into the side of the zombie's head. He wasn't sure where the other seven zombies had gone, and quite frankly didn't care, as long as he could get to the stairwell.

Reaching the double doors at the end of the hall, he took a moment to listen against the doors for movement in the room. He couldn't hear anything, and he tried to visualize the space from his visit here about ten years ago. He remembered the room being about one hundred feet across, with the doors he needed to access at the far end, and a large number of cubicles and offices throughout the room.

He pulled his keycard out from under his sweat-soaked shirt and touched the radio frequency (RF) pad on the right side of the door. The door clicked unlocked, and he pushed it open quietly. He had no ammo, so wanted to sneak into the room and through it. There were about thirty undead standing motionless towards his left.

At his right stood a desk, and on the desk was an old government-issue desk stapler that looked like it was fifty years old, and weighed nearly as much. Cliff picked up the stapler and threw it over the heads of the undead, crashing it against the far wall. They snapped out of their trance and began lurching towards the new noise. Cliff ducked behind a cubicle wall and moved quickly and quietly in a crouch towards the doors at the far wall. About halfway across the room the undead lost interest in the stapler, and Cliff broke out in a sprint for the doors.

Reaching the doors, the moans growing louder behind him, he slapped his keycard against the RF panel and the doors opened with a satisfying click. He burst through the doors and leaned against them until he heard the click of the lock re-engaging. Standing in the dimly lit concrete stairwell, Cliff tried to slow his breathing. He was almost there, he thought. Maybe his chances were starting to look up.

CHAPTER 41

Big Bend National Park, Texas

Sandra stood security watch, and as the sun began to rise she put their trusty blue enamel kettle on the Coleman stove for the morning coffee. It was bitterly cold in the desert this morning, but it still felt better than the last few mornings. She had come to terms with the terror of the previous afternoon, and felt that the group had reached a point where they could take hold, stake a claim, and survive for their future. As light dawned across the clear winter sky, she knew the kids wouldn't be asleep much longer. Even at the end of the world, toddlers slept in for no one. She dug through the food stored in the FJ, taking out what she needed for Will and Keeley's breakfast. Milk for both kids was reconstituted from powdered milk.

Just as the water for the coffee began to boil, Jessie emerged from her and Bexar's tent, yawning. Jessie had sat the first night watch and had therefore had the longest uninterrupted sleep, but she still felt like she needed to sleep for a couple of days just to catch up.

"Hey Jess, if you don't mind taking care of the coffee, I want to dig through some of the books we took yesterday. Maybe I can find something useful to help us out here," Sandra greeted her.

Jessie nodded silently, and Sandra walked to the Scout to the pile of books that had spilled across the backseat. She pulled them out one-by-one, making stacks of books on the trailer, separating the non-fiction from the novels. She was hoping to find something that would make identifying edible plants easier, or something similar. Most of the books were coffee table-type books with photography and local area art, which was interesting but of little survival value for the group. She hoped one day that she would once again have a coffee table to place books on.

She stopped when she found a book titled "The ARRL Handbook for Radio Amateurs," and set that apart from the others. They had found a handheld amateur ham radio in Malachi's cache in Maypearl, but hadn't used it yet since none of them knew how to operate it, nor had they had the chance to try and figure it out.

By now the boys were awake and up, as were the children. Leaving the rest of the books piled around the Scout, Sandra brought the amateur radio book over to the group. Holding it up, she asked, "Don't we have a ham radio from Malachi's cache? If anyone else still has one working, maybe we could find them?"

A huge grin spread across Jack's face. "That's exactly what I need! Malachi was the commo expert, I never did more than just dabble with some two-meter radios a long time ago. I hadn't planned on losing him, so I never really spent any time learning about it."

Jack spent the entire breakfast with the book in his lap, reading as he ate. The mood in the group was much higher than it had been for days. Sandra took Jack's finished plate from him, and he went to the FJ and turned on the Yaesu radio. He switched the radio over to the 70cm band and began slowly cycling through the channels. After nearly five minutes, everyone held their breath as a weak voice came through the radio's speaker.

"... yeah, well, Marfa's pretty much burned to the ground, and Terlingua is once again a ghost town, but I think there are a few families scattered out on their ranches that are still surviving ... no ... rumor ... biker gang ... Odessa ... south ..."

They never heard the other side of the conversation, and the transmission they were receiving kept garbling in and out, but now they knew for a fact that there were other survivors in the area. They weren't all alone in the desert.

Bexar looked up, realizing he was staring at the radio speaker, and found everyone else doing the same. "Well, the good news is that there are at least two other people out there who are surviving, but the bad news is that it sort of sounded like the bikers might be near Odessa and heading south from I-20. That might mean they're headed towards El Paso, but that could also mean they're headed towards Fort Stockton."

"Do you think they're headed here? How could they have followed us?" Jessie said.

"I don't know Jess, besides the lone biker scout we shot at, I'm not sure they knew we were there, much less where we were headed. I mean, we drove across a lot of Texas to make it here, and if they were really following us, why did they go up to Odessa instead of down the road following us?"

"What do you think we should do?" Sandra asked Bexar.

"Well, I'd love to get somewhere we can get better reception and see if we can communicate with the people we heard on the radio today. Then we can decide if we want to stay here, or keep running. If we stay, we'll need to decide if we try to lay low and hide, or if we should build up and fortify our position."

Jessie asked, "So where can we get better reception?"

"I'm not sure, babe," he replied.

"What about Emory Peak?" said Jack. "That's the highest ground we have."

"Sure Jack, but we'd have to go through the Basin first to get to the trailhead, and we just got run out of the Basin by a bunch of hungry zombies."

"What if we took a few days and cleared them out systematically, with a better plan and better tactics than before," Jack replied. "Then we can still relocate up to the cabins like we wanted to in the first place. I know I'd feel safer surrounded by the mountains than out here in the desert. Besides, it would be a shorter hike to Emory Peak from the cabins than from here."

It was a lively discussion that lasted for the better part of an hour, but in the end they agreed to continue using their current camp near Cattail Falls as their base, but to start clearing the Basin. They weren't going to run any longer; this was going to be their home.

Groom Lake, Nevada

Cliff glanced at his watch and saw that it was now seven o'clock in the morning, nearly five hours since he had clung to the pipe in the ceiling for his life, which included nearly an hour of hide-and-seek with the undead quartermaster in the storage area before he was finally able to get some more ammo for his rifle and pistol. Cliff had finally beaten the zombie to death with a heavy-duty government desk chair that looked like it had been made before FDR was president. Cliff giggled, remembering his chair-bludgeon, and realized that his mind was slipping due to stress, lack of food, and lack of sleep.

He topped off the magazines for his pistol and his rifle, and switched out the batteries for his weapon lights, night vision scope, and flashlight, all of which used CR123A batteries, by design. He then put two more twelve-count boxes of batteries in his go-bag, and since he was alone and the quartermaster was really dead this time, Cliff took the luxury of digging through a case of MREs to find the meal he liked best, the Chicken Fajita entrée. Normally, you got to eat what you got to eat and that was it, but he felt he deserved an extra perk for his morning's efforts.

CHAPTER 42

February 2nd
Groom Lake, Nevada

One month had passed since Cliff had first entered the underground facility at Groom Lake. At the time he hadn't realized that the entire complex was a death zone; not a single person was left alive; instead, several hundred undead wandered around the secret facility.

The food supply had been cached with the intent of keeping approximately two hundred people alive and fed for over a year. There was no way Cliff could ever consume that much food before it started to go bad. Checking the date stamps, he estimated that he had about five years left on the MREs. Beyond that, there were enough weapons and ammunition to start a convincing religious cult, and there were even crates of the old woodland battle dress uniforms, or "BDUs," so he was also set for clothing.

Even with all the time and effort he'd spent over the past month fighting and killing the undead trapped in the halls, rooms, and passageways in the facility, he still hadn't been able to access the Kali Project labs four levels below him. Nor had he made it out to the full communications room, the "hut," that was near the aerials above ground. The hut was accessed through a tunnel from the third level and was nearly a half-mile long. There was limited communications access in the bunker, but full access could only be found in the hut, and full access was the only way to contact any of the other facilities, that is, if they were still operational. Because he knew from first-hand experience that the two premier and best-equipped facilities, Denver and Groom Lake, were both dead zones, Cliff didn't hold out much hope for the others. NORAD wasn't even a hardened facility anymore and it was close to Denver—he'd barely made it out of Denver alive.

Taking an educated guess as to the number of people who would normally man the facility, he thought he was getting close to having the place completely clear of the undead, but he still wouldn't completely let his guard down. Today he thought he might finally have a chance to access the Kali Project labs and hopefully find the Yama Strain information. If anyone else was still alive, and if there was any hope of overcoming this, the information in the labs would be the key.

Before opening the door, Cliff prepared with the room-clearing tactics he'd developed over the past month. He would open the door slowly and check for any undead at the door. If it was clear, he would wedge a big yellow doorstop under the door to hold it open and bang on the door loudly. Backing away from the open door, he would wait for any undead to come to him, while he stood on the "safe" side of the door. If there was a large group of undead, they would bottleneck at the doorway, slowing their approach, and preventing a swarm.

Cliff carefully opened the outer lab door, and as he wasn't immediately greeted by any undead, and with doorstop in place, he began banging on the door and yelling before taking ten steps away from the doorway. A chorus of moans erupted from the darkness on the other side of the doorframe. He raised his M4 and peered through the EoTech sight. With a near-unlimited supply of .223 and a large cache of SOPMOD M4 rifles, Cliff had built out an AR platform with the tools he needed for his mission, including the optic and a suppressor. He had even found a set of Peltor electronic hearing protectors, but as long as the suppressor lasted he wouldn't need the hearing protection.

After his near-death adventure by running out of ammo shortly after arriving at the facility, he now carried nearly three hundred rounds of .223 on his chest rig and belt, plus what was in the rifle. All that ammo was heavy, but heavy was better than dead. He was happy he wasn't humping a full combat load through the mountains of Afghanistan anymore; this was easy work compared to some of his previous missions.

The first zombie made it to the door; it was another former security officer. After a previous hard-learned lesson about the undead piling up in the doorway when you shot them, Cliff now let the first handful through the door before putting them down.

Four undead security officers and eight undead scientists later, the stream of zombies coming through the door had stopped. Cliff banged on the door a few more times and waited for a response, but there was none. Shining the rifle-mounted Surefire light through the doorway into the darkness, he didn't see any movement or any other undead. Slowly entering the doorway, he reached out with his left hand and flipped on the light switch. With the nuclear reactors, the facility should have an ample supply of electricity for at least another twenty years, and in moments like this he truly appreciated what a luxury electric lights were. If the power was out here like it had been in the Denver facility, this would have been an impossible task born in hell.

Ten minutes later the front sections of the lab were clear, and all the lights turned on. He came to a heavy door that was locked with an actual physical lock, instead of the RF chip-encoded electronic locks in the rest of the facility. Cliff tried the door, but it was secure. Banging on the door with his fist did nothing—the door was solid like a concrete wall. Grabbing a metal trashcan from the front room, he loudly banged the can on the door, which rung like a heavy gong. Laughing, he yelled, "AMWAY, YOU WANT TO BUY SOME WORTHLESS SHIT?" He dropped the trashcan and had started towards the other rooms to look for keys that might work on the door when he heard a heavy latch turn over on the other side of the door.

As the door slowly cracked open, Cliff spun around and dropped to one knee behind a desk, M4 up and pointed towards the opening door.

"Amway? Down here? Bullshit. They don't have clearance. At least you didn't try to tempt me with some Girl Scout cookies ... holy shit man, relax! I'm not a zombie."

Inching through the opening doorway was a scruffy-looking dark-haired kid, about in his twenties. Surprised to find another living person, Cliff lowered his rifle to the SUL position and stood. "Hey!" he blurted. "I'm Cliff, and I'm OGA. I've been sent here to retrieve any remaining scientists, secure this facility, and help facilitate their research with the hope of restarting our country."

"Well, Mr. Other Government Agency operator," the kid said, "I'm Lance Weisinger, and I'm an overqualified lab technician recruited about nine months ago after completing my doctorate in molecular biology. I've been underground ever since, and I've been trapped back in that lab for nearly six weeks—what took you guys so long?"

"Bad news, Lance," replied Cliff. "There aren't any other guys, it's just me, and I've been underground here for a month fighting my way down to you. You're the first living person I've found. Is there anyone else with you?"

"No, just me," Lance replied. "There were two others in the secure lab with me, but they reanimated so I locked them in one of the other bio-labs. I've been in the front lab trying to survive ever since. I did try to leave the lab a few weeks ago, but there were about a dozen reanimates between me and the door over there, so I stayed put and hoped for a rescue. What helped is that we kept a couple cases of MREs down here because many of the researchers would spend days at a time in the lab, so I've been able to ration out my food and survive. Since I was trapped, I kept working on the project."

"Did you find how to stop this madness?" Cliff asked.

"No, not yet, but I think we have a chance. It's going to take a lot more time, and it's really slow with only me to take care of all the work."

"What about the other two reanimates you locked up? Show me where they are and I'll put 'em down for you."

"No, no," said Lance, "they're locked up, and I need them for my research. Without them, I wouldn't have fresh infected tissue to experiment on."

"Okay Lance, for now though, come with me to where I've set up shop. We'll get you some fresh clothes, and see if we can contact anyone else that could help."

Lance nodded. "Oh good. I've developed a bad rash from these clothes. I tried washing them in the sink but it hasn't helped. Who are we going to contact? I thought you said everyone here was dead."

"Yeah, everyone here is, but with your help we can take control of the commo-hut and see if there's anyone on the other side of the radio."

CHAPTER 43

Big Bend National Park, Texas

Jack had been stalking his prey through the woods since before dawn. He wished it had gone up the trail instead of down. If he could get the kill, it would be extra work dragging the carcass back up the mountain. The sun had just began to peek over the top of the mountains to the east, and it would only be a few more hours until the stiff cold winter air was broken by the heat of the sun. Jack stopped to scan and listen to the area around him. Hearing movement in the brush to his left, near a small stream, he raised his rifle and aimed towards the disturbance in the woods. Almost holding his breath, he waited for his prey to be shown. A sudden fury of movement exploded from the brush about twenty yards in front of him; tracking the movement with the muzzle, he fired his rifle, felling a mule deer.

Over the past month of living in the Chisos Basin, the group had been forced to flee for their lives from an undead horde and take refuge on the desert floor near Cattail Falls. After regrouping and establishing a camp and a plan, they had flushed the roaming undead out of the Basin over the course of two weeks, burning the bodies in a dumpster by the tent camping area. It took another full week of work to clear each of the cabins, the motel rooms, and the support buildings of trapped undead. They had hoped, through all of the dirty fighting and burning dead bodies, to find some survivors, but there were no survivors at all.

Only in the past few days had they been able to relocate from their temporary camp on the desert floor to the CCC cabins at the top of the basin, near the trail for the South Rim and Emory Peak. Their cache of stored food was beginning to dwindle, so Jack had set out to kill a mule deer because he had the most hunting experience. They hoped the cold weather would help the meat keep while they set about preserving it.

While Jack hunted for food, Bexar was at the cabins watching the kids. Sandra and Jessie had taken the Wagoneer down to Panther Junction to scout the homes where the park staff had lived. The girls were looking for any signs of survivors, but they were also looking for any canned food, salt, or anything else that could be useful. The homes hadn't been cleared of the undead yet, so the girls were playing it safe, using tactics the group had developed during the past month of undead clearing.

After the park personnel's homes were raided, the next step would be to check the big RV camping spots in the Park, like the Rio Grande Village. Where there were big recreational vehicles there were generators, hopefully some that had been unaffected by the EMP.

Jack finished field-dressing the deer and built a drag using some 550 cord and wood found by the creek. A car horn honked twice from the direction of the cabins. Sandra and Jessie were back from their scouting trip, and he needed to get his fresh kill back up to the cabin. Hopefully the girls had found a large barrel of salt; they would need it to preserve all of this meat.

It took Jack nearly thirty minutes, but the deer was at the trailhead and across the hood of his FJ. A few moments later he pulled up to the front of their cabins. Sandra, Jessie, and Bexar were organizing the raided supplies, which included a large stack of canned goods, a few large boxes of kosher salt, and a bunch of mason jars with lids, but that wasn't the most exciting find.

"Four groups of solar panels, probably five feet across, all mounted on poles next to the homes!" Jessie reported excitedly. "We just didn't know how to take them apart and bring them back. Besides, we haven't cleared that area or the visitor's center yet either."

For the past two weeks they had been trying to come up with a way to power the pumps at the water tanks in the basin. Water pumped up from a well on the desert floor near The Window to a series of tanks, then pumped to another series of tanks, and eventually to two large tanks hidden in the woods behind the cabins. All the equipment appeared to be in good order, it just needed electricity. If they could power the pumps, they would have a lifetime of fresh water on tap. With the water, javelina, and deer in the area, they would have everything they needed to survive for the foreseeable future.

With the group settling into a comfortable routine, they made a plan for two of them to go up the trail to Emory Peak the following week. That couple would hike to the top of the mountain with the ham radio and shortwave radio, enough food and water for their stay, and the charged car battery from the Scout to power the radio. They would spend two days on the mountain trying to reach any other survivors, or gather more information about what had happened to the world over these past weeks. Whoever wasn't on the mountain would watch the kids and keep up the work at their base camp.

Besides the radio work on the mountain, everyone was excited for the little overnight trip. It had been nearly six weeks since either Bexar and Jessie or Jack and Sandra had had a chance of enjoying a date night. They were, in fact, so excited they had to rock-paper-scissors to determine who got to go up the mountain first. But now with the new find of solar panels, the communications plan might be delayed a few days.

CHAPTER 44

February 3rd
Groom Lake, Nevada

Lance and Cliff made their way back to the supply room, which was about the size of a high school basketball gymnasium. It was divided into sections by shelving units, with some more secure areas in large locked fence cages that were about twenty by twenty feet. Luckily, the undead quartermaster had the keys on his belt, so Cliff now had the keys to the whole storage facility.

Over the past month spent killing the undead in the underground base, Cliff had procured one of the fenced-in cages and turned it into a shelter, removing what was stored and making it a safe place for him to sleep. With a cot, some blankets, a few cases of .223, and two cases of MREs, even if he became trapped by the undead in the cage, he could easily survive while systematically killing them all. He had even hung netting on the fence to obscure the view into the cage.

Now with Lance joining him, Cliff began gathering supplies for the young scientist: A fresh set of BDUs, underwear, socks, boots, t-shirt, and a belt. He left Lance to change and discard his well-abused clothes. Cliff set out emptying the fenced cage next to his own. Lance returned in his new clothes and helped organize his new "room" much like Cliff's.

"Know how to shoot?" Cliff asked.

"Yeah, well, not really. I played a bunch of Call of Duty, and I shot a friend's shotgun a few times, but that's about it," Lance replied sheepishly.

"Okay, well, let's get you a pistol and some ammo, and I can start teaching you the basics, but I'll do the heavy lifting when it comes to taking down any threats.

You're the last guy here who has a chance at the Yama Strain, so you need to learn how to survive, and I need your help."

"I thought you wanted me in the lab working on our problem?"

"I do," agreed Cliff, "but first we need to clear the commo-hut and see if anyone else is still showing green, then we can try to find you some help. I know the President's dead, I verified that personally. The VP too. Hopefully one of the other facilities is up and running and somebody survived. My mission is to facilitate the continuity of government and the restart of leadership, and to help anyone involved succeed in saving what's left of our country. If I was to guess, I'd say there's probably pockets of survivors, especially military personnel, out there in the wild, but that's just a hunch. Since leaving Denver you're the first living person I've spoken with. To be honest, we're pretty much goat-fucked, but we have to succeed in my mission if there's any hope of survival at all."

Lance thought about it. "I get why here at this facility, but how do you fit in, why you?"

"I'm one of a handful of people who were selected and trained to complete this mission, assuming this scenario happened," replied Cliff. "Although I wasn't supposed to be here, I was supposed to be in Denver; there's another member of my team that was supposed to be here. The Denver facility is a tomb; I barely made it out alive. I'm hoping that some others of my team survived and made it to their responsibilities. Mount Weather has a good chance of survival, but it's also well-known publicly, so if survivors flocked there and turned, it would have easily been overrun. This place is a sealed, secure location, and it was overrun, so who knows. Not counting here and Denver, that only leaves Waxahachie and Napa Valley."

"Waxa-what?" said Lance.

"Waxahachie, Texas. Do you remember the super-conducting collider they built underground ringing the city?"

"Vaguely."

"Okay, well, the collider was real, they really built it, but it was also a cover for the construction of another underground facility. The story was that the boring machines used to build the collider were turned and discarded underground, but in reality they started the excavation process to build something very similar to what's here. Except that the lake they're built under isn't dry, it's really a lake with water in it, and they're built much deeper than we are here."

"Damn, didn't know about that one!" said Lance. "And I figured it was the shit to work at Area 51. Thought I would learn about secret aliens and stuff. Guess I was wrong."

"There are no aliens, guy," Cliff said, shaking his head. "Most of those stories were made up and perpetuated by our own government to give the public something to latch onto and distract them from what we were really doing. Besides, when you have unbalanced people telling the story for you because they deeply believe it, the general public sees it all as crazy, just because of the storyteller. Either way, none of it matters if we can't get our communications up, or if there's no one to answer them. We need to get to work so we can get into the commo-hut tomorrow."

"So what are we doing the rest of the day?" asked Lance.

"You're going to learn how not to shoot yourself, or more importantly, not shoot me."

CHAPTER 45

Big Bend National Park, Texas

The group's morning began as usual, with breakfast and planning for the day. First they would tackle clearing out the park staff's homes and the visitor's center, which should only take a couple of hours. Then Bexar and Jack would continue on to the Rio Grande Village and RV camping area to scout and recon the area for any survivors, or any supplies they might need. Jessie and Sandra would stay by the homes, the kids with them, and attempt to safely remove the solar panels from their mounts. The cabins would be left unguarded, but they believed that with the terrain, if they closed the gate across the road in the mountain, the undead would have a hard time getting up there. Besides, they were relatively confident that the undead in the Basin had been completely eradicated.

The kids played in the back seat of the Wagoneer as Sandra and Jessie loaded Bexar's tool kit in the back and started out of the Basin. Bexar and Jack followed in the FJ, stopping only to shut the gate behind them, securing it with a length of 550 cord. Bexar and Jack had every fuel can the group owned, along with the hose and the hand-cranked pump. Both the Jeep and the FJ had been topped off that morning, and the gas cans were now empty.

There were two gas stations in the Park, one near the visitor's center, and another in the Rio Grande Village. Neither had been checked for fuel in their underground tanks, as there hadn't been time until now, so Bexar and Jack would fill the group's gas cans if possible. Worst case, there would hopefully be some abandoned vehicles or gas-powered RVs they could siphon gas from in the RV park.

The group convoyed down the mountain and towards the visitor's center, passing the gas station on their right. The first task was the undead in the visitor's center, then clearing the homes behind it. The kids stayed in the Wagoneer, and Sandra climbed onto the roof for watch. Jessie and Bexar took firing positions in the parking lot, while Jack pulled the piece of rebar out from the door handles to unlock the visitor's center. Jack pushed against the doors, holding them closed, and looked back at Bexar and Jessie.

"You guys ready?"

"Yup," Bexar replied.

"Yeah," echoed Jessie.

"Okay, here we go!" Jack pounded on the doors then ran perpendicular to the line of fire to clear the doors. Within seconds the first undead burst through the unlocked doors, and the group held their fire, letting the walking corpse clear the doorway. As the third zombie came out of the visitor's center, Bexar fired the first shot, exploding the skull of the zombie closest to them. Systematically the process continued, with Jessie and Bexar methodically killing each undead that shambled out of the dark building until a dozen bodies littered the parking lot and no more emerged.

Rifles up, Bexar and Jessie moved slowly towards the doorway and paused long enough for Jack to join them, then banged loudly on the doors again and held them open. There was no response from inside. Bexar and Jessie switched on their weapon lights and walked into the darkness. A few minutes later they came back out and declared the building clear. In the Basin they had taken the time to burn the bodies of the undead they'd killed, but here they would leave them where they had fallen, and let the animals of the desert take care of the carcasses.

They loaded back into their vehicles and followed the road into the first group of homes in the housing area behind the visitor's center. Repeating the process they had used with the visitor's center, they had cleared all the homes within three hours. They hadn't found any survivors, but thirty walking corpses were put down for good. The service buildings and other homes further on would need to wait for another day; there was still work to be done.

Jessie and Sandra fed the kids and tried to get them to lay down for a nap in the back of the Jeep before starting their project of dismantling the solar panels. Jack and Bexar drove back to the gas station in their FJ.

The small service station had a selection of fan belts and radiator hoses, as well as a good selection of gas station snacks, so the few belts and hoses that would fit their vehicles went in the back of the FJ, as did boxes of beef jerky, some candy bars, Gatorade, and Red Bull. The keys for the underground tanks were found in the service station office, next to the chart the attendants used to keep track of the tank stick measurements, which saved Bexar and Jack the effort of having to cut the locks. It also gave them the ability to re-lock the tanks and take the keys with them.

Twenty minutes later the red gas cans were full and the underground gas tank was secured. They used the measuring stick they had found to measure the tank, and by referencing the chart in the office, noted that there was another seven-hundred gallons of fuel in just that one tank, so they should be set for some time, at least until the fuel started to go bad. Loaded back in the FJ, the boys headed out towards the Rio Grande Village.

Ignoring the forty-five-mile-per-hour speed limit signs, it took about thirty more minutes to reach the ranger's station just outside the Rio Grande Village. Jack stopped the truck in the road and they both exited with rifles in hand. In the parking lot was a single Park Services truck, which was to be expected. The window next to the front door was shattered and dried blood covered the sidewalk. With no movement outside the building, Jack held cover on the front door while Bexar walked up, opened the front door, and propped it open with a rock from the parking lot. He then banged loudly on the door and yelled inside, and was instantly answered by a loud and angry moan. Bexar ran quickly out of the line of fire before making the loop back to join Jack, keeping his rifle in the SUL position while scanning the area for any other threats and leaving Jack to engage the emerging zombie. Two shots later the zombie lay truly dead by the shattered window on the sidewalk. They quickly searched the ranger's station but didn't find anything except for some stale donuts, a lot of dried blood, and some park maps.

Safely back in the FJ, they drove the short distance to the edge of the Rio Grande Village. The convenience store and laundromat were on the left, with the parking lot in front of them, and the smaller RV park to the right, through the trees. The parking lot had a handful of vehicles, and it looked like there were a lot of RVs parked on the other side of the trees. They couldn't even see the main RV park, which was further down the road. Jack turned the FJ around, pointing it towards their exit in case they needed a quick escape.

"Cars first, or the store?" asked Bexar.

"Let's do the store," replied Jack. "If they're in the cars they'll stay in the cars."

"Good call."

It was Jack's turn for door duty, so Bexar took a firing position, resting his rifle across the bed sides of a pickup parked sideways in front of the store. The windows to the store were intact and Jack found the doors unlocked. Taking a rock from a planter outside, he propped open one of the doors and banged loudly on the other door before running around the front of the truck Bexar was using as a shield.

"Holy shit," was all Jack said as he recoiled and fell to the ground, his rifle clattering on the pavement.

"What the hell, are you okay?" Bexar asked, reaching down and handing Jack his rifle.

"Yeah, look," said Jack, pointing at the truck's passenger window where a toddler was beating at the window and moaning. An undead toddler.

"Damn! Hey, look alive, they're coming out."

Jack turned and took a firing position next to Bexar; five undead had already come through the door, unnoticed due to Jack's excitement. Quick rifle work and the undead were permanently dead on the ground in front of the store. Bexar swapped magazines in his rifle, putting his slightly used magazine back into his chest rig last in line for use, in case he needed the couple of rounds left in it later. He and Jack walked into the store.

"Damn, everything's gone."

"Probably the folks in the RV park, Bexar. They probably raided the store after this all started."

"Yeah."

A few minutes later the pair exited back into the midday sun only to see three undead stumbling across the parking lot from the RV park.

"They must have been drawn by the gunfire, or you yelling like a girl," Bexar said.

"Fuck you," said Jack, "and it was probably the gunfire."

"Where there's two there's three, and where there's three there's thirty ... stay or go?"

"Stay. You've got left and I've got right?"

"Sure."

"Great, ready? Annnnnnnnnnd GO!"

The friends snapped their rifles up from the SUL position and began taking shots in their area of responsibility—Bexar the left half of the parking lot, and Jack the right. The first three undead were killed quickly, but more kept streaming out of the RV park.

Bexar and Jack had spent considerable time practicing with their ARs over the past five years; both had attended top-quality tactical rifle courses more than once. With that much practice you became accustomed to how your rifle feels when something changes, like when the recoil buffer pushes against the spring in the buffer tube but fails to fall forward back into battery, due to being stopped by an empty magazine.

Bexar yelled, "OUT" while he rotated the rifle in front of his face, depressing the magazine release button with his right index finger, his left hand dropping to the next full magazine on his chest rig.

Jack replied, "COVERING" and began firing at the closer zombies in Bexar's area of responsibility. Bexar slapped the fresh magazine into the magazine well and thumbed the bolt release to drop the bolt forward, while bringing his rifle back into a firing position and yelling "UP!" Jack went back to covering his half of the parking lot with Bexar covering his half for only three more shots before the process restarted with Jack yelling, "OUT!"

Three magazine changes apiece later, with their rifle barrels smoking in the cold winter air, no more undead came out of the RV park.

"Holy shit, were you counting, Jack?"

"Nope, but damn, that's a lot of people."

"Gather, and I'll cover."

"Rog-o," Jack replied, bending down to gather the pair's empty magazines, "let's top off and then we can check the crowd."

Jack gave Bexar his spent magazines and they walked to the FJ to reload and top off. Walking back to the parking lot now scattered with bodies, Jack took his hatchet in hand and Bexar grabbed a large flathead screwdriver, and they began checking the undead for any that were still moving. Two of the dead were still undead, which was quickly remedied.

"How many more do you think are in the RVs over there?" Jack asked.

"Shit Jack, I have no idea," Bexar replied, "but maybe a couple of the travel trailers are in good shape and don't have any bodies in them. If we needed to leave the park, we could do it in style! But if we're going to clear them, we need something to mark the ones we clear so we know if we come back."

"Yeah, tell you what, I'll hold cover if you want to check the store for something we could use," Jack said.

Bexar nodded and walked back into the store. A few minutes later he came back out into the parking lot holding a roll of duct tape.

"We can use the tape to make an 'X' across the door frames of the RVs we clear, then we'll also know if they were opened by someone else when we come back."

Jack and Bexar climbed in the FJ and moved it closer to the RVs. Once again they turned the truck so it faced the exit and began to clear the mobile homes. It took ninety minutes of banging on the sides of twenty-two different pull travel trailers and fifth-wheels, but thirteen more undead were freed from their aluminum tombs and sent to their final resting place in the parking lot. During the process they found two nice Honda generators that still worked, and ten more five-gallon red plastic gas cans.

Even with the access to the underground tanks at the gas station, they would need as many gas cans as they could carry in case they needed to leave the Park. Their thoughts now turned to using one of the generators to run a refrigerator or a freezer to help stretch their food supplies. The sun was setting in the mountains, so they loaded the FJ with the new supplies and drove towards the sun and back to their camp in the Basin. The much larger Rio Grande Campground RV area would have to wait for another day.

CHAPTER 46

February 4th
NORAD, Peterson AFB

"Major! Groom Lake just made contact, they're back online!" Technical Sergeant Arcuni yelled across the room to a weary Major Wright. So far NORAD has been able to remain secure by taking some drastic steps as soon as the Chinese bombers and the ICBM launches were first detected.

Close to a dozen of their men were dead by their own hand, not able to come to terms with the new world around them. Most of the men who had committed suicide had families on the outside, and had lost hope when they checked on their homes using SATINT, real-time satellite imagery, only to find them destroyed. One had even identified the bodies of his two young daughters in the street in front of his home.

Another five men had been lost on supply raids outside of their building. The base was completely overrun by the undead and, as far as they could tell, they were the last airmen on duty.

"Sir," Sergeant Arcuni continued, "he identified himself with the code word 'Lazarus.'"

"Alright, let me look it up."

A few moments later, Wright returned. "He's supposedly OGA, tasked with ensuring the continuity of government."

Major Wright crossed the room to Arcuni's terminal and turned on the external speaker so he could hear the radio traffic.

"Lazarus, this is Major Wright, what is your current status, over?"

"NORAD, SITREP follows. Most of the facility is secure, however, all personnel but one KIA. I am requesting any help you can offer. We need personnel to continue our mission, even if civilian, how copy?" SITREP was military-speak for a situation report.

"Clear. Copy Lazarus, unable to provide any information on relief; in fact, we're in very bad shape here as well, over."

"Roger that, Major, we are well supplied and secure if you can rendezvous, over."

"Lazarus, not sure how to facilitate transport ... look, I don't know how you're set over there, but we're in really bad shape here. Most of Peterson is destroyed, burned, and overrun by undead. We have twenty-eight men left, and we are scavenging for food and water, with little success."

Lazarus replied, "Major, we need your help, and it sounds like you need us. I drove to my location from Denver; it wasn't easy, but it might be your only choice."

Wright put down the handset and looked around the room at his men. They looked rough. None of them had showered since the beginning, nor had they been able to shave. Most had lost at least fifteen pounds from stress and a lack of food.

"Okay guys," Wright finally said, "we've all seen the SATINT. I think it would be near suicide to attempt the trip by truck or on foot ... if we can find a plane—no bullshit—can any of you fly?"

Arcuni looked up at Wright. "Sir, I can."

CHAPTER 47

NORAD, Peterson AFB

"Gentlemen, take every Sat-Phone you can fit, and get both SeeMe systems packed and loaded," Major Wright directed his remaining airmen as he oversaw the evacuation to Groom Lake.

Over the past few weeks, the airmen had only been able to scavenge the destroyed air base for supplies. To accomplish this, they took the only two five-ton, six-axle M939 trucks and three HMMWVs (Humvees) they could find that were still functional. The rest had been burned, wrecked, or destroyed in the lost battle for the installation against the dead. According to "Lazarus," Groom Lake was well-stocked, so Wright opted to leave behind their dwindling cache of MREs to save weight and room. Even with the five trucks, space was very tight for the twenty-eight remaining men and all the gear they needed to bring.

Major Wright wasn't sure if Groom Lake had the capability to direct and retrieve satellite imagery, but the new Space Enabled Effects for Military Engagements (SeeMe) systems could; at less than a year old and nearly a million dollars apiece, the Major deemed them an absolute necessity. If Groom Lake wasn't mission-capable with the dozen Key Hole KH-11b and the three new KH-12 satellites currently in orbit, then without the SeeMe systems, they wouldn't be able to use any of the current technology satellite imagery. Wright guessed they had only two, maybe three more years of use out of the Key Hole systems before the lack of course corrections and the high possibility of a collision with the other orbiting piles of electronics left them forever in the dark. Beyond that, he also figured they only had about three years of reliable GPS service before the same fate befell those satellites, so they should use the technology while they still had it.

Before setting his simple plan in motion, Wright had a long discussion with Arcuni. While stationed at the USAFA (Air Force Academy), Arcuni, an avid private pilot, had befriended the pilots who flew the DHC-6 Twin Otters for the skydiving teams. Over the course of three years, he had accumulated over two hundred hours of flight time sitting in the right seat with the lead pilot. He had also snuck in about one hundred hours of flight time sitting right seat with one of the Lockheed C-130 Hercules transport aircraft crews after being stationed at Peterson. If Arcuni and Wright had attempted their plan of egress just three months ago, they both would have landed an all-expenses-paid "vacation" in Leavenworth, Kansas. However, with the "rotters," as they had started calling the undead, in command of the base, the plan to take a C-130 and fly it to Groom Lake was set in motion.

Wright oversaw the preparations to leave while Arcuni, set up with a SeeMe system, examined a nearly live digital feed from a KH-12 satellite overhead. Out of the dozen aircraft on the ramp, Arcuni picked the two C-130s that looked the most promising, with the first choice being the one closest to a start-cart. The men in their five trucks would leave in a convoy, attempt to evade the roaming undead, and load and start a C-130 and fly to Groom Lake. If their attempts to take the aircraft failed, the convoy would have no choice but to evade overland to Nevada, a prospect that none of them looked forward to.

In the previous weeks Wright had established a set protocol for tracking and maintaining intelligence estimates on the undead throughout the country, and so far the undead had mainly stayed clustered near the larger cities. In the beginning, he had only been able to gather information on cities between the Rocky and Appalachian Mountains because the East and West Coast's imagery was obscured by smoke from the large uncontained fires, but in the past few weeks they had been able to initiate an analysis of the major coastal cities. What they'd found was horrific—near total destruction on an unimaginable scale.

For now though, his priority had to be escaping to Groom Lake. The overland route from Colorado to Nevada contained a roaming mob of undead, plus a large number of "unassociated undead." About three weeks earlier the undead had begun moving in large groups the airmen referred to as "herds"; they even took to assigning numbers to each of the primary herds (and in a few cases, nicknames). Each herd totaled an estimated 75,000 to 125,000, with one near Dallas, Texas totaling at least 200,000 undead. The only upside was that these large herds were relatively slow-moving so they could be outmaneuvered, but the undead needed no rest. Always moving, anything in the herd's path was destroyed by the crush of undead bodies.

Still using near-real-time imagery, Arcuni plotted the convoy's route through the base to the flight line. Besides having to drive across a large section of the base, which involved dealing with the large number of undead roaming the base, there was also a fence that separated the base from the flight operations.

On the bright side, they were relatively well-armed—Wright's airmen were able to scavenge about a dozen M4s from the handful of armories, and what they had found discarded on the ground where the undead had overrun a defensive position on the base. They also located two cases of .556 ammunition, roughly two-dozen magazines for the M4s, four M9 pistols, and a box of 500 rounds of 9mm ammunition. Major Wright kept one pistol, gave one to Arcuni, and distributed the other two to the reservists who had been police officers out in the "real world." The M4s were distributed to the airmen who claimed the most proficiency with the weapon. Wright really wished he had some PJs in his group; these Air Force special operators, called pararescuemen or pararescue jumpers, could have made the tactical side of his plan much easier.

"Major, we're loaded, and have four hours until sunset," Arcuni reported.

"Alright," said the Major, "let's shut all of this stuff down and get the trucks started, it's time to roll!"

CHAPTER 48

NORAD, Peterson AFB

"CONTACT LEFT!" came from the cargo area behind Major Wright. The distinct chatter of an M4 firing rapidly shattered the brief optimism. The convoy had only made it to the edge of the block south of their building.

"Orduna, speed us up, we need to break contact and conserve ammo," ordered the major. "Arcuni, relay to the convoy to pick their shots and only shoot when they absolutely have to. We have to evade the undead and conserve ammo."

"Roger, Sir."

"CONTACT RIGHT!" The rate of fire picked up. Major Wright was in the lead HMMWV (Humvee) with Airman Orduna at the wheel; looking over his shoulder to see what his fellow airmen were shooting at, Orduna never saw the group of rotters shambling out from behind a burned-out pickup ahead of his truck.

"ORDUNA!" Wright yelled, causing the airman to look forward and jerk the steering wheel hard to the right to avoid the undead. The first one bounced off the front bumper of the truck, and the HMMWV's front right wheel struck the burned-out pickup truck in the road. The HMMWV lurched hard and spun sideways as the second Humvee slammed into the driver's door of the lead truck, causing a horrific crash.

The rest of the convoy slid to a stop, smoke rising from their too-hot tires and brakes. Three airmen from the first M989 trailer jumped out of the back of their truck and ran to the collision to check on the major and their fellow airmen for injury. "Sir," said one, "you're injured, give me your arm and we'll get you out of here." Wright's vision slowly came back into focus. At first he wasn't sure where he was, but about halfway to the M989 he started to realize what had just happened.

"Orduna, Arcuni, Holt, are they okay?"

"No, sorry sir, Orduna and Holt are dead. Arcuni's unconscious, and he's already in the back of the truck."

"Shit, what about the second Humvee?"

"Combat loss sir, no KIA, just some bumps and scratches."

"Clear," Wright replied, "salvage gear and get rolling."

Three of the airmen began retrieving gear, while four others provided cover fire with their M4s to the convoy. The undead, drawn to the sound of the crash and the prospect of a fresh meal, began to amass onsite. Two pistol shots rang out, and the remaining airmen climbed aboard their trucks.

"Sir, Orduna and Holt will not reanimate, we made sure of that."

"Good man," said Wright, "thank you, they would've appreciated that."

Ten minutes after the collision, the now smaller convoy barreled towards one of the southern gates to get out on the flight line. The C-130s were at that end of the ramp and there was no time to waste. Wright was sure that the gathering of undead at the collision would soon follow the evading trucks.

The large vertical stabilizers of the parked C-130s loomed in the distance on the other side of the fence. They would have to move fast. Wright estimated they had only fifteen minutes to pick a plane, load it, and take off before the undead began flooding onto the flight line and runways. Hitting them with their large truck was bad enough, striking one with their plane would stop their evacuation before it could really begin.

In the cargo hold of the first M989, Wright poured water from a bottle onto Arcuni's face. "You back with us yet?" he asked.

Coughing, Arcuni opened his eyes. "Yes Major, but I'm dizzy, and my head feels like it's going to explode."

"You probably have a concussion, at the very least, but we don't have any time for that. We have fifteen mikes to get in the air. We load and hold perimeter, you pick the plane, make sure we have enough fuel, and get us in the air."

"Roger."

"Hold on back there, about to breech the gate!" came through the opening in the cab where a small rear window had been before.

The five-ton truck shifted and began to pick up more speed. After hitting the fence gate at forty miles per hour, the truck jerked left and right but stayed upright. It screeched to a halt near the C-130 that Arcuni wanted to check first. Not knowing yet which plane on the ramp they were going to load, the airmen exited the trucks and formed a defensive perimeter, leaving their gear on the trucks. Once Arcuni spun the turbo-props, those airmen without rifles would begin loading the plane.

Arcuni tried to jog to the first C-130 Hercules, but he still couldn't focus his vision and fell to the ground, vomiting what little food he had in his stomach. Another airman ran to him and pulled him up, saying, "Shit man, come on," practically carrying Arcuni towards the aircraft. Once seated in the cockpit, Arcuni turned on the master and the fuel gauges lit up, but the needles barely wavered off the bottom.

"Out, out, out, to the second plane!" he yelled.

He climbed down and was once again half-carried by his teammate to the second plane. This time the fuel needles climbed a little higher. It was still not a lot of fuel, but he thought it might get them to Groom Lake, or at least he hoped it would. His buddies holding security began engaging the approaching undead and the tempo of the rifle fire increased.

"Get the major, plug up the APU, pull the chocks, and get this bitch loaded!" he commanded.

The airman ran through the cargo hold to the back of the plane and flipped the handle to drop the hydraulically controlled ramp. Seeing this, Wright jumped into the Humvee that the auxiliary power unit (APU) had been hitched to and drove towards the plane. Those airmen not on guard with M4s drove the rest of the trucks to the plane for loading. The APU coughed to a start, throttled up, and the C-130's turbo props roared to life, one at a time.

Disconnecting the APU, Major Wright climbed into the cockpit of the aircraft. Sitting in the left seat, Arcuni pushed the controls, working his way through a shortened pre-flight checklist. Not wasting any time, his fellow airmen were peppered by wind and dirt as Arcuni set the brakes and ran up the engines while the plane was still being loaded.

"How do we look?" Wright asked.

"Shit sir, I don't know," said Arcuni. "There's a couple of warning lights on, but I really have no idea what they mean. Everything feels okay, but I'm not sure how it'll all play out."

"This is the girl we brought to the dance, Arcuni," Wright replied, "we'll have to dance with her. If we don't get in the air now we're screwed, buddy."

"Rog-o, sir."

One of the other airmen tapped Wright on the shoulder. "Major, we're loaded and closing the ramp now. There are probably two hundred rotters through the fence and more behind them."

"Time to go, Arcuni," Wright replied.

Arcuni released the brakes, pushed the right engines a bit more forward than the left side, pushed with his left foot, and spun the big turbo-prop plane to the left and towards the taxiway on the edge of the flight line. Taxiing at over fifty Kts (knots), the plane lurched forward as Arcuni slowed to make the next left onto the taxiway before shoving the throttles forward.

"A taxiway is not a runway, but who gives a shit today, right sir?"

Pushing forward with the yoke to keep the aircraft on the ground, Arcuni watched the indicated airspeed climb to one hundred Kts before pulling back on the yoke, causing the big plane to practically jump into the air and generating hoots, yells, and cursing from the cargo hold. A gentle turn to the left to point west, and they had escaped Peterson AFB.

Arcuni leveled out the climb at 12,000 MSL (mean sea level) to be confident he could clear the surrounding mountains. He had no navigational charts, and wasn't sure how high he would have to be to clear everything, but he was betting this would be a safe altitude, while still remaining low enough to lower the danger of becoming hypoxic. Once level, and with the throttles set at a safe cruising airspeed, he took the opportunity to program the coordinates to Groom Lake into the navigation. Even without navigational charts to plan waypoints and identify dangers, he could at least get there using the navigation system, and he'd also have an idea of how long the flight would take.

Thirty minutes into the flight Arcuni began to feel better. He wasn't as dizzy, and his vision had focused. The cold winter air made the flight smooth and almost enjoyable, if it wasn't so loud in the aircraft. The all-too-brief moment of tranquility shattered at the sound of a screeching buzzer that accompanied a new warning light on the panel between Arcuni and Wright.

"Damnit, outboard starboard engine lost oil pressure," Arcuni yelled to Wright, and as if on cue, the aircraft began to shake.

"Shutting it down—Major, pull that red handle, the one with the number four on it, it's the fire suppression."

The plane's airspeed slowed noticeably with the loss of the engine, and it took some finesse for Arcuni to throttle the port side engines just right to keep the controls neutral, the fourth engine's propeller feathered and turning like a windmill in the air.

"Sir, we're about forty-five mikes before we begin descent. Try raising Groom Lake on the radio, we're not going to be able to overfly the runway to check for obstacles, they'll have to check it for us."

Groom Lake, Nevada

"Well shit," exclaimed Cliff.

"What?" said Lanoo.

"The guys from NORAD found a plane. They're on their way, about forty-five minutes out."

"That's great," replied Lance. "What's the problem?"

"They lost a couple of guys on the evac, but they also lost an engine and will be limping it in. They need us to go topside and make sure the runway's clear for them."

CHAPTER 49

Big Bend National Park, Texas

"Good luck up there, I hope you get us some good news!"

Sandra and Jack shared hugs with Jessie and Bexar before they started up the trail towards Emory Peak. The plan was for Sandra and Jack to be on the mountain for four nights, unless bad weather drove them back down to the camp. In the meantime, Bexar and Jessie's goal, besides watching both kids, was to attempt to get the water pumps for the system of tanks pushing water into the Chisos Basin back online. With both kids to watch, that task would be harder, since both children were exceptionally good at "unhelping," as all children tend to be. Regardless, it was a good trade, because in seven days Jessie and Bexar would have a chance to be alone on the mountain at the listening post. It wasn't exactly a nice spa treatment at the 7F Lodge, but it would be nice to have some alone time in beautiful surroundings.

"And they're gone. Let's gear up and get that travel trailer from the Rio Grande RV park, then we can scrounge around the rest of the RV park for anything useful."

"Okay, but I don't want to be gone all day, Bexar, I don't like being out of the Basin after dark," Jessie replied.

"Right. I'll gather the kids if you want to gather some ammo and some food for the trip. Also, I'll get the empty jerry cans; we can refill at Panther Junction on our way through."

In twenty minutes, Jessie, Bexar, and both kids were loaded up and on their way to the Rio Grande Village. Two hours later the travel trailer was hooked up to the Wagoneer and they were headed back to the Basin.

"Do you think the RV will make the road up into the Basin?" Jessie asked Bexar. "The sign says nothing over fourteen feet in length."

"No Jess, I don't think it will, but we could leave it outside the gate at the turnoff."

"What if we put it down at Cattail Falls with the Scout? It could be a bug-out shelter."

"That's a good idea, I like it," Bexar said.

The turnoff for the Basin passed by Bexar's window, and they headed towards the unmarked gravel road leading to the Cattail Falls trailhead.

Another two hours passed, and the trailer was secured at their original campsite in the desert. After arriving, they decided to leave the trailer connected to the Wagoneer and drive the Scout back to the Basin with the kids. Bexar didn't think the Scout was heavy enough to pull the RV very well. To complete the bug-out shelter, Bexar left five full jerry cans of fuel on the Wagoneer with the plan to rotate their fuel stock to keep the gas fresh. After returning to the Basin, Jessie gathered the remaining MREs, a five-gallon container of fresh water, and some other supplies to stock the bug-out RV.

"Do you think they made it to the peak yet?" she asked Bexar.

"Hell no," he replied. "When you and I did that hike the first time it took us nearly seven hours to get up there from the tent camping area. I think they'll probably make it to the top about supper time."

Emory Peak

As predicted, Jack and Sandra made it to the very top of Emory Peak just as the sun dipped low in the western sky. They had needed to do a little bit of light bouldering, but made it to their destination without any problems. The big wall tent was too big and too heavy to carry up the mountain trail, so they'd left it with the base camp. Jack climbed back down to set up a basic lean-to shelter on the last section of trail before the short climbing section to the narrow peak. The wind on the peak was stronger than they anticipated, but what they hadn't remembered from their previous hike up the South Rim were the solar panels powering a radio repeater, enclosed in a metal box, on the top of the mountain.

Once the lean-to shelter was erected with the help of some 550 parachute cord and dinner had been eaten, Jack climbed back up to the peak to begin setting up their ham radio, as well as the small hand-cranked shortwave radio. Sandra started cranking the shortwave to generate power while Jack broke into the metal box containing the radio repeater equipment.

"If Malachi was still alive, he'd be able to figure out this setup, and we could probably have radio communications from the cabins."

"But he's not, Jack," Sandra said quietly.

"I know," Jack replied, and fell silent.

"Sorry babe," Sandra interrupted his thoughts. "Tell you what, it's getting dark, let's just try tuning through the shortwave, and in the morning we can get the ham set up properly."

"Sounds like a plan."

The shortwave produced nothing but static while the two sat there, holding hands and watching the sky turn from red to a deep purple over the desert floor. Alone and safe, the husband and wife made love for the first time since their world had come apart.

Groom Lake, Nevada

Cliff and Lance made it topside without any problems, but once there they found the base eerily quiet.

"Weren't there close to a thousand people who worked up here? Where did they go, man?" Lance asked.

"I have no idea," replied Cliff, "but I doubt they walked off base to safety. If we're lucky we might find a couple of survivors, but when I came on base last month I watched from a distance, and even then I didn't see any movement or signs of life. Forget about it, keep sharp and stay frosty, remember what we've practiced. Keep your M4 ready in the SUL position, safety on and finger indexed—if a rotter pops up, get on target, thumb the safety, and press the trigger to the rear."

Lance held his M4 with the ACOG sight and felt the safety lever with his thumb to make sure it was still flipped up and safe. Cliff led the hike, Lance falling behind about twenty feet, both of them walking in the middle of the road. It was strange for Cliff to be out in the open and in the middle of the road. He was used to using the buildings and their shadows for cover and concealment, but new enemies required new tactics.

The truck, now one hundred yards in front of them, appeared to be just as Cliff had left it. In his rucksack he carried a twelve-volt car battery from one of the backup systems that he thought should be enough to jump-start the truck, which had been sitting out in the open desert. Reaching the truck, Cliff opened the door, put the transmission into neutral, and pushed the truck forward to reveal the keys hidden under the front left tire. Before attempting to connect the jump-start battery, he tried the ignition and was surprised when the truck turned over, coughing to life with a loud backfire.

Lance joined Cliff in the cab of the truck and they started towards the runways carved out of the dry lakebed. Foot to the floor, the needle hovered at just over eighty miles per hour, but in the large expanse of the dry lakebed it felt like they were practically standing still. After reaching the end of the exceptionally long lakebed runway, Cliff turned the truck around and pointed it back towards the base. A handful of minutes ticked by before he finally brought the old truck to a stop on the flight line near the aircraft hangars. Cliff climbed into the bed of the pickup truck, leaning against the cab and preparing to wait while keeping an eye on the sky. Ten more minutes of careful sky watching passed before the overly large tail of a C-130 Hercules came into view over the mountains.

Cliff watched the plane descend in his binoculars and called down to Lance, "Looks like only the two port side engines are working. If they're coming in for a straight-in approach, it'll be a downwind landing. Shouldn't be a problem for a Herc though, we have enough runway to land the Starship Enterprise."

"Cliff?"

"Huh?"

"CLIFF!"

Cliff lowered the binoculars and turned around to see what Lance was so excited about. Shambling from between the hangars and onto the flight line were about fifty undead.

"Damn, didn't hear them with the wind blowing," said Cliff. "Well, we'd better stop 'em before they get out on the runway and cause a lot of problems for our arriving guests. Lance, why don't you stay with the truck. When the Herc lands, drive out there and don't let them taxi up to the flight line. Oh, and give me two of your magazines for your M4."

"Where are you going?" asked Lance.

"I'm going over there to see a man about a horse. Where the fuck do you think I'm going? Go help those guys on the plane get to the safety of our underground facility, I'll be back later."

Before Lance could respond, Cliff had jumped over the bedrail of the truck and was trotting towards the approaching undead.

Cockpit in the C-130

"Arcuni, do you see that truck on the runway?"

"Yes sir. Hopefully he won't get in our way, but this Herc is landing now, whether we want to or not."

The rudder trim was pushed all the way over, trying to keep the big turbo-prop flying straight with only two engines. Arcuni moved another level and the flaps descended, followed by the landing gear. With very little experience with the big cargo plane, Arcuni flared the landing a little late. The Herc slammed into the ground hard with too much forward speed, blowing out the tires on the right-side main landing gear. He pushed hard on the opposite side brakes while flaming the two remaining engines to feather. The pickup truck, driving fast across the lakebed, slammed on the brakes and slid to a stop just as the Herc skidded by, the nose gear failed, and the plane began a large carving skid across the lakebed. It finally came to a stop, and Arcuni started breathing again.

"Holy shit!" he cried. "Major, if we were on a regular runway we would've gone off the tarmac and onto the grass, which would have rolled the plane. The lakebed saved us!"

"Luck favors the prepared, and also the stupid. Let's get moving. We need to get everyone un-assed, and get all our gear unloaded," Wright said.

"Roger that, sir."

Arcuni finished shutting down the two remaining functional engines. The old C-130 had gotten the crew to Nevada, but it would never fly again. The guys in the back lowered the cargo ramp as the major made his way to the rear opening of the aircraft. In the still desert air they were greeted by a long-haired, scrawny civilian and the sound of sporadic rifle fire in the distance towards the flight line.

"Hey there," said the civilian. "Nice crash. We need to get your gear and get you underground."

"Right, who the fuck are you and what's going on?" replied the major.

"I'm Lance, the last remaining scientist. That guy over there is Cliff, and he has a goodly number of undead he's trying to keep away from your plane."

"Okay Lance, we'll get unloaded. Take these six guys in the truck and go help Cliff," Major Wright said, pointing at six of the airmen who were carrying M4 rifles.

"But Cliff said ..."

"No buts son, do it now."

Lance shrugged and climbed into the cab of the truck while the six airmen climbed into the truck bed, and they drove off in the direction of the gunfire. The major and his remaining men had the plane unloaded in less than ten minutes, which seemed strange to them since it had felt like it had taken less than thirty seconds to load the plane under duress.

Shortly after the rifle reports had stopped, the truck returned with Lance at the wheel. Major Wright accompanied the fifth and final truckload of equipment to the service elevator that lowered them into the underground facility. The six airmen that had helped Lance and Cliff were already in their new living quarters and enjoying their first hot shower in over a month. New sets of old-style BDUs from the storeroom were provided for all the new arrivals.

Cliff strode over to the major. "Hi Major, I'm Lazarus, but Cliff's actually my name, and I'm sure glad you made it safely."

"Me too, Cliff," the major replied, shaking Cliff's hand. "It was really hit or miss, but compared to how we were living at Peterson, this place you've got is a five-star resort."

"I understand. You'll find that this facility is very well-stocked, and we have the necessary equipment and containments for Lance to continue his and his former colleagues' work. Our communications, however, are severely lacking. I don't think we can communicate outside of a handful of military channels, and I have no idea what's left out there beyond what I passed driving here from Denver."

"In that case, Cliff," said the major, "you're going to really like the shiny new toys we brought with us, but I know you won't like the answers they'll give you."

CHAPTER 50

February 5th
Emory Peak, Big Bend National Park, Texas

The sun had just begun to break over the eastern sky when Jack finished cranking the shortwave radio's charging handle. He consulted the list of known channels in the ham radio book, and after trying the frequencies listed for broadcasts from the U.S. with no success, he turned his little radio to the BBC channel, where he was greeted by a faint voice.

"Sandra, found one!" he called out.

Sandra sat next to the open equipment box on the mountain top, with the solar panel and battery disconnected from the radio equipment they didn't know how to use. Leaving her task, she sat next to Jack to listen to the shortwave radio broadcast.

"*... from Germany is that the government has apparently collapsed, and an estimated two million survivors are stranded without help, food, water, or power while the irradiated undead roam the cities. Berlin is reported to be a complete loss, and officials are still trying to determine the direction and strength of the radiation fallout with our limited information and dwindling resources. The quarantine in the United Kingdom has thus far been successful, with only a reported two percent reanimation and infection rate in the population. We remind you again to remain indoors, and to report immediately any family members who take ill. Take no chances with the dead or the undead—only head trauma will stop the threat. Although they may have once been a loved one, they are no longer human, and pose a great danger. Any bite or scratch will infect you, and you will most certainly*"

. 211 .

die and reanimate. In other reports, engineers continue to work around the clock to restore power, with electricity already restored to a reported thirty percent of the United Kingdom. Stay calm, stay strong, and we will survive once ag..."

"Jack, what happened?" Sandra asked.

"I don't know," he said, "the signal just faded out."

"What was that about radiation fallout? Bexar said that EMPs don't produce fallout, that we didn't need to be worried about that."

"It shouldn't," replied Jack, "but that report makes me think there may have been a nuclear incident or attack, if Berlin is gone and the U.K. is in trouble. I wonder who else is left. From what we've seen on our drive to Maypearl and then to here, I think we've lost a lot more than just two percent of our population."

"Jack, I think it's more likely there's only two percent of us left," Sandra said wearily.

"If you want to get back to work on the solar panel for the ham radio," he replied, "I'll keep trying to find more news."

Groom Lake, Nevada

Cliff usually wasn't impressed very easily, but the systems that Wright had brought with him from Colorado were impressive. The SeeMe system now gave them the capability to track the large herds of undead while also looking for signs of survivors, all in near-real time. Although it seemed like using satellite imagery to find survivors was akin to trying to figure out which haystack in all of Oklahoma had a needle in it, it seemed like the SeeMe system could do exactly that.

Big Bend National Park, Texas

The sun hung low across the desert as Bexar finished wiring the first water pump from the holding tank near the bottom of The Window, along with a small battery bank. He held his breath while flipping over the breaker, hoping that his "McGyvered" solution would work. It did, and he could hear the pump humming and the sound of water moving up the pipe. Tomorrow, if he could repeat his success with two more water tanks and pumps, the cabins would have running water.

CHAPTER 51

February 10th
Groom Lake, Nevada

Lance and the airmen he had selected as assistants had not been seen in nearly five days. Cliff rode the elevator down to the laboratory level and found Lance asleep on the couch in the lounge. He kicked his foot to wake him up.

"Dude, seriously, WTF?" Lance mumbled sleepily.

"Haven't seen or heard from you in a few days," Cliff replied. "Everyone still alive down here?"

"Yeah, but I'm not very confident we'll be able to do this," Lance said. "Yama is much more complicated than we thought."

"How's that?" said Cliff.

"Well, we know the general history of the virus, that it came from spores recovered near Tibet by the Nazis, that the Soviets took it at the end of the Second World War and tried to modify it but were unsuccessful, and that then the Chinese took control of it when the Soviet Union collapsed and completed a lot of bio-engineering on the little SOB. I can only imagine how many people they killed getting the virus to this point."

"Okay, so what does that mean for us?" Cliff asked.

"It's like this," said Lance, sitting up and lacing his fingers behind his head, "in the initial attack with the spray planes, the virus didn't actually kill you, it was just that if you died you would reanimate. But then the virus mutated, and now if you contract the new strain of the virus through bites or deep scratches, it will kill you, and you'll still reanimate. From what I can tell, it can take anywhere from about thirty minutes to a few hours for the new strain to kill you after infection."

"Bites or deep cuts only?"

"That and other fluid transfer. I recommend wearing protection if you're going to fuck one of those things, and if you have any open wounds, fluid spray from gunshots, for instance, could infect you as well."

"Shit."

"Yeah, shit is right," Lance continued, "and I'm not sure how we're going to be able to stop this in time to save anyone, if we can stop it at all. Some of the models we've run in the past couple of days have made it look like nearly a ninety-nine percent mortality rate, *globally*. This is a mass extinction event."

"Okay, where do you think we're at right now?"

"My best guess, a bit over a month into it, is probably about ninety percent mortality. If we actually find any survivors out there, we're going to need to quarantine them for at least two days after a physical search for bite marks, just to keep ourselves safe."

"Got it. Anything else you could use down here?" Cliff said.

"Yeah, let me take my nap and leave us alone to work," Lance replied.

"Roger that. Let me know if you need anything else. I have some airmen to train in tactics and marksmanship, a facility to run, and we still need to clear the dorms in the sister facility next to this one."

CHAPTER 52

Chisos Basin Campground, Big Bend National Park, Texas

It took more time than he'd anticipated, but Bexar finished getting the other two water pumps online and the cabins now had running potable water. The hot water heaters were still on his list, but he simply didn't have enough electrical power to run a hot water heater without running a generator. If the group needed hot water they could heat it on the fire. As of late, in an effort to conserve the limited Coleman fuel for their lanterns, they were cooking with fire rather than on their old Coleman stoves.

Bexar didn't expect Sandra and Jack to come back down the mountain until tomorrow, but he wouldn't be surprised if they came down early if they had news, or If they missed their little boy too much. Regardless, he was excited to hear what they'd found on the mountain top, and if they had made contact with anyone or heard any updates on the shortwave.

Emory Peak

"Roger Texas, we read you five-by-five, how are you set for provisions?"

"Copy Groom Lake, we're set for now and surviving fine. Do you have any news outside of Texas, or any news of anything at all?"

"Texas, we have information that most of the people between the Appalachian and the Rocky Mountains are either dead or infected. We are currently tracking three large herds of undead swarming in three different sectors. The closest herd to you is in Texas and moving away from the Dallas area."

Jack and Sandra looked at each other, mouthing the word "herds?" at almost the same time, then Sandra shrugged and said, "Copy that, Groom Lake, where are they now and which way are they traveling?"

"The last track showed a herd of about 200,000 undead approximately fifty miles southwest of the Dallas area, following I-20 west."

Sandra, mic in hand, looked at Jack. "If they're going south they're basically headed towards us. Two hundred thousand? We'll never be able to defend against that many."

Jack nodded, reached for the mic, and keyed, "Groom Lake, if we're in the path of the moving horde, what do you advise?"

Across the country, in a dark room illuminated only by the harsh light from electronic screens and computer monitors, Arcuni looked at the airman sitting at the radio and shrugged. The airman keyed the radio. "Texas, we can only advise you flee a herd, but if you're unable to, get hidden, get secure, be quiet, and hope they pass around you."

"Clear, thank you Groom Lake, station Texas is out for now. Will check back in two hours if you continue to monitor."

"Wilco, two hours."

Jack looked at his wife. "What do you think? If we bug out again, I feel like it'll never end, and we'll always be on the run."

"Can we secure the camp? There's only the one road into the Basin, unless you think the undead can travel over the mountains."

"I doubt they could do it without the road." Jack looked at the horizon and up to the sun. "It's about noon, let's wait and check back in with Groom Lake in two hours, then we can get back down the mountain and discuss it with Jessie and Bexar. I bet we could make some sort of roadblock and secure ourselves in the Basin."

"So, we've got two hours then?" Sandra smiled at Jack and began unbuttoning her jeans.

CHAPTER 63

Groom Lake, Nevada

Arcuni handed the mic to the airman in the radio hut with him. "Okay, keep monitoring, I'm going to let Cliff know what we found out about our new friends in Texas."

Twenty minutes later, Arcuni found Cliff topside, leading five airmen from NORAD with him in immediate action drills with M-16s. Arcuni walked up to the group and waited until the drill was done, then caught Cliff's attention. After the last series, Cliff let the class relax with a water break and walked over to Arcuni. "Hey Technical Sergeant Arcuni, how's life out there in Radioville?"

"Sparse," replied Arcuni, "but we did make contact with a small group of survivors in rural Texas on a ham frequency."

"Yeah? That's great!" said Cliff. "Where are they, and how many are there? Are they well set?"

"They said they were very well-provisioned, there's four adults and two children. Best I can figure is that they're in a wildlife area or a state park or something, but out in the desert."

"Right, well, there's a lot of west Texas, could be Big Bend, or could be some random area out there in the Lone Star State."

"They sounded like they were well prepared. I told them about the herd outside of Dallas and they were very concerned about that, but I didn't really have any advice to give them. They're supposed to check back in on the radio in two hours."

"Great, okay Arcuni, let me know if you make contact with anyone else."

Arcuni nodded and climbed back underground, grabbing two cups of coffee to share with the airman in the radio hut.

Chisos Basin Campground, Big Bend National Park, Texas

Two hours later Jack made contact with Groom Lake again and had a brief conversation with the man who said his name was Arcuni. Arcuni was very inquisitive about their position, and Jack assured him that although it might be a few days until another from his group could check in on the radio, they would be in touch.

Jack and Sandra made their way down the mountain, arriving at the camp earlier than Bexar and Jessie had expected. Dinner was slow-cooking on the smoldering coals of their fire.

"Hey you two, welcome back!" cried Jessie. "We didn't expect you back so early, but we have something neat to show you."

"Yeah, well, we have something to tell you too," said Jack. "Why don't you go first?"

Three hours later the sun had sunk below the desert mountains, turning the cold sky purple and red. The children were in bed, fighting their bedtime but falling asleep almost immediately after being read a story from one of the books stolen from their stop in Marathon.

"Well sure, Bexar," Jack said, "we could barricade the road, but how would we bug out if we started to get overrun?"

Bexar said, "We'd take the Window trail and take the split to end up down at the Cattail Falls trailhead. We stashed the pull-behind RV there along with the Wagoneer. It would take a few hours to get over the trail, but once we reached the Jeep and RV, we could take one of two routes out of the Park. Hell, we could even drive to Boquelles and down into Mexico; if Mexico's in the same shape as the U.S., I'm sure the Federales wouldn't notice."

"Sure, but how are we going to barricade the road and still leave it open for us to travel in the meantime?"

"I don't know," said Bexar. "Maybe we could pull more RVs back up here and block the road?"

Jack thought for a moment. "Well, we have the actual gate that the National Parks Service uses to close the road to the Basin and that's a start, but what if we also drag a couple of dumpsters onto the road from the tent camping area? We could offset them so we can drive around them, but we could also push them together using the front bumper of one of our rigs if we needed to."

"I like it Jack, that could work," Bexar said, "but I think we should also fill the dumpsters with rocks or dirt or something so they're really heavy. If they're empty you could probably push one by yourself, and a shitload of undead could easily brush it out of their way."

"Yeah alright, we'll do it first thing in the morning. We also still have a few of the shotgun blanks trip alarms. I think we should put some across the road high enough that a javelina won't trip it, but a person would, dead or not."

"Good idea," Bexar said. "In the morning we'll also rig the traps." He continued, "Listen Jack, this is great stuff, but we need to have a Plan C in case Plan A and Plan B don't work."

"You're right," Jack agreed, "we have to assume that the zombie horde will come through here at some point; we can't rely on just two plans."

CHAPTER 54

Bexar and the rest of the group were up before sunrise. One would think that with the end of the world, and the resulting loss of routines and timekeeping, it would be easy to sleep in until sunrise. But children have a way of ruining sleep regardless of what the rest of world is doing. By the time the group's typical breakfast was eaten and cleaned up and the other morning routines completed, the sun was over the mountains. Bexar and Jack set out to put their new security plan in motion. The regular National Park Services gate that was used to close the Basin was already secured, locked with a metal clasp; it had been set that way for the past week, but that was no longer enough security for the group. Due to the size and weight of the dumpsters with their heavy bear-proof lids, it took Bexar and Jack until shortly after noon to drag the dumpsters out of the tent camping area with the Scout and up the road to the gate.

Moving the dumpsters and then filling them with dirt and rocks proved to be hard, slow work, but as the sun began to set on another day, the two fathers and husbands were finishing the work needed to protect their families. The dumpsters rested with about a ten-foot gap between them so the group's vehicles could traverse the opening, but the opening could also be quickly closed by pushing the rear dumpster forward with one of their vehicles.

Early tomorrow, Jessie and Bexar would hike up to Emory Peak, excited by the possibility of reestablishing contact with their new friends at Groom Lake.

CHAPTER 55

February 12th
Groom Lake, Nevada

"Hey Sarge, our friends in Texas are back on the net," the airman called out.

"I thought they weren't supposed to be back on until tomorrow, did something go wrong?" Arcuni asked.

"No, I think they were excited to make contact again and get more intel from us. You want to talk to them while I get Cliff?"

"Yeah," said Arcuni.

Arcuni took the proffered mic from the airman and unplugged the headphones from the console so the transmissions could be heard over the external speaker. "Howdy Texans, you're back early, is everything okay?"

"Howdy to you, Groom Lake, yes, we're fine. The guy you spoke to a couple of days ago told us about the Dallas horde so we started making preparations. Do you have any updates on that?"

"I think we do, we sent for our officer in charge and he'll have all the details for you, but for now I have to ask, where are you guys holed up at?"

Jessie looked at Bexar and silently shook her head no, but Bexar keyed the radio. "We're in Big Bend."

"Good country out there," Arcuni replied. "Find any other survivors yet?"

"No, just us four and our two kids, but we're prepared to help any other survivors with food and water if you send them our way."

Fort Bliss, Texas

"Hey Twardo, get over here, you're not gonna believe this shit!"

Twardo pushed the teenaged Mexican girl off his lap, zipped up his pants, and walked out of the hotel room to join Russell, the club's sergeant-at-arms. "This better be fucking good, asshole, or I'm going to beat you until you piss yourself."

"Prez, I caught a conversation on the civilian radio channels—there's a small group of survivors over in Big Bend National Park who say they're well-supplied. There's only four of them, and two kids."

"Shit yeah, how far from here?"

"Probably nearly a two-day ride."

"Put ten guys together to be ready to ride in the morning. The rest of the club will stay with the VP, the bitches, and the gear. Get a prospect to drive the van, and another to drive the truck to bring back what we can loot."

Groom Lake

"Texas, my name is Cliff, and I was tasked by our government to help any survivors in any way I can," came a new voice over the radio. "Is there anything you need?"

"Hi Cliff," Bexar replied, "I'm Bexar. I didn't know the government was still intact, how exactly could you help us?"

"To be honest with you Bexar, the government isn't exactly intact. So far, we've found my group is one of the last remaining official representatives, but we're trying to complete our mission of helping other survivors. If we can do that, maybe we can save our country for the future. We're prepared to take other survivors here; we have food, water, and other provisions."

"Where exactly is Groom Lake?"

"Nevada."

"Nevada? Wait, Area 51? You're shitting me!" Bexar said incredulously.

"Nope, I am one hundred percent serious," Cliff replied, smiling.

Arcuni opened the door to the commo-hut. Cliff slid his thumb off the push-to-talk button and said, "What's up, Sergeant?"

"We're not going to have another pass over that part of the country until 08:00 our time tomorrow, and then we'll need to review the imagery and prepare a Sitrep for you."

Cliff nodded and keyed the mic. "Bexar, we don't have anything new for you as of right now, but we are updating our information and will have something for you by about noon your time tomorrow."

"Uh, okay thanks," replied Bexar. "I guess we'll check back in at noon our time tomorrow."

Emory Peak, Big Bend National Park

"That was strange," Jessie said. "Why do you think it's going to take so long?"

Bexar said, "I bet they're trying to get a plane or a satellite overhead first.

"Okay, but what are you going to do until tomorrow?"

"You."

Two hours later, the sun was descending over the mountains as Bexar and Jessie woke up from their nap. Bexar started heating up dinner on a fuel tablet while Jessie began cranking the shortwave radio.

"... no further communication has been received from the continent since the day before yesterday. As of now, the Crown is waiting and hoping that contact will be reestablished, and is extremely concerned for the rest of Europe. MI-6 has confirmed that most of central and eastern China experienced heavy fallout from the retaliation nuclear strike initiated by Russia and the United States against North Korea. Iran and most of the Middle East are also feared lost due to a nuclear strike thought to have been conducted by Israel. MI-6 has thus far been unable to confirm any previous attacks against Israel before their attack on their Muslim neighbors. There has been no contact with any North American officials since Z-Day plus-three. In other news, the Ministry of Health reminds all subjects to immediately report any persons displaying signs of infection, or any bite marks. King Harry has also sent notice to this station to remind all Britons to "Stay calm and carry on." The empire will survive; it must survive, for we may be the only ones ..."

"Holy shit, Jess, it's like 'On the Beach'!" Bexar exclaimed.

"Like what?" she said.

"The novel 'On the Beach' by Nevil Shute, where the last place on Earth to be killed off by nuclear fallout was Australia, and they were living large and loose trying to enjoy their last few months of life before the radiation killed them all too."

"That sounds horrible. What did they do?"

"Mainly they drank all day and held dangerous car races where no one cared about safety. I think all we had in the U.S. were EMPs."

"Can we get fallout from those?"

"I don't think so."

CHAPTER 56

"Cliff, the SATINT is mostly complete," Arcuni reported.

"Any surprises?" Cliff replied.

"The Dallas herd has grown larger and is covering an incredible amount of distance in a short amount of time, but there are also some smaller groups splitting off from the herd."

"Okay, where's the main group now?" Cliff asked.

"About three hundred miles southwest of Dallas. The horde is still following I-20 west, but one of the larger factions that split off is moving south along I-35."

"How far away are they from our Texas friends?"

"Assuming that they would have to deviate course to travel south from I-20, probably seven to ten days."

"Any other survivors?"

"We picked up a group of people on motorcycles traveling east on I-10 about two hundred miles east of Fort Bliss."

"Anything from Bliss?"

"No, nothing, except that there are a few buildings on fire, and fifty-three motorcycles parked next to a motel on the eastern side of the base. There are also people in the parking lot, but we haven't been able to determine if they're alive or reanimates."

"How many riders are in the group traveling east, and any indication what their destination is?"

"Twenty-three riders, and we don't have any indication of their destination, but they're traveling in the general direction of the other survivors from Big Bend."

"Should we tell our Texas friends about the motorcycles?"

"Not yet, they're still well away from the Park, and we don't even know if they're headed there. Monitor the motorcycles' progress and see if we can plot possible destinations. When's the next KH overflight?"

"Tomorrow at 10:02 local time."

Emory Peak, Big Bend National Park, Texas

Bexar was quite sure that he and Jessie hadn't had this much sex since the romantic Alaskan cruise they had taken as a "let's get pregnant" trip nearly three years ago. It was hard to believe that it had already been three years since before they were pregnant, or had their precious little girl. Condoms were in short supply in their provisions so Bexar was pulling out; he and Jessie weren't sure they could bring another baby into this brave new world.

Jessie scanned the ham frequencies, but they were unable to make contact with anyone, and she couldn't even find any evidence of other transmissions. It was over a month since the other two survivors in the area had been heard on the radio. Bexar wanted to believe that those two old cowboys were still surviving, and that there were other survivors out there to be found, but the endless static was beginning to erode his hope.

Jessie set the ham on the frequency they'd been using to communicate with their new friends in Area 51, and powered up the shortwave radio. Scanning through the known frequencies, Jessie suddenly heard a voice, and stopped the scan to listen.

"Listen Bexar," she said, "it's just a woman reading random numbers. That's really creepy."

"Those 'number' channels have been around for a while," he said. "Some channels are random numbers, some channels will have random words, some letters, and some a combination of them. The conspiracy theory types on the interwebs believe the channels are secret government communications to spies out in the field, although in this day and age that doesn't seem likely, with the ability to communicate with the Internet."

"So we don't know who's broadcasting them or who would be listening?"

"Nope, no one seems to know who or where with those channels. The conspiracy theories range from American spies to the Bilderberg group to alien bases under Denver International Airport, but that's crazy. Who knows, hell, Cliff says he's at Area 51."

"Do you think he is?" Jessie asked.

"I don't know. He could be, or he could be psychotic. I can't imagine that the end of the world with the dead rising to hunt the living could be good for anyone's mental health."

Jessie looked at the sun nearing the middle of the sky overhead. "I think we have time for one more before we're expected on the radio, if you're up to it, lover boy."

Bexar smiled and nodded, and Jessie pulled her blanket aside, revealing her naked body.

Groom Lake

"Okay Sarge, it should be about noon their time, I'll get Mr. Cliff." Arcuni nodded and the airman left the commo-hut. Arcuni pushed a frequency preset and the radio changed from a scanning mode to the frequency used thus far to communicate with the group in Texas.

Twenty minutes passed before Cliff opened the door to the commo-hut with the airman in tow.

"Nothing yet, Cliff."

Cliff nodded and sat down next to Arcuni, donning a headset for the radio. Nearly ten minutes later, the speakers crackled with Bexar's distant voice, "Good afternoon secret alien base, are you on the net?"

Arcuni looked at Cliff, who smiled and shrugged. "Roger that Texas folks, any updates in your status?"

"Nothing of note, but we are away from our base camp, up on one of the mountains to get reception for radio communication."

"Copy that. We have some updates for you. The Dallas herd continues in a southwesterly direction, following the I-20; however, some smaller groups of undead have broken off from the herd. The largest of those is traveling south following the I-35."

"Do you think either of those will affect us at our location?"

"We're not sure yet, but we don't think so. We will continue to track and keep you updated."

"Thanks, Area 51. We picked up a BBC broadcast on the shortwave. It said that the British thought most of Europe was a total loss, followed by some discussion on nuclear fallout. Do you have any more information about that?"

Arcuni once again looked at Cliff, who shrugged. "We are just now getting up and running after pulling together some other survivors. We've been focused on the CONUS and will have to investigate further."

Bexar shook his head at Jessie in disbelief, and keyed the radio again. "Also, Area 51, we picked up one of the old 'numbers' broadcasts on the shortwave, is that you guys?"

Cliff looked at Arcuni. "Shit, we need to get a shortwave in here to monitor that. If that's not an automatic relay and they're still up and broadcasting, we might have some problems."

Arcuni started to ask a question, but Cliff's raised hand motioned him to be quiet as he keyed the radio microphone. "No Texas," he replied, "that's not us, it's probably just an old recorded message on repeat. Can you contact us again tomorrow at noon your time?"

"That's affirmative, Area-51, contact you noon our time. Texas out."

CHAPTER 67

Marfa, Texas

"PROSPECT UP!"

Two prospects, wearing smooth leather vests with a single "Prospect" rocker on the back, ran quickly to Russell, the sergeant-at-arms.

"You two get the crank pump and fill the bikes, then top off the gas cans and the support cages."

"YES SIR!" One prospect ran to the van to get the hand-cranked pump they used to pump gas out of the underground gas station tanks, while the other started pushing the full members' motorcycles towards the access hatch for the tanks.

Twardo approached Russell. "How far out are we now?"

"Two hours or so. We'll be there by dinner time."

"Good. I'm hungry, and I want to taste their food. There isn't shit in this goat sneeze town; let's get everything we can from our friendly Texans and get the fuck out back to Fort Bliss."

The one-percenters' break lasted just long enough for the prospects to fuel up all the motorcycles, the van, and the truck. The full members used the break to smoke, both tobacco and marijuana. Each full-patched member received at least a carton of cigarettes from every gas station and grocery store the club raided; the prospects had to scavenge the leftovers. Twardo was sure that everyone would have to quit smoking cigarettes cold turkey before too much longer; there were only so many cigarettes left in the world.

Emory Peak, Big Bend National Park, Texas

"How far away are they, Bexar?" Jessie asked.

"I don't know, probably a full day's drive before the world ended. Nowadays it'll take much longer, probably a solid week of travel. Depends on if there are any other legions of the undead, and where they are. Anyone would be seriously screwed if we got caught by one of those."

"I say we make contact with Groom Lake one more time, then head down the mountain to discuss it with Jack and Sandra, maybe start our escape plan," she said.

"Okay, we can talk it over, but I really don't think we should leave the Park unless it becomes absolutely necessary. We have a good thing here, Jess, and it could support our family for many years to come."

Jessie nodded in agreement before turning the shortwave radio back on. Bexar turned on the ham radio and checked that it was tuned to the right frequency to contact Groom Lake. Between him and Jessie, they had figured out how to wire the solar panel to the battery in the radio box, and the battery to their two radios. Without consulting Jack or Sandra, they decided to leave the ham radio in the sealed, weatherproof metal box on the mountain. Since they couldn't transmit any signals in the Basin, it would be easier to leave it on top of the peak than to carry it up and down the mountain with each crew rotation. At least with the shortwave, there was a chance of receiving a transmission while still in the Basin.

Groom Lake, Nevada

"Really? I didn't expect the herds to move that quickly. Sorry, Arcuni, continue your brief," Major Wright said. He and Technical Sergeant Arcuni, Cliff, and all of the remaining NORAD airmen had gathered in one of the larger rooms for a briefing. Lance and his assistants were still buried in their work in the laboratories.

Arcuni continued, "The leading edge of the Dallas herd is now nearing where I-20 and I-10 meet in west Texas, with the bulk of the herd reaching the interchange in the next two days. Denver has given birth to another herd, which is moving south, roughly following I-25. Same with Houston except that herd is moving north roughly following I-45. Our working theory is that the herds begin to form when no new food sources are found. The reanimates travel in the direction with the least amount of obstacles—so smaller roads to larger roads and to even larger roads. That would explain why they're ending up on the Interstates—no lakes, no trees, no buildings, nothing but cars and more undead to join their ranks."

"That makes sense," Cliff said. "Good thing I got here early or I might have had a harder trip than I did, since I basically followed the Interstate out of Denver. Any updates on the fires?"

Arcuni clicked to the next slide in the PowerPoint presentation, showing a large overhead photo of North America followed by red dots in many locations. It looked to Cliff like America had a bad case of chicken pox.

"Gentlemen, as you can see with our overlay, we have found a significant number of unchecked fires still burning. The list is long, but it includes much of Dallas, Denver, Tucson, San Antonio, Oklahoma City, Lincoln, Austin, Indianapolis, Columbus, Fort Worth, Chicago, Phoenix ... to put it bluntly, if it's a city name you'd recognize, it either is or was on fire."

Major Wright looked at his notes and back to Arcuni. "Any theories as to why the substantial amount of fire?"

"Yes sir, but they range from utilities such as power plants and gas lines failing, car crashes, aircraft crashes, trains, buses, to even a cow kicking over a lantern. We have a bunch of ideas, most of them likely, but we just don't have the hard intel to figure that out yet."

Cliff nodded. "It isn't important yet, Major?"

"I would tend to agree," the major said. "Arcuni, please continue."

"Thank you. So far our radio operators have made contact with roughly two-dozen survivor groups spread out across middle America. None of them are in any city of any size, although some fled larger cities into the countryside. We're confident that we will continue to come into contact with more."

Cliff nodded in agreement again. "That's great news. Make sure that all of the survivors we contact have an open invitation to our location. With that in mind, Major, would you put together a working group to develop a security plan for receiving survivors, including a quarantine period, and a way for a group to make contact with us once they arrive topside?"

"No problem. Are we expecting any arrivals in the next seventy-two hours?" Major Wright asked.

"No idea," said Cliff. "Arcuni?"

"Not that we know of, but the topside lighting is still on, so if survivors pass near here they might be drawn to it. Same with the reanimates. Our security patrol has been encountering a stark increase in the undead. We should consider extinguishing topside lighting."

It was Wright's turn to nod in agreement. "Good idea, get on that when we finish here."

Cliff stood and walked to the lectern. "Guys, so far we've made incredible progress, and have confirmed that there are other survivors. Eventually we will form expeditionary groups to go outside the wire and search for survivors, or help them arrive safely here, but we're much too short on manpower to do that now. Thank you for the good briefing, Arcuni, everyone is dismissed."

Cliff looked at his watch and walked out the door towards the commo-hut. A few minutes later he walked into the room that was humming with electronics. "Any contact from our group in Texas?"

One of the airmen raised his hand and waved Cliff to his station. "Here sir, they just came online."

The radio operator handed Cliff the headphones and the mic. "Hello Texas survivors, how are you faring?"

"We're doing well, Groom Lake. Do you have any updates for us?"

"We do. The Dallas herd is nearing the I-10 and I-20 split out west, and there's a smaller herd traveling north from Houston on I-45. The good news is we've been able to make contact with other survivors in other states."

"That's great!" Bexar replied. "Make contact with anyone else in Texas?"

"No contact, but we did locate a group of people on motorcycles traveling easterly on highways south of I-10 nearing Big Bend National Park."

Bexar shot a nervous look at his wife and keyed the mic, "A motorcycle gang?"

"We don't have any means to determine that; we only found the riders during a satellite pass of the region."

"Groom Lake, are they riding spaced out or are they riding side-by-side, and do they have any other vehicles following them?"

Cliff looked over at an airman sitting at one of the computers in the room. "Can you pull up the overhead I flagged with the motorcycle riders?" He hit the mic again. "Standby, Texas, we're pulling the photo back up."

After a moment, Cliff spoke again. "Okay, they're riding side-by-side, and there's a van and a truck following behind them."

"Groom Lake, we ran into a motorcycle gang while en route here; they were herding the undead and using them to attack survivors and communities."

"They don't appear to have any reanimates following them. They're moving fast like they have a destination. There are a few small towns in their path, as well as the National Park."

"Okay, thank you, Groom Lake, I'm signing off, and it'll be a few days before we can make contact again. If the motorcycles are headed to the Park, how much time would you estimate before they arrive there?"

Cliff looked at the airman at the computer again. "How much time until the motorcycles reach Big Bend National Park?"

"Uh, looks like about four hours, if they stay on course and speed."

"Texas, we're estimating four hours."

Emory Peak

"Christ, babe, we've got to get moving. I wish we could talk to Jack and Sandra and send them a warning."

Jessie turned off the ham radio, unclipped it from the batteries, and stuffed it into the metal cabinet before picking up her pack. Bexar picked up his pack and his rifle and stopped.

"Hang on a second babe, going hot."

He pointed his AR in the direction of the cabins and pulled the trigger three times.

Chisos Basin Campground, Big Bend National Park, Texas

"Did you hear that, Jack?"

"Hear what?"

"I thought I heard a rifle."

"Maybe Bexar bagged a deer or something up there," he said.

"Why would he? We have enough here, and we just killed another javelina before they left. I don't think he'd do that. What if something's wrong?"

"If it is, Sandra, I'm sure he'll come down the mountain and tell us."

"What if they need us to come help them, should we go up the trail to see?"

"No, if something's wrong they'll beat us down before we can make it up there. Here, in a bit I'll check the dumpsters and the gate just to make sure everything's okay."

Jack went back to tending the afternoon fire, burning down his small pile of wood to make good cooking coals for the Dutch oven. The javelina stew was already in the cast iron pot. An hour later the Dutch oven was sitting on a hot bed of coals, with more hot coals piled on top of the lid. Jack looked at the sun in the western sky and estimated that the sun would have dipped just behind The Window by about the time the stew was done.

Jack left dinner cooking on the hot coals, grabbed his rifle, and drove the Scout towards the dumpsters and gates in the road to the Basin. Arriving at their defensive dumpsters, Jack disconnected the shotgun popper alarms and used the Scout to push the dumpsters together. Tomorrow he and Bexar could drag the dumpsters apart again, but it would probably be good to have the road closed, just in case.

After about thirty minutes of work and observing the road out on the desert floor, Jack strung the shotgun popper alarms across the road about ten feet in front of the dumpsters, so if something came near the roadblock, they would at least have some warning. Just before he climbed into the Scout to drive back to the cabins, he heard a low rumble bouncing off the mountains.

Jack looked at the sky, but could see no storm clouds. Grabbing the binoculars from the passenger seat of the Scout and climbing on top of the dumpsters to get a better look, he could nearly see Panther Junction, although the angle was wrong. The sound grew louder and more distinct in the distance, but still nothing entered Jack's narrow field-of-view. Eyes widening, Jack finally recognized the sound as it became clearer—motorcycles.

"Damnit, the bikers! So probably the undead too. Damnit!"

Jack jumped off the dumpsters and drove up the mountain towards the cabin as fast as he could negotiate the turns in the Scout.

CHAPTER 58

Chisos Basin Campground, Big Bend National Park, Texas

Jack skidded the Scout to a screeching halt in front of their cabin.

"Sandra get out here, we've got to get ready!"

"Shush Jack, Keeley's still down for her nap in Bexar's cabin, and Will's still napping in ours; if you wake them it's your ass."

"No, we've got problems, there are bikers in the Park, we've got to get ready!"

"That's probably what the rifle shots were about. What now?"

"Hopefully Bexar and Jessie are headed down the mountain, so let's hope they make it fast. I pushed the dumpsters together and set up the shotgun alarms. We need to put our go-bags in the Scout and load anything else we might need to bug out. Then I want to head back down the road and set up at the dumpsters to watch for any of them coming into the Basin. Maybe I can start picking them off before they can make it to the gate."

"What about the kids?"

"Let them nap for now, but if you hear any more shooting, get them in the Scout and be ready to roll."

"If they come up the only road in and out, how do I drive out?"

"I don't know. We'll have to play it by ear. We might have to drive fast, run them down, and hope for the best."

Jack gathered some supplies in a backpack and threw it over his shoulders, then grabbed the go-bags and tossed them into the Scout before getting in the FJ and leaving for the dumpsters. Sandra continued to load the Scout with two cases of .223, some pistol ammo, and some of their preserved venison jerky. She knew that they had the new cache site by Cattail Falls, but any extra supplies she brought could only help. The kids were still asleep, and the Scout was loaded as much as she dared. She looked at the cabins and began thinking about finding a good place to set. If she could get the kids safe in one of the back cabins, she could snipe the bikers or undead if they got past Jack. She wasn't going to leave without him.

Jack stopped the FJ at the dumpsters and turned it around so he could drive back towards the cabins quickly. He took off the backpack and placed it on top of the dumpsters, along with his rifle, and climbed up with his gear. In the backpack he had ten loaded 30-round Pmags, two bottles of water, and the binoculars. Jack sat up, the rifle in his lap, binoculars to his eyes scanning the roads ahead, and waited.

Panther Junction, Big Bend National Park

Twardo stopped his group of bikers where the road came to a three-way stop in front of the Ranger's station at Panther Junction. He knew from the radio conversations that his prize lay somewhere referred to as "The Basin," but he didn't know where that was in the Park. Twardo had never been to this part of Texas, since there weren't any motorcycle rallies or club chapters down here. The large brown sign at the intersection had an arrow pointing right that read "Chisos Basin," with the distance shown in miles. Bingo.

"Russell, send a scout to follow that sign."

Russell looked around and pointed to one of the least senior club members. Without a word, the man started his motorcycle and sped off in a cloud of dust in the direction the sign pointed.

Chisos Basin

Jack could hear the sound of the motorcycles in the desert getting closer until they stopped. It sounded like they were in the direction of Panther Junction, even though it was out of his view. He then heard a single motorcycle start and take off in a hurry. The sound increased in volume, and Jack's suspicion was confirmed a few minutes later when he saw the motorcycle approach the turnoff for the Basin. The bike slowed and then turned left, traveling towards Jack and his roadblock. Jack stashed the binoculars in his backpack and lay prone on the dumpster with his rifle, flicking the lever on the lower receiver from "Safe" to "Fire."

To Jack it felt like an hour had passed before the motorcycle finally came into view, but in reality it only took a couple of minutes. Coming suddenly upon the closed gate, the biker slammed on his brakes and came to a skidding stop. He switched off the motorcycle's ignition, drew a pistol from under his vest, and began walking towards the closed gate and the dumpsters.

Jack held his breath, waiting for the biker to see him, and waiting to see if the biker was from the same gang the group had encountered before. A deer broke out of the woods, running across the road behind the biker, causing him to spin in place, pistol raised. The three-piece patch on his vest was now clearly visible to Jack. That was the confirmation he'd been waiting for; slowly letting out his breath, he squeezed the trigger to the rear. But he was nervous and jerked the trigger slightly, so the round went low and struck the biker in the middle of the back. The biker cried out in pain and fell to the pavement. A few moments later he appeared to die.

"Shit, now we're in trouble," Jack said out loud to himself, climbing into the FJ to return to the cabins.

Panther Junction

Twardo turned to Russell. "That was a rifle. John only had a pistol. Looks like we've found our new friends. Saddle up!" he said, making a circling motion in the air with his right hand. The bikers mounted their motorcycles and the group sped off, the angry sound splintering the quiet desert air.

Chisos Basin

Sandra heard the rifle report and saw the FJ driving up the road into the Basin. Will had just woken up from his nap and was playing in Sandra's cabin, but Keeley was still sleeping in Bexar's cabin. Sandra ran out and met Jack at the FJ as he pulled to a stop. "What happened?"

"It's them Sandra, the same bikers from Comanche. One of them rode up to the dumpsters and I killed him. I didn't see any undead and I couldn't see the rest of their group, but after I fired my shot I heard a bunch of motorcycle start near Panther Junction—I don't know how many of them."

"Damn. Okay, I prepped two shooting positions, one on the roof of our cabin and the other on the roof of the motel out front."

"Perfect. Hide the Scout behind the cabins, I'll take the spot on the motel. You're the last line of defense. Keep our little boy safe!"

Sandra nodded, and Jack jogged towards the single-story motel across from the Ranger's station in the Basin. Once on the roof, he had a clear view of the road as it came up from the tent camp area. Counting his magazines, Jack had a total of twenty loaded 30-round Pmags, minus the single shot he had just fired at the dumpsters.

Twardo signaled the group to a stop when they came in view of John's parked motorcycle.

"Give me two prospects up front!"

Two prospects obediently climbed out of the van and jogged up to the club president.

"You two go up the road on foot, find John and figure out what happened, then report back."

The prospects nodded and, pistols in hand, began walking towards the motorcycle, disappearing out of sight around the bend in the road.

Shortly after losing sight of the prospects, the valley echoed with a shotgun blast, followed by both prospects running back down the road towards the rest of the club.

"What the fuck was that?"

"Sir, we didn't see John but there was a bunch of blood on the road, which is blocked by two dumpsters. When we got close someone shot at us from nowhere, so we ran back down here."

"You fucking pussies, go back up there and figure it out!"

The prospects were visibly shaken, but they started back up the road, pistols raised but moving slower than last time. About ten minutes passed before they reappeared.

"We couldn't find John, but the dumpsters are full of rocks and dirt, and there's no one around. We'll need the truck to pull them out of the way."

Twardo nodded. One prospect retrieved John's motorcycle, the other drove the truck past the group to the dumpsters before pulling out some heavy chain from the bed. Less than five minutes later, one of the dumpsters had been pulled out of the way.

Before riding past the roadblock, Russell walked around the dumpsters and stopped.

"Hey Prez, check this out."

Twardo joined Russell, who continued, "Someone set up a trip wire, see? It's attached to this thing over here with a shotgun shell. I bet the prospects set another one off earlier."

Twardo circled his right hand above his head and the bikers mounted their motorcycles once again.

Emory Peak

Bexar and Jessie were out of breath and sweating in the cool winter air, but they were getting close to where the trail came out behind the cabins. The echoing shotgun blast stopped them both in their tracks. They instantly knew it was the trip alarms at the dumpsters, and without a word they continued down the trail at a jog.

Chisos Basin

Lying on the roof of the motel with the binoculars up to his face, Jack saw a biker walking up the road into the parking area. It was the biker he had killed, now reanimated. He decided not to put it down and risk giving away his position. Then he heard the pack of motorcycle engines start.

The group still rode side-by-side as they entered the parking area in the Basin. Twardo saw a burned-out building to his left, a couple of motels, some cabins, some other buildings on his right, and John walking across the parking lot. Twardo turned off his motorcycle and walked towards John, who was moaning and quite obviously dead.

"Well shit John, you went and became a goddamned zombie."

Twardo pulled a pistol out from under his vest and pointed it at reanimated John's face. Suddenly, it was his own face that exploded, the sharp rifle report echoing a split second later.

Undead John didn't notice or care about the rifle, or that Twardo had just died, he simply bent over and tore a chunk of flesh from his president's shoulder. Russell, still standing next to his motorcycle, yelled, "Holy shit, get the deuce out of the van and kill those motherfuckers!"

Two prospects ran to the van, swung open the rear doors, and dragged an M-2 with a tripod base out of the back, carrying it towards a large rock in the parking lot for cover. A third prospect pulled two green ammo cans out of the back of the van and was starting towards the M-2 when the side of his head exploded outward and he fell to the ground. Another biker went down as he ran towards the Ranger's station, falling to the pavement, screaming and holding his stomach, blood pouring out of the rifle wound.

Russell yelled behind him, "You get the truck and get up there to flank him." As the truck drove up the road next to the motel, Jack fired a full magazine into the truck. He missed the driver, but the truck gained a flat tire and a bunch of bullet holes in the side.

Russell yelled at the prospects just finishing loading the M-2, "That asshole's on top of the motel there, kill that piece of shit!" The M-2's report was fast and deep, echoing in the Basin. Tracer rounds walked up the front of the hotel, 50-cal holes crumbling the front wall.

Jack grabbed his backpack and slid down the back of the motel's roof. He ran west, away from the crew-served weapon and towards the trail that would lead to the back of the cabins. Three shots from an AR rang out near the cabins, and as Jack turned the corner he saw the biker who'd been driving the truck fall to the ground dead, three bullet holes in his chest. That biker would soon reanimate, but he had other things to worry about for now.

The prospects only stopped shooting the motel once they had emptied an entire can of 50-cal chain-fed ammo. The motel was smoking, about to catch on fire from the tracer rounds, but they didn't care. They figured the guy on the motel was probably dead because he wasn't shooting at them anymore.

Russell pointed at two club members behind him and said, "You two, go up there and make sure that guy on the roof's dead."

The bikers jogged forward, giving undead John a wide berth as he continued to eat their former club president. Going to the back of the motel, one hoisted the other up onto the roof, where they found an empty AR magazine and a bunch of shell casings, but no shooter. Standing on the roof, they saw the club's truck parked in the road with a lot of bullet holes, a flat tire, and no driver. They whistled and waved at the other Pistoleros, motioning them to come forward. The bikers moved their motorcycles out of the road and into the parking lot by the motel, the van following.

Bexar and Jessie were getting close. The gunfire could be heard very clearly, as could the long bursts from a fully-automatic big caliber gun. Neither of them had been in the military, so they didn't know the distinct sound an M-2 makes, but both knew that the sound was very bad.

The bikers, away from their motorcycles, walked up the road in a loose group towards the abandoned and bullet-riddled truck. As the first biker passed the truck,

Sandra shot him in the throat. The rest of the bikers dove for cover and started shooting at the cabin, not knowing that Sandra was on the roof.

Will sat in the cabin, crying, scared, and alone. His mother had told him to stay in there no matter what. Sandra knew the cabin was his best protection, and she was never going to let the bikers get near the cabin anyways. But he was just a little boy who wanted to find his mom, so he opened the door and ran out of the cabin into the open. Russell saw the little boy running across the parking lot and shot him twice, sending his little body tumbling to the ground.

Jack rounded the back of the cabins just in time to see his only child run out of their cabin and die in the parking lot. He stopped, and an anguished howl tore from his guts. Blinded with hatred and rage, he ran around the cabin toward the bikers, shooting wildly. Two of those rounds found two different bikers before his bolt locked back on an empty magazine. Taking advantage of the break in the shooting, Russell shot Jack with his pistol, and continued shooting until Jack's body fell in a growing pool of blood.

Sandra's body went ice cold, and she began slowly taking aim, firing on one biker at a time. The prospects finished moving the M-2 about the time that Sandra started back into the fight, opening up on the cabin where she lay on the roof.

Bexar and Jessie were close enough to hear the gunfire and Jack's bone-chilling scream, but came down the trail just in time to see Jack lying dead by his son's dead body, and to see the M-2 begin firing on Sandra, decimating their cabin and killing her in a hail of gunfire. They both stopped behind the last row of cabins.

"Holy fucking shit, Jess, they're all dead!" Bexar was shaking, his face white.

Jessie stood motionless, tears streaming down her face.

"Jess, find Keeley, check our cabin. I'm going to kill these bastards, then I'll meet you at the RV."

Jessie's feet felt rooted to the ground, but her need to protect her child shook her loose from her catatonic state and she began running towards their cabin. If Keeley was in Sandra's cabin she would probably be dead, but she prayed that her little girl had been hidden in the cabin further back.

Bexar took a kneeling position behind a large tree and tried to slow his breathing while taking aim at the bikers. His first target was the biker behind the big machine gun, and as he squeezed the trigger twice, the biker's head exploded brain matter all over his fellow prospects. Moving slightly, he did the same with the biker holding the ammo belt, and then the biker next to the open ammo can.

Seeing his prospects being picked off, Russell ran down the road towards his parked motorcycle. The two remaining bikers who were still alive turned to follow Russell, but both were shot twice in the back by Bexar. They dropped to the pavement, screaming in pain. Bexar took aim on the last biker, but he turned the corner out of his view before he could take the shot.

Bexar stood, rifle up, and slowly made his way to where Jack and Will were lying on the pavement. Both were dead, bullet holes riddling both of their torsos. Bexar couldn't fathom his best friend and his little boy reanimating, so he drew his pistol and shot them both once in the head. He then went to Sandra's cabin and climbed onto the roof from the picnic table in front. Sandra was also dead, but mercifully a round had found her skull and he wouldn't have to shoot another close friend.

He climbed down from the roof and walked back to where Jack's body lay to retrieve the backpack. In the bag, he found eight loaded Pmags and a broken pair of binoculars. Bexar tossed the field glasses out of the bag and walked to the Scout, where he retrieved Jack and Sandra's go-bags, a couple of cases of ammo, and the venison jerky. He then put the two cases of .223 ammo in the large backpack, shouldered the bag, and went to his cabin to retrieve his go-bag before jogging towards the trail to The Window.

Before starting down the trail, Bexar did a tactical reload, swapping a fresh magazine into his AR. Rounding the corner by the western edge of the motel that was now on fire, Bexar saw a handful of bikers, reanimated and stumbling aimlessly around the parking lot.

"Fuck you all, you deserve to stay zombies."

Bexar made his way to the trailhead and hopefully towards his family.

CHAPTER 50

On the trail to The Window

Bexar passed a large boulder to his right and found himself staring down the barrel of a pistol. Jessie stood in the middle of the trail, Keeley hiding behind her legs. When she saw it was her husband, she holstered the pistol and started crying, hugging Bexar.

"I found Keeley hiding under the bed in our cabin. Since our cabin was in the back of the group the bikers never made it back that far."

"Thank you Jessie, I love you. Jack, Sandra, and Will are all dead, but I made sure they wouldn't reanimate. One of the bikers got away, but I killed the rest of them."

The stars were beginning to come out in the night sky. Jessie kept Keeley hidden while Bexar made a safety sweep around the RV. It was still hitched to the Wagoneer and all their cached supplies were safe.

Jessie laid Keeley down to sleep in the RV before joining Bexar outside in the cold winter air. Even though the RV was well-hidden off the main road, they sat in the dark quietly discussing their future.

"Bexar, I don't think I can stay here any longer, not with our friends killed. I don't want to see their bodies, I don't want to see that sweet little boy's dead face. I just can't."

"Yeah, me neither. We can leave in the morning if you want, or we can wait."

"We need to leave now," Jessie said. "What if that biker comes back, what if he brings the undead, what if we can't defeat them next time? We need to go, but I don't know where to go anymore."

"Jess, the only place I can think of now is Groom Lake, and hope that Cliff wasn't lying to us. The radio is still on top of Emory Peak, but I don't want to hike back up there to get it. We'll be on our own and out of contact, but we can do it."

Fort Bliss, Texas

Russell came roaring into the biker's camp at the rundown hotel outside of Fort Bliss near midnight, the lone survivor from the botched raid at Big Bend. Walking towards the club vice president, Russell pushed the naked woman dancing in front of the VP to the ground. "Those fuckers killed everyone. Saddle up, we're going back!"

The VP looked at the nude woman on the ground, then back up at Russell. "It can wait 'til tomorrow," he said.

Russell drew his pistol and shot the VP in the face.

"Okay assholes, load up, we roll in thirty minutes. If you don't like it, take it up with your VP!"

CHAPTER 60

February 14ᵗʰ
Big Bend National Park, Texas

Physically and emotionally drained, Jessie and Bexar startled awake before sunrise to the rumbling sound of a large group of motorcycles. They grabbed their rifles and bolted out of the RV.

"Holy crap!" said Jessie, "that was fast, they're back already!"

"Yeah, but it sounds like they're heading up into the Basin. Get Keeley and get in the Jeep, I'll get the RV ready to move. We're leaving now. We'll head towards Terlingua and try to miss them."

Bexar cranked at the leveling jacks and broke out the trailer's tail lights while Jessie returned to the RV to carry a still-sleeping Keeley to the Jeep. With one last glance up towards the backside of The Window, Bexar climbed in the Wagoneer and put it in gear. Driving to the paved surface, Bexar turned his new convoy to the right on Ross Maxwell Scenic Drive and towards SH385 and Groom Lake, Nevada.

Holding Jessie's hand as he drove, Bexar just hoped that this major trek would be easier than the last two. He looked at his wife beside him, and said, "By the way, Happy Valentine's Day. I love you, Jessie."

Smiling tiredly, she replied, "I love you too, babe."

WINCHESTER PREY

Book Two

PROLOGUE

February 17, Year 1

Chivo lay prone on the side of the mountain, surrounded by trees and desert shrub grass. He should have had his ghillie suit, but there were a lot of things he'd gone without and this would have to be another. It didn't matter; the mission came first. Without a laser rangefinder or a spotter, he made some guesses for target distances, doped the conditions and dialed in the adjustments on the optic mounted on top of his big rifle. Motorcycles were parked by the cabins, while three white males meandered between the cabins and the parking area. Chivo had no idea what the target of interest looked like. All he knew was that it wasn't a biker and there was a good chance the target was in this part of the national park.

Three women in various stages of undress stepped out of the middle cabin, the woman in the middle being nearly dragged by the others. She was completely nude with her hands tied behind her back. All three women shook, but Chivo didn't know if it was from the cold winter air or from fear.

A rifle shot cracked through the cold air, echoing off the mountain walls, followed by another rifle shot and then another. *Sounds like an M4*, Chivo thought. A man who looked like a member of the motorcycle gang fired wildly with a pistol.

I can't identify which is the target. I can't see who is friend or foe. I can't engage yet.

Chivo panned his rifle to the left, dragging the narrow field of view seen through the rifle's scope, just in time to see a man with a beard wearing tactical pants and other tactical kit running towards the main parking area from between the long row of cabins to the south. The man with the beard didn't look like a biker. The man stopped running, knelt and continued to fire an M4 at the bikers. The guy with the beard had to be his man.

Time to get to work, Chivo thought while making some minor adjustments to the scope on his big rifle. Target lined up, Chivo slowly exhaled and gently pressed the trigger to the rear. The powerful rifle barked sharply, filling the air around him with dirt and grass kicked up from the shockwave of the projectile exploding out of the end of the long barrel. Through the scope Chivo watched the target's head disappear into a red mist.

CHAPTER 1

Little Rock, AR
December 26, Year 1 (before the attack)

Early morning light filtered into the second-story bedroom of the historic home in Pulaski Heights. Only the two golden brown cocker spaniels broke the silence of the morning by wagging their tails against the nightstand. Her children were with her ex-husband and his new girlfriend, skiing in Colorado for Christmas. The kids would have fun even if she was ten years too young for him. A hot cup of tea, a big fire in the fireplace, and a small stack of Jules Vern novels comprised her entire plan for the day.

Both of her dogs' tails stopped wagging, their attention snapping towards the outside window. Amanda reluctantly stepped out of her warm bed and peeked around the curtain of her window. A dark-colored Tahoe with deep window tint stopped in the circle drive at the front of her house. She stepped into her slippers and pulled a thick bathrobe on while stomping down the stairs. Her dogs happily plodded down the stairs before her, racing to the door. *I finally have a single day of peace and quiet and the department is going to ruin it.* The dogs barked in response to the stern knock at her door.

Amanda opened the heavy wooden door. "What is so damned important that it couldn't wait until next week?"

Two men stood on her front porch, both wearing dark suits, white shirts and dark ties. Sunglasses covered their eyes. Amanda looked at their feet. *Cheap shoes, hallmark of the FBI.* Amanda's suspicions were confirmed as the man on the right opened a worn leather case which contained a gold badge and a photo ID with FBI emblazoned in large blue letters.

"Madam Secretary, I am Agent Smith and this is Agent Johnson. Would you step outside, please? I'm sorry, but you will need to come with us."

"Excuse me? Come with you for what? It's the day after Christmas, nor am I dressed."

Agent Johnson removed his wool overcoat and held it out for Secretary Lampton. "I'm sorry, ma'am, but you must come with us. You can wear this for now. We already have a change of clothes waiting for you, as well as an overnight bag."

"You have what for me already? I demand to know what is going on and will not step a single foot outside of my home until you tell me what it is."

"Madam Secretary, *Babylon Shield* has been initiated. You must leave with us immediately."

Amanda's eyes went wide. "We are under attack?"

"Yes ma'am, as we speak. And we have no time to waste."

United States Secretary of Agriculture Amanda Lampton stepped into the frigid air, taking Johnson's proffered overcoat, and shut the door behind her. Agent Smith climbed into the driver's seat of the still-running Tahoe while Agent Johnson held the back door open for Secretary Lampton.

Once seated, Smith put the Tahoe into gear and accelerated sharply while flipping two switches on the SUV's dash. The siren wailing from behind the Tahoe's grill, punctuated by the flashing hidden emergency lights, shattered the affluent neighborhood's peace.

Agent Johnson turned in his seat and pointed to a duffel bag on the back seat. "Ma'am, in the bag you will find a change of clothes. Would you please get dressed?"

"Now? In here?"

"Please."

Amanda opened the duffel and found a new pair of tan cargo pants, a black t-shirt, a sports bra, panties, socks and a pair of running shoes, in addition to a sweatshirt and a North Face jacket. Smith was driving extremely fast and the Tahoe bounced sharply, making it difficult for Amanda to get dressed. It wasn't until she lay down in the back seat to pull on the cargo pants that she realized that the bra and panties were her own. That realization was a little unsettling, but she decided that questioning how the agents had retrieved her own under clothing could wait. *Besides, these two field agents would have no idea.*

Sitting upright, Amanda realized they were already on I-630. She saw the speedometer's needle hovering near ninety miles per hour. Agent Smith drove very aggressively, sweeping across the Interstate onto the inside shoulder to rocket past two large semi-trucks driving side by side in the two inside lanes. Amanda cringed at the sight of the Tahoe's mirrors nearly scraping the semi-truck and the concrete barrier on the other side. The Tahoe continued to weave through traffic, the heavy SUV rolling from side to side with each gut-wrenching near miss.

The SUV suddenly lurched forward. Smith had stomped hard on the brakes before releasing to turn, barely making the exit ramp for I-30 South. Once on the ramp, the SUV accelerated hard. Amanda bounced against the interior of the Tahoe, her head hitting the side window before she could steady herself in the seat long enough to latch the seatbelt.

The wide sweeping ramp onto I-440 pushed Amanda against her door, the tires squealing in protest to the speed of the SUV, which settled for only a moment before swerving hard to miss another large truck. Agent Smith exited for Airport Road, siren still blaring and lights flashing, before turning hard left through the intersection, indifferent to the red light and other drivers' honking protests. Through the windshield Amanda saw one of the smaller commuter aircraft taking off on the runway in front of them. Smith continued to accelerate hard.

Everything in the Tahoe became quiet. Only the sound of the tires rolling on the pavement vibrated through the interior. Smith slammed the gear selector to neutral while turning the ignition key on and off rapidly to no effect, before stomping on the brake pedal with both feet while pulling on the steering wheel.

The anti-lock brake system had disabled with the rest of the vehicle. All four tires began to skid across the pavement. The Tahoe bounced across a raised median, narrowly missing two other vehicles, which were rolling through the intersection out of control. Amanda's seatbelt locked her into her seat and the last thing she saw before the Tahoe launched into a drainage ditch was the same commuter plane above them, its tail pointed straight down, falling.

CHAPTER 2

Jake and Sara relaxed in their home on the south end of town, a fire burning fiercely in their living room fireplace. Both sat on the couch in thick cotton robes with mugs of coffee steaming on the tray table between them. Sara intently read a book on her iPad, feet curled under her body. Christmas was always the best time of year. Although they didn't have any children to build the Christmas spirit with, Sara was able to enjoy her break from her middle school students. Science and teaching were her passions, although she was often frustrated by the fifth graders she taught. Jake typed on the MacBook perched in his lap. He had no Christmas break, but he also had no *real* job. He worked as an independent journalist, author and photographer. That meant he had the opportunity to be sent to the far-flung reaches of the world for an assignment, but that also meant his working hours were much less defined than most people's. While not on assignment, at least, he worked from home. Though Sara enjoyed the arrangement, she often wished she could reclaim the formal dining room of their home from the stacks of Pelican cases holding tens of thousands of dollars in professional photography equipment.

The lights flickered once and went off, leaving Jake and Sara to the light of the fireplace. Losing power in Colorado in the winter wasn't all that uncommon, except that Jake's MacBook and Sara's iPad both went dark at the same time.

"What the hell? My iPad died; your MacBook too? Why would that happen when the power went out?"

Jake sat silent for a moment and watched the orange flames dance in the fireplace.

"Honey, look outside and see if anyone has any lights on. I have a bad feeling. I'm going to unlock *the* room and get the shortwave radio out of the faraday cage."

"No. You don't think ... that?"

"I don't know yet, but why else would our electronics go dark along with the electricity? Sort of an odd coincidence, isn't it? I think we should probably get dressed and G.O.O.D. ready."

Jake stood and walked towards the back of the house. Sara looked out the front window and across their snow-covered lawn. A couple of her neighbors stood in their front yards looking a little bewildered.

"Jake, looks like everyone's power is out."

"OK."

Jake sat back on the couch twenty minutes later, fully dressed and holding a hand-cranked shortwave radio in his hands. "Time to see if the cages worked if it was an EMP."

Jake turned the shortwave on and dialed in the first FEMA emergency broadcast channel to be met with a computer-generated voice: "... remain indoors and avoid contact with any other persons. If a person or family member becomes ill or begins to act strangely, immediately leave the area or quarantine the individual and contact local emergency responders. If unable to reach emergency personal, hang a sheet or large towel on a front-facing exterior door and passing patrols will stop to render aid. This is not a test ..."

The broadcast repeated.

Sara looked up from the radio Jake held. "What do you think they meant by 'acting strangely'?"

"I don't know, babe, but sounds like a contagion outbreak, and I think we might have had an EMP even though they didn't say anything about it."

Jake tuned the shortwave radio into the BBC's frequency and found a distressed voice—a real voice, not a computer—reading a broadcast:

"... Reports have been sparse but initial reports indicate that a wide-scale attack has been carried out against the United States, the UK and other nations of the European Union. Some reports have spoken of a strange oil-like substance falling from the sky, trailing from large aircraft formations. These reports have been coming to us across most of Western Europe and the UK. Contact with the States has failed and a Ministry official confided to the BBC on the basis of anonymity that there has been a possible nuclear strike against the United States or that multiple nuclear warheads were detonated high in the atmosphere above North America. We have not been able to confirm those reports but will bring you updates as we can gather them. Stand by, I'm being handed a new report ... It reads 'Remain indoors and avoid contact with all other persons. If a person or family member becomes ill ...'"

The transmission faded into static.

Jake looked at Sara, his brow furrowed. "EMP and some sort of biological or chemical attack. Finish getting dressed while I get the plastic and duct tape. We need to seal up until we can find out more of what's going on."

Sara left for the bedroom to finish getting dressed, while Jake went to their spare bedroom. The locked door was a heavy exterior door with a numeric punch lock. Jake pushed the five-digit key and entered the dark room. The room was lined with shelves of supplies. In the corner sat a large maroon gun safe. Jake spun the dial, quickly unlocked the safe and opened the heavy door. He took a deep breath and let it out with a heavy sigh. He and Sara had prepared for society to collapse, for some natural disaster or attack to disrupt their lives, but if he was honest with himself, deep down he never thought it would actually happen.

Already on his thick nylon belt was a holster, and in it went the Glock 17 after he loaded it and made ready with a round in the chamber. Jake retrieved his AR-15, loaded it and propped it against the wall next to the safe. He wanted it ready and nearby, but he and his wife needed to tape up and seal the home's windows and doors.

The fireplace would remain open for now, as the fire's heat would most likely destroy any airborne pathogens falling down the fireplace. At least Jake hoped it would, and hoped there wasn't any nuclear fallout. However, if the attack was a high-altitude detonation to generate an EMP, there shouldn't be any fallout. An hour after the lights went out in the Sells' home, they were secure and sheltered in place.

Little Rock, AR

Amanda slowly opened her eyes. She blinked hard and couldn't remember where she was. She turned to look out her window and saw it was missing with grass and dirt in its place. Slowly her mind caught up to her surroundings and the nightmare crash started to regain focus. Over the sound of her heartbeat booming in her ears, she began to be become aware of someone else talking.

She looked left and saw Agent Smith leaning into the Tahoe's interior. "Ma'am, unlatch your seatbelt and take my hand."

Complying, she unlatched her seatbelt and stood upright to reach Smith's hand hanging through the shattered side window. Amanda stood on the inside of the door, the Tahoe having come to a rest on its side. Once outside of the ruined SUV, after having climbed off the top of the upturned Tahoe, she remembered seeing the airplane falling out of the sky just before the crash. Amanda turned to look behind her and saw thick black smoke billowing into the sky a few hundred yards away.

Smith and Johnson wrestled the rear doors of the Tahoe open and retrieved two large Pelican cases before stripping out of their ruined dark suits. Amanda stood silently, too confused to protest and too uninformed to ask any questions. Everything had happened too fast. Only fifteen minutes ago she was lying comfortably in her warm bed, and now she stood next to a ruined SUV in a ditch watching two men she didn't know strip to their underwear. Smith and Johnson both began pulling clothing and gear out of the heavy plastic cases. Soon they were dressed in black tactical clothing and began strapping on body armor and holstering weapons. Smith handed Amanda a military-looking backpack that felt like it weighed at least thirty pounds.

"You'll need this. Please put it over your shoulders."

Smith and Johnson retrieved similar-looking bags from the back of the Tahoe, but both of their bags were considerably larger and appeared to weigh much more than Amanda's bag.

Amanda, still in shock although her thoughts were starting to catch up with what she'd just seen, finally spoke. "What ... what happened?"

Smith released the charging handle on his M4 rifle with a loud metallic thunk. "EMP, ma'am."

"EMP? What is an E-M-P?"

"Electromagnetic pulse. It's from a nuclear detonation, which releases a strong magnetic wave that pretty much destroys anything electronic that isn't shielded."

Amanda looked nervously towards the sky and back to Smith. "What about nuclear fallout?"

Smith shook his head. "If the devices were detonated high enough in the atmosphere, then we won't have to worry about that."

Smith walked up the embankment and out of the ditch to the roadway, where he paused and scanned the area before waving Johnson and Amanda to follow. Once she climbed out of the ditch and back onto the roadway, Amanda tried to take in the scene before her. Large fires and thick black smoke could be seen in every direction.

"What happened to all the planes?"

"Just like how the EMP fried the computer in the Tahoe and it quit running, so with the aircraft. Everything from the engines to the flight systems are computer controlled. Basically, the planes stopped flying."

Amanda looked around her at the pillars of thick smoke that now filled the sky. "What are we going to do?"

Johnson smiled. "We have a plane to catch." Before Amanda could ask how that was possible, he answered her question. "Military plane. It's shielded against an EMP. Or at least it is supposed to be."

The three of them walked briskly towards the terminal in the distance, which also appeared to be on fire. The damage had been caused by another aircraft crashing into it, and the parking lot was marred by the obvious path of destruction of the downed plane. Smith walked with a slight limp. Amanda couldn't remember if he had the limp before the crash or not, but she hadn't seen him walk very far before now.

Johnson climbed on top of the large "Bill & Hillary Clinton National Airport" sign, removed a large pair of binoculars from his bag and scanned the area.

"The G-Five is hard bent."

Smith cursed.

Amanda waited for an explanation, but Johnson gave none and continued to scan the area with his binoculars.

"Agent Smith, what is a *G-Five* and what is *hard bent*?"

"It means something is broken beyond immediate repair. We were to meet a Gulfstream V over at the General Aviation side of the airport. With it we were to escort you to Denver to the secure facility there. Looks like we're going to need alternate transportation now."

Johnson pointed towards the airport's control tower. "Looks like an old Bronco parked by that tower. It might be serviceable."

Johnson jumped off the sign and placed the binoculars back into his heavy pack. "We better hurry before the owner or someone else decides to use it to bug out."

Amanda fell in behind Smith, who walked towards the tower at a very brisk pace, although limping. Johnson walked a few yards behind Amanda and held rear security for their designated person, only stopping when they saw several large aircraft fly overhead in a wide formation. Dark trails followed their path, and moments later the three of them were covered in an oily substance that fell from the sky like rain.

Lampton wiped the oil off her face and rubbed it between her fingers. "What is this?"

Johnson tersely replied that he didn't know and exchanged a concerned look with his partner.

CHAPTER 3

Cortez, CO
January 25, Year 1

"Jake, we have three more families requesting shelter with us."

"Thank you, Sara. Have Mike do a weapons check and inspect the men for any bites. If you wouldn't mind taking care of the women and children, I would appreciate it. Oh, and make sure they completely understand the rules."

"Will do, baby." Sara kissed Jake on the forehead, the notebook ledger of supplies open on the desk in front of him for the daily inventory. Candlelight flickered across the smudged pages. Jake never meant to be a leader; in fact, with the exception of his articles, he preferred to be seldom seen and heard, but his good nature and kind heart became his downfall. Jake and Sara were well prepared for the end of the world as they knew it, their spare bedroom stocked with supplies, food, and water. They planned for society to collapse, for the loss of electrical power and the absolute need to survive on their own without any assistance from the government, but they had not planned for the dead to rise to hunt the living. They also didn't expect that other survivors would somehow find their home and come in desperate need of help. Jake should have locked the door and turned away everyone that came calling, but the first to arrive was a young husband and wife that Jake knew from his local volunteer work. The teenagers, Jason and Jamie, were married a week before they graduated high school and eight months later they'd confided that they were trying to start a family. Jake knew they needed help. They weren't prepared for life, much less the end of the world.

But those two loved each other more deeply than Jake and Sara had seen in many others, and they couldn't turn away such good-hearted people.

The next family was another married couple in their mid-thirties with three young children. The children tugged at Jake's heart. Already in the past month, Jake had been forced to put down a handful of undead children who'd ventured into his yard, and he just couldn't stomach the thought of seeing any more. In the coming weeks the number of survivors, most of them families, reached thirty-eight, and quickly the expanding group was well out of room in Jake and Sara's home.

The middle school became the next logical location. The classrooms were divided among the families with areas for central meeting locations, supply storage and in-processing facilities. The group now had the ability to accept many more refugees, more survivors.

"Jake, could you come out here please?" Sara called from the hallway. That was odd, but Jake didn't question Sara, especially when she asked for help. He simply obeyed her request and carried his candle into the hallway.

"There are three men wearing matching button-down shirts and ties asking us to repent and convert to their church."

Jake looked surprised. "Convert? Like missionaries? You're kidding."

"Yes, missionaries, and I'm not kidding."

Jake sighed. "OK, well, let's see what they're really after."

Jake walked through the hall, shielding his candle from the movement, and entered the old middle school gym, which had been converted into the group's secure processing area. The metal doors closed behind him with a heavy click.

Jake tried to take in the scene before him. Standing side by side were three men dressed in matching white shirts with red ties. The men stood calmly, each of them holding a small book that looked like a Bible in his left hand. The hair on the back of Jake's neck stood. These men felt dangerous, but he couldn't figure out why.

"Hello, my name is Jake. Sara said you wanted to ask me some questions."

"Yes, good morning. I'm Brother Chris. This is Brother Matt and this is Brother William. We're with The Chosen Tribe of God and we've come to call your group to repent your sins and join us under the teachings of The Prophet."

Jake stole a glance at Sara. "Thank you, gentlemen, but I think we're full up on religion here."

"Can we pray to The Prophet with you for your safety and conversion?"

"No. No, I don't want you to pray for me or to pray with me, and quite frankly I have a hard time believing that God still cares for us down here on Earth anymore after everything we've been through."

"Could we speak to the others who reside here? They may be willing to open their hearts to the truth so they won't be damned like you are."

Jake's heart rate quickened and his eyebrow raised in surprise. *Damned like we are?* His right hand thumbed open the locking snap of his holster.

"No, you may not. And if you would be kind enough to leave, I would appreciate it."

The three men from The Tribe looked at Jake like his hair was on fire, a look both quizzical and judging, and walked out of the gym back into the cold morning air.

"Sara, those guys are going to be a problem. I think they were serious. Group meeting in the cafeteria in twenty minutes. Please pass the word. I've got to sit down for a minute and try to figure this out."

Sara stood on her tippy toes and kissed her husband on the cheek before unlocking the metal gym door and disappearing into the dark interior of the school.

CHAPTER 4

The past four weeks had proved to be perilous for Amanda. A knock on her door early the day after Christmas began it all. She was a fast riser, the youngest Secretary of Agriculture for the United States in the history of the position, but for all her professional ability she wasn't prepared to be able to dodge the series of bad hands that were continuing to be dealt. One of the commuter jets disabled by the EMP attack had crashed through the General Aviation side of the airport in Little Rock, which destroyed the military hardened Gulf Stream jet. That abruptly changed their plan of escape. The first vehicle they stole to flee towards Denver was an ancient Ford Bronco that still ran after the EMP, but that survived only until being ambushed by a militant group of survivalists outside of Texarkana. The second vehicle, an old Chevrolet Suburban, smoked so badly that it looked to be on its last leg when they found it. After the near disaster of Texarkana, Smith and Johnson decided to stick to the little-traveled Farm-to-Market roads around the eastern side of Tyler until reaching Highway 49 south of town. An old road atlas that unfolded to the size of a small table top was currently half-folded in Johnson's lap while he traced the route with his finger.

"Follow this road until you reach Highway 31 and then turn west. We'll stay on that road for about an hour."

As they approached Highway 69, the knocking emanating from under the hood of the Suburban became sharply louder. White smoke billowed from under the hood and with a loud metallic crunch the motor stopped abruptly.

"Well, fuck me."

Amanda raised her eyebrows at Johnson's remark.

"Sorry ma'am. I'll double check, but I think the motor just threw a rod and our ride is hard bent."

Johnson climbed out of the driver's seat and Smith exited the front passenger's door with his M4 at the ready. White smoke continued to pour from the sides of the hood. Johnson raised the hood and tried to fan the smoke enough to see into the engine bay.

"Damnit. Well, Smith, it looks like we're on foot again."

"And after last time, our supplies are still low. We need gear, but more importantly, we need to replenish our food and water."

Amanda climbed out of the Suburban and held her AR-15 at the ready while scanning the surrounding area. During the fight in Texarkana they were able to liberate a civilian-made AR from one of the militants they killed. Each night after setting up camp, Smith used the spare time to teach Amanda how to use it. She was a fast learner, but the new world in which they lived demanded that people be fast learners, or they would die only to shamble perpetually as corpses.

Johnson closed the hood and climbed up the front bumper and onto the roof of the Suburban, scanning the area with his binoculars before climbing down to discuss their options with the group.

After a heated discussion, Amanda told the men she'd seen a sign for Gander Mountain for this exit and suggested they could raid the store for the supplies they needed. With no better suggestions, the trio shouldered their bags from the back of the SUV and started walking north towards the general direction the sign pointed.

Thirty minutes of walking later, they knelt in the wood line on the south edge of the parking lot of Gander Mountain and surveyed the scene before them. It told the story of the early days after the attack. Parts of bodies lay in the parking lot, the scraps left by turkey buzzards and other animals to rot in the open. The glass at the front of the building was shattered and at this point none of them thought there might be much left for them to scavenge. They formed a loose column and walked along the edge of the tree line towards the rear of the store and around to the loading docks. A tractor-trailer sat abandoned at the dock, but the loading dock's rollup door stood open, so they had a way in.

They circled up and began to formulate a plan. Johnson started, "I think the front of the store is probably wiped out. I say we ignore that and just check the back room for anything overlooked. Perhaps in the trailer as well. For tonight, if we can't find a new vehicle we can recon the neighborhood across the highway and try to find a house that isn't full of the previous residents."

With little discussion, Smith and Amanda agreed, and quickly their plan was set in motion. Inside the loading area and storeroom stood pallets of merchandise that was still boxed and wrapped in plastic to be secured for transport. Twenty minutes passed but the three of them were able to cut the boxes free from their wrapped pallets and look for items they could use. Luckily, they found much of what they needed. A bit over one thousand rounds of .223, which would work in Amanda's AR as well as the two agents' M4 rifles. They also found new boots, clothes and socks for each of them. A lightweight backpacking tent, sleeping bags, and a compact backpacking stove with fuel rounded out the surprises. It felt like they'd won the lottery, met Santa Claus, and had a birthday all at once.

With the new gear distributed, they climbed off the loading dock quickly, wanting to get back to the safety of the tree line without being seen. They were walking along the edge of the semi-truck when Johnson let out a muffled yelp followed by a single shot from his M4. The upper torso of a reanimated corpse lay face down on the pavement, black fluid pouring from its ruined skull. Johnson sat on the ground and rolled his left pants leg over his calf. The zombie's teeth had punctured his pants and the skin of Johnson's leg. His death warrant had just been signed in blood.

Smith and Amanda stared at Johnson in disbelief.

"Looks like I'm going to take that boat ride across the river before you do, buddy."

"Yeah. Shit. I'm sorry, brother."

"Nothing to be sorry about. I should have been more careful. I'm not sure how long I've got, but let's try to find you guys some wheels before I turn. I'll take lead. That way you won't be surprised when I turn. Will you put me down when I do?"

"I promise you I will."

The two men hugged before forming in a column again, this time with Johnson taking the lead.

The neighborhood across the highway from Gander Mountain looked promising, with most of the cars in the driveways being older models, and only twenty minutes later they found an early 1980s GMC van. The A-Team van it was not, but after some work Smith hotwired the van and it ran. It ran poorly, but it ran. Thirty minutes and four backyard metal sheds later, three five-gallon gas cans had been located and the group was driving back onto the highway where their disabled Suburban still sat.

Johnson and Smith stood at the back of the Suburban and transferred the rest of their gear to their "new" van. Johnson gave Amanda his M4, his body armor, magazines and the rest of his gear that she might find useful. His face was ashen and his clammy skin betrayed the cold winter air. Johnson was going to die soon, and Smith had one more duty of love to carry out for his brother-in-arms. He and Johnson hugged, and Smith kissed Johnson on the forehead before Johnson turned to face away from his friend. Smith drew his pistol, muttered "Till Valhalla, brother," and pulled the trigger once. The bullet entered Johnson's head at the base of his skull, which killed him instantly and prevented him from rising from the dead as a walking corpse. Tears welled in Amanda's eyes and the famous speech from Henry V fell into her thoughts: "We few, we happy few, we band of brothers." This was the saddest, bravest and kindest act of love Amanda had ever witnessed.

CHAPTER 5

A dusty gloved hand reached into the large hole in the concrete floor and helped Odin climb out. From their location, surrounded by crates and fifty-five-gallon drums, the warehouse was pitch black in the very early morning before sunrise. The interior appeared grainy green, visible only to the four men kneeling in the middle next to the hole in the floor. They looked like aliens with their Night Observation Devices, NODs, hanging from their helmets, flipped in front of their faces.

Odin spoke in a hushed voice. "Yeah Chivo, it goes about a hundred meters north and then nothing. It doesn't look like a cave-in, it looks like someone demoed it already. We're just lucky the river is low or the tunnel would probably be full of water and goddamned rats."

The pale squat warehouse near Bulevar Juan Pablo and the Rio Grande River in Juarez, Mexico didn't look like much, but for Chivo and his four-man team, this building had been their best hope. For the past four months the four men known as Chivo, Odin, Apollo and Zennie had been operating illegally in Mexico. Former American Special Forces sheep-dipped into the CIA, they worked for a front company named Overland Shipping Consultants and were in the interior of Mexico battling the powerful drug cartels. The teams fought against the cartels' ultraviolent regime and tried to disrupt the constant flow of narcotics into the United States. Since the attack on the United States nearly seven weeks prior, the four-man team had fought their way north, trying to return to U.S. soil. The reports of the EMP event in the United States were less pronounced in Mexico; however, a lot of technology had failed. But now, trapped in a warehouse used by the drug cartels to smuggle drugs under the Rio Grande, they were surrounded by thousands of undead. They were in trouble.

"Chivo, what do you think? I'm not sure we're going to be able to get to the river and sneak over the fence without being detected," Apollo whispered.

Chivo shrugged. "We might have to double time it, run and gun and hope for the best."

Undead corpses scraped against the side of the building, dragging pieces of the fence and building off as the mass of bodies flowed like a river burst from a dam. The moans were so loud that the four men could barely hear each other's voices, but still they whispered for fear of being detected by the passing undead.

"Well mano, either way we can't hold up here. I don't think the building is going to remain intact for much longer. We've got to get back to CONUS and figure out what the fuck happened." Chivo was interrupted by the sound of the heavy metal fence around the building twisting and breaking. "Zennie, check the overhead door on the northeast corner. Make sure it's safe to open and see if there is a way to open it quietly. As long as we have stealth on our side we'll use it, but we'll break with bounding overwatch if we have to. As long as we make it across the river and through the fence, I think we'll be OK from the swarm."

Zennie nodded and evaporated into the shadows, walking to the roll-up door like a ghost. The other three team members moved towards the overhead door but took defensive positions in case they had to immediately engage any threats beyond the door. Through the grainy green world shown to Chivo through his NODs, he watched Zennie check the door for any IEDs. The business that operated this warehouse was only to provide a front for the cartel and to house the tunnel that crossed under the Rio Grande and into El Paso and the United States. The cartel was worse than the terrorists in the sandbox that Chivo fought before, more ruthless and driven only by money and power, not by any sort of moral code.

Zennie gave a thumbs-up with his left hand. The other three were in place with their M4 rifles held ready to immediately engage any threats, dead or living, once the door started to creep up.

BOOM!

Ears ringing and dizzy, Chivo was the first of his teammates on his feet, most of the force of the blast deflected by the large forklift he had been using for cover. A gaping hole remained where the northwest corner of the building once stood, moonlight flooding into the warehouse.

Stealth lost, the teammates checked in with each other, yelling across the ruined warehouse.

"Apollo, clear."

"Odin, clear."

"Chivo, clear."

Zennie didn't check in. Chivo, in a tactical crouch with his M4 rifle up, moved rapidly towards where the roll-up door once stood. Loud moans of the undead echoed in the large building and radiated through the bones of each of the team members. Chivo found Zennie's body, both of his legs missing below the knee, his left arm gone, and his neck bent at an impossible angle. "Dammit brother, now what the fuck are we going to do?"

Chivo grabbed his dead teammate and hefted him over his shoulder in a fireman's carry just as Apollo and Odin made it to the blast site. The mass of undead was already stumbling over the brick and debris through the hole that opened the building to the street.

"Contact left!"

"Contact right!"

Odin and Apollo called out at nearly the same time as they began engaging the approaching dead. The staccato sound of the team's rifles was drowned out by the sheer number of the dead shambling down the street and into the destroyed building, all of them attracted by the loud explosion. Only a quarter mile stood between the team and the relative safety found on the United States' side of the heavy border fence, but even then they would only be away from this group of zombies and would be on the edge of El Paso. Large cities spelled trouble.

The Special Forces community never left a teammate behind if at all possible, so, trusting his teammates, Chivo let his M4 hang on the sling and carried Zennie's body on his shoulders. Chivo's shirt, his plate carrier, and the rest of his gear became drenched in blood. After the previous forty-nine days, the three men were exhausted and could only keep a pace just faster than the dead shambling after them. The team made it away from the destroyed warehouse and to the four-lane blacktop of Bulevar Juan Pablo. Abandoned on the road were a handful of cars and trucks left to rot on the desert highway after the EMP attack disabled them. Rounding the corner of a large box truck, Chivo ran chest first into a walking, rotting corpse. Already off balance carrying Zennie's body, Chivo fell forward with a loud grunt, knocking the walking corpse to the ground beneath him. Zennie's body fell over Chivo's head with a wet thud onto the pavement. Instinctively, Chivo pushed himself up on the undead's stomach with his left hand, but his hand sank into the rotting flesh while his right hand drew the Glock pistol carried on his right thigh. With a single shot, the undead's skull exploded into a slimy black mass on the roadway.

Chivo quickly reholstered his pistol and retrieved his dead teammate's body. "Sorry brother, but we're at least going to get you back home to American soil."

The steady rhythm of Apollo and Odin firing their rifles was interrupted only by calls of "Loading!" and "Covering!" whenever either would have to rapidly change magazines. The undead horde behind them was staggering in number and the smell was nearly overwhelming. Flies buzzed like a thick black cloud over the walking undead.

The team trudged over the desert berm and down into the dry river bed of the Rio Grande. Feeling closer to their goal, they jogged up the other side of the riverbank and onto American soil. If they were going to die at least they would die together and on home soil. The three men moved quickly to a large gate used by the border agents for their patrols. Chivo leaned Zennie's body against the fence and pulled a pair of bolt cutters out of the pack on his back. He cut the links of the fence as fast as he could. There would be no way for them to open the heavy gate, so they were reduced to cutting a hole in the fence and securing it the best they could once they passed through.

Apollo called out "Loading!" and dropped another empty M4 magazine into his dump pouch before reaching to the front of his armor carrier to retrieve another fresh magazine to reload his rifle. His hand swept across the front of his carrier and found no magazines. He was out of ammo. Apollo turned and ripped a fresh magazine off his dead teammate's gear and quickly brought his rifle back into the fight—none too soon, as one of the walking corpses was only ten feet from Chivo's back.

"Chivo, you might want to hurry the fuck up. Things are starting to get a little sporty out here."

"Easy mano, I'm almost done."

Chivo pushed a three-foot-tall hole in the bottom of the fence open and crawled through before grabbing Zennie's body and dragging him through with him. Apollo and Oden climbed through the fence with only seconds to spare, the first of the horde of walking corpses only yards behind them. Oden stuck the barrel of his rifle through a link in the fence and continued to drop the undead at the leading element of the horde, while Apollo took four pairs of plastic quick cuffs and secured the hole in the fence as best he could using the plastic handcuffs like zip ties.

Chivo pulled the remaining fully-loaded M4 magazines off Zennie's gear and passed them out to Apollo and Odin. In a loose defensive circle around their dead teammate's body, facing outward and watching for new threats, the team took a moment to discuss their next move.

Odin spoke first. "OK guys. SITREP, whatcha got?"

"We need ammo," Apollo responded.

"We need wheels in a bad way," Chivo chimed in.

"First I think we need to find a spot to hunker down to see if that horde passes. I'm afraid that even with the fence, more undead from this side will be attracted to the commotion. Besides, we need to take care of Zennie's body," Odin replied.

Something clamped onto the back of Chivo's pants, causing him to jump forward and away from his teammates. Zennie was back and moving but he was not with the living. "Shit!" Chivo drew his pistol and fired a single shot, striking Zennie in the skull.

"Fuck dude, a man can't even find peace in death anymore."

Chivo pulled Zennie's body back onto his shoulders, now that he was dead for good, and pointed to the neighborhood to his right. "Let's grab one of those houses, lay up for a bit and see if we can figure out what our next move is. If we're lucky, we'll find some food too."

The other two nodded and took off in a slow jog, spread out in a defensive line, towards the homes across the highway, hoping they would find a safe place to regroup.

CHAPTER 8

Near Corsicana, Texas
February 13, Year 1

The situation continued to deteriorate. Low gray clouds blocked the early morning sun, the start to another flat day of barely surviving. Clint Smith stood on the roof of the 1972 GMC van and surveyed the road ahead of them through his binoculars. Amanda stood at the rear of the van, Johnson's former M4 rifle in her hands, watching for any undead to catch up that were following the van as it passed. Clint climbed down from the roof and thumbed through a much-worn DeLorme Texas atlas. The atlas was an absolute godsend; they'd found it after the first large folding atlas was destroyed.

Only the day before they'd found the ancient but still-running van outside of the town of Athens. The fight they'd endured to clear that town was staggering, but they were beginning to get close to their destination. In the forty-nine days since the attack, Amanda estimated they'd traveled just over three hundred miles, and twenty-five of those days were spent covering short distances on foot.

Originally the plan had been to travel north out of Little Rock and to I-40 towards Colorado, but the fighting was so intense that they were forced to travel south. The first few days after the attack and the oily chemical sprayed by the large flight of aircraft that passed overhead, the number of the undead grew exponentially. On the small highways found in the piney woods of east Texas, the number of undead seemed manageable, but near the Dallas/Fort Worth area the number of abandoned vehicles on the road and the shambling corpses increased starkly, sapping any positive outlook Amanda had still clung to.

Clint pointed east. "If we take that road to the right we should be able to skirt around Corsicana, but I don't think we'll be able to skip having to travel on I-45. How much ammo do you have left?"

Amanda looked at the M4 magazines in the carrier around her midsection, Johnson's own armor carrier that was given to her just before Clint shot him. "About two hundred rounds."

"Shit. We're probably going to need every last one of them."

Clint climbed into the driver's seat, quickly joined in the passenger seat by Amanda. With the windshield missing, both of them were quickly soaked by the cold rain. Farm-to Market 1128, thankfully, was devoid of undead in the road, as was FM 3041—that is, until they reached the feeder road for I-45. Clint stopped the van, engine still running, and climbed onto the roof again with his binoculars.

"Southbound is a damn parking lot. Looks like there was a wreck south of us, probably before the EMP hit. Northbound isn't too bad, but I can see movement between the vehicles."

Amanda grimaced. Movement on the highway could only be the undead. Returning to the driver's seat, Clint turned the van right, drove down the feeder road and onto the Interstate. They were able to drive around the disabled vehicles and the small groups of undead, but the driving was slow, about fifteen miles per hour, as they weaved from shoulder to shoulder to pass all the vehicles and walking corpses. Three vertical strands of cable separated the northbound and southbound lanes. Even though the cable was in place to prevent a vehicle from crossing the median and causing a head-on collision, it wasn't effective at stopping the undead, but it did cause the walking corpses to fall face forward into the grass as they tried to walk through the median to follow the passing van.

After the weeks of incredible hardship, Amanda giggled at the bodies tripping over the wire and no longer retaining the cognitive ability to even attempt to catch their fall. Each of the corpses broke its fall by planting its face into the dirt. Clint looked at Amanda suspiciously, believing—and rightly so—that she was beginning to have a bit of a mental breakdown.

Thirty minutes of slow driving passed before Clint took the exit for FM 1126. The north Texas farmland, sparsely populated, left few people to be killed. Some of the homes they passed looked like they had wisps of smoke coming out of the chimneys. Amanda assumed survivors probably lived there, but after their last run-in with a survivor group, she simply did not trust them to be benign. Clint swerved the van around another group of undead as they turned onto Highway 287. Those were the last shambling undead that Amanda saw before they turned onto TX-34 and drove across a bridge spanning a small lake.

Clint turned after the lake and followed the small road through the countryside. Neither of them spoke. Amanda curled up in her seat, shivering from the cold rain coming through the windshield. Clint stopped the van at a gate, blocking the road next to a small guard shack with a sign reading "Waxahachie Creek Park."

"Here? This is where we're going?"

A half-dozen undead shuffled towards the van from inside the park.

"This is a backup facility. It's fairly new and hopefully it's still intact."

Clint didn't worry about how to raise the pole acting as a gate across the road. He simply drove through it, breaking the fiberglass arm from its base. Amanda drew her pistol and shot the two undead closest to the van through the gap left by the missing windshield. The van turned right and Clint drove quickly onto a gravel drive, stopping by a large metal shed. More undead began approaching the van from the darkness of the woods in the park.

"And here we are, Madam Secretary."

"You're back to calling me Madam Secretary now, baby?"

Clint smiled.

"A metal shed. Really? The new secret government facility is a metal shed?"

A rare smile spread across Clint's face and he gave Amanda a wink. "Do me a favor and keep the welcoming party off me. It will take me a little bit of time to get the shed open."

Amanda had no choice but to believe him, even after his confession three weeks prior that he and his dead partner Chuck Johnson weren't really with the FBI but were in actuality highly trained agents working for another government agency that he would only refer to as "another government agency." She really was Alice, and this new world was her rabbit hole.

She climbed over the dash and onto the roof of the van, quickly scanned the approaching threats, and laid two full M4 magazines on the roof in front of her. Then Amanda lay down on the top of the van in a prone firing position. Taking aim at the closest walking corpse, she concentrated on slowing her breathing and gently pressed the trigger to the rear. For a woman who had never had any sort of formal training in firearms, she was thankful that Smith and Johnson did at least take the time to teach her how to handle an M4, which she'd put to more practice than she ever could have guessed.

Clint walked to the side of the metal shed and opened the electrical fuse panel. He flipped a few of the breakers and the whole box lifted up from the building to reveal a keypad like that of an old telephone. Between shots engaging the approaching dead, Amanda tried to steal glances as to what Clint was doing. Clint tapped in a long series of numbers quickly from memory, like he would punch in his PIN at an ATM.

Clint lowered the box and closed the cover before taking a firing position, leaning across the short hood of the van. Amanda felt like she missed with every other shot, but Clint was quickly thinning the approaching undead to a manageable level when Amanda was startled by the sound of water erupting into the air in the lake like a geyser two hundred yards away. The water being blown into the air was visible over the top of the thick trees. A full minute later the geyser stopped, and with a loud hiss the metal shed slid backwards on its foundation to reveal a concrete ramp leading to a large well-lit area that looked a bit like a parking garage.

"You have got to be shitting me."

Clint smiled again. "Nope. Get in the van. We should drive in before we attract any more welcoming committee friends."

The van easily cleared the concrete roof as it drove underground, following a series of ramps back and forth, continuing deeper underground before leveling out in a large flat open area. The area was staggeringly cavernous. Clint stopped the van at the bottom of the last ramp, rolled down his window, and punched another series of numbers into a keypad. High above them and with a loud hiss, the metal shed slid back into place, sealing the entrance.

"Welcome to Osiris, the new land of the living."

Amanda looked side to side in awe. The open area they were in appeared to be at least two hundred yards long and at least as wide, all of it well lit with overhead lighting. Clint drove to a large metal door with another keypad. After entering another series of numbers, the large metal blast door slowly swung outward.

"The geyser of water in the lake was from this place," said Clint. "The interior was sealed with pure nitrogen to preserve everything, to keep any contaminants out and to prevent any organisms from taking home."

"OK, fine, but why here? Why this part of Texas? I don't understand."

"Do you remember the Superconductor Super Collider that was canceled back in the early 1990s?"

"Yeah, vaguely."

"OK, this is the result of that project. From the beginning, the entire project was a front to build this facility. The scientists didn't know that, the workers didn't know that, no one knew it except a small number of people cleared into this black project. The SSC was never intended to be completed, so cost overruns and some skillful manipulation of the media helped push public pressure to cancel the project, just as we planned. The tunnel-boring machine continued with a new series of contractors past the publicly known fourteen miles of tunnel to here, which is under the lake we drove across. Just a bit over two hundred feet below the lake, actually."

"Is there anyone else here?"

"Can't be. When the startup sequence started, the geyser you saw was the nitrogen being purged and replaced by air we can breathe. Before that happened, the air inside would have killed anyone trying to breathe it."

"What do we do now?"

"We go inside, take hot showers, put on new clothes, have a hot meal and try to figure out if any of my other teammates from my project survived. We have a mission to complete."

"What project is that?"

"Project Lazarus."

CHAPTER 7

Cortez, CO
February 13, Year 1

Jake stood on a table in the middle of the cafeteria, addressing his group of survivors. As of this morning, with the birth of a healthy baby girl, the number of souls in the school-turned-survivor-commune had grown to forty-two. Scavenging operations were planned in detail and now had the added needs for a newborn. They were carried out by rotating teams of men. While one team held the operations slot for three days, another team provided compound security for a day shift, and the third held the security job for a night shift. A fourth team stood down for three days of rest and family time. The three day rotation seemed to work well now that there were enough people to man the teams and keep the rotation running. Perhaps as more people arrived and became a part of the survivor group, the rotations could be spread out with more down time. That would be a welcome logistical problem to overcome, but the other side to that coin was with more people came the need for more supplies. For the past nine days the scavenging teams had been harassed by The Tribe. So far the religious fanatics hadn't attacked the middle school, but they were laying ambushes for the scavenging team while they were outside of the fence.

From the roof of the middle school the security teams could see the highway west of the football stadium and had a clear view of approach, but the scattering of homes to the east gave The Tribe cover to move for an attack. During the past four weeks special scavenging trips had been completed for supplies and a chain-link fence was now erected surrounding the school grounds from Maple Street down to

Second Street and Pine to tie into the fence already standing around the athletic complex. So far the fence has been successful in keeping the walkers out of the school building and off the property, although there had been an increase in the number of walkers coming to the fence line.

For Jake, Sara, and the others in their group, life was going as well as it could be given their current situation—that is, until the religious nuts showed up. Not a single person in their group had heard of The Tribe before the attack and theories abounded as to their origin. Some said they were in town but lived in secret; others said that their proclaimed prophet organized his cult after everything went to hell.

Jake looked at the people gathered in the cafeteria. The only members missing were the ones currently assigned to the security patrol. Jake had briefed each of them personally an hour before while they stood their post.

"As all of you know, the mounting attacks continue to hamper our scavenging teams. Supplies are exceptionally low and starting tonight we are reducing rations in an attempt to make what we have last."

Moans rumbled through the group.

"We have to decide what our plan of action will be. After much thought, the only options I could come up with were we hunker down and let The Tribe try to lay siege to our compound, we go on the attack against them, or we flee and relocate away from their area."

Jake looked at the men, women, and older children standing around him. He considered each of them his family. "We'll raise a vote if no one has any other suggestions."

"All in favor of relocating?"

None of the members raised their hands.

"All in favor of going on the offensive against The Tribe?"

Some of the men and a few of the older children raised their hands, seven in total.

"All in favor of hunkering down and trying to ride them out?"

The rest of the group raised their hands, winning the vote.

"OK, well, the group has spoken, so if each team leader would confer with their member families about further suggestions for our chosen plan of action, please report to me by sundown. We have a lot of work to do."

CHAPTER 8

Odin crossed over the low concrete barrier of the Cesar E. Chavez Border Highway before helping Chivo pull Zennie's body across and onto his own shoulders. Blood continued to drain out of Zennie's mangled body and Odin was quickly soaked in his blood. The vehicles on the highway were sparse, but after the running gun fight and Chivo's experience on the Mexican highway, the three of them gave each vehicle a wide berth as they crossed the four-lane highway. Reaching the sandy road shoulder, Chivo took out his bolt cutters and began cutting the chain-link fence separating the neighborhood of smaller houses ahead of them from the highway behind them. Not concerned about a horde of zombies in pursuit, Chivo took the time to cut the entire fence from top to bottom to make it easier to carry Zennie's body through.

Apollo climbed through the fence first and squatted on the small residential street, rifle up, scanning for any potential threats, living or dead. Odin quickly joined his teammate, still carrying Zennie's body. Joined by Chivo, Apollo whispered, "OK, which one?"

"Mano, that brown one on the right has a Marine Corps flag on the porch. I choose that one."

Odin quickly agreed. "Maybe that Marine has supplies or ammo or who knows what. You never know with those crazy fuckers."

Apollo took point, M4 at the ready, scanning. Odin, the least able to fight, stayed in the middle while he carried Zennie's body, and Chivo brought up the rear of their loose column. The small one-story home was surrounded by a low chain-link fence, but the gate across the driveway was unlocked. Once entering the yard, Chivo was careful to quietly reset the gate's latch. Odin leaned Zennie's body against a newer Chrysler four-door car that sat in the driveway. Apollo checked around the corner of the backyard and found an old, rusted brown pickup behind the home. Chivo checked the small shed in the backyard and found a small riding lawn mower, a full gas can, and a line trimmer. Odin slowly turned the knob of the side door for the home and was relieved to find it unlocked. Their hopes of a death-free home were quickly dashed when Chivo pointed to a window. "Flies, lots of damn flies on the inside of the window."

"Fuck, Chivo. What do you think?"

Chivo shrugged and loudly tapped on the glass of the window before stacking with his teammates at the door for a fast entry.

Chivo squeezed Apollo's shoulder. Apollo leaned forward to Odin and whispered, "Lots of flies, probably a dead body."

"Sure, but nothing reacted to the knocking, so maybe we'll be lucky. Slow and steady on this one."

Odin gently pushed the door open and the smell of weeks-old death immediately overwhelmed the three. Apollo shook his head, flipped the NODs on the front of his helmet down, and pulled the shemagh around his neck up to cover his mouth and nose. M4 raised, Odin slowly walked into the house. Apollo and Chivo followed. Once inside they found the house neat and well-kept. The three small bedrooms were quickly cleared and the reason for the smell and the flies was also found. A bloated corpse, skin rippling from the insects underneath, lay dead in the blood-splattered bathtub. Most of the man's skull was missing and a blood-covered chrome revolver lay on the floor next to the tub. Odin shut the door to the bathroom.

Chivo went outside and returned with Zennie's body, carried him to the master bedroom and lay his brother-in-arms on the bed while he searched the dresser in the room for any supplies. A box of .38 +P ammo was found in a sock drawer, presumably for the revolver lying on the floor of the bathroom. Chivo set the box of ammo on the dresser and figured that no one would want to take the revolver and they didn't need ammo for a gun they didn't have.

Odin stood in the living room looking at a shadow box sitting on the shelf above the TV. He pointed to it. "Guys, check this out. Looks like this guy was a staff sergeant in the Marines and was a Vietnam Vet. Guess after all of that, this new world was too much of a fight for him."

Apollo pointed to the case next to the shadow box. "Hand me that American flag."

Oden opened the wooden flag case, removed the American flag, and handed it to Apollo. The three of them walked to the master bedroom with the flag. Chivo and Odin unfolded the flag and draped it over Zennie's body. The three of them stood silently over their fallen teammate's body before leaving the room and shutting the door behind them.

Searching the rest of the house for supplies took very little time as the home wasn't very big. The cupboards were completely bare of any non-perishable food; in fact, no food was to be found at all. Odin shrugged, "Well, I guess we know one of the reasons why the old guy decided to check out.

"I'm going to check that old truck in the backyard. Maybe we'll get lucky. It's old enough that it should have survived the EMP." With that, Apollo made for the door, but stopped.

Even from inside the house the three of them stiffened at the sound of the moaning undead. Chivo gently pushed the curtain across the front window aside. "Amigos, there's probably two dozen walking corpses out there."

"Is the fence still up and closed?" Apollo asked.

"Yeah, looks like it."

"Good. I'm still going to check the truck."

Apollo walked out of the side door and returned about ten minutes later. Chivo still stood by the front window with the curtain pulled aside.

"Hey, it's an old Ford Ranger back when that was a full-sized truck. The battery seems to be good and I poured the lawn mower gas into the tank. The dash lit up and the gauge showed half a tank, but who knows if that's right or if that gauge still works. I think we now have wheels, but the Chrysler is in the way and we've got to do something about the walkers at the fence."

Odin spoke first. "If we clear out the walkers, we can push the car out of the way."

Chivo turned away from the window. "Sure, but there are more of those fuckers shuffling our direction. We don't have the ammo for this. We need a distraction. But we don't have a plan yet. Once we leave here, where do we go?"

Apollo answered, "Fort Bliss. We hit a couple of supply shops, get some MREs, some ammo, and maybe we can get some commo gear. Then we get out in the open desert, get safe, regroup, and try to find out who is left in charge. If there is anyone maybe they already have a plan in action. I think we should wait for sunrise to save our NODs, and besides, it'll give us a chance to rest for a minute. I don't think we're going to get to rest again for a while."

CHAPTER 8

Near Terlingua, TX
February 14, Year 1

Bexar kept the old Jeep Wagoneer's speedometer as close to fifty miles per hour as he could in an attempt to conserve the gas they had. The trip ahead of them was very long. The Reed family—Bexar, Jessie, and their young daughter Keeley—were fleeing Big Bend National Park; their friends had been killed by the Pistoleros, a biker gang who survived after the fall of man by plundering and looting survivors. Pulled behind the Wagoneer was an RV that Bexar had scavenged from one of the RV parks in the confines of the national park. The owner was missing and presumed dead, so Bexar didn't have to kill any living person to take it, and to Bexar that was a significant distinction.

As isolated as Texas Highway 118 was, Bexar constantly checked his side mirrors, worried that the bikers would come rumbling up behind him. Bexar's plan was to take his family and skirt along the Rio Grande to stay away from the major highways as long as possible in an attempt to elude the biker gang while trying to reach Groom Lake, Nevada. A man calling himself "Cliff" promised shelter, supplies, and a safe haven for the Reed family. All they had to do was get there. Bexar turned left and onto FM 170, towards the ghost town of Terlingua.

Keeley played happily in the back seat, oblivious to the horrors of the previous day when she had been sheltered in Bexar's cabin. In the cabin she was protected from the gun battle that killed Jack, Sandra, and their son Will. In the distance ahead of Bexar's Wagoneer, a lone motorcycle rider was only a speck on the horizon, blending in with the asphalt. The morning sun glinted on the motorcycle's chrome and caught Jessie's attention.

"Bexar, do you see that?"

"Yeah, looks like something in the road. Maybe a motorcycle. Or maybe what's left of one."

"It kind of looks like it's moving. Do you think it's moving?" Jessie asked.

Before Bexar could answer, the Jeep's windshield exploded inward, showering the interior with shards of glass. The report of the rifle reached their ears just after the glass hit their faces.

"Fuck! Jessie, are you hit? What about Keeley?" Bexar yelled over the wind noise.

Keeley, fastened into her safety seat, screamed in terror. Jessie told Bexar she was OK as she climbed over the front seat to get into the back with her daughter. A lone figure stood in the middle of the highway, away from the parked motorcycle, with a rifle shouldered and pointing towards the approaching Jeep. Bexar had no cover, no place to hide and protect his family, so he pushed the accelerator pedal all the way to the floor. The old Jeep's engine roared in protest and even with the RV in tow the speedometer needle steadily rose past sixty miles per hour and then seventy miles per hour.

The biker fired three more shots from his large AR-10 rifle before trying to dive out of the way of the Jeep. Bexar's face bent in anger at the man attacking his family and followed the lone rifleman with the steering wheel of his Jeep.

The impact of the man against the front of the Jeep was much harder than Bexar expected. Jessie screamed. Blood exploded from the biker's skull as he bounced off the hood of the Jeep and fell forward. The front left tire ran over the man's body, jostling the Jeep. That tire exploded in a shower of rubber chunks. The Jeep lurched hard to the left. Bexar fought to correct the action with the steering wheel, but the RV swung out from behind the Jeep, momentum overruling Bexar's frantic efforts to keep control of the vehicle.

The rest of the windows in the Jeep exploded, shattering while the Jeep fell to its side and began to roll. The RV came off the hitch, and the safety chains keeping it attached to the back of the Jeep pulled the back end of the Jeep in an arch following the heavy trailer's path. Jessie fell over the front seat and flopped onto the front floorboard of the Jeep. Bexar gripped the steering wheel as hard as he could and watched the horizon spin with each roll. Finally it stopped. Everything stopped into an incredible silence that lasted only a breath before being pierced by Keeley's screams. Bexar brushed the pieces of broken safety glass off his face before opening his eyes and seeing his wife's body crumpled on the passenger floorboard. Luckily, the Jeep had landed upright.

"Fuck. Damnit, Jessie, talk to me." Bexar unlatched his seatbelt and leaned over to check on his wife. Jessie was breathing and her pulse was strong. Bexar took a deep breath and tried to open the driver's door with no luck. Three hard kicks later, Bexar forced the door open and climbed out of the destroyed Wagoneer. The RV's safety chains broke and the RV lay in a shattered mess of fiberglass and insulation about one hundred feet from the road in the desert. Keeley continued to scream. Bexar gently brushed the glass off her face while checking the rest of her body for any obvious injuries. He found none. Stealing a glance at Jessie, he could see she was bleeding badly.

Bexar forced himself to take a deep breath and try to think through the next step. To the north he saw a small motel and a road going up the hill. The road to the Terlingua ghost town. Ahead, about a half-dozen undead, attracted by the rifle fire and the incredible wreck, staggered out of the desert and down the hill from Terlingua towards Bexar and his family.

Bexar climbed into the Jeep and dug around the mess of gear for his rifle. The AR-15 was in the back of the Jeep, having been tossed there during the collision. A quick check and it appeared that the rifle was undamaged. Bexar felt dizzy and tried to shoulder his rifle. Unsteady on his feet, Bexar leaned against the crushed hood of the Jeep and took aim at the closest walking corpse. Three shots later, he was able to move on to the next approaching threat. Bexar's aim was badly shaken and it took a full magazine of .223 to put down all the zombies, but all the threats were resolved for now.

Keeley, still screaming in her car seat, was Bexar's first priority. Jessie would have to wait, but since she was unconscious, hopefully any more approaching dead wouldn't notice her. Bexar cut the car seat's harness and gently pulled his daughter to his shoulder with a hug.

"It's OK baby, we're OK. Daddy's got you and you're safe."

Keeley in his arms, Bexar jogged towards the hotel and stopped at the door to the first room he came to. The door was locked. Bexar drew his pistol and kicked in the door, Keeley held tight against his shoulder with his left arm. He was relieved to find that only the smell of stale air and bedding. Bexar made a quick check to make sure there were no surprises under the bed or in the bathroom before he sat Keeley at the foot of the bed.

"I've got to get Mommy. I'll be right back. Try to be quiet. I love you."

Bexar pulled the broken door closed and hoped it would hold closed. Keeley screamed and banged on the door with her tiny hands. Bexar tried to jog back to the Jeep, tripping several times, still dizzy from the wreck. Reaching the Jeep, he pulled his go-bag from the back seat and placed it on the cracked asphalt before climbing into the front seat to get his wife. Bexar made a fast blood check and found that the blood covering her face was from a deep gash on her head. If the world were still normal they would be headed to the hospital to get stitches, but for now all they had were each other.

As gently as he could, but quickly, Bexar extricated his wife from under the Jeep's dash and laid her unconscious body on the road next to his go-bag. Digging in his bag, he retrieved the trauma kit. Bexar decided against the Quikclot, since this wasn't an arterial bleed, and pressed a large wad of gauze onto the wound before wrapping her head with an Israeli bandage to hold it all in place. Bexar shouldered his go-bag, knelt, and picked up his wife. Struggling, he was eventually able to get her on his shoulders in a fireman's carry. Bexar moved as quickly as he could while still being careful not to fall. His vision was blurry and he thought he might throw up. Reaching the hotel room where Keeley was, he heard her screams from outside the door.

So had two more undead.

Bexar slowed his walk and drew his pistol. As quietly as he could, he walked up behind the two zombies clawing at the hotel door, put the muzzle of his pistol against the back of the skull of the first, and pulled the trigger before turning and shooting the second zombie in the face at point-blank range.

Pistol reholstered, Bexar looked back at the wrecked Jeep. He should have chosen a room that couldn't be seen from the highway. Bexar left Keeley screaming in the hotel room without opening the door and walked further away from the road to another hotel room, one that couldn't be seen from the road, and banged on the window. There was no reaction from inside the room from the noise. Bexar gently sat Jessie on the ground and leaned his unconscious wife against the wall while he kicked in the door and quickly cleared the small hotel room. Bexar pulled his wife into the room and laid her on the bed before leaving and running back to the first hotel room to get his daughter. She was no longer screaming but was sobbing, being scared and alone. He picked Keeley up and was greeted by her little arms squeezing his neck in a big hug. Bexar was sure that in under an hour she would probably be laughing and playing. Little kids rebounded so quickly.

"OK baby, Mommy needs you to snuggle so she'll feel better, and she needs you to be extra quiet so she can sleep. Do you think you can do that?"

Keeley's little head nodded yes, her face wet with tears. Bexar sat Keeley on the bed next to his wife, shut the door, and returned to his destroyed Jeep. Fearful that another passing biker would find them and they would lose what little provisions they still had, Bexar needed to gather all their gear and he needed to get it hidden quickly.

CHAPTER 10

Big Bend National Park
February 14, Year 1

"Prospects, get your asses up here!"

Six prospects ran from the back of the group of motorcycles to the front where the Pistoleros new club president, Russell, was standing at the entrance to the Basin, the dumpsters still partially blocking the roadway.

"Where the fuck is Stinky?"

The prospect standing closest to Russell spoke up. "We don't know, Prez. He stopped to patch his tire and never caught back up."

"OK, whatever. You six get up there and kill every motherfucker you find. I want these assholes dead, and I want our brothers who are dead put down for good. Secure the deuce and anything of value you find. Honk four times when it's clear and you're done. Got it?"

Russell and the rest of the full-patch members of the motorcycle club hung back by the dumpsters that Jack and Bexar had used to block the road into the Basin. Russell didn't know that Bexar and his family had already escaped. All they knew was that the club had intercepted radio transmissions between some people here and some guy named Cliff, and that the group here was loaded with supplies, food and ammo. The motorcycle club wanted what they had and they came to take it. They would kill whoever had it, but for the first time since the start, this group fought back. Russell survived by retreating back to the club's base camp for help.

The eleven fully patched members of the club waited with their president in the cool high desert air, smoking cigarettes and drinking lukewarm beer from the saddlebags on their motorcycles while they waited for Stinky to show up. They had nothing else to do while they waited for the prospects to kill all the remaining people in the Basin without risking any more full members.

To Russell and the rest of the men drinking beer by their motorcycles, the morning passed slowly. Sporadic gunfire echoed off the mountains above them. Seven beers into his waiting, Russell finally heard a car horn honk four times. That was the sign, so the men threw their empty bottles on the side of the road, started their motorcycles, and road into the Basin side by side in a column of two.

"Where the fuck are the rest of you?" Russell growled after shutting off his motorcycle.

"Jake and Fungus got bit so we put them down. They're over there with the rest of our brothers." Tiny pointed to a row of bodies with motorcycle vests laid over each one.

"Fine, where's the dickhead who started all of this?"

"We found him, his woman and a kid. All dead."

"Were they walkers?"

"No, just dead, shot in the head."

Russell walked to where the prospect pointed and looked at the body. "You dumbass, he was already dead when he was shot in the head! Find the guy who shot him! Find the other guy!"

Russell looked across the pile of bodies and around to the motels and the Ranger Station nervously before walking over to the bullet-riddled motel. He ducked under the walkway, trying to hide from an enemy sniper he believed was hiding in the trees on the hillside.

Another prospect ran up to Russell. "Prez, you're going to want to see this. We just found a bunch of good shit in one of the cabins!"

Russell followed the prospect up the hill towards Bexar and Jack's cabins.

"The water works, the toilets flush, there's two vehicles and there's a bunch of other shit."

"Great. Go get me Buzzer."

Russell stood near Bexar's cabin, looking at all they had found, when Buzzer walked up.

"Buzzer, you're the new VP. Get someone to go find Stinky. Send some prospects to get the others, the women, and the rest of the gear. We're moving Church here. Also, get me a couple of scouts. We've got to find the asshole who did all this."

Buzzer nodded and walked off, yelling for prospects.

CHAPTER 11

Groom Lake, NV
February 14, Year 1

Cliff walked into the radio hut. Major Wright and the airman on duty sat with their backs to the door, both wearing headphones plugged into the radio console. The airman made notes on his yellow notepad while speaking to someone on the other side of the microphone, while Wright zoomed in the satellite's latest photo over a location that Cliff didn't recognize.

On the wall to their left hung an old large paper map of the United States. Where the airman had found the old paper map was anyone's guess. Colored push pins were placed sporadically across the map, each pin representing a group of survivors that the radio operators at Groom Lake had contacted since their arrival on the C-130 from Peterson AFB in Colorado. That aircraft sat disabled in the middle of the dry lake bed above them after being damaged on landing.

Quickly counting, Cliff found more than sixty pins spread across the U.S., mostly in the middle of the country between the Rocky and Appalachian Mountains. The different colored pins represented the approximate number of survivors in each group. If Cliff remembered what Wright told him correctly, that would mean that there were currently a little over two hundred survivors that the airmen had contacted and accounted for. That was good news for Cliff. If there were survivors, then there was a country to save, and that was his mission.

Wright sneezed loudly, breaking his concentration from the computer screen, and he noticed Cliff standing in the room. The Air Force major waved Cliff over to the console and removed his headphones.

"Cliff, we're contacting more and more survivors daily. It's very strange. I don't think the EMP affected every area the same. There seem to be pockets where some of the electronics survived. Or at least there are a good number of individuals finding access to radio equipment that was shielded enough to survive."

"Major if that's the case, there's a good chance that there are many more who survived with no way to contact us. We're going to need to formulate a plan on reaching out to those we can't contact." The airman at the radio snapped his fingers, interrupting their conversation, and waved them to his console before pushing a button to activate the external speaker.

A women's frantic voice filled the room. "He's back and he's trying to get inside. We ran out of ammo a week ago. I don't know what to do!"

The airman tried to sound calm and hopeful for the woman. "Can you get into the attic to hide? Take water with you if you can, but the important thing is to be out of sight and be as quiet as possible. They usually lose interest and leave."

Wright pointed to a house on his computer screen. "That's the house she's in. This image is thirty-seven hours old and it is the latest pass we have. Her name is Jamie. She's thirty years old and in a town just south of Houston, Texas. Her neighbor was apparently a bit of a prepper and took Jamie and her husband into his home to shelter about a week after the attack. The neighbor was bitten about a week ago while repairing the radio antenna on his roof. He brought the radio online, hence their being able to contact us, but he died shortly after. She and her husband made contact with us about three days ago. They are nearly out of food and are completely out of ammo, so her husband left yesterday to scavenge for supplies. He has since returned as a walking corpse and has brought some new friends with him."

Cliff and Wright turned their attention back to the radio when the speaker crackled to life again. Loud banging and the moans of the undead came through the open mic clearly, followed by a loud crash.

"Oh my God, oh my God, they're inside now ... Mark, no, please don't. Mark, it's me, it's Jamie, please don't, don't ..."

The radio hut filled with sorrowful screams of pain before the radio went silent, the microphone's push to talk apparently released. The airman sitting at the radio console looked pale. Sweat dripped down his forehead.

"Will, why don't you take ten minutes. I'll take care of things here until you get back."

"Thanks, Major."

The airman shakily rose to his feet and walked out of the room, looking slightly ill.

Wright walked to the paper map on the wall and replaced the white pin just south of Houston with a black one. "That's the fourth person we've heard die on the radio like that."

Cliff shook his head. "We've got to figure out a way to help these people. We need to come up with a plan, a way to get survivors here where they'll be safe. Or at the very least we need to figure out a way to get them the supplies they need, be it food, water, ammo or whatever."

Wright nodded. "To do that we need a helicopter, but even then without any refueling assets we couldn't get one all the way to Houston and back. Besides, all we have for pilots is Arcuni, and he could barely fly what we came here in, much less a helicopter. What we need is another plane, something we can land on rough roads and short strips."

"Like another C-130?"

"Yes, but the one sitting on the lake bed above us won't fly again without a serious amount of parts and skilled work, neither of which we have."

"OK Major, since you volunteered, why don't you start looking for something we can take? Something that a small team could drive from here to get and bring back. Something close."

CHAPTER 12

Terlingua, Texas
February 14, Year 1

Across the parking lot from the small hotel room where Bexar had left his still unconscious wife and his daughter stood the hotel office. Leaning against a low stone wall next to the building was a wheelbarrow. Bexar jogged across the parking lot, righted the wheel barrow, and moved quickly to the wrecked Jeep and destroyed RV. Reaching the Jeep, Bexar quickly began loading the wheel barrow with the meager supplies they had escaped with from Big Bend.

After returning to the hotel room with the first load, Bexar dumped the wheelbarrow outside the door. He looked at the zombies he had killed moments before and realized that one of them didn't look too bad, like he was a freshly turned walker. With a new idea, Bexar hefted the corpse and dumped him into the wheelbarrow before returning to the Jeep. Out of breath but scared to be caught in the open if the bikers came looking for their missing club member, Bexar dumped the corpse by the driver's door of his Wagoneer. He then lifted the corpse into the front seat, put the seat belt on him and let him slump over the steering wheel before bending the damaged door closed.

Bexar hoped that if he was lucky and if someone found the wreck, they would assume that he was dead behind the wheel and leave it at that. It might give him the chance to hide his family. Two more trips with the wheelbarrow later, everything the family had to survive with was off the road and in their tiny hotel room.

Opening an MRE, Bexar gave Keeley the cracker and the brownie, which finally helped slow his daughter's crying into weak sobs while she ate. Bexar wet a towel with the water left in the tank of the toilet in the bathroom and started wiping the drying blood off his wife's face. Bexar worried about what to do. If she had any serious injury or even just a minor internal injury there were no hospitals left and no doctors, and if she died, Bexar wasn't sure he would be brave enough to put his wife down. He would end up like Malachi. Bexar looked at Keeley, who with a full stomach was playing with the TV remote quietly on the floor, and smiled. He had to survive. Keeley needed him to survive.

"Don't worry, little one, I'll always be here for you." Bexar kissed his daughter on her head and was greeted with a sweet smile. Bexar thought of the world she would be forced to grow up in. The smile broke his heart.

Faintly, Bexar heard the low rumble of motorcycles. He leapt out of his chair, picked up his AR-15, and carefully pulled the corner of the curtain open to peer outside. The rumbling exhaust note of the motorcycles grew louder and Bexar realized he was holding his breath. He forced himself to take a deep breath and to try to keep his heart rate under control.

The seconds felt like they slowed to hours as the sound of motorcycles drew closer and they finally appeared in Bexar's view. Two motorcycles slowed as they approached the wreck and appeared to stop by the motorcycle parked on the shoulder. The hotel's office mostly blocked the view. A van pulled up behind the motorcycles and Bexar recognized it as the same one the biker gang had in the Basin, the one with the big machine gun. Two men climbed out of the van and joined the other two, who had dismounted their motorcycles. Two of the men carried the dead biker and put him in the back of the van; another carried the damaged AR-10 rifle and put it with the body in the van. Bexar couldn't be sure what they were doing, but after a few minutes the motorcycles started with a roar and rode off back the way they'd come, followed by the van and one of their men riding the dead biker's motorcycle.

Bexar continued to watch out of the window for a full minute after they rode out of view and realized he was holding his breath again. With a loud sigh, he left the window and sat on the edge of the bed. He took his unconscious wife's hand in his and said, "Jessie, I'm sorry, baby. We've got to move. We can't stay here. We're too close to the highway. We need to hide."

CHAPTER 13

El Paso, Texas
February 14, Year 1

"That's the dumbest plan you've ever come up with, Odin."

"Fine, Chivo. Tell me why *you* think it won't work."

"Oh no, I think it will work, but it's still fucking stupid. Stupid white-trash tricks. What the hell is it with your people and riding lawn mowers?"

"They're multipurpose. You can mow your yard and then ride it to Walmart for more beer. A very versatile machine, the lawn tractor."

They found the key for the Chrysler hanging on a nail by the side door. Odin pushed the riding lawn mower out of the backyard shed. Apollo unlocked the Chrysler, put the car in neutral, and waited for the signal from Chivo in the front yard. Chivo walked to the far corner of the yard away from the driveway, the group of undead following him, excitedly bouncing off the fence and trying to reach their fresh meal. He raised his rifle and took aim at the closest walking corpse.

The triangle reticle of the ACOG on his rifle rested on the rotting forehead seen through the optic, his chosen first kill. Chivo pressed the trigger to the rear and the plan was rapidly set in motion by the loud bark of his rifle. The shattered skull fragments and rotting brain matter covered the other walking dead in the group, and before the first kill's body hit the ground, Chivo's second shot exploded another rotting skull.

Apollo ran to the gate which was closed across the driveway, pushed open the latch and threw both sides open while the riding lawn mower coughed to life in a cloud of white smoke. Odin laughed wildly as the lawn mower roared past Apollo, who ran back to the front of the Chrysler. Legs pumping, Apollo pushed the big four-door car down the driveway before it bounced into the street. Chivo ran past Apollo and to the old truck behind the house, climbed into the cab and turned the key to the sound of an old tired motor turning over slowly. Chivo turned the ignition off and back on again, pumping the gas. Rifle fire from the front of the house filled his ears while he tried to get the old truck to start.

Three tries later, the old truck burst to life with a loud backfire, a heavy cloud of black smoke pouring out of the exhaust pipe. Chivo jammed the selector to reverse and slammed his foot on the gas pedal, spinning the tires and hitting the shed with the truck. He jerked the selector to drive and spun the tires down the driveway before sliding to a stop on the road in front of the house. Apollo climbed into the passenger seat, cranked the manual window open, and hung out the open window with his rifle, quickly engaging the mob of new rotted bodies pouring into the street towards the truck from behind the surrounding houses.

"What the shit, Chivo? I thought you grew up stealing cars in Laredo."

"Fuck you, punta, and don't fucking shoot Odin."

Chivo punched the accelerator and jerked the old Ford around the large group of undead following the riding lawn mower before pulling alongside Odin. Odin tossed his rifle into the bed of the truck before he grabbed the bedrail and leapt into the bed headfirst. The mower's kill switch stopped the motor immediately, and the following herd of undead crashed into the stopped mower before turning to follow the truck as it sped around the corner. Chivo made the block and bumped across the sandy ground and through the section of fence to the highway that they'd cut down to get to the house, before they bounced onto the Cesar E. Chavez Border Highway.

Taking a couple of deep breaths, Chivo resisted the urge to drive as fast as he could. Instead, he kept the truck's speedometer on thirty miles per hour so he could outpace the following dead but still easily maneuver around the debris, abandoned vehicles, and shambling dead that appeared in their path.

None of the team members were intimately familiar with the surface streets in El Paso, although they knew the basic layout of the highways. The only way they really knew how to get to Fort Bliss was right through the heart of the city and into one of the main gates. Odin stood in the bed of the truck, leaning on the roof of the cab with his rifle, dropping the undead that posed an immediate threat to his teammates. Apollo attempted to help Chivo navigate while leaning out of the passenger's side window, firing his rifle.

Ten minutes later Apollo was out of ammo for his M4 and began pulling loaded magazines from the pouches on Chivo's armor carrier. Chivo took the exit ramp for Patriot Freeway, swerving around more abandoned vehicles on the flyover. As they approached the zoo, Odin banged on the roof of the cab and yelled "Stop the truck!"

Chivo slammed on the brakes and the truck slid to a stop.

"What the hell, Odin?"

"Look on the other side of the highway, up on the top of the sign." Odin pointed even though his teammates In the truck couldn't see him. Standing on the supports of the exit signs spanning the highway was a woman waving both arms above her head. A low guardrail and a small chain-link fence separated the other side of the highway, so the closest Chivo could get the truck was next to the base of the sign between the lanes. Below the woman two dozen rotting corpses stood reaching towards her, moaning, their hands grasping the air above their heads, trying to reach their prey.

Odin shouldered his rifle and began thinning the swarm of undead. Apollo left his rifle in the truck, climbed out and drew the pistol holstered on his right thigh. Walking quickly around the front of the truck, his feet rolling heel to toe, the muzzle of the raised pistol glided perfectly flat through the air as the slide rocked back with each fired round. One by one each of the staggering undead fell to the pavement, spattered with skull fragments and rotted black brain matter.

Reaching the base of the sign, Apollo called up to the woman. "Are you OK?"

"Yes," she responded weakly.

"Are you bit?"

"No."

"Can you climb down?"

"I don't think I can."

Chivo stood at the front of the still-running truck, scanning outward for any new threats, and saw a white panel van about ten yards away with "Garcia's Painting" on the side.

"Apollo, hang on for a sec."

Odin looked to where Chivo gestured and ran to the van to help retrieve the ladders bungeed to its roof. They brought back the longest extension ladder to the base of the sign and extended the ladder as far as it would go.

"Can you get to the ladder and climb down now?"

"I'll try"

The woman visibly shook while climbing through the middle of the big metal span, carefully stepping on each metal brace. Reaching the ladder, she climbed over the edge and slowly climbed down one rung at a time. Once on the pavement, she collapsed. Apollo carried her back to the old Ford, Chivo picking off the curious undead that were shambling towards the truck.

Odin climbed into the bed of the truck while Apollo set the young woman on the bench seat of the cab beside Chivo and climbed in behind her. Her face was badly sunburned, her lips cracked and her hair matted. She looked severely dehydrated. Chivo put the truck in drive and continued towards Fort Bliss.

"My name is Tyrone but everyone calls me Apollo. That's Chivo and behind us is Odin."

Weakly she nodded and said, "I'm Lindsey."

"How long have you been stuck up there, Lindsey?"

"Nineteen days."

Apollo looked at her with disbelief. "Did you have any food or water?"

"No. I had a few Powerbars, but those only lasted four days. Each morning I scrubbed the frost off the metal for water."

"How did you end up on the sign?"

"My scooter ran out of gas and I was chased up there by those things."

Apollo reached into the cargo pocket on his filthy pants and retrieved a mashed Snickers bar. Lindsey took the candy bar but couldn't eat it, her mouth too dry to even chew. Chivo handed her the tube of his Camelbak, from which she quickly took long drinks of water.

"Slow down, senorita. You'll get sick if you drink too much water too fast."

Lindsey nodded and nibbled on the Snickers bar as quickly as she dared.

CHAPTER 14

Terlingua, Texas
February 14, Year 1

Bexar looked out the window of the little hotel room, the desert floor turning a deep shade of purple from the setting sun. No more motorcycles had ridden past on the main road, but there was undead activity down near the Jeep. Bexar guessed that all the noise of the gunfire and the wreck that morning had drawn them out of the desert and wherever they had come from before that. Jessie finally regained consciousness around midafternoon, but was still nauseous and dizzy with an obvious concussion.

"Jess, I think we need to move up the hill and away from the main road. We can hide up there until I can find us another vehicle to use."

"OK, but when do you want to go up the hill?"

"Once the sun goes down some more. There aren't any clouds in the sky so I should be able to see, but I want the darkness in case any more bikers come by."

Jessie lay on the bed with her eyes closed, trying to will the headache away. The only pain relievers they still had were a handful of Extra Strength Tylenol, and they simply weren't extra strength enough. Bexar sat on the floor playing with Keeley, checking out of the window every few minutes.

With the setting sun the hotel room grew darker and before long Bexar decided that it was dark enough outside to start his plan. "Keep the rifle. I'm taking my pistol and knife. I'll tap on the door four times when I come back."

Bexar helped his wife to a chair by the door, handed her his rifle, kissed her gently on the forehead, and slowly opened the door. Once outside he closed the door as quietly as he could and smiled when he heard the hotel security latch slide closed behind the door. As Bexar walked quickly across the parking lot, a single corpse, a nude and quite heavyset woman, stumbled toward him. Bexar closed the distance and plunged his heavy CM Forge knife through her right eyeball, deep into her skull.

The eyeball burst with pus around the blade of the knife as the body went limp and flopped to the ground. The pus smelled wretched and Bexar wiped the thick fluid off his knife on the woman's skin as best he could before turning to walk up the hill towards the Terlingua Ghost Town.

Bexar resisted the urge to use the buildings as cover, choosing to stay in the middle of the street so he couldn't be surprised by any more walking corpses. As he passed the sparse buildings, silence flooded his ears. Within a few minutes he reached a bar and grill on the side of the road. The inside of the windows looked dirty in the moonlight, like they were smeared with dried blood, and although Bexar couldn't see movement in the dark windows, he seemed to feel it, the hairs on the back of his neck standing. Bexar decided that if there were undead in that building, they could stay there. Besides, Bexar thought, if he cleared the building with it being so close to the main road, it would be a sign that someone living had been through there.

Ten minutes later Bexar stepped onto the long front porch of the Starlight Theatre. He started at the left end of the building with the trading post. The front door was unlocked. Bexar retrieved a rock from the parking lot, opened the door, and threw the rock into the dark interior with a loud crash. Immediately, a loud moan erupted from the dark doorway.

With another rock, Bexar propped the door open and waited on the front porch for whatever was inside to shamble outside to meet him. Inside it sounded like the walking body was slowly getting closer to the front of the store, crashing into displays and knocking things over. Eventually an old man stumbled through the open doorway, face slack and dead eyes locked open, torn skin hanging in sheets from his ruined neck. Bexar plunged his knife into the bridge of the man's nose, through the nasal cavity and deep into the skull. The old man crashed onto the wooden porch.

Bexar reached into his pocket and retrieved the Surefire light and stepped into the dark store, closing the door behind him. Close to five minutes later he was finished clearing the store, confident that the old man was the only one who had been inside. Returning to the front of the store, Bexar was greeted by another corpse, an old man standing at the door and peering through the glass. Bexar walked away from the door to one of the large front windows, tapped on the glass, and shone his light at the undead man. He took the bait and stumbled away from the door. Bexar turned off the light, rushed outside and drove his heavy knife into the right temple of the second old man. The rotted body fell to the porch with a wet thump, and Bexar stepped over it to continue to the Starlight Theatre.

The restaurant and bar was also unlocked but empty. Bexar smiled, seeing that the bar had not been raided and the liquor bottles twinkled in the light cast by his flashlight. Outside Bexar was happier still to see that he'd remembered correctly and that the hotel was comprised of little cabins spread out in the area. Bexar walked north to the closest cabin and found it unlocked and empty of anyone living, dead, or otherwise. Satisfied he could safely move his family to their new accommodations, he turned and walked down the hill back towards the highway and the small hotel.

Fifteen minutes later Bexar held a sleepy Keeley in his arms while Jessie held onto his shoulder for support as they walked up the hill towards the Starlight. Once they were settled in their new cabin it took Bexar three more trips with the wheelbarrow to move the meager supplies and provisions they still had to their new cabin. The moon hung high overhead and Bexar wasn't sure what time it was, but he felt like it was well after midnight. Back in the cabin, Bexar found his wife and daughter asleep before falling into a dream-filled fitful sleep in a chair by the door himself.

CHAPTER 15

El Paso, Texas
February 1, Year 1

The old truck sped along the Patriot Freeway northbound towards Fort Bliss, the U.S. Army installation. With the heavy concentration of abandoned vehicles and undead on the road, the thirty miles per hour that Chivo worked to maintain made it feel like they were driving at breakneck speed. As they approached I-10, the roadway became even more congested. Apollo and Odin stopped trying to shoot the undead in their path, their numbers being far too great and the team's ammo reserves falling dangerously low. Chivo did his best to drive around as many as he could. More than a few times undead bounced across the front of the truck only to be dragged off by the grinding pavement below.

The exchange for I-10 with the flyover ramps above them looked bad, but they could see below that I-10 was much worse off than they were. The Interstate was completely clogged with abandoned cars. It looked like the undead stumbled through the cars by the thousands. Seeing such a large concentration of walking corpses draped a feeling of hopelessness across the truck and it felt like the air was sucked right out of the cab of the truck. Lindsey sobbed, her head buried in her hands. Apollo looked at her and wanted to comfort her, but he simply didn't know how to or if she would even be OK with a pat on the shoulder from a man she just met.

With a loud thump and crash, the windshield burst into the cab of the truck. A walker had fallen off the overpass above them and slammed onto the hood of the truck, its head crashing through the windshield. Apollo, jammed against the door, had no room to draw his pistol for the jaw snapping at their hands. The glass behind their heads burst inward, the barrel of Odin's M4 punching through, followed by the deafening report of his rifle firing inside the cab of the truck. The undead's skull exploded, covering Chivo, Lindsey, and Apollo in black slime and skull fragments that smelled horrific. Before Apollo or Chivo could start cursing their teammate, another loud crunch hit the truck, this time at the back, followed by Odin yelling and rapidly firing his rifle.

"Fuck fuck fuck fuck fuck FUCK!"

Apollo twisted in his seat and pushed the shattered back glass out into the bed. Odin sat in the bed, rifle by his side, a woman's rotted corpse bent over the side of the bed. Odin clutched his left shoulder, blood oozing from between his fingers.

"Odin! What the fuck, dude?"

"The bitch got me. She fucking bit me."

Apollo looked at Chivo, who glanced over his shoulder at Odin and sped up. They knew their teammate was a dead man; it was just a matter of how long it took for the virus to kill him. They also knew it was their duty to their brother to put him down once he turned.

Apollo climbed through the open hole in the back of the cab where the glass had been, leaving Lindsey on the bench seat, curled up in a ball and sobbing. Sitting in the bed of the truck with Odin, Apollo pulled latex gloves out of another pocket, snapped them on and pulled the EMS shears from his chest carrier to cut open Odin's shirt and expose the bite wound. Moments later Apollo finished with the field dressing to help with the bleeding.

Odin looked sadly at Apollo. "I'm sorry, brother."

"I'm sorry too. You're not gone yet, but I'll make sure you won't turn when it's time."

"Thank you."

The truck swerved widely around an overturned and burned-out tour bus. Close to thirty undead with charred skin and clothes formed a mass in the road ahead and turned towards the approaching truck. Chivo pushed the truck's gas pedal to the floor. White smoke billowed from the damaged hood. Chivo drove the truck down an on-ramp and off the highway, and the tires squealed in protest as the truck slid to a stop. The entry gate to Fort Bliss stood ahead, sandbags and a machine gun emplacement blocking the road. A half-dozen hulks of destroyed cars sat on the fire-scorched pavement and were riddled with large-caliber bullet holes.

Numerous bodies lay motionless on the pavement, turkey buzzards still peeling flesh off the rotting corpses.

Chivo looked left and saw that part of the brick and iron fence by the gate was missing. He turned the wheel, mashed on the accelerator, and bounced the truck over the curb into the parking lot, passing the entry gate's last stand.

Behind the gate were two large MRAPS and a burned-out Bradley sitting dormant. More dead bodies lay on the pavement. Apollo pounded on the roof of the cab and yelled over the wind noise. "Go up eleven streets, take a right, go about two hundred meters and stop. It's been a few years, but they should still store the brigade's commo gear in that building."

Chivo nodded and slowed the truck, trying to limp it to their destination. The sun was beginning to set and some of the buildings they passed also had sandbagged positions in place. Undead shambled through the street, turning to follow the truck as it passed by in a cloud of white smoke. Vehicles stood in the roadway at each intersection, clearly marked as Military Police (MP). Some were burned; some looked abandoned. The undead giving chase to the passing truck mostly wore ACUs. Some were geared up with M4s and M16s bouncing on their slings, but all of them had shoulder pieces identifying them as MPs.

Odin watched the undead gather in strength, falling in behind the passing truck. "Chivo, stop for a minute."

"What?"

"Fucking stop. I have an idea."

Chivo stopped the truck in the middle of the intersection. Odin and Apollo jumped out of the truck's bed with their rifles up. "What sort of new fucked up white-trash idea do you have now? See another riding lawn mower?"

"Nope, but our following fan club have M4s, M16s, and magazines on their armor carriers. If we put some down we should be able to gather some more ammo."

"OK, I can see that. Pick off the first few. I don't want to get caught by the whole group."

"Roger that. Let's go."

Apollo and Odin fist bumped before moving at angles away from each other, towards each side of the street, M4s up and ready. Chivo stayed in the truck to protect Lindsey, hoping to keep the truck's motor running. The smoke was getting thicker and the noises coming from under the hood weren't of the good variety.

Each man's rifle barked a dozen times before they ran to the bodies of the men they just put out of their undead misery. Some of the magazines they pulled from the carriers were crusted with dried blood, but neither man cared. They desperately needed ammo.

The larger mass of undead bodies was beginning to get close, and they were coming from all directions towards the truck. Before the corpses reached the truck, Apollo and Odin climbed into the bed and Chivo drove away from the approaching horde. Odin's face was pale, his lips ashy, his breathing fast and shallow. Apollo passed six full magazines to Chivo. Odin pulled all but two of his magazines out of his carrier and handed them to Apollo, along with the ten extra magazines he'd scavenged from the soldier's bodies.

"I have another idea. The truck is shit-canned. You're going to need new wheels and you need to ditch our following parade. When we get to your spot, you guys get out and haul ass. I'm taking the truck and leading our new friends in a new direction."

The truck turned hard without slowing and slid to a stop in front of the building Apollo had described, which sat behind an empty fenced-in area that normally held a large number of Humvees.

Odin climbed out of the bed, hands shaking, and took Chivo's spot behind the steering wheel.

"OK boys, last stop. See you fuckers in Valhalla!"

Apollo and Chivo both kissed Odin on the forehead before he shut the door and drove back the way they had come, honking the horn and yelling like a madman. Chivo took one more look at the smoking truck speeding away before he cut a small hole in the bottom of the chain-link fence and crawled through. Lindsey followed with Apollo behind her.

Apollo pointed at a small squat building. "That storage building should hold most of the un-mounted commo gear. We can shelter inside with Lindsey while one of us finds our merry little band some new wheels."

Chivo tested the door and found it locked. Apollo pulled a small zippered pouch out of a bag on his chest and knelt in front of the door with a set of picks and rakes.

"This should only take me a few minutes."

Five minutes later, the desert sky was dark purple from the setting sun, and the unlikely trio were safe inside a dusty storeroom, surrounded by racks of Hardigg and Storm cases.

CHAPTER 18

Groom Lake, Nevada
February 15, Year 1

Major Ben Wright walked through the maze of corridors of the complex deep below the surface in Groom Lake, Nevada. Approaching Cliff's office, Wright knocked sharply and walked through the door without waiting for an answer. The strong smell of coffee filled the small office.

"Cliff, we checked Nellis AFB first. Surprisingly, there are two C-130s on the ramp. One of them is really peculiar in that it is parked on the helipad on the north end of the field. The helipad where the Pararescue Jumpers (PJs) are based. I believe that aircraft was parked there after all of this started. The consensus is there may be survivors there. We've tried raising them on the frequencies we believe they would be using or monitoring, but we have had no luck with contact."

"Great, Ben. Put together a two-man team, including Arcuni of course, who are willing to take a road trip with me. I'm going to lead a quick expedition outside the wire to see if that aircraft will fly, and if it does, bring it back here. Tell the men we'll take my truck and the meeting to go top side is at 0600. They can check out any gear from the stores that they need, but remind them we're moving fast and not planning on staying the night. Heavy on the ammo, light on the food."

Wright nodded, turned and left the office to find Arcuni. Although the major had grown to know his enlisted men quite well since the attack, he couldn't guess who Arcuni would want to take with him for such a dangerous trip. Cliff almost seemed excited to get above ground and outside the wire, and after the harrowing trip to get to Groom Lake, Wright simply didn't see the allure of the "adventure."

Cliff watched the office door close as Wright left his office. He stood and drew the pistol quickly from the holster on his right thigh, his whole body quickly setting into a strong shooting stance that spoke of thousands and thousands of repetitions. His right thumb depressed the magazine release button and Cliff set the loaded magazine on his desk before locking the slide open and catching the live round ejected from the pistol's chamber. Quickly Cliff fieldstripped the pistol before retrieving a rag and a small bottle of Break-Free from his top desk drawer. Cliff wiped down his already spotless pistol and oiled it before putting all the pieces together. The pistol empty, Cliff reset the trigger, stood in his shooting stance, aimed at the 6 of the clock on the wall and smoothly pressed the trigger to the rear, dry firing the pistol. A resounding click seemed to echo in Cliff's ears and the front of the muzzle didn't even move a fraction of an inch. Cliff reset the trigger and did the dry firing practice again. Then again and again, a dozen times more, each time the front of the pistol never wavering or flinching with the trigger pull. Cliff seated the loaded magazine, chambered a round, and replaced the now-missing round from the magazine before verifying the weapon was loaded with a press check. He reholstered his pistol.

Reaching for the M4 rifle leaned against the corner of the wall behind his desk, Cliff fieldstripped the rifle and repeated the same process he'd completed with his pistol. After lubing the working parts and reassembling the rifle, Cliff repeated the dry firing practice with his rifle before inserting a loaded Pmag and making the weapon ready. The fire selector flipped to "safe," Cliff slung the rifle across his chest and walked into the corridor to the stairwell and down two flights of stairs to where his berth was located. Each piece of gear that Cliff had on his mental checklist came out of his footlocker and was laid on the blanket of his rack. The chest rig, each magazine, bump helmet, NODs and med kit all lay disassembled. One by one he cleaned and checked each piece of gear to make sure that it contained all it needed and functioned properly, all the while in Cliff's mind he could still hear the gruff voice of his instructor at The Farm "gently reminding" him of what would happen if he failed to complete his proper preparation for each mission, no matter how routine it may seem.

As hard as that training was, as tough of a time in Cliff's life as it had been, the emotional and physical challenges beyond what he could have ever imagined, his instructor was right. Besides, Cliff's prior missions proved harder than the training ever was, and his current mission was harder than his worst nightmares.

An hour later all of his gear was cleaned, reassembled and verified to be complete and working. The rifle magazines were reloaded and placed in a row on his rack with the rest of his gear. Ten minutes later Cliff walked into the cavernous storeroom, found a medium-sized ALICE pack, opened a box of thirty-round M4 magazines, and claimed ten more, loading each one full with XM193. The loaded magazines were placed in the three large outside pockets of the ALICE pack. In the main space went a poncho liner, space blanket, two chem-lights, three sets of spare batteries for his NODs, and two MREs that he promptly stripped to save room. Cliff wasn't sure what he would encounter on the road to Nellis Air Force Base, but if it was anything like his trip to Groom Lake, the more ammo he could carry, the better.

Loaded for his mission, Cliff dropped his new gear by his bunk, taking his M4 and pistol with him, which was the standing rule for everyone in the facility in case of a breakout of undead. He found Arcuni coming out of the radio hut. "Hey Arcuni, got a sec? Walk with me."

Arcuni turned and followed Cliff back into the radio hut.

"Hey Wright, when's the last time you heard from our friends at the national park in Texas?"

Wright picked up a clipboard and flipped through a few pages before finding the notation he was looking for. "Looks like it's been two days."

"OK, when is the next SAT pass there?"

"Should have one tomorrow morning about 0700 our time."

"Great. Do me a favor and try to reach them. If you can't reach them, check the SATINT and try to figure out why, I just remembered the bikers and I'm concerned about them."

"Got it."

Cliff turned and walked out of the radio hut with Arcuni in tow. "Alrighty, Arcuni. Have you decided who you want to come with us tomorrow?"

"Garcia is my pick if he's up to it."

"Have you checked out any gear yet?"

"Haven't had the chance. The major broke the news to me just before I saw you."

"OK, let's get Garcia and make sure he's on board. Then I'll take both of you to the storeroom and help you get kitted up. Then we need to go topside to prep the truck and get a bunch of extra gas from the fuel bowser."

CHAPTER 17

Terlingua, Texas
February 16, Year 1

"Daddy, I'm hungry."

Keeley's little hand patted Bexar on the leg. Bexar lurched awake with a gasp, still sitting in the chair by the door. His dreams were a constant loop of his having to shoot Jack and Will in the head to keep their dead bodies from returning to life. It took Bexar a few moments for his head to clear and to realize where he was and what had happened. The unfamiliar interior of the new cabin confused him before he focused on his daughter climbing into his lap.

"I went potty and now I'm hungry."

"Went potty in here?"

"Yes."

"Good. You need to stay inside the cabin unless Mommy or Daddy are with you."

"I want waffles."

"We don't have any waffles, baby. We have some MREs left and that's just about all we've got."

"I don't want an RME. I want waffles!" said the toddler, stomping her feet.

Jessie stirred and walked unsteadily into the sitting room of the little cabin suite before kissing Bexar on the forehead.

"How's your head, babe?"

"Hurts. I still feel dizzy, but at least I don't feel like I'm going to throw up anymore."

"That sounds better. Here, take my rifle. I'm going over to the trading post to see if there is anything in there I could scavenge for breakfast. If possible, I want to try to save what little we have left."

Bexar handed his rifle to Jessie, who took his spot in his chair. He pulled the corner of the curtain back and peered outside, watching for a few minutes before pulling his heavy knife out and slowly opening the cabin's front door into the cold morning air.

Moving slowly, Bexar scanned the area around him. The bodies of the zombies he'd killed last night still lay on the porch of the Starlight Theatre and the trading post. Walking onto the porch, Bexar stepped over the bodies and stopped at the front door of the store. He tapped on the glass with the butt of his knife. He couldn't be too careful. He couldn't risk getting bitten by some undead body he had missed the previous night.

Waiting and seeing no reaction to his noise, Bexar opened the door and stepped inside. The store looked different in the daylight. It had a lot of knickknacks, tourist stuff like gemstones, walking sticks, t-shirts and the like. The store also had a small selection of camping and hiking gear. In the middle of the store sat a small cooler with sodas, bottled water, and Gatorade. Bexar slid the cooler door open. The air smelled stale, but nothing smelled rotten. The sealed bottles should be fine.

From behind the counter, Bexar retrieved two shopping bags and filled them with Gatorade and bottled water. On a shelf near the cooler were some dry goods and camping food, including pancake mix and a handful of small cast iron skillets. Another shopping bag was retrieved and in went the food, skillets, and pancake mix. Next to the camping supplies were some cheap binoculars for sale. Cheap binoculars are better than no binoculars, so Bexar removed them from the package and hung them around his neck.

On the way out the door Bexar saw a small stuffed javelina and some t-shirts. Bexar had never been able to resist buying his baby girl a new stuffed animal, so the javelina went into the bag, as did two t-shirts in her and his wife's sizes.

Bexar stepped onto the porch and heard the distinct rumble of motorcycle exhaust, the sound coming from down the hill, from the highway below. He glanced towards the road but couldn't see more than just a small section through the ghost town. Bags in hand, he ran down the porch and through the walkway to his family's cabin. After startling Jessie by throwing the door open and dropping the bags, Bexar took the rifle from his wife, told her to lock up, and bolted out the front door.

Bexar jogged down the dirt road towards the highway before he stopped and hid behind the crumbled wall of an abandoned ghost town house. The sound of the motorcycle engines grew louder before the first motorcycle burst into view on the highway. Five motorcycles and two old vans drove past. One of the vans Bexar recognized from the day before. The convoy was headed towards the park. At least this time, none of them stopped to inspect his wrecked Jeep.

Behind the ruined house, Bexar stayed kneeling, scanning the road and the area with the binoculars for another ten minutes before standing to walk back to the cabin. That was when the first undead man teetered into view on the highway below. Quickly Bexar knelt behind the crumbling wall as the faint moans of the undead reached his ears. Trying to count the walking corpses as they passed, Bexar saw men, women and children, some of them grotesque, some of them obviously rotting, but some of them looked like freshly dead bodies. Dozens passed by Bexar's wrecked Wagoneer. Another ten minutes passed before the stream of undead began to relent. The carrion smell of rotting flesh wafted in the air, noticeable even up the hill away from the road where Bexar knelt. As slowly and as quietly as possible, Bexar turned and walked out of view from the road in a crouch before jogging back to the cabin to tell Jessie what he had seen.

Keeley sat on the bed in the back room, wearing one of her new t-shirts and playing with the plush Javelina.

"We're still not safe here, but I don't think you're in any condition to attempt to walk anywhere yet," Bexar told his wife as he mixed the pancake mix in an empty water bottle.

"Bexar, I don't think it would be smart for us to try to walk anywhere. We need to find another vehicle."

"Yeah, I agree, but I have no damned idea where we'll find another vehicle that still runs. The Scout and the FJ are still in the park, but good fucking luck getting back there and getting them back from the bikers."

Jessie frowned at her husband. "I bet someone in this little town has an old Jeep or Bronco or truck or *something* that still runs. Surely. I mean I don't remember seeing a bunch of shiny new trucks here last time we visited a couple of years ago."

"OK. You're probably right. I really think I should wait until dark to go looking. I don't want to get caught out in the open if the bikers go by again."

The small fireplace in the cabin already had a pile of dry woodchips in it, waiting for the next guest to check in, so Jessie started a fire to chase the chill out of the cabin and to cook the pancakes.

CHAPTER 18

Cliff, Arcuni, and Garcia had loaded the truck the night before. Their heavy packs mostly full of ammo lay in the bed of the truck, along with six five-gallon jerry cans full of gasoline, filled from the facility's fuel bowser, which had also filled the truck's fuel tank. The single-cab truck would be cramped, but they decided it would be best if they all rode in the cab together. The freezing temperatures on the high desert had more to do with that decision than any grand plans or tactics. Cliff, leader of the expedition to Nellis, designated himself the driver. Garcia sat passenger, and an unhappy Arcuni sat wedged in the middle on the bench seat. He was the only person who could fly the plane, so he sat in the most protected "VIP" seat for the trip.

The concentration of undead on the surface of the base above the underground installation was light, and each member of the team had the chance to "warm up" their rifles by putting down the dozen zombies they encountered before driving across the dry lakebed. The wrecked C-130 that Arcuni and his fellow airmen had used to flee Peterson Air force Base lay dormant in the distance where it had originally come to rest. Retracing the road that Cliff had used to drive over the mountains and into Groom Lake when he first arrived, the trio emerged onto NV-375, the Extraterrestrial Highway, and turned right.

The open desert highway was practically devoid of signs of life from before the attack, the group only passing four abandoned vehicles on the road before they reached the small town of Crystal Springs. Cliff kept the truck at sixty miles per hour to conserve gas while in the barren expanse of open desert. He watched the sand blow across the roadway ahead of the truck. As they passed through the town, Cliff slowed and drove around three reanimates standing in the middle of the road. The undead turned to follow the passing truck, the first movement the walking corpses had seen in weeks, but the truck soon passed out of view. Beyond the town, Cliff turned onto US-93. This road was also mostly deserted, except a few more abandoned vehicles, but the highway was still easily negotiable. The small town of Alamo passed without incident and Cliff was thankful that this trip was not like his last, and that he also had people to talk to while driving.

Nearing I-15 the road became clogged with abandoned and burned-out cars. Cliff slowed and drove the truck onto the sandy sides of the highway off the pavement, undead meandering through the parking lot of cars that was the highway. A destroyed truck stop lay in their path before they could turn onto I-15, and the SATINT he'd reviewed indicated that there was a high concentration of undead in the area. Cliff wanted to pass through as quickly, quietly, and safely as possible. He did not want to chance another collision with a walking corpse like on his previous road trip in Colorado.

Burned bodies lay in grotesque positions on the road, unmoving. Parts of their bodies were missing, devoured by the undead, buzzards, or other animals; Cliff wasn't sure. With the truck stop on their right, Cliff abandoned any hope of keeping the truck on the paved surface and turned towards the open desert. Nearly one hundred yards into the desert they were able to avoid most of the shambling undead, attracted to the truck from the highway by the noise and movement. The truck bounced across the access road and bounded up the on-ramp onto I-15 before turning to travel southbound. Most of the morning was already gone, the sun sitting directly overhead, but they were near their destination. The truck stop could be the easiest adventure they had on the trip, as Nellis AFB sat on the edge of Las Vegas and the SATINT was very clear that the entire city was a complete loss, overrun by the undead.

Arcuni and Garcia nervously press checked their M4s, both verifying that their rifles were loaded and the selector was still on "safe." Without any distractions, both of them fidgeted nervously while the conversation faded to silence. Cliff fought to keep the truck's speed above forty miles per hour, but that was proving difficult as they neared the Las Vegas Motor Speedway and took the exit for NV-604.

Cliff drove the truck back and forth across the highway, dodging abandoned cars and the shambling undead. "OK, the gap in the concrete barriers should be up here on the right. Garcia, do you have the bolt cutters ready?"

"Yeah, boss."

"Arcuni, you ready with the zip ties?"

"Sure, but I don't see how the zip ties could hold the fence if enough of them press against it."

"It might hold, it might not, but it should slow them down enough to give us time to complete our mission. Regardless, it's better than doing nothing and hoping they don't follow us in."

Cliff glanced in the rear-view mirror, then pointed over his shoulder. Arcuni twisted in his seat and looked out of the truck's rear window. In the near distance he saw a large number of undead stumbling and following the passing truck. In the truck they far outpaced the dead, but the dead would eventually catch up when the truck stopped.

Garcia pointed. "There!"

Cliff slammed on the brakes and turned the wheel. The truck drove across the highway onto the sandy shoulder and stopped directly in front of the chain-link fence that ringed the air base. Concrete K-barriers lined the inside of the fence to prevent someone from driving onto the base, but, using the SATINT, Wright found a spot that had a gap large enough for the truck to drive through. Garcia jumped out of the truck, followed by Arcuni. Arcuni's cargo pocket bristled with large zip ties. He provided security with his M4 while Garcia used bolt cutters to cut the fence. Quickly, the fence was cut free and pulled out of the way for Cliff to drive the truck through. Once through, Arcuni and Garcia made quick work of putting the fence back in place, zip ties through each piece of the cut chain-links.

They both climbed back into the cab and Cliff drove forward, the truck bouncing through the short distance into a parking lot and then onto Ellsworth Avenue. The large tail of the C-130 rose above the buildings to the south. Cliff drove to the edge of the flight line, where another chain-link fence was in their way. Garcia made quick work of this fence, but since they were on base, the fence remained cut and unrepaired.

The C-130 sat in front of them with no visible activity around it. No APU was in sight, but Arcuni didn't mind. As long as there was enough fuel on board to make the quick hop to Groom Lake, they would be fine. The aircraft could start under its own power and there was plenty of fuel for the plane in storage at Groom Lake. He only had to get it home safely.

The truck stopped by the open tail ramp of the cargo plane and all three of them climbed out. Garcia stayed by the truck and provided security, his M4 at the ready. Cliff and Arcuni cautiously walked up the cargo ramp towards the cockpit. They found the aircraft empty. Arcuni sat his rifle on the co-pilot's seat, climbed into the left seat, and flipped the master switch on. The dash lit up like a Christmas tree. Turning on a few more systems, Arcuni found the fuel tanks more than half full, and as long as the engines would start they could easily make it home to Groom Lake.

Arcuni smiled at the whine of the starter motor as it spun up the turbine of each motor in sequence. The clicks of the igniters were followed by the deep *fwomp* sound of the fuel igniting before being drowned out by the whining turbine motors and large propellers beating through the air. One by one, each engine started. Cliff looked out the open tail ramp of the cargo plane to see Garcia waving frantically before he turned, raised his rifle and fired through a full magazine very rapidly.

"Get turned around and get taxiing! We're going to have to clear the way and we'll meet you at the end of the runway!" Cliff yelled over the sound of the engines before he ran towards the back of the plane, where Garcia was rapidly firing through another magazine of ammo.

The ramp rose about a foot off the ground. Arcuni watched over his shoulder to see that Cliff had exited before slowly letting the brakes out and steering the nose wheel hard left. To help make the tight distance, Arcuni pushed the right engine's throttles forward, rocking the lumbering giant into a sharper turn. The helipad was simply not designed with the intent of turning an aircraft like a C-130 around, and the nose wheel dropped off the pavement into the hard-packed sand while turning. Movement out of the right of the windshield caught Arcuni's attention. Three undead were running out of the hangar towards the plane, and he hoped they wouldn't get close enough to catch one of the spinning props. It took him a minute to realize that undead do not run; they can't run. Those must be survivors.

Sand blew across Cliff and Garcia, pushed by the aircraft's propellers. Even ducking their heads into their hands, their exposed skin was being blasted raw by the blowing sand. Once the worst of the prop blast subsided, Cliff and Garcia's rifles were up and they were rapidly engaging the growing numbers of walking corpses shambling across the sand and from the other buildings along the flight line.

"Garcia, you drive the truck. Keep us in front of the plane. We've got to clear a path. I'll take the bed and shoot as we drive. Keep it smooth—"

Cliff was interrupted by the unmistakable sound of a rifle round snapping through the air as it passed in front of his face. Cliff turned and saw an undead airman fall to the pavement just ten feet from where he stood. On the right, three men in full tactical kit and desert uniforms were running towards the truck.

"Garcia, get in the truck! We've got to go. They can join us if they want, but we don't have any fucking time to talk about it."

Garcia climbed into the truck just as the trio of new arrivals passed by the wingtip of the C-130. Cliff waved to them to climb into the truck as he jumped into the truck's bed. He turned, faced forward, laid his rifle on the roof of the truck's cab, and began firing at the quickly approaching horde.

Garcia drove slowly, watching the three new guys run to the back of the truck in the mirror. The truck bounced, followed by Cliff pounding on the roof of the cab, so he sped up. He could hear four rifles being fired rapidly.

Cliff looked at the man next to him, pointed to the three ALICE packs in the bed, and yelled "AMMO!" over the deafening noise of the C-130 taxiing behind them. The new man nodded, knelt, and began passing out loaded M4 magazines to his teammates. The truck crossed onto the main flight line and drove straight; the C-130 turned and rolled towards the end of the runway. Garcia kept the truck creeping along at a smooth pace, just faster than walking speed, the four men in the bed of the truck burning through ammo alarmingly fast.

The approaching undead horde appeared to be in the thousands, staggering from around the hangars and buildings onto the flight line ahead of them. Behind the truck Cliff heard Arcuni running up the engines of the C-130, preparing for maximum power for takeoff. Cliff turned and looked at Arcuni high above the runway through the windshield of the big plane and made a big circling motion in the air above his head. Arcuni nodded, pushed the throttles all the way forward, and released the brakes. The C-130 lurched forward and began rolling faster on the runway.

Cliff pounded on the roof of the truck, leaned over to the open driver's window, pointed, and yelled "CATCH THAT FUCKING PLANE!" Garcia nodded and slammed the gas pedal to the floor. The men in the bed of the truck gave up trying to engage any other threats and just grabbed ahold of the truck as tightly as they could to keep from being thrown out. The truck's tires squealed in protest of the high-speed turn as Garcia pushed the truck from the taxiway onto the runway and slowed, the C-130 barreling towards them. Just before the nose of the plane rumbled by, the power and force of the plane shaking the truck, Garcia pinned the gas pedal to the floor and swerved behind the passing plane. The cargo tailgate of the C-130 stood open, nearly touching the tarmac speeding beneath it. Quickly the truck gained on the aircraft, closing the gap between the truck and the tailgate. With a jolt, the front tires of the truck bounced onto the ramp and the truck skidded to a halt in the cargo hold of the aircraft. The front bumper of the truck crashed against the forward bulkhead just as the plane leapt into the air, the cargo ramp closing behind them.

CHAPTER 19

Big Bend National Park
February 16, Year 1

"Buzzer, have the scouts returned?"

"No Prez, not yet."

Russell sat on the back porch of the large westernmost cabin on the hill, overlooking the valley floor below and The Window. The sun was beginning to set behind the mountains, painting the sky shades of purple, pink, and red. The cabin contained ammo, food, and clothes folded neatly in the dresser drawers. The clothes appeared to have belonged to a man, woman, and a little girl, so Russell knew for sure that the man, woman and small boy that they found dead probably weren't the only occupants of the cabins. The contents found two cabins over seemed to belong to the dead family. The large cabin between the two was the most interesting. It stored a significant amount of gear, including a large amount of venison jerky, water, ammo, and some sort of canvas tent besides a bunch of other gear. This was the club's most incredible find since they'd raided the Army Reserve Station outside of El Paso, killing the men taking refuge there as well.

The Pistoleros fought their way across Texas, using zombies as a weapon, and it looked like they had a place they could stay for a long time, if not a permanent home. There was still a lot of work to be done, though. The club needed to find and take more girls and women. They needed booze and they needed some pharmacies. Pseudoephedrine in large quantities was hard to find in the middle of nowhere west Texas, and there was no way they could last long without the basic ingredients needed to cook more meth.

The sound of big V-twin motorcycles resonated off the valley floor and mountains around them, interrupting Russell's list of instructions for Buzzer, who by default was the club's new vice president.

"That should be the rest of the group and the women showing up now, Prez."

Russell tossed his near-empty bottle of Shiner Bock over the edge of the porch to shatter against the other empty bottles on the desert floor below. Buzzer and Russell walked through the cabin and into the parking area as the returning party shut off their motorcycles.

"Well?" Russell asked, lighting a cigarette.

Mike, a young and recently patched club member, walked from his motorcycle to Russell. "We found Stinky. Some guy ran him over with an old Jeep, but Stinky killed the guy before he was hit."

"Did you find any other bodies?"

"No, but there was an RV blown apart in the desert from the wreck. We didn't look through that. The others were probably in there."

Russell jabbed the cigarette into the corner of his mouth and stomped back into the cabin. He returned shortly holding a small pink shirt.

"Do you think the guy Stinky killed could have worn this fucking shirt, dumbass?"

"No, Prez."

"Then get your ass back on your fucking bike and go look in that fucking trailer. Buzzer, you go with him. Bring me the woman, bring back the girl, kill anyone else with them and don't fuck this up!"

Buzzer nodded, walked to his old Harley FLT Tour Glide, and left in an angry roar of a wide-open throttle. Mike scurried to start his bike and catch up to the VP. The old van and other club members remained in the parking area. A half-dozen partially clothed women, heads held low, climbed out of the back of the van. Their long hair partially hid the bruises on some of their faces. Russell pointed at the women. "Two of you whores get in here with me. You're going to earn your keep," he ordered before he threw the cigarette onto the ground and walked back into the dark cabin.

The prospect standing next to the van pushed two of the women forward. They kept their heads down and walked towards the cabin, one of them crying softly.

Buzzer and Mike rode across the desert floor side by side, burning up the asphalt at seventy-five miles per hour. Their front tires pointed towards the setting sun, glowing an angry shade of red across the open sky. If they were going to be back by midnight, they would have to hurry.

CHAPTER 20

Groom Lake, Nevada
February 16, Year 1

Lumbering across the mountains, the C-130 descended to the south of Groom Lake and turned final for Runway 32R, flaps extended and engine power reduced. Obviously the flight back was much quicker than the drive to Nellis. By the time the passengers climbed out of the truck in the cargo hold and strapped it to the anchors in the decking, it was time for them to seatbelt in for landing. Arcuni brought the cargo plane to the tarmac with a thump, but unlike last time, all the tires held and he was able to taxi the aircraft safely towards the hangars. He taxied past the disabled and abandoned "Janet Airline" Boeing 737 on the main ramp and taxied to the north end of the flight line. The plane made a large U-turn and stopped next to the hangar that housed the main entrance to the underground complex. The cargo ramp opened and one by one Arcuni shut down each of the four engines.

Standing on the tarmac outside the hangar were two airmen with M4 rifles in their hands facing outwards from the parked aircraft. Near where they stood lay the bodies of a dozen undead former employees of the secret base at Groom Lake. Positive that the sound of a landing aircraft would encourage more undead curiosity, Cliff wanted to get his truck out of the cargo bay and into the hangar quickly, then get everyone safely below ground.

The three new arrivals attached the loading ramps typically used to drive vehicles up the cargo ramp, which had some minor damage from the truck's hard entry into the cargo hold without the extra loading ramps. No time was wasted before the truck was released from the cargo tie downs and driven into the hangar. With the new silence of the aircraft engines turned off, Cliff could hold a conversation without having to yell. The three new arrivals introduced themselves to Cliff, whom they guessed correctly to be the leader.

"I'm Rick, this is Chris and Evan. We're with the 66th Rescue Squadron."

"So you're PJs?"

"Yeah. So who the fuck are you and what's up with stealing our plane? Where are we, Groom Lake?"

Cliff smiled a rare smile. "You can call me Cliff. Yes, you are now at Groom Lake. I'm sorry to say we don't have any aliens or flying saucers, but we do have a large underground complex and well-stocked shelter. We took your plane because we are in contact with a number of other survivors. Some of them need supplies, some of them need extract, and since Arcuni here knows how to fly a little bit, we took the Herc so we had a way to help those survivors. Also, thanks—I'm not sure if we could have cleared that horde of undead back there without all three of you helping."

The three Pararescue Jumpers nodded and exchanged looks with each other. Rick shrugged. Planned or not, the three of them were along for the ride. They followed Cliff into the hangar and into the large freight elevator, which lowered them below ground.

Terlingua, Texas

"Baby, we can't think about that. We've got to focus on the here and now. Find the basics and then we can figure it out from there."

"Fine, but then what? How are we going to get all the way to Nevada? What about that biker gang?"

"We can't focus on that yet; we just need to remain hidden. For now, we need to focus on water, food and shelter. We have the shelter for now, but I don't think we'll be able to stay for too long. We're too close to the park and too exposed. We only have a little food, the MREs and the rest of the five-gallon container of water."

"We're in the desert. Where are we going to find water out here?"

"There are options. The Rio Grande is nearby, a short drive if we had a vehicle. The buildings in this town should have well water, but I'm not sure if we can hand pump it."

"You need to find us another Jeep. You said there's some food and more bottled water in the store over there. So you need to focus on getting us out of here."

"You're probably right, Jess. The sun is setting. I'll go out tonight and try to find us something."

Jessie smiled and kissed her husband on the forehead.

CHAPTER 21

Fort Bliss, Texas
February 16, Year 1

"Apollo, what did you find?"

Lindsey sat quietly at a desk stuffed between floor to ceiling shelving units stacked high with hard cases of all kinds of equipment. Chivo and Apollo combed through the gear, opening each case one by one.

"I've got a 117 Foxtrot. Now help me find the SATCOM antenna for it."

The PRC-117F radio was exactly what they were looking for and what they needed, assuming they could find someone on the other end of the line to answer their call. After seeing the absolute destruction in El Paso and on base, and the throngs of undead swarming in the streets, Chivo began to hold serious doubts that there would be anyone left for them to reach out to for help. Apollo took the Hardigg case and set it on the desk where Lindsey sat, watching Chivo's flashlight dance in the darkness on the far end of the building.

"Apollo, found one! We're in luck!"

"OK, bring it up. Let's get outside, get a good line overhead and see if anyone picks up."

Chivo sat the small case with the SATCOM antenna next to the door, extinguished his flashlight and snapped his NODs to the mount on his helmet. After pausing a moment to let his eyes adjust to the grainy green images, Chivo slowly pulled the door open inch by inch, watching out the widening crack into the darkness outside. After a few seconds, Chivo pushed the door closed, holding the door handle open so it wouldn't make a loud click sound.

"We're overrun, mano," Chivo whispered.

"What?"

"Yeah, I guess the fence didn't hold or there's a breach in it or something, but there has to be at least twenty-five of those dead fuckers shambling around out there."

"Shit, we don't have the ammo for all of this. And once we start putting those down, more will come to join the party, then more after that. What the fuck, man."

"We need to get away from the middle of this post. Maybe get out into the desert, out into the maneuver and training areas."

"On the upside, we have a bunch of Humvees and up-armored vehicles in the area that we can choose from."

"Sure, but the downside is that they get gallons to the mile, they break all the damn time, and we won't have any support vehicles. What we need is another non-standard vehicle, something light and fast."

Lindsey broke her silence, startling the two men planning their escape. "What is a non-standard vehicle?"

Chivo smiled, even though that was lost on Lindsey behind his thick beard and the darkness. "A non-standard vehicle is like a civilian vehicle, something that the military doesn't issue, like that truck we had. Back when Apollo and I were in the Stan, we always used Toyota 4-Runners or a Hilux because they blended with the locals and you couldn't kill one. Much more reliable than a Humvee."

"Couldn't we take a Humvee to go find a Toyota or truck or something since there seemed to be a lot of military trucks sitting around when we drove in?"

Apollo agreed. "We're going to have to do that, Chivo. The next question is which one of the trucks out there has a full tank of fuel, will start, and will actually run long enough for a quick escape? Seems like most of them were broken most of the time."

"We start with the last intersection where the MP parked his. You figure it had fuel and worked a few days ago when he drove it there."

"OK, we do that, but do we bring Lindsey and the 117 with us, or leave them and make a return trip?"

"Don't leave me. Please don't leave me alone again," Lindsey half cried.

"Well Apollo, guess she's coming with us. Might as well bring the radio too. How many mags do you have? I'm down to two."

"I have three."

"Shit, mano. This is starting to get bad."

"Not as bad as Tripoli."

"No, not as bad as Tripoli, but worse than Sukkur."

They both chuckled with that thought.

"OK, want to bet there are some walkers near that Humvee that have some mags on their carriers?"

"No bet, but maybe if we stay here tonight and each put an empty mag under our pillow the ammo fairy will visit and fill them with 5.56 for us."

"The only fairy I believe in is your mom, which explains you."

Lindsey couldn't see Chivo and Apollo in the darkness and wasn't sure they were joking. "What is wrong with you two?"

Chivo laughed. "OK, Apollo, back on task. We get the Humvee, search for ammo, find more ammo on post somewhere, maybe some MREs and haul ass. Am I leaving anything out?"

"Yeah, the 117F. Take it now or come back for it later?"

"I can carry the radio, but I'll be down to a pistol for the half-click jog to the intersection. If we can move fast enough, it shouldn't be a problem."

Apollo gave Chivo a thumbs-up. "Lindsey, stay between us, keep moving no matter what, and we'll get through this together."

After stowing the SATCOM antenna in the case with the radio, Apollo placed the case by the door. A spare battery for the radio went into each of their packs. Chivo also stowed a spare antenna and handset in his pack with the radio battery. Chivo stood behind the door's opening path and slowly turned the handle. Inch by inch, he quietly pulled the door open. Apollo stood back from the opening door, M4 up, NODs flipped in front of his face, and raised his left hand with his palm flat. Moonlight flared in Chivo's goggles from the opening door. Chivo stopped and held the door still. Apollo switched off his NODs and flipped them up away from his face. The moonlight was bright enough that he didn't want to waste the battery power, Chivo followed suit.

A thumbs-up and Chivo slowly pulled the door all the way open, held it in place with his foot, and picked up the heavy radio case before giving his partner a thumbs-up. Apollo looked at Lindsey and smiled before sliding out of the open door so quietly he could have startled a ghost. Chivo's M4 hung on the sling across his chest, his pistol in his right hand, tucked against his chest.

Apollo glided left and immediately saw why the undead milled in the previously secured area. The fence had collapsed inward where they had previously cut a hole. The shuffling feet of the thirty walking corpses by the building sounded like death's hand knocking, but they mostly ignored the three living people that stepped out into the moonlight until the door snapped shut behind them with a loud clack.

All thirty pairs of dead eyes locked onto the three living intruders and the moans of the dead drowned out the shuffling feet, each horrible face clicking its teeth in excited anticipation of a fresh meal. Lindsey wanted to close her eyes, she wanted to stop and hide, but behind her Chivo's voice was hard. "Move! Do not stop! Keep up and move!"

Apollo's rifle report pierced the night, "Contact front! Pick up the pace, buddy!"

Apollo stepped on the chain-link fence, which now lay flat on the ground, and began moving in a half-jog. Lindsey locked her eyes on his back, running to keep up while trying to ignore the sea of death surrounding them. The sharp snap of Apollo's rifle was punctuated with the flat sound of Chivo firing his pistol as quickly as he could, putting down the undead closest to the group. The pistol's slide locked back on an empty magazine. "LOADING!" Chivo yelled over the rifle fire. Not willing to stop and not willing to drop the radio case in his left hand, Chivo jammed the empty pistol into the top opening of his armor carrier so he could let it go. He then pushed the magazine release button and dropped the empty magazine into his dump pouch before retrieving a fresh mag from his carrier and slamming that into the butt of the pistol. Grasping the grip, Chivo thumbed the slide release, bringing the reloaded pistol into battery as the pistol's slide slammed forward. "UP!" Chivo yelled to Apollo, who could now bring his focus away from having to cover Chivo's area of fire.

Apollo reached the Humvee and went immediately to the driver's door, which stood open. The dead body of the MP slumped into the floorboard. A large and bloody bite mark to his left shoulder gave reason to the apparently self-inflicted gunshot wound to his head. Dried blood, skull fragments, and brain matter were sprayed across the interior of the Humvee. Apollo pulled the body out of the truck and to the pavement. Chivo opened the back door and pushed Lindsey onto the back seat, followed by the radio case, before slamming the door shut. Chivo turned and immediately shot two more undead that were nearly touching him.

"We've got to get, mano. Hurry it the fuck up!"

Apollo grabbed two full M4 magazines from the dead MP before climbing into the driver's seat and shutting the door. His gloved hand grabbed the large three-way switch. He put his foot on the brake, put the transmission in neutral and flipped the switch over to the start position. The big diesel motor coughed to life and Apollo was relieved to see the fuel gauge needle bounce to just past the three-quarter mark. Chivo climbed into the passenger's seat as Apollo mashed his foot on the accelerator.

"Dude, lights."

"Yeah." Apollo pushed the buttons below the starter toggle to black out all the external lights. They didn't want any more attention than they already had.

"Where now, Chivo?"

"North mano, north towards the ranges. We need more ammo pronto."

CHAPTER 22

Terlingua, Texas
February 16, Year 1

The moon provided a surprisingly bright light. Bexar left Jessie and Keeley in their new cabin so he could try to find a vehicle that still ran after the EMP. Bexar walked slowly in the moonlight, holding his AR-15 loosely, tired and letting most of the weight rest on the padded sling. The last two days had been incredibly hard on Bexar, and he simply didn't have the energy or focus to be as vigilant as he should. Fifteen minutes was all it took for Bexar to walk around the back of the Starlight Theatre, hoping to be lucky enough to find a working vehicle close by. Bexar really wished he still at least had the hand-cranked shortwave radio with the hope of hearing some updated news. It would simply be too much to also wish for the HAM radio stowed in the metal cabinet on the top of Emory Peak.

An old F-100 caught Bexar's eye, but it had been abandoned for a long time and quite obviously had not run for even longer. Bexar, giving up hope of finding anything close, turned and started to walk down the hill towards the highway. He didn't remember seeing any usable vehicles the previous night, but he wasn't really focused on looking for one either. Thirty minutes later, Bexar was in the parking lot of the bar and grill he'd passed by the first night, steam rising off his head in the cold winter air. An old Jeep CJ sat in the parking lot, which raised Bexar's hopes, but when he opened the hood he found the owner had performed an engine swap. A new fuel-injected V-8 wouldn't work now. If only the owner had kept the original equipment. Shaking his head, Bexar gently set the hood back in place. In the dark windows of the restaurant behind him, the shadows moved. Bexar didn't want to excite the zombies trapped in the restaurant or have to deal with them tonight. He felt like he was on the edge of a nervous breakdown and he wasn't sure he could take any more problems.

Bexar continued down the hill and was standing across from the small hotel nearly to the highway when he heard the thundering pops of motorcycles riding in fast from the north.

"God dammit," Bexar whispered to himself. He jogged to a horse trailer parked in the sand near the hotel and lay prone on the ground, his rifle pointed towards the highway. He didn't want to risk running up the hill and being seen. Bexar hoped the bikers would just pass by their location. He lay motionless, frustrated that he couldn't get away from the damn bikers and get his family to safety. Adding to his anger was the sight of his lovingly built bug-out vehicle, the Jeep Wagoneer he'd owned since high school, sitting on the road in front of him, totally destroyed from the wreck. The sound of the motorcycles continued to grow louder, and then Bexar saw the headlights appear over the hill and approach his wrecked Wagoneer. Bexar took deep breaths, exhaling through his nose while trying to keep his heart rate and mind in control. He was nearly sure that if the bikers turned the motorcycles off, they would be able to hear his heart pounding in his chest.

The two riders stopped by the Wagoneer and appeared to be talking, but they left their bikes running and Bexar couldn't hear them. Bexar stopped breathing when he saw the older biker with a long beard point up the hill towards the ghost town and his cabin. The riders turned and began riding up the hill towards him. Bexar's right thumb pushed the safety on his AR down and he smoothly pressed the trigger. One of the motorcycles swerved sharply, the rider falling off before the bike fell and slid in a shower of sparks on the pavement. The second rider skid to a stop, drew a pistol, and fired wildly in the direction he thought he saw a muzzle flash. Bexar began snapping his trigger sharply, firing the AR rapidly as the biker turned and left in a full throttle cloud of dust and fury of sound. Bexar felt a sudden burning pain in his right thigh. With all of the adrenaline flowing through his body, it felt like someone snapped a rubber band against his bare skin. Bexar thought he saw the bike shudder and swerve, but the rider remained upright and rode over the crest of the hill back towards the park at a high rate of speed.

Bexar stood and walked to where the downed biker lay on his back, his face bleeding from road rash and clutching his shoulder where blood oozed around his fingers from the bullet wound. The biker began to speak but Bexar fired a single shot into the man's face. The heavy crimson blood flowed out of the hole in the man's skull, painting the pavement. Bexar was too angry to show mercy. Angry that the bikers ruined everything. Angry that the bikers killed his friends, and angry that the bikers made him flee and hide his family. The motorcycle lay in the sand on the side of the road, still running. As Bexar walked to the bike, the pain in his right leg grew in intensity, each step resulting in a painful limp.

Although the headlight was smashed and the gas tank now had a large dent in it, the bike appeared to be rideable. If it weren't for Keeley and the gear, he and Jessie would be set for transportation. Bexar flipped the kill ignition switch off before pushing the motorcycle upright. With a deep breath, Bexar switched on his flashlight and looked at his right leg. His pants leg was soaked in blood.

Bexar looked up the hill and wasn't sure he could walk up it. He sat on the motorcycle, started it, and rode up the hill to the cabin. Careful to park the motorcycle out of view behind the cabin, Bexar limped to the front door and softly knocked four times. "Jessie, it's me."

The door latch clicked open and Bexar limped into the cabin.

"Oh my God, Bexar! What happened?"

"Help me get these pants off. I think I'll be OK."

The wound on Bexar's leg appeared to be a grazing wound. Thankfully, they wouldn't have to worry about a round lodged in his leg. He and Jessie used a washrag from the bathroom and the med kit to clean the wound as best they could. Jessie squeezed about half a tube of antibiotic ointment into the wound and pressed the white cloth hard against his leg before wrapping duct tape around the makeshift bandage.

"Thank you, baby. There were two of them. I killed one, but the other got away. I'm not sure if I nicked him or what, but I tried."

Outside the cabin, they heard the unmistakable sound of the moaning walking dead.

"God dammit. If things weren't bad enough, all of the noise brought us more fucking zombies."

CHAPTER 23

Near Terlingua, Texas
February 16, Year 1

The highway was pitch black. Without a working headlight only the moonlight glowing off the asphalt lit his way. Being so remote, the road would have been just as dark before the end of the world, but that fact was lost on Buzzer. His right hand pinned the throttle of his old Harley all the way back, the motor spinning as fast as it could, but the world around him moved slowly by. For three days, Buzzer had not slept, smoking more meth when he started to crash. He was quickly running out and wasn't sure when the club would be able to cook more, but that didn't matter now. What mattered was that he was going to kill that asshole, but first he had to get Russell and some more men for the fight.

While near El Paso, the club had raided every pharmacy they found, taking large bags full of Vicodin, Viagra, Xanax, and pseudoephedrine. The pseudoephedrine was used to cook meth. The rest was just to party.

The old Harley sprayed oil out of the top of the motor, the valve cover having been caught by one of Bexar's widely fired AR rounds. The spraying oil drenched Buzzer's left leg, but it was also coating the rear tire of the motorcycle in a thick layer of oil. Nearing Study Butte and the turn for Highway 118, Buzzer flew up on a large gaggle of undead shambling westward, following the path he and Mike had taken earlier. Buzzer pushed on the handlebars and felt the rear end of the motorcycle slide out from under him. He grabbed a fistful of brake lever, but it was much too late. The oil slick tire slid out from under the motorcycle, violently throwing the motorcycle on its side. Buzzer's right foot caught under the crash bars.

The motorcycle slid into the walking corpses at seventy miles per hour, knocking them off their feet like bowling pins, which could have been funny if the sparks from the sliding motorcycle hadn't caught Buzzer's oil-soaked pants and motorcycle on fire. Bodies bounced off the motorcycle and over Buzzer.

Eventually the motorcycle slid to a stop, Buzzer's right leg shredded from the grinding asphalt and his left leg on fire from the oil. Punctured in the crash, the gas tank caught, and Buzzer burst into flames, trapped under his motorcycle as the undead approached. Buzzer screamed as the dead, unfazed by the fire, bit into his body, ripping away chunks of flesh while he burned. Ribbons of burning flesh hung from the zombie's mouths as they began to catch fire as well, the burning fat popping amidst Buzzer's screams until eventually he lost consciousness.

Groom Lake, Nevada

Cliff escorted the three new arrivals to the large cargo elevator that descended underground to the first underground level, where there was a heavy blast door that secured the main entrance to the facility. The door stood open and they were greeted by an angry looking Major Wright, who stood next to the door holding an M4 rifle.

"Cliff, we've had an outbreak. I believe we have it contained to the bottom two floors. It started in the lab. I think Lance might be trapped or dead."

Cliff's face showed no emotion or reaction to the news, but his anger raged under his disciplined demeanor. Lance was the only remaining scientist associated with the Kali Project–the only person who had a chance at deciphering what the Chinese had engineered from the ancient virus. Cliff's mission to help stop the spread of the Yama Strain was over, leaving his underground facility in the wilds, like Fort Apache, to give aid to anyone needing it. The secondary plan, the absolute worst case, was now in effect.

"OK, Ben, how many?"

"Eight if you count the specimens that Lance kept in the lab," said Wright, just now noticing the three newcomers to the facility. "Who are these guys?"

"Sir, we're with the 66th Rescue Squadron. This guy stole our plane so we hitched a ride with him."

"Well, welcome aboard. We are in need of medically trained people, so it would seem."

Cliff looked at the PJs. "If you guys wouldn't mind giving me a hand, we need to take care of this problem before it gets any worse."

Once Arcuni and Garcia walked past the heavy blast door, followed by the airmen who were providing above-ground security, Wright pushed the big red button on the inside wall. Hydraulic rams pushed the door closed, and heavy steel pins pushed outward into the steel and concrete doorframe with a resounding deep thud.

Cliff guided the trio of Air Force special operators to the south stairwell and began making his way down the stairs. "The bottom floor is a research lab. They were working on the Yuma Strain, which is what caused all of this, since before the attack."

"So there's a cure?"

"Not yet, and now it doesn't seem like there will be if Lance is dead."

On the landing above the second to the bottom level, the floor above the lab, Cliff found an airman standing with an M4 pointed towards the heavy metal fire door. The new arrivals could see dents pushed through from the other side of the door. The sound of pounding fists from the other side of the metal door resonated in the concrete stairwell, punctuated by the muffled moans of the dead.

Standing at the top of the landing, Cliff spoke to the young airman. "Greg, when I give you the word I want you to open the door, sprint up the stairs, and stand behind us. Got it?"

"You want me to let them out?"

"Yes. We need to put them down, and the stairs will give us some safety. They usually trip on the first step and have to crawl up the rest of the steps."

Greg gave Cliff a look of disbelief, but nodded and walked down the stairs to the door.

"Guys, hold fire until the first one trips on the stairs. We need to let the first few out of the doorway so they don't jam up, making us go in after them. Also, head shots only please." The three PJs each responded with a thumbs-up.

"OK Greg, now."

Greg pushed the door handle down, turned, and sprinted up the stairs to stand behind Cliff and the other three. The door exploded into the stairwell, the first walking corpse falling forward from the door suddenly giving way. The second undead stepped through the doorway and tottered towards the stairs only to trip on the first step.

Cliff fired the first shot, a single shot, and the corpse on the stairs stopped moving, its head cracked open by the M4 round. Rick fired his rifle, as did Chris and Evan. Four undead lay dead for good in the stairwell, skull fragments and black rotted brain matter covering the painted concrete.

"Greg, after we go inside secure the door. We're going to clear the lab before doing secondary searches of each level."

Greg replied that he would and followed the four men down the stairs, careful not to slip in the oozing black brain matter that lay on the floor.

"OK guys, lab level. There should be four more if Wright correctly accounted for everyone. Beyond the landing are some offices followed by a slightly open area that leads to the lab's sealed doors. I had to clear this damned place by myself the first time and the way to do it is like we just did. Give the undead a path, make some noise, and let them come to you. It's too easy to get swarmed if you try to enter and clear a room fast."

The metal fire door on the bottom and last landing also had dents from the inside, but this time there was no banging on the door and no moaning dead to greet them.

"All right, stand easy for a minute. Let me get the door ready and then come back up the stairs with you."

Cliff walked to the door and pulled a large rubber doorstop out of the cargo pocket of his BDUs before quietly opening the door. He propped the door open with the door stop, trotted up the stairs next to the PJs, and used the muzzle of his rifle to bang on the pipe-metal handrail of the stairs. The stairwell resonated like a gong, and out of view on the other side of the open doorway, moans immediately erupted in response.

The first zombie that shambled through the doorway was Lance, part of his right forearm missing. It appeared that he wasn't a recently killed undead. His left eye hung out of his face, held on by parts of rotting flesh, and part of his lips were missing. Cliff fired a single shot, putting Lance down for good. Three more undead staggered out of the doorway into the stairwell, each put down with single headshots by Cliff.

"Damn. Well, you three do a sweep of this floor and the next, then get Greg to show you to your bunks and get some showers. On the way, stop by the storeroom and get some new BDUs. You guys smell like ass. Meet me in conference room D-1, Delta-One in ninety-mikes. We've got to discuss some stuff with the rest of the crew."

The PJs looked at a clock on the wall and mentally counted off their ninety-minute deadline.

Cliff didn't wait for an answer. He turned and jogged past Greg, tersely saying, "Stay put," as he passed.

CHAPTER 24

Cortez, CO
February 16, Year 1

"Jake, I think this could be our golden ticket. We can't do anything but take them at face value. I mean, what else can we do?"

"I'm not sure what good it would do us. They say they're in Nevada, Sara. I can't even start to wrap my head around how we could move all our families safely across the country to what is basically a mystery group who 'claim' that they are the good guys. They could be anyone and anywhere for that matter."

"Baby, I'm not sure that the vote to stay was the right one. Right now the attacks are light, but I don't think the problem of The Tribe is going to go away on its own. I think it will only get worse."

"I know, and I'm starting to agree, but the group voted on our course."

"It's time for another vote."

"Maybe."

Jake wasn't sure anymore. Bill, one of the older survivors, had spent the last four weeks slowly scavenging all the pieces he needed to repair his HAM radio to the point of finding butane-fired soldering irons and physically replacing pieces damaged by the EMP. The solar panels and deep-cycle batteries needed to power certain desired amenities was another pet project of Bill's, and with no surviving family members, he was generally left alone to work on his projects in his spare time and off-duty days. No one believed he would be successful until he received a news broadcast from the BBC on a shortwave radio frequency. Quickly, the group came to realize that the broadcast was old and on an electronic loop, repeating every three hours. However, it did give everyone hope of finding other survivors outside of their small Colorado town. Contact with a group claiming they were authorized government agents operating out of Nevada shot through the Colorado group like a bolt of lightning. Initially, many of the members wanted to immediately leave for Nevada and the promise of a better life, but then the magnitude of the logistics, the realization of how hard an overland journey would be set in, and the original spring of hope was quickly replaced by a deep well of despair.

To make the low morale worse, the attacks on the scavenging teams by members of The Tribe were increasing in frequency, as were probes into the group's defenses. Jake was certain that before long they would have to fight off a full-scale siege by The Tribe.

Bill burst into the room. "Jake! Part of the fence is down and there are walkers in the compound!"

Jake bolted out of his chair, joined by Sara. They ran out of the room, each armed with a machete or an axe. Bill continued through the old middle school, raising the alarm with all the other members before joining the group on the south side of the school grounds where the fence was breached. The children remained in the school, secured in an interior classroom with two of the older women, who gladly took the job of protecting the group's young.

Outside, Jake found that nearly fifty feet of fence was down and approximately sixty walking corpses shambled through the opening. Down Pine Street, he saw men in an old truck herding the zombies towards the school and anger raged through his veins. The religious cult had gone too far.

The fight for the school's courtyard lasted for nearly an hour. Two of their group were lost to bites, a man and a woman. Each of them left behind a spouse and a child.

After the fight, drenched in sweat, Jake turned to Sara. "This is too much. The Tribe has gone too far. Once the team repairing the fence is done, have everyone meet in the cafeteria for another vote. It's time we hunt these jackasses down."

CHAPTER 25

After each building they passed, more and more undead appeared around the edges, closing in on the sound of the Humvee rumbling by slowly. The group found each intersection manned by a now dead or missing MP, only the vehicles or dead bodies left behind. The bridge over the Liberty Expressway was not blocked, but after crossing it they ran into the fenced western edge of the Army Air Field's flightline.

"Around or through?"

Chivo shrugged and looked at the shambling horde that was just starting to crest the top of the bridge.

"Those fuckers just won't quit. They won't give up, will they?"

"No Chivo, they won't."

"The airfield looks clear and we've got to get on the other side of the runways."

Apollo gunned the motor and the big desert tan truck lurched forward towards the fence before following the road left and to an open gate that crossed the road. He stopped the truck just past the gate and both men climbed out of the Humvee. The undead horde, relentless, still approached, but they had a little bit of time.

Chivo closed the double gate and set the pin in the asphalt before wrapping the chain hanging on the gate around the gate poles twice. His last pair of flex cuffs went through the chain and through the fence to secure the gate the best he could.

"Too bad they didn't leave the lock. That was my last pair of flex cuffs."

Apollo shrugged. They returned to the Humvee and continued north, crossing over the rail spur that the Army used to transport their vehicles, and sped along at a blistering speed of forty miles per hour. They could see no movement in the dark desert around them, dead or alive.

Driving through the rail depot, Chivo pointed to a dark strip of road on their left. "I'm not sure this road makes it to the range, but I seem to remember that one does."

Apollo took the next left and the next right to turn onto Chaffee Road. With the moonlight, they could see a large number of undead trying to turn and follow the passing Humvee on the other side of the fence that lined the perimeter of the Army Post.

"Chivo, this whole fucking place is dead. How are we going to find any survivors?"

"We survived. Lindsey survived. There have to be others that survived too."

They drove in silence across the large expanse of the post for twenty minutes before they approached a highway crossing over their small road. Cars and trucks sat dormant on the road and Apollo never slowed the Humvee, trying to clear from under the bridge as quickly as he could after losing Odin to a falling corpse. Apollo slammed on the brakes and turned onto a dirt road; Chivo watched in the sideview mirror as three bodies fell off the bridge to follow them. He didn't see if any of them got back up and he hoped their legs were shattered from the fall and they were unable to walk or follow their passing truck. One more fence was all that separated them from Purple Heart Boulevard. More dormant and abandoned vehicles lined the road.

"Left here." Chivo pointed to a dirt road to the north and Apollo followed.

"OK, you'll see the shooting berms around the range in a second. Go right and we can go around them into the desert."

"Wait, what is this? This isn't an Army range," Apollo asked.

"Sort of. It's the Rod and Gun club. It's the closest place I could think of where we could find ammo and maybe some other gear. If we're lucky, it hasn't been looted yet. If we're really lucky, no one is in there, because it was closed for Christmas when the attack hit."

Apollo slowed, driving the Humvee off the dirt road and into the desert, following the tall dirt berm of a rifle range before turning to drive across the back of the ranges towards the middle of the complex. They drove through the clay shooting range and stopped close to the rear of the building, parking on the range. Apollo turned the Humvee to point towards the open desert in case they needed to make a fast escape before moving the selector switch to "OFF."

Chivo climbed out of the passenger seat and crouched by the rear tire with his rifle up, sweeping the back of the dark building with the muzzle of his rifle. Apollo climbed out of the driver's seat and walked around the front bumper, rifle up, taking position next to his teammate. He opened Lindsey's door and whispered, "Do you want to stay here in the truck or do you want to come with us?"

"I don't want to be alone again."

Lindsey climbed down from the Humvee and crouched beside Chivo. He pulled his pistol out of the holster and handed it to Lindsey. "You know how to work one of these?"

"Sure, I guess." Her right index finger snaked into the trigger guard.

"Hang on. Keep your booger flinger out of there, off the trigger and along the side of the gun until you're ready to shoot. Otherwise you'll end up shooting one of us by mistake. Good. Now keep the pistol tucked up to your chest like this. We'll take care of anything towards the front. Just make sure nothing shuffles up behind us. Got it?"

Lindsey looked over her shoulder to the desert expanding into an endless black hole and looked back at Chivo with wide eyes, who smiled and gave her a quick thumbs-up.

"If you two are done playing tea party, we need to clear this building and get secure."

Apollo and Chivo glided silently towards the building, each with his M4 raised, carefully watching their own slice of the pie in front of them and to the sides. The back door of the building was not closed all the way. Chivo slowly pulled the door open and held it open with his foot. Apollo stepped forward and waited. Chivo put his left hand on Apollo's shoulder, who waited for Chivo to squeeze his shoulder to give him the ready signal.

Chivo shook Apollo's shoulder, the sign to wait. Apollo glanced over his shoulder at Chivo with a confused expression, not understanding what the holdup was and why they weren't making entry. Chivo picked up a piece of a brick that was by the door and threw it into the dark building, which resulted in a resounding crash piercing the still winter's night.

Immediately the sound was responded to by a dark moan that erupted deep inside the building, followed by more crashing and the sound of chairs being knocked over. Chivo picked up another piece of brick and propped the door open before signaling Apollo to fall back away from the door. Lindsey stayed behind

Chivo, facing towards the Humvee and the desert, trying to keep rear security, but she kept looking over her shoulder nervously and shuddered with a soft whimper when the walking corpse crashed towards the open door.

Chivo squeezed the pressure switch on his M4's vertical grip, activating the weapon-mounted light, and illuminated what used to be a very overweight middle-aged man stumbling towards them. Chivo backed up, bumping into Lindsey, who quickly scurried out of the way. Chivo let the corpse fall through the doorway before firing a single shot into the zombie's skull, putting the man down for good.

They all waited for another full minute before stepping over the rotted corpse by the door and into the back of the Rod and Gun Club. Slowly, Chivo and Apollo swept each room, checking every closet and every place a person could hide. The smell was nearly unbearable. The small restaurant in the building must have been stocked with food before the EMP hit and all of it had rotted. The smell was so bad it even masked the smell of the rotting corpse just outside the back door. Twenty minutes later Chivo and Apollo were confident that the building was clear and they found what they were looking for: ammo.

Flashlight held in his teeth, Apollo stacked boxes of civilian .223 in a pile on the counter next to the cash register. Chivo ripped open the cardboard packaging and dumped the rounds, one twenty-round box at a time, into an empty green ammo can.

"Are you keeping count of how many boxes you're opening?"

"Yes, but if you keep interrupting me I won't be able to."

"Twenty, thirty-three, fourteen, seventy-two ..."

"Damnit, you ass."

Chivo and Apollo both chuckled, their first chance for real humor since Zennie died.

"OK, looks like we have right at three hundred rounds."

Chivo looked at the loose rounds in the bottom of the ammo can.

"Shit."

"Yeah, well, it's still better than nothing and much better than what we had before."

"Lindsey, how about we get you your own pistol so I can have mine back," Chivo said, pointing at the glass case she was sitting on. In the case lay a single pistol, a Glock 19. The rest of the case was empty. In a drawer under the glass case, Chivo located the pistol's case and the two magazines that came with it. Also in the drawer was a fifty-round box of 9mm, and the good luck continued when on the wall behind the glass cases they found a display of holsters, including one for a G19. A few moments later, Lindsey was now the proud new owner of a Glock 19, loaded and holstered on her right hip.

"You didn't even have to wait seven days, chica."

Lindsey smiled at Chivo, who busily got back to work reloading his empty M4 magazines.

CHAPTER 26

**The Basin, Big Bend National Park
February 16, Year 1**

Russell pushed the nude woman off the bed and onto the floor where she fell with a thud and woke with a scream. He backhanded her across the jaw and she fell silent, staring at the floor, scared to look up at him while he pulled his dirty jeans on. The motorcycle club president pulled his long hair into a tight ponytail, lit a cigarette, and walked out of the cabin into the cold morning air. The sky over the mountains to the east glowed faintly orange with the rising sun; Russell hadn't slept in three days, flying high on crystal meth. He pulled a large zip-top bag out of the saddle bag on his motorcycle, which was full of smaller bags of Xanax, Vicodin, and Viagra, and a handful of smaller "one hit" bags of crystal meth. His supply was dwindling fast. The decongestant was cooked down into crystal meth for the club members, and if he was getting low then he knew everyone was getting low. If they ran out of drugs, the club members would tear themselves apart.

"Where the fuck is Buzzer?" Russell yelled to no one in particular, his voice echoing softly against the mountains.

"Give me a prospect!"

Two scraggly men leapt out of the old van in the parking lot and ran to where Russell stood.

"You two get another prospect, take the van north, and knock over as many pharmacies as you can find. Get back here before sundown tomorrow, and you better come back loaded with gear."

"What, leave now?"

"Yes, god dammit! Leave fucking now!"

The two prospects ran back to the old van, yelling another man's name before starting the van and driving down the road towards the exit of The Basin.

Russell walked to the row of smaller cabins on his right and opened the door to the first one he came to. Brad, whom everyone called Dirty Dick or DD for short, lay flat on his back, feet on the floor, passed out on his bed with a lit cigarette in his mouth. Russell kicked DD's foot, startling him awake.

"What, Prez?"

"Have you seen Buzzer?"

"Naw, he and Mike haven't gotten back yet."

"Get someone and go find them."

"Right, Prez."

DD pulled on his boots, walked out of the door, pissed on the bush in front of his cabin and sauntered off to get another club member. Ten minutes later the mountains echoed with the thundering exhaust of the two motorcycles leaving The Basin towards Terlingua in search of Buzzer and Mike.

Russell walked back to his motorcycle and pulled out his bag of drugs and a small glass pipe. He needed a boost to make it another day.

Groom Lake, Nevada

Cliff entered the conference room. Wright, Arcuni, and four other airmen, along with Chris, Rick and Evan, the newly arrived PJs, sat waiting around a large table in the middle of the room. The PJs were dressed in brand new woodland BDUs and were freshly showered, which they took no small joy in after having had to endure such a long time without running water while stranded at Nellis AFB.

Cliff walked to the front of the room by a large smart board and began, "Lance is dead."

Most of the people in the room looked shocked. Wright was the first to speak, "What happened and what are we going to do now?"

"Unless by some miracle of God or Buddha or The Flying Spaghetti Monster or whatever deity anyone can believe in anymore we find a microbiologist or a virologist or someone else who is similarly trained, we will have to assume that there is not nor will there ever be a cure for the Yama Strain. The Kali Project is now officially over." Cliff met the face of each man. The feeling of defeat filled the room.

"Our mission now, what we must accomplish, is to redouble our efforts to find survivors. We have to help them in any way we can. We need to bring survivors here so we can protect them and help them survive. We are no longer fighting to save what is left of the United States. Our fight now is against the extinction of the human race."

"Ben." Cliff pointed to Major Wright. "What is our current status board of survivors?"

Wright sat up and flipped through the pages on his clipboard. "We currently have contact with two hundred and nineteen known survivors in sixty-seven groups that are confirmed through radio contact on the civilian amateur radio bands. We have located another hundred possible survivor group locations using the SeeMe SATINT system."

"Anything on the military bands? Any contact with any of the remains of our military?"

"We have only caught brief bursts of encrypted transmissions, but we didn't have the right crypto to intercept and decode."

"Keep trying. Broadcast in the blind on the military freqs as well. If we're going to make this work, we are going to need more than just the civilian survivors. We're going to need trained men and women to fight the undead to protect our facility first, then to branch out into the surrounding areas."

Cliff stopped for a moment. "What about our first group, our friends in the national park in Texas? Do you have the new imagery yet?"

Wright pointed to one of the airmen sitting further down the table. "Have you had a chance to evaluate the latest?"

"Not yet, sir. We just got it downloaded from the last overhead pass before coming to this meeting."

Cliff pointed to the smart board behind him. "Can you pull it up now? Put it up here? I want to take a look at it."

The airman said he could and walked to the computer on the table against the wall. The group continued to discuss finding more surviving military members when Evan, one of the PJs who had been silent thus far, joined the conversation.

"Nellis was completely dead. We had to scavenge the base for supplies and four teammates were lost during those operations. We didn't find a single survivor. Maybe there are others, maybe there were better equipped bases, or our Navy not in port might still have living souls on their ships, but out of our entire base I'm confident that we were the last three living persons."

The airman by the computer cleared his throat. "Cliff, the latest imagery is up." He dimmed the lights and a large photo taken from the satellite that passed overhead filled the screen. It showed The Basin in Big Bend National Park, but was too far zoomed out to see more than just the general outline of the roads. The airman zoomed in the image, panning up the road towards the standing structures and stopping on what looked like a small group of people congregating near a vehicle before zooming in further.

"What the hell?" Cliff pointed to the group of undead bent over something in the middle of the road. "Is that a child?"

An uneasy silence fell on the room before the airman used a laser pointer to begin talking everyone through the evaluation of the imagery as he completed it.

"That appears to be a crew-served weapon, those are motorcycles, and yes, I believe that is a group of walking corpses feeding on a small child. That appears to be the remains of another body near the child and I think that is another body on the roof of this building here." The red dot pointed to the overhead view of the roof of one of the cabins.

Cliff stood and walked closer to the screen. "Zoom out. We need to see if there is any evidence of survivors."

The photo zoomed out slowly. The roads were quickly lost in the expanding view of the desert.

"Wait, pan north and zoom in a little along the road to the north. The projected screen zoomed into the road and panned slowly, following the empty road.

"Wright, which direction did those bikers come from again?"

"They rode in from the west."

"OK, follow the intersection road west."

The airman continued west, following the empty desert road before stopping on a view with a vehicle in it. Without being asked he zoomed in, filling the screen with the overhead photo of an SUV pulling an RV traveling westbound.

"OK, that has to be them," Cliff said, a rare smile creeping onto his face. "When is the next overhead pass?"

Wright looked at the clock on the wall. "Four hours."

"Great. Go back over past imagery and figure out where that RV and truck came from, then find out where it went. I want to know what happened to our friends."

CHAPTER 27

Cortez, Colorado
February 16, Year 1

"I have no fucking idea where they found something like that!" Jake yelled.

Jake and Bill hunkered behind a concrete retaining wall, while automatic rifle fire strafed the ground above them. The plan to fight back against The Tribe was failing miserably. Seven of his men lay dead. Their school, their sanctuary, was under siege, and they were pinned down in an ambush while trying to sneak back into the school after a scavenger run. This was wrong on too many levels. The Tribe wasn't supposed to win; they were the bad guys. Jake thought of Sara and his anger raged. His wife, his best friend, had been taken and was being held captive by the violent cult. If she were alive, that is. Most of the women who had taken refuge with Jake and Sara at the school were missing, either captured or possibly killed. The men who remained fought hard, but were armed only with axes, machetes, and improvised weapons. Those worked well against the zombies, but against The Tribe, Jake simply felt helpless.

Jason, the married teenager who was the first to seek refuge with Jake, had left a few minutes before, running away as fast as he could from the machine gun fire, zigzagging as he ran before ducking through a row of houses and towards a construction site to the south. The sound of a large diesel motor rattled through the silence. A manual gearbox ground and crunched with each shift, rattling the air with the approaching sound of an old semi-truck. Accelerating as quickly as the worn motor could muster, an ancient semi truck burst into view, black smoke pouring out of the twin stack exhausts over the back of the cab as if the truck were burning coal instead of diesel.

The machine gun erupted into a new barrage of fire. Approaching from the rear, Bill and Jake watched The Tribe's fire dance around the truck, but they couldn't bring their rounds to target. The truck's windshield shattered as the truck roared by the pinned-down men.

The automatic rifle fire abruptly stopped, the machine gun silenced. Jake peeked over the top of the retaining wall to see Jason climb out of the bullet-riddled cab with a bloodstained machete in his hand. Jason walked to the rear of the truck where the two ruined bodies of The Tribe's attackers lay in grotesque horror, killed by being run down and driven over by the truck's heavy wheels. Surprisingly, only one of the rear dual tires on the trailer appeared flat; the rest of the truck appeared serviceable.

Jason walked to the first man's body and with a hard overhead swing cleaved the man's head in two. He walked to the second body and repeated the same motion with his machete. Jake and Bill joined Jason and found the offending machine gun lying on the ground under the truck's trailer, the barrel sharply bent.

"Damn, that would have been handy to have."

"Sorry, Jake. This was the best I could come up with."

"Jason, no, don't be sorry. You did great. You saved Bill and me. But how did you know the truck would start?"

"I didn't. I took a gamble. I remembered seeing this truck at the construction site while out on a scavenge, but we never investigated to see if it worked. We just assumed it didn't work like all the other vehicles. But I figured that being old, it might be old enough to still work. I couldn't think of anything else to try so that was all I had."

"Well good gamble, let's get your new beast back to the school. We're going to have to figure out the next step."

CHAPTER 28

Terlingua, Texas
February 16, Year 1

Indifferent to the end of the world, and just like before the EMP attack, the little girl of the Reed family rarely slept in to what could even be considered a normal time, although they had no working clock anymore. Bexar parted the curtains slightly and saw the eastern horizon growing faintly lighter, the sun just starting to rise. The moans of the undead had subsided during the night, and Bexar really hoped that a rat or a javelina or something had distracted them and led the zombies away from the cabin and his family.

Bexar pulled the curtains open a little further and saw some of the undead standing near the cabin as if they were in a trance, not moving, just standing there like they were waiting for something to happen. Keeley was smart for her age, but she was still a toddler, and Jessie worked very hard to keep her playtime quiet or at least quiet enough that she wouldn't be heard through the thin, rock-constructed walls.

"Jess, I don't know why they're like that. Maybe because it was night time? But we've seen them move at night before."

"Maybe because it's really cold out there and they slow down in the cold? It's really cold in here too."

"Fine, start a fire, but keep it small in case we need to put it out in a hurry. And I don't want too much smoke in the air above us."

The small wood-burning fireplace in the corner of the living area still had a stack of small cut logs next to it with a pile of wood chips to help get the fire started. Before the fall of civilization, this would have been a romantic getaway destination. It only took a few minutes for the wood to begin popping, and soon Keeley joined her mother close to the fire, trying to chase the chill away.

"What are you going to do?"

Bexar stood with a grimace. His leg hurt—it really hurt—but it didn't hurt as bad as he would have thought. As a cop, he'd always wondered what it would feel like to be shot and deeply longed to never find out. Thankfully, it had only been a grazing wound. He shuddered to think what would have happened if it had been a devastating shot like what happened to Amber, Malachi's wife. Actually, he did know what could have happened—he would have died just as she had and hopefully Jessie would have been strong enough to put him down for good before his reanimated corpse could bite her or Keeley. The thought of being a corpse condemned to walk the earth in death made Bexar realize he no longer feared death. He feared becoming a part of the undead.

"I'm going to take the motorcycle and lead our new friends outside away from the cabin. Then I'm going to ride to Lajitas to see if I have any better luck finding us a new vehicle."

"If you could get another motorcycle, I could ride with Keeley in my lap."

"We really don't want to do that. We would have to give up what little bit of gear we have left and we would be at the mercy of the weather, never mind having no protection from the undead on the roads at all. Besides, you don't even know how to ride."

"I figured you could teach me. Anyway, how come their motorcycles work when nothing else does?"

"I'm not sure. Malachi probably would have known, but I can say that the motorcycle I took from the guy I killed seems really old. I'm not sure what year it is, but I seriously doubt it has any electronics on it at all. Regardless, I learned to never underestimate a hard-core biker's ability to cobble together some bullshit to keep a beat-up old Harley running with nothing but electrical tape and some barbed wire."

Jessie ignored the comment. "How are you going to get to the bike with the undead standing around out there?"

"That I haven't figured out yet, but I was thinking you could throw something out the front door while I sneaked out the back. But I don't know what."

Jessie picked up a fake plant in a small ceramic pot. "I bet this would make some good noise when it crashed and broke."

Bexar smiled while he unpacked his go-bag to rearrange for a quick day-trip. Down to a single AR-15 between the two of them, Bexar took the majority of loaded Pmags, twelve in total. That left a few behind, but he was torn between carrying all the ammo he could and the weight if he needed to move on foot, limping as slowly as that may be. Bexar also chose his multitool, a stripped-down MRE, two bottles of water, the medical trauma kit, and the cheap binoculars he'd taken the night before. Bexar looked around the room and took one of the surplus green wool army blankets off the bed and cut a hole in the middle.

"Why did you do that? Now our blanket has a big hole in the middle."

Bexar winked at Jessie before putting on his chest rig and shouldering his go-bag. He slung the rifle across his chest and put the big CM Forge knife back in the sheath on his belt next to his pistol. He tossed the wool blanket over his body, sticking his head through the hole that he'd cut in the middle. Some 550-cord made a quick belt around his waist to hold the wool poncho down against the wind.

"See, now I won't freeze to death on the ride. If you didn't notice, I don't exactly have my heavy riding jacket or face fleeces with me, so I needed something. I should be home by sundown. If something happens and I'm not, hold the fort; I'll be back soon."

Jessie kissed Bexar before he limped to the back door. She took the fake potted plant in her hand. She glanced out the window to make sure there wasn't a surprise right outside the door before opening it quickly and throwing the ceramic pot, fake plant and all, into the parking lot, where it landed with a loud crash. Bexar pulled his big knife and exited out the rear door onto the back porch. An undead teenager stood facing the desert, away from the door, in his underwear, looking a bit like he'd had too much to drink at an underage party. Bexar crept slowly behind the walking corpse and drove the knife into the back of his skull.

The body fell, the teenager's ruined skull hitting the pavement and the knife falling with him, pulling Bexar off balance and onto the ground on top of the body. His right leg throbbed sharply from the sudden movement. Bexar rolled off the body, fighting back the urge to throw up. He stood as quickly as he could and brushed the maggots off the front of his poncho before wiggling the knife back and forth to free it from the skull. Working it loose, Bexar bent to wipe the blade off on the only piece of clothing the kid was wearing, a pair of underwear, but he noticed that the cotton briefs were caked and stained with blood and dried old shit. The thought hadn't crossed Bexar's mind before, but bodies release their bowels when they die and apparently that was true even if the body reanimated afterwards.

Bexar shuddered, brushed the remaining maggots off his poncho, and added to the gore by wiping his knife on the green wool. The old Harley was right where he'd left it and surprisingly there was no puddle of oil under it. It started without much effort. The straight pipe exhaust made Bexar's skin crawl, the noise accosting his tactical sense of the absolute need to be quiet to avoid the undead. Side stand up, Bexar gently rolled on the throttle and blipped the motor a few times as he pulled past the front of the cabin to make sure that every pair of dead eyes were on him.

Regardless of the reason, Bexar was happy to be in the saddle again. Motor-cops are motor-cops because they love to ride, and Bexar was no different. He didn't realize how much he had missed being on two wheels. Slowly, Bexar rode down the hill towards the highway, blipping the throttle often, leading the undead out of Terlingua like the pied piper. Once on the highway and with a little bit of time before the following mob of walking corpses could reach him, Bexar feathered the clutch, toed the rear brake and began riding in tight circles, tighter and tighter with each figure eight on the asphalt, the floorboards scraping the pavement. Bexar's head snapped left and right with each turn. The undead continued to close the gap, relentless, so Bexar pointed the front wheel south, rolled on the throttle, and shifted gears. Each time his left heel kicked the shifter into a higher gear, Bexar grabbed another handful of throttle, riding faster and faster while laughing, able to forget his worries for just a short amount of time with an early morning ride through the desert.

Study Butte, Texas

Two motorcycles riding side by side slowed and stopped in the middle of Highway 118 where it intersected with Highway 170. A motorcycle lay in the road, mostly burned. The undead near the burned motorcycle took notice of the new arrivals disturbing the peace of the feeding dead and began shambling towards the two bikers.

"DD, isn't that Buzzer's bike?"

"Yeah, and what's left of that asshole is still under the bike. Fuck, man. Russell is going to be pissed."

Before the walking corpses could reach them, the two riders turned around on the highway and rode back to the park as fast as they could.

Near Lajitas, Texas

The scenery of the highway meandering through the desert was incredible. The mountains in the distance, the sun rising over the desert floor ... Bexar would have really enjoyed the ride if the need to find a vehicle and get back to his family wasn't his immediate thought. It was a blessing that they were in such an isolated part of Texas. The highway was nearly devoid of any abandoned cars or trucks and Bexar didn't see a single undead walking on the highway. He shuddered to think what Waco or Dallas was like now.

Bexar passed a fireworks stand on the side of the highway outside of town and stopped the bike. December 26. He hadn't thought about the fireworks stands being open, selling for New Year's Eve when the attacks came. Bexar found the stand completely abandoned, but hundreds of Chinese-made fireworks remained on the shelves. Bexar grabbed four big boxes of Black-Cats and a box of sparklers and stowed them in a saddlebag on the still-running motorcycle. Movement from across the highway caught Bexar's attention. Two elderly corpses walked towards him.

"Loud pipes save lives, my ass. All they do is call the dead to the hunt!" Bexar said out loud to no one before gingerly climbing back on the bike, his right leg still throbbing, and continuing his ride to Lajitas. A handful of modern trucks were parked in the lot for the state park's visitor center and Bexar really had no desire to investigate it by himself—especially after the fiasco of the first day he and his friends had upon arrival into Big Bend. That memory was still raw. Bexar continued to ride until reaching the edge of Lajitas, near where the resorts were located just off the highway. He rode the motorcycle off the road and parked it on the side stand behind the sign for the Maverick Ranch. Even with basically no chance of passing traffic, he wanted the bike to be slightly hidden from anyone who might pass. So far every other survivor he had met wasn't someone who wanted anything good. Bexar began towards the highway before returning to the bike and stuffing a small box of Black-Cat firecrackers in his cargo pocket.

Bexar walked in the middle of the highway, approaching the local resort and spa on his left, his right leg throbbing with each step. He turned to walk into the parking lot, uneasy about the hotel and buildings. He didn't see any movement, but that didn't mean he was alone. He felt eyes following him through the parking lot. Bexar pulled the front of his blanket poncho aside and held his rifle at the ready.

The landscaping near the entrance to the parking lot had an old wagon in it. Bexar moved to the wagon and crouched down, trying to stay concealed from anyone at the hotel while he tried to figure out his next step. Bexar couldn't shake the feeling that he was being watched, but there was no movement that he could see. Retrieving his binoculars, Bexar scanned the parking lot. He counted twenty-three vehicles in all, but not one of them looked old enough to have survived the EMP. Bexar saw a new, well-outfitted four-door Jeep Wrangler with two fuel cans on a rack by the spare tire. If he could find a vehicle, he needed fuel.

Bexar stowed the binoculars and crept slowly around the decorative wagon and into the parking lot, careful to stay away from the vehicles and anything that could have a walking corpse hiding behind it. A decorative fence separated the parking spots, so Bexar couldn't easily cut between parking spots; he decided to walk down the edge towards the Jeep. Parked next to the Jeep was a newer Chevy Tahoe with tinted windows. Bexar edged up to the back of the Jeep and gently tapped on the metal Jerry cans with the back of his knuckles. One of the cans still had gas in it!

Trying to be as quiet as possible, Bexar unlatched the gas can and set it gently on the pavement. Behind him, something slammed into the glass of the Tahoe with a wet thud, startling him. He fell backwards over the metal gas can with a rattling crash. Suddenly, from between the buildings, the feeding call of the moaning undead erupted in the still air. In the rear window of the Tahoe, a child was slamming her head against the glass. Bexar looked again and finally realized that the child was not living; she was beating her head against the glass trying to get her next meal.

The first undead appeared from between the cars by the building. Bexar raised his AR and fired two rounds. The undead body dropped to the ground, no longer moving. The muzzle of Bexar's rifle followed the movement caught in the corner of his vision. He aimed two more shots and another walking corpse fell to the ground. More moans filled the air. Dozens of undead began to appear, shambling from around the buildings of the resort and the vehicles in the parking lot, from nearly every direction. Bexar dropped his rifle to hang on the sling and pulled the firecrackers out of his pocket and his old Zippo out of his other pocket. He lit the fuse and paper before throwing the Black-Cats towards the approaching undead.

Bexar grabbed the fuel can and jogged as quickly as he could, limping in pain, back towards the motorcycle as the firecrackers filled the air with noise and violence. He cut the corner across the landscaping towards his motorcycle and barely missed the outstretched bony hands of an elderly corpse. The undead face flashed in his memory, ears missing, bottom lip missing and dried blood covering the front of the man's sweater vest.

As Bexar reached the motorcycle, he noticed his right pant leg was turning red with his blood. He was thankful he parked so close. He wasn't sure how much further he could have jogged, as bad as his leg hurt. He sat the gas can on the ground and looked at the motorcycle, blinked hard a couple of times and stared at the back of the bike. There was no sissy bar, he had no bungee cords, he had no way to quickly get the gas can attached to the motorcycle. The sound of scraping rocks and the approaching moans brought Bexar back to the present. He peeked around the sign and saw the approaching mass of undead bodies.

"FUCK!"

Bexar climbed into the saddle, started the bike, and rode back the way he came, the gas can left on the side of the road. The peaceful morning ride to Lajitas now became a pain-filled angry return ride in the mid-afternoon sun. After the previous weeks, Bexar still wasn't sure how long a group of undead would follow after they lost sight of their prey. He hoped they wouldn't follow for long. Bexar headed towards Terlingua and his family, the day's mission a complete failure. He would have to ride to Alpine or Marfa next; he had to keep trying, and he couldn't think that he wouldn't be able to find a replacement vehicle at all. Bexar didn't know how much longer they could remain hidden from the bikers if they stayed so close to the park.

CHAPTER 29

Fort Bliss, Texas
February 16, Year 1

Chivo glanced out of the windows near the Rod & Gun Club's small restaurant; the sky over the eastern mountains glowed orange with the approaching dawn. Lindsey and Apollo were still asleep. Chivo wished he could have slept longer, but with only two of them, they had to split the night watch in half. Neither of them trusted Lindsey with the task of keeping a security watch; besides, she desperately needed a full night's sleep after being stranded over the highway for so many days. Besides the ammo, next to the rotting kitchen, they found the dry goods storeroom with two cases of bottled water and a case of Gatorade. They were in desperate need of water and were thankful for the lucky find, even though the smell of the rotted food and the lingering smell of death from the previous occupant still turned their stomachs.

Chivo kicked Apollo's boot, waking his teammate before kneeling next to his head and whispering, "I need to set up the coms and see if we can reach anyone. I'm guessing it might take me half of the morning to click through our freqs and also check some of the back channels. I really have no idea who might still be listening on the other end."

Apollo agreed. "Yes, if we can't reach anyone, we need to raid some of the homes across the tracks for food. Actually, we might need to do that anyway. Also, we need better transportation and more fuel. I don't trust the Humvee not to break and the gas mileage is horrid."

"Right. Well, come give me some cover while I get our coms setup."

Chivo and Apollo shouldered their rifles, leaving their heavy packs behind, and crept out of the back door towards where they'd left the Humvee. Frost covered the plants and tables on the range, but there was no sign of any movement. The only body they encountered was the one they'd killed the night before, which still lay by the back door.

Reaching the Humvee, Chivo opened the back door and retrieved the case with the radio. A few feet away from the big truck he opened the case, connected the handset, and set up the antenna. The radio powered up and the battery showed a full charge just as it did when they'd left the small warehouse the night before, but both men had field experience during which radio batteries decided it was time for an early retirement without any warning.

Chivo punched in the first set of frequencies, took an educated guess at the line of sight for the communications satellite that should be overhead, and began a process of broadcasting and waiting multiple times before moving on to the next channel in his memorized list.

The door behind them burst open. Apollo spun around, immediately raising his rifle, and saw Lindsey running towards them crying. Apollo lowered his rifle and she ran straight to Apollo and started hitting him. "I thought you two assholes left me! I woke up and was all alone, you dick!"

"I'm sorry. We needed to set up the radio and attempt to make contact. We have to be outside to do it and I thought you needed the sleep."

Lindsey stopped hitting Apollo and sat down next to Chivo, her face wet with tears. Apollo raised his eyebrows at Chivo, who looked over his shoulder at him. Chivo shrugged and went back to his task.

Groom Lake, Nevada

After the meeting and the stark news of Lance's death, Ben Wright walked back to the radio hut, the airman accompanying him. They had a big task ahead of them; they needed to prioritize the list of known survivors for their needs, what sort of supplies they could be provided or if they needed to be evacuated. Then, they had to plot those groups in terms of the C-130's effective fuel range. There would be no inflight refueling now, if ever again, and the thought of landing on an unknown airfield in an attempt to fuel the aircraft just did not seem like a good idea.

Wright was also tasked with finding where the SUV with the RV had gone in Texas, which could be miles and miles away from the previous spot by now and in just about any direction. The tasks themselves were not unusual in Wright's professional experience with the Air Force. What was unusual was the complete lack of manpower he had to accomplish it.

Wright looked at the map on the wall, colored pins spread out across Middle America. "Any of you guys remember the operating range of a C-130?"

"I think it's about two thousand miles lightly loaded, sir."

"OK, so roughly nine hundred to a thousand miles out so it can make it back, with light winds at altitude."

Wright took his compass, spread the legs to the scale on the map for a gap of one hundred miles and ticked off ten spots from Groom Lake and made a mark on the map. With a piece of string he drew a circle from Groom Lake and that spot across the map. Nearly half of the pins lay outside of the circle and outside of how far they could fly.

"You don't happen to know how much fuel it carries, do you?"

"Yes, sir. Almost eight thousand gallons."

Wright turned around. "OK, Mr. Dean, how and why do you know that?"

"Memorized all that stuff when I was a kid. Always wanted to go into the Air Force. Made models of all sorts of aircraft and practically wore my VHS of *Iron Eagle* out from watching it so many times."

Wright smiled. The airman was nearly ten years his junior, but as a child of the 1980s, Wright knew what it was like to be pulled to the Air Force from watching *Iron Eagle*. The first one, at least.

"How long would it take to put that much fuel in the tanks?"

"You got me on that one, sir."

Wright looked at the map again. They would have to figure out which fields they could fly to and refuel. They needed to know how long it would take to fuel the plane and how heavy the concentration of undead was in the area. The fuel pumps were probably electrically operated and non-functional, so they would have to figure out a way to power them. The task seemed insurmountable, but they had to do it. First, though, there were survivors in the circle who needed help.

Wright pushed the speaker button on the phone next to him and punched in a four-digit extension.

"Cliff, go ahead."

"Cliff, Wright. How soon do you want to send a mission?"

"As soon as we can. Get Arcuni topside. Tell him to take the PJs with him for security and get a fuel truck to the Herc. In fact, new rule: after landing from a mission, refuel the plane in case of a priority rescue mission."

"Will do. Do you want a supply drop or a rescue for the first op? I think we have good candidates for both now, both within the plane's flight range."

"Both if you can. We have a lot of fuel stored here, but it isn't an infinite supply. Besides, with each flight, we take a risk breaking something on the plane that we won't be able to fix. The more we can do at once, the better."

"Right. Once we have the op logistics planned, I'll give you a brief, and I assume you're taking care of the tactical side?"

"Yes, well, sort of. I'm not going outside the wire on this one. The PJs will take care of the tactical side of the op. Get with Arcuni. He could probably use a hand up front and you'll need another guy to act as a loadmaster. I'll brief the PJs on their roles and send them to you for the details. You get with Arcuni and figure out the rest of the crew."

Wright pushed the speaker button and ended the call, finishing up the barely legible notes scribbled across the yellow pad of paper on the desk.

"Guys," Wright said, pointing to the map on the wall, "try to make contact with anyone in this circle. See if any of them are in desperate need of food, ammo, or gear and see if any of them need an evac. List them in order of needs and check the overheads for any airstrips that can handle the Herc near their location—which is how long, Dean?"

"Uh, four thousand feet or better to be safe."

"OK, four thousand feet or longer runways. Civilian fields are OK, but they need to be close to the survivors. Either we have to go get them and bring them to the field or they have to get to the field. For supplies, we still have to land. We don't have the rigging for an air drop, nor do we have anyone who knows how to rig it. We'll have to land and offload ourselves. Once you have that list, plot them to see if we can hit more than one of them in a single trip. We are limited to daylight ops, and Cliff wants the first op wheels up as soon as we possibly can. I'll be back in ninety minutes to check on progress. Oh, and check for undead concentrations near the fields."

Wright looked at the clock and figured they had about ten hours until sunset. "If we can be wheels up in four hours, we can fly out to a location in range, in time."

"Major, are we allowing for night landings here, or do we need to be back here before local sunset?"

"I don't have that answer. We have to check the lights up top to see if they work, but I think we can."

Wright started out the door and stopped. "One of you figure out if one of the weather birds is still in orbit and still working. We can't send Arcuni into a damn storm."

The door shut behind him and the room erupted in activity.

CHAPTER 30

Marathon, Texas
February 16, Year 1

"I don't see any signs. I don't think they got shit in this town."

The three men with leather vests drove through the small-town streets, dodging walking corpses. "Damnit, the sign says Alpine is that way. Is that town any bigger?"

"Not really. Turn around. We have to drive to Fort Stockton."

The motorcycle club prospect who was driving turned the old van around and headed to Highway 385. He lit another cigarette off the burning end of the one he already had in his mouth, burned nearly to the filter. His gaunt face and his eyes were wild, typical of someone addicted to crystal meth. The back of the van smelled strongly of burning marijuana and gasoline fumes. Five plastic five-gallon cans of gasoline sat at the very back of the van. The thought that it might be dangerous to smoke with so much gasoline in the back of the van never occurred to the three of them, but not much ever did.

Next to the gas cans sat a crate half-full of blocks wrapped in brown paper labeled "Peno," with an orange diamond-shaped warning placard. There was also a box with a small label indicating it held blasting caps, a box labeled as M60 Igniters, and a spool of green cabling.

The desert highway was mostly deserted, with only a few abandoned cars and an oil field truck that the van swerved around at close to eighty miles per hour. It was still well before noon when the van crossed the railroad tracks and ran the stop sign to turn onto West Railroad Avenue, continuing the northern route.

"Turn here. Something has to be on business I-10." The van lurched left and onto West Dickinson Boulevard. The trio traveled a few blocks before the driver slammed on the brakes and turned into a parking lot of a small pharmacy. The pharmacy was more general store than medical supply, and the front window was full of merchandise.

"Bingo."

The driver left the engine running and the three piled out of the old van. The driver carried a shotgun, the other carried an M4 rifle, and the third held a large military-style duffel bag. The driver walked up to the front door. It was locked, so he broke the glass out. All three of the men took deep breaths. The interior smelled stale but it had no smell of death, so the three climbed through the broken glass. The customer windows at the back of the store were blocked with a pull-down gate, but three quick shotgun blasts gave the three entry into the secured room via the employee door.

Ten minutes later the duffel bag was heavy with large bottles of Xanax, Viagra, and Vicodin, and every package of nasal decongestant the store contained. When they climbed back through the shattered glass at the front of the store, they found the running van had attracted six undead with the noise of the motor. The driver picked up a large rock from the parking lot and threw it through the other large window at the front of the store. The loud crash of the shattering glass drew the undead's attention, causing them to shamble away towards the van, leaving the van clear for the three bikers to climb in. Before the walking corpses could turn and follow, the old van drove out of the parking lot, a black cloud of exhaust pouring out of the tailpipe.

"How much did we get?"

The man in the back of the van lit a cigarette and sorted through the bottom of the duffel.

"Enough for one batch, maybe."

"Shit, we need a bigger store."

"We need a bigger town."

"We need that fucking Walmart," the man in the passenger seat said, pointing at a sign further up the road.

Nearing I-10, the van pulled into the Walmart parking lot, which was choked with abandoned cars. Undead shuffled through the parking lot.

"Shit man, I'm not going in there."

"No way. Lead them off and we'll blow the drive-through window."

The driver drove slowly through the parking lot, honking the horn, while the front passenger cranked down the side window and yelled at the undead crowd. Every rotted face in the parking lot turned to look at the van and then the dead lurched into motion, following as quickly as they could.

Hundreds of undead followed the van out of the main parking lot exit and into the street. The driver accelerated sharply, turned right, and made the block around to the rear of Walmart, then to the side of the store where the pharmacy drive-through window was located. A car sat abandoned at the window, empty with the passenger door open. The three quickly put the car in neutral and pushed it out of the way using the front bumper of the van.

The man handling the duffel bag opened the back of the van and pulled a handful of the brown paper-wrapped blocks out of the cardboard box. Unwrapped, the blocks looked like off-white modeling clay but were really civilian C4 explosives stolen from a mining operation near Buffalo, Texas. He handed off the explosives with a roll of duct tape to the driver, who taped four of the small blocks on the corners of the thick bulletproof glass of the drive-through window. Next, the spool of green cord was unrolled, four lengths cut, ended with blasting caps and shoved into the soft explosives. The three made quick work of rigging, and forty feet away, they attached one of the M60 Igniters, hiding behind the other side of their van before firing the explosives.

The explosion knocked the three men to the ground and shattered all the windows of the van. The ringing in their ears blocked out the approaching moans of the undead. Peering around the damaged van, they could see the drive-through window was missing, and there was a ten-foot hole in the exterior wall. Brick and shattered glass covered the ground.

They stood shakily, feeling dizzy, but once they retrieved their dropped weapons and the duffel bag, the three of them staggered into the large pharmacy. Walmart's much larger stock of the drugs they wanted quickly filled the duffel to the top. To carry out the rest of the over-the-counter pseudoephedrine, they filled six plastic shopping bags. The club was set for a good while with all the meth they could cook from this haul.

The three of them were inside the building for only five minutes, but stepping back into the sunlight, they were met by more undead than they could count, some already tripping through the rubble and towards the gaping hole in the wall.

The driver shot the closest walking corpse with the shotgun. Its rotting head vaporized into a cloud of black diseased mist. The man with the duffel bag over his shoulders and the plastic bags in his hands stayed back, letting the other two take care of the approaching death. The man with the M4 pushed the selector switch past fire and to three-round burst, jerking the trigger back and firing wildly while walking towards the van. He was immediately swarmed and brought down by a dozen undead clawing at his skin; he screamed in pain while their rotted teeth tore chunks of flesh from his arms, neck, and face.

The driver kept pumping his Remington 870, firing the 00 buckshot as rapidly as he could work the action, until an audible click echoed in his ears. Another four undead pulled him to the ground, the shotgun clattering to the pavement. As he brought his hands to his neck, blood sprayed the rotted faces of the zombies ripping into the warm flesh.

Fear overwhelmed the man with the drugs. His hands were frozen shut holding the shopping bags, the duffel bag still on his shoulders. He ran. He ran as fast as he could past his screaming buddies, who were finding death one painful bite at a time. He kept running until he dove headfirst into the open rear doors of the van and pulled the doors closed against the clawing blackened hands of the hungry dead, their rotted fingers crushed between the closed doors. He clambered swiftly into the driver's seat.

Glass fragments on the dash blew into his face as he drove through the mass of dead bodies in the parking lot. Black smoke blew out of the exhaust; the gasoline sloshed in the cans next to the box of explosives. An undead whose hand was crushed in the rear doors was dragged along the pavement. As the van accelerated, the undead's arm ripped at the elbow, leaving the forearm stuck in the door. The prospect lit another cigarette and drove the old van as fast as he could towards Big Bend and his club.

CHAPTER 31

Big Bend National Park
February 16, Year 1

Two motorcycles roared into The Basin, past the motels and up the road to the cabins. The riders turned the engines off, leaned the bikes on their side stands, and stood to see Russell walk out of his cabin towards them. DD lit a cigarette, afraid of what he had to tell his club president.

"Well, where's Buzzer?"

"He's dead, Prez. Crashed and taken down by walkers."

"Both of them? What about Mike?"

"No, just Buzzer. We didn't go past the walkers. We left to come tell you."

"Damnit! Those assholes are where they found Stinky! You fucking idiots didn't even get far enough to check. Get everyone out here. It's time for Church and we're going to kill that fucking family!"

DD ran towards the cabins. His partner went to get supplies out of the cabin next to Russell's. Twenty minutes later all the club members and prospects stood in the road in front of Russell's cabin. There were only fifteen of them left. Some of them smoked and some drank beer, even though it was barely noon, and most all of them were high.

"You take that old 4x4 and put the deuce with ammo in the back. The rest of you bring your rifles and grab some ammo. We're going to round up some walkers and take revenge. Buzzer is dead. DD, you're the new VP. Load it up! We ride now!"

The prospects ran to get the M2 out of the supply cabin, along with two heavy green cans full of ammunition and the tripod for the crew-served machine gun, and loaded it all into the back of the Scout that had been Malachi's. Bexar had left it by the cabins when he bugged out, along with the FJ, but the club didn't care about the history of the vehicles. They didn't care about the families who had spent their hard-earned money and time building the vehicles to help with their survival; the club was only going to use them like they used everything else they stole.

The mountains echoed with a dozen old Harleys cranking to life, straight pipes popping loudly. Russell waved his hand above his head and rode down the hill. The rest of the club fell in formation, riding in twos, the Scout at the rear of the motorcycles.

Highway 170

Bexar rolled off the throttle and gently slowed the motorcycle to a stop. He had a flat tire. He must have picked up a nail or a screw or something in the road. After leaning the motorcycle on the side stand, he checked the rear tire, which sat flat against the rim and pavement. The tire was a tubeless tire, so if he had a plug he could plug it, but Bexar still had no idea how he would air the tire up enough to ride.

Bexar opened the left saddlebag, removed the remainder of his fireworks, and dug out a couple of dirty rags and a small glass pipe he recognized as something an addict would use to smoke meth or crack with. He threw the pipe across the road and it shattered with a satisfying crash. At the bottom of the saddlebag was a can of Fix-A-Flat. He shook the can and it felt full. Before the EMP there was absolutely no way he would have used a can of Fix-A-Flat on a motorcycle tire, but he had to get back to his family. Maybe the store in Terlingua had tire plugs and he could still plug the tire when he returned. He rubbed his hand on the tire, trying to find what punctured it, but he couldn't find anything. He realized that he'd never checked the other saddlebag. Bexar opened it and dug through the contents. He found two dirty t-shirts emblazoned with the Pistoleros' logo and a zip-top bag full of other bags. In the bags, he could identify marijuana, something that looked like meth, and a handful of different pills. The Norco he recognized, the pill colored yellow with "Watson" embossed on one side. The little oddly-shaped blue pill he could identify as Viagra, but he didn't know what the other pills were. Bexar chuckled at the Viagra. Maybe he should keep it and see if Jessie would let him try it out with her. But he had no use for the meth or the marijuana. Bexar was nearly falling over with the pain from the bullet wound in his leg and realized he was lucky to find the Norco, a narcotic pain killer. He dug out one of the yellow pills and a bottle of water from his go-bag and swallowed the pill, then stuffed the bag of pills into his go-bag.

Glancing up and down the highway, Bexar didn't see any movement or any undead, but he didn't want to stay stranded in the middle of the road for long. He unscrewed the valve cap on the rear tire, screwed on the Fix-A-Flat, tube and pressed the button. The foamy glue hissed into the tire, raising the motorcycle's rim off the pavement. Bexar pushed the sidewall of the tire with his thumb and decided to add a little more. Happy with how full the tire seemed, Bexar kept the half-used can and returned it to the saddlebag with his fireworks, started the bike, and continued the ride back to Terlingua. The hydrocodone was starting to make Bexar feel a little spaced out, but the brunt of the pain in his right leg was starting to fade.

Terlingua, Texas

Russell signaled the club to stop when they approached the wrecked Wagoneer still sitting in the highway. He shut off his motorcycle and walked to the Jeep's driver's door. The corpse sitting in the front seat had a bullet hole in the front of his skull and his lips were missing. Russell knew right then that the body in the Jeep hadn't been a living person when it was shot, and the walking dead don't drive. Someone had put the corpse in the driver's seat.

"You dumbasses! This body was a walker before it was shot and put in the fucking Jeep."

He looked around and pointed to the small motel a few hundred yards away. "Prospects, go check that motel." The three prospects left the Scout and moved towards the hotel, pistols in their hands. Russell dug a fresh pack of cigarettes out of the carton in his saddlebag, slapped the pack a few times to pack the tobacco, and lit a fresh smoke. He watched the prospects kicking in the doors to the motel rooms, finding nothing along the way.

Fifteen minutes later, they walked back to the club and to Russell. "No one is there, but there's two rooms that have been broken into already and there are a couple of dead walkers in the parking lot."

Russell looked up the hill, scanning for where his rabbits could have run. A small trail of smoke whispered in the wind above the hill. "That's them. It's got to be. Prospects, drop the tail gate of the 4x4 and put the deuce together in the back. DD, lead the way. Prospects, follow behind. Let's get this asshole."

DD rode up the hill, skirting around a small group of undead who had been attracted by all the noise. The Scout bounced along behind DD's motorcycle, the thick barrel of the fifty-caliber machine gun sticking past the rear bumper, and the rest of the club followed on their motorcycles.

DD rode slowly, expecting to get ambushed. The road split towards the top of the hill and a few hundred feet in front of him stood a cabin, a light trail of smoke rising from the small chimney. He stopped and shut off his motorcycle, leaned it on the side stand, and stood. DD pulled the M4 rifle slung across his back off his shoulder and pointed the prospects towards the cabin. The curtains by the front door moved. Someone peeked out the window. DD waved at the prospects and pointed at the cabin.

The fifty-caliber machine gun ripped the still air open, chunks of stone exploding off the walls from the force of the large bullets. Some of the club members were firing their M4s at the cabin, the much smaller rounds popping against the stonework, barely audible above the din of the rapid-firing machine gun. The M2 stopped while the prospects tried to clear a misfeed. The sudden silence was startling.

The back door of the cabin flew open and a small girl burst from around the back of the cabin, in view of Russell, running as fast as her little legs could carry her. Russell thumbed his rifle to three-round burst and, leading the running toddler, yanked on the trigger. The girl fell to the ground, tumbling through the dirt, the impacting rounds knocking her over. A woman ran screaming to the girl. The woman made it a few feet and collapsed to her knees, pulling the crumpled little body to her chest, blood pouring out of the limp body onto the woman's clothes. She screamed in agony, rocking the dead body in her arms. As she brushed her daughter's hair from her face, the girl's unblinking eyes stared back at her.

Russell walked to the woman, drew a pistol from his motorcycle vest, pointed it at the back of the woman's head, and began squeezing the trigger. Then he stopped. He slowly released the slack in the trigger, drew his arm back, and struck the woman in the side of the head with his pistol. Unconscious, she fell over the dead girl's body.

Russell faced the club. "Toss the house, fucking burn it to the ground, and then get back to camp. Put this bitch in the 4x4 and bring her back. No one else gets to fuck her. She's my trophy."

CHAPTER 32

Groom Lake, Nevada
February 16, Year 1

Conference room D-1 was full of people again. Arcuni, joined by Sam Garcia and Ray Johnson, sat across the table from Chris, Rick, and Evan, the newly arrived PJs, who were some of the Air Force's most elite and highly-trained special operators. Major Ben Wright started the briefing and was quickly joined by Cliff, who walked into the room a little late.

"We have identified two groups of survivors that are close enough to a proposed flight path within the Herc's range. The first group is located north of Amarillo, Texas, in a town called Dumas, and are requesting an evac. They are in no danger of being overrun, but they are out of food and nearly out of water and have no means to resupply themselves."

Wright tapped the keyboard and the slide refreshed with a tight overhead view of a small airport.

"This is the Dumas Municipal Airport. They are currently en route to the airfield and are instructed to shelter in the Quonset hut located here." The view zoomed in, showing an old half-barrel-shaped Quonset hut hangar near the larger of the two runways.

"The group is labeled Texas-Bravo-19, or TB19, and contacted us on a civilian HAM frequency a week ago after picking up our blind broadcasts on the shortwave frequencies. We have not informed them, however, that the undead group Zed-Alpha 2, or ZA2, is approaching from the south. Our estimates have the leading elements of ZA2 reaching Dumas in approximately twenty-seven hours. So for their survival, it is imperative we have an immediate evac."

Wright tapped on the keyboard and the next slide came on the large screen, showing a wide view overhead with a red blob labeled ZA2.

"Current estimates is that ZA2 contains approximately three hundred thousand walking corpses. The latest imagery shows a path of destruction left in their wake on par with an Old Testament locust plague. Quite literally, everything in its path is completely destroyed. If we can't rescue these ten people and the four children, they will not survive. Any questions?"

No one spoke, so Wright clicked to the next slide in his PowerPoint presentation.

"The next group, designated Colorado-Alpha-2, or CA2, is located near the Four Corners region in a town named Cortez, Colorado. Their group contains approximately forty members and some children. Their numbers have fluctuated and we haven't been able to find out why. They claim to not need extraction and are only in need of weapons, ammo, and some food. Johnson, have you prepared their requested items?"

"Yes sir, forty-eight cases of MREs and ten thousand rounds of XM193 are on pallets and plastic wrapped for transport. A crate of M-16A2s is also loaded."

Wright clicked to the next slide, which showed a zoomed-in high-resolution overhead image. "This is the municipal airport in Cortez, Colorado. This group has access to a truck that was unaffected by the EMP and will meet the plane here." Wright pointed to a turnoff from the taxiway on the north end of the hangars. Offload the cargo and remind them they are welcome here and they will be more secure as well. Any questions?"

Wright pointed to Arcuni. "Mr. Arcuni, if you would, cover flight ops, and Rick will follow up with the tactical and medical briefings."

SSC Facility, Bardwell Lake

Amanda awoke with a start. The privacy curtain on her metal bunk blocked out the low light in the large room, which was lined with identical bunks and lockers. The room was so still and quiet that she started to imagine noises. Only the faint humming of the HVAC system could be heard. It would take her some time to get used to sleeping safely again. In fact, she might not be able to enjoy a deep sleep again for the rest of her life. Johnson's old M4 rifle lay on her right side. Amanda gripped the rifle before sliding open the edge of the heavy privacy curtain. She didn't see any movement in the room, just row after row of empty bunks.

Amanda slid off the bed, already dressed in the new ACUs that she and Clint had retrieved from the storage room the previous night. She'd thrown her old clothes in the trash promptly after taking a very long and hot shower the night before. She slid the ammo carrier over her head. It was much heavier than it had been in a long time, now that all of the M4 magazines were full of ammo for the first time in weeks. She slung the rifle and walked towards the large restroom to brush her teeth and enjoy using a real toilet again. Amanda looked in the mirror and couldn't believe how old she looked. Forty-two years old and she didn't look a day younger than sixty. The weeks on the road had left her face hollow looking and too thin, even though before the attack she would have been happy with all the weight she'd lost.

A few minutes later, Amanda found Clint sitting in the cafeteria, the smell of hot coffee filling the room. His rifle was propped against the table while he ate an MRE for breakfast.

"What's the plan for today, guy?"

"Well, first we're going to finish breakfast, and then I'm going to the communications room and attempt to get our coms online."

"Who is left to talk to? I thought the EMP would have disabled all the radios."

"Maybe, maybe not. Besides, there are other facilities similar to this one. Chuck and I weren't the only two members of the project. We should find the Denver facility up and running, and if we're really lucky, they'll be able to evac us and fly us there to join them."

CHAPTER 33

Terlingua, Texas
February 16, Year 1

Miles away Bexar saw the thick black smoke rising above the mountains. The flat tire had cost him valuable time and even though he knew that the tire full of Fix-A-Flat wasn't really safe on the motorcycle, he rolled hard on the throttle and leaned over the tank, trying to get every last bit of performance out of the old beat-up Harley. Sparks flew with each sweeping turn, the floorboards under his feet scraping against the asphalt as Bexar ignored the highway's painted lines and took each turn apex to apex as if on a racetrack.

The closer he got to Terlingua, the more the pit of despair grew in the bottom of his stomach. Bexar's mind raced faster than the motorcycle. *If Jessie caught the cabin on fire they might be OK, but if the bikers found her ...* The throttle wouldn't roll any further backward. It was wide open, and Bexar pushed the motorcycle recklessly fast on the narrow highway.

Reaching the turnoff for Terlingua, the back wheel of the motorcycle shuddered with the hard braking to make the turn. After he cleared the turn-off, he saw it. The cabin was a burned-out shell. Only part of the rock walls stood, and over two dozen undead shuffled around the ruin. Bexar stopped the motorcycle where the road split at the top of the hill, shouldered his rifle, and began putting the walking corpses down for good. Thirty rounds and a magazine change later, the twenty-five undead were down. Every time Bexar took aim, he was scared that he would see his wife's face, snarling in anger and death, but she wasn't among the walkers. He left the motorcycle in the middle of the road and jogged, limping, to the cabin.

In the dirt next to the cabin lay his little girl, the t-shirt he'd given her the night before from the store next door soaked in blood, her tiny body partially eaten by the dead.

Bexar yelled. Tears poured down his cheeks and he collapsed to the ground. He had no idea how long he sat next to his daughter's mangled body, but eventually he stood and walked through the smoking ruin of their cabin. Jessie's body was not in the cabin, and he didn't find her body anywhere nearby. Bexar walked across the parking lot to the Starlight Theatre, which was empty, as was the store, but large bullet casings and links littered the parking lot. Bexar had no military experience, but he instantly thought of the bikers and that big fifty-cal machine gun they'd used against them in the park.

Mindlessly, he kicked the shell casings around before walking into the store and returning holding a souvenir beach towel. Bexar walked to his daughter's dead body and wrapped her in the cheap towel. He gently picked her up in his arms and walked down the hill towards the old Terlingua Ghost Town cemetery and found an empty space. The rocky soil was too hard and he couldn't dig a grave, so Bexar spent the next three hours gathering rocks from a crumbling wall of a long abandoned house in the ghost town, gently laying the rocks on her body, making a mound of a grave the best he could.

The sun hung low against the western sky when Bexar was finished and walked back up the hill, his clothes covered in dirt and dust, his face wet with sweat and tears. Bexar walked into the Starlight Theatre and behind the bar. He only had the supplies in his go-bag, he had no idea where his wife was, but he guessed she was probably dead. Or maybe the bikers took her. If they took her, possibly they went back to The Basin, but a dark blanket of depression fell over him, realizing that his little girl was dead, and he blamed himself. Bexar took the bottle of Gentleman's Jack down from behind the bar, poured three fingers of the brown liquor into a dusty glass, and downed the whiskey in one long drink before pouring another one. The whiskey burned his throat and he started to feel his muscles relax. He needed a plan. A plan to rescue Jessie. But first, he had to find her. He tried to concentrate, but he couldn't focus. His sweet little girl's body, half-eaten by the dead, filled his mind. Bexar drank the second glass and poured another.

Groom Lake, Nevada

"Where's Cliff?" Wright asked the airman that walked into the radio hut.

"I think he went topside to see the mission off and he isn't back yet."

"Get up there and bring him to me. He'll want to see this."

The airman nodded and walked out the door. Wright leaned in towards the computer monitor. The SUV was on the road and looked badly damaged; the trailer was off the road and quite obviously destroyed. A body lay in the road behind the Jeep and two more bodies were in the parking lot of the buildings to the north. Wright had no idea what it was, but the building looked like it could be a hotel or maybe some storage units. For all the power the satellites had, Google would have made finding out more information cooler.

Cliff burst through the door and walked to Wright and his computer.

"Here is the SUV; it's about twenty miles west of the park. It looks like it wrecked, but with those two bodies in the parking lot away from the wreck, I think someone survived."

Cliff nodded. "What about the park and the motorcycles?"

"The interior of the park is here. Looking at past overheads, our best guess is that our friends were set up in these cabins on the south side of the parking area. You can see now, there are a number of motorcycles near the cabins and a pile of bodies to the north in this other parking lot."

The airman at the radio console snapped his fingers sharply to get Wright's attention before waving him over. The airman scribbled notes on the yellow pad of paper in front of him, but his handwriting was so bad the major couldn't read it. Wright pushed the button on the console that activated the external speaker. The man transmitting refused to give his location and referenced a handful of code words that meant nothing to Wright or the airman. The airman shrugged at Wright, but Cliff reached for the handset and keyed the mic.

The airman pointed to the computer screen. The transmission was being made over an emergency SATCOM channel that was reserved for theater-wide communications in Afghanistan. That was peculiar, but Wright assumed there had to be military survivors all across the globe. The airman made a few clicks with his mouse and located the geostationary satellite being used for the transmission, which was positioned over the United States. So that meant the transmission had to be from inside CONUS, or at least North America. The communications system should have a GPS lock as well, but that feature wasn't functioning for some reason.

Fort Bliss, Texas

Chivo sat on the roof of the Humvee after moving up there for safety when Apollo left to explore the rest of the area on foot for supplies. The sound of an engine approaching caused an instant reaction from Chivo. He spun towards the sound on the roof while simultaneously raising his rifle. Off the end of his barrel, he saw an old Land Rover drive around the side of the building and towards the Humvee. Apollo was behind the wheel, grinning like the Cheshire Cat, Lindsey in the passenger seat.

Chivo lowered his rifle and turned back to the radio to continue trying different channels on the SATCOM. The first few hours Chivo tried the predetermined channels to contact the project director and handler for the anti-drug mission they had been on in Mexico. Those had no response. Chivo tried some of the theater-wide channels from when he was in Iraq and Afghanistan. One of the channels used in Afghanistan some ten years ago had a response. He didn't know who it was, but at least there was someone else out there. The clipped conversation went back and forth, but Chivo was unwilling to reveal too much about himself or his location without positively identifying whom he was speaking with. Luckily, he had remembered to disable the locater.

Apollo climbed out of the newly found Land Rover and walked to the side of the Humvee where Chivo was waving frantically at him.

"Apollo, this guy says he's Lazarus Actual."

"You're shitting me. He trained me at The Farm. Let me have that." Apollo climbed on the roof of the Humvee and took the handset from his teammate.

"Lazarus Actual, this is Mule Spike Six. Do you still have that scar?"

Groom Lake, Nevada

The external speaker activated, Wright and the airman looked at Cliff, who seemed to recognize the voice and showed a rare smirk. "Mule Spike Six, yes I do. And your mother says hi."

Using a bit of code, they agreed on using another SATCOM channel since neither had any way of knowing who could be listening, if anyone was listening at all. After the channel switch and over the next few minutes, Apollo relayed their status, their location, and a quick rundown of how they'd fled from Mexico.

Cliff turned to Wright. "How far away are they from our friends in the Texas Park?"

Wright took his map compass and ticked off the scale distance with the map on the wall. "Call it two hundred fifty miles as the crow flies."

Cliff scribbled down a location on a pad of paper and handed it to Wright. "Figure out a way to get Mule Spike from Fort Bliss to this location before they head to the park. Keep them away from ZA2 and away from I-10 if at all possible." Cliff wrote down a list of instructions, including a twenty-four-digit key he wrote from memory.

Fort Bliss, Texas

Apollo took the small notepad and pen out of his shirt pocket and began taking notes

"All right, Chivo. We've got an op."

"An op? Doing what, staying alive? We're a bit understaffed and undersupplied at the moment."

"Cliff says he has an inland resupply cache. These are the directions and this is the code to get in."

"Pyote? Where the hell is that?"

"No idea. We'll have to follow the directions. But he wants us to leave immediately and get to the supply cache pronto."

Chivo held his hand up to the sky. Four fingers separated the sun from the horizon. "We've only got about two hours until dark, mano."

"Yeah, so we need to hurry it up and we need some containers to siphon the diesel from the Humvee so we can take it with us for our new ride."

"Do we still trust this guy? It's been years since he was at The Farm."

"I caught a rumor that he was with a project called Osiris."

"What the hell is that?"

"No idea, and I knew better than to ask."

"Fuck it, my little Mexican buddy. What else do we have to do?"

Chivo packed up the antenna and the radio and put it in the back of the Land Rover before walking inside with Apollo and Lindsey.

CHAPTER 34

Dumas, Texas
February 16, Year 1

The C-130 turned for the downwind leg of the landing pattern over the hangars, the four big turboprop engines roaring through the desert landscape. Arcuni brought the cargo plane across for a short base to final and put the wheels down just before the first hash marks on the runway. Taking the middle turnoff for the taxiway, the big plane taxied alongside the old Quonset hut. The ramp lowered and Rick, Evan, and Chris trotted out of the back of the plane to meet the people running from the hangar towards the plane. Arcuni left the engines running while ten survivors and their four children were met by the PJs.

"Where's the rest of you? I thought there were fourteen."

"There were."

"OK, all of you can come with us, but once we get back to the facility, you will be strip-searched for bites and quarantined for forty-eight hours. All weapons must be declared, but you will keep them and you will be required to be armed at all times. You will also be required to earn your keep on our base. Do you understand?"

One of the men, who introduced himself as Jake, shook Chris's hand and the group all walked towards the ramp of the Herc. The PJs fanned out, providing security on each side and towards the rear of the group.

Once everyone was in the plane, Garcia pointed to the cargo net seats towards the front for the new passengers before raising the ramp. Arcuni taxied to the runway. Some undead were visible, shambling towards the plane from the highway, but they were far enough away that Arcuni knew he would be airborne before they became a problem. Arcuni pushed the throttles forward and the big plane bounced down the runway until rotating and lifting into the sky as he banked to the right to turn for the next group of survivors on their mission.

Arcuni didn't have the luxury of a winds aloft report, a full weather report, or even all the charts he needed to fly safely, but he did at least have the charts for his flight today. He'd found them in a big binder stuffed behind the right seat. They were outdated, but at least he had something. The airspace markers really didn't mean anything anymore and they were ignored, but the elevation markers and the rotating plotter navigation ruler he'd also found were needed and used. Assuming neutral winds aloft, the flight to Cortez should be about an hour. It was also nice that the cabin pressurization system worked and he didn't have to worry about everyone getting hypoxic from the lack of oxygen on the flight.

Looking out the windshields at twenty thousand feet and across the expanse of the southwest, it was easy to imagine that none of this had happened and that everything below him was normal. However, if everything were normal, he wouldn't be flipping through an aircraft's manual trying to learn the systems while flying for a dangerous operation where others' lives depended on him. Arcuni turned the last plotted waypoint and toggled the lights in the cargo hold on and off twice to signal his passengers to seatbelt in as he started the descent.

Cortez, Colorado

Black smoke poured out of the twin exhaust stacks of the old Peterbilt semi-truck, the engine pushing the truck as hard as it could. The trailer's doors were tied open and three men of the group were lying on the floor of the trailer firing the only three rifles they had as rapidly as they could at the trailing pickup trucks. A gray C-130 roared overhead, seeming to float on a string, nose down, hanging on the props as it flew the final approach into the small municipal airport in Cortez.

Two old pickup trucks raced after the semi. Men stood in the beds of the trucks and fired rifles over the cabs towards the fleeing semi-truck. One of the men in the trailer yelled in pain, hit in the top of the shoulder. He accidently dropped his rifle, which clattered out of the back of the trailer only to be run over by the first chasing pickup. The driver of the semi downshifted hard; the truck lurched forward before leaning sharply as the truck bounced and shook around the corner onto Airport Road.

The cargo plane taxied back towards the center of the airport and onto the flightline by the beat-up hangars before turning back onto the taxiway, tailgate lowering towards the approaching semi. The three PJs jumped off the lowering ramp, rifles up and ready for action, as the semi-truck burst through the fence and bounced through a ditch. If this had been an operation before the EMP, overhead air support would have neutralized the threat before landing, but the PJs adapted and overcame for the new world. Impossibly slowly, the big old truck lurched hard to the left and crashed onto its side, sliding to a stop on the pavement by the first hangar.

Chris, Evan, and Rick jogged towards the overturned truck but threw themselves to the ground when the first rifle round cracked overhead, barely audible over the loud turboprop engines behind them. The two trucks bounded through the hole in the fence created by the semi and stopped. The first person to appear out of the semi was a teenage girl, and a man standing in the back of the first pickup shot her. Rick watched the girl drop to the ground, clutching her stomach; he thumbed the safety of his M4 down and squeezed the trigger. The shooter's head snapped back and his body fell in the bed of the truck. Chris and Evan followed suit, quickly firing their rifles and killing the seven men in the pickup trucks before running towards the overturned semi and the injured girl.

Rick climbed the cab of the truck and found the driver, a middle-aged man, dead, his neck obviously broken. Evan ran to the teenage girl, who rolled in the dirt, crying in pain. Blood flowed out from around her hands as she clutched her stomach just above her jeans. Chris went to the back of the trailer and found twelve other men with various injuries, one of them dead.

"Is anyone seriously hurt?" Chris yelled into the trailer.

No one responded. "OK, everyone out. The plane is waiting. Where is everyone else? Are any more coming? Is there anyone else chasing you?"

A teenage boy with shaggy hair nodded. "Yes, there are more in our group. They're not coming. We barely escaped those gunmen."

"OK, everyone up and move fast. Get to the plane. We'll be right there with you."

The group of men, including the teenager, left their dead with the truck and half-jogged towards the waiting plane. Chris jogged past Rick and Evan, waving his left hand in a circle above his head, and got in front of the group to lead them safely into the aircraft. Rick and Evan knelt next to the teenage girl and lifted her off the ground. They fell in behind the group, carrying the injured girl with them, moving towards the open cargo hold of the aircraft.

Garcia stood at the tail ramp, M4 in his hands and his headset plugged into the communication port at the rear of the plane. Once Evan's boots hit the ramp, he half-yelled into the headset for Arcuni to taxi. Arcuni hadn't seen the firefight behind the plane, but he did hear the excitement in Garcia's voice. He also saw three more old pickup trucks driving towards the airport at a high rate of speed. He put two and two together and decided it would probably be best to take off as quickly as possible. Arcuni didn't bother to taxi to the runway. He pushed the throttle all the way to the stop. The big plane rumbled down the taxiway and into the dirt before he pulled back hard on the controls. The powerful plane, lightly loaded, launched into the sky and quickly left the pursuing trucks behind.

In the back of the plane, Garcia got the cargo ramp closed just before the C-130 leapt into the air. The newly arrived passengers fell onto the floor, exhausted and dirty. Chris and Evan knelt over the teenage girl, an EMS trauma bag open between them. Chris started an IV while Evan cut off the girl's shirt, bra, and jeans with a pair of shears. They rolled her on her side and checked for an exit wound, but found none and rolled her back face-up. The girl cried in pain before Chris could get a dose of morphine injected into her arm. Evan packed her wound with gauze and applied pressure, trying to stop the bleeding. Normally, they fought to keep someone alive to get the patient to a field hospital for immediate care, but there was no hospital. There was no other help. They were the only ones who had any chance at saving this girl's life.

Chris wrapped a blood pressure cuff around her arm. Her breathing was getting shallower. She was going into shock. They both worked hard and methodically, doing all they could to help the girl, but it wasn't enough to save her. A loud gasp followed by a rattled breath, and the girl was dead. Evan closed her eyelids and pulled the silver space blanket over her head. They didn't have half the gear they normally carried in the Pave Hawks, much less a body bag.

The teenage boy hung his head and cried into his hands while the man beside him hugged him and tried to comfort him. The two pallets of supplies turned out to be worthless. The large group of survivors they'd come to resupply now sat in the cargo hold of the aircraft in silence and in much smaller numbers. Rick wanted to ask them some questions about their attackers, but there would be time later. There were some ground rules he had to tell the new arrivals. Rick walked to the group, who now huddled close together around the teenage boy.

"I'm sorry to bring this up now, but there are a few things I need to tell you. When we arrive, everyone will be submitted to a strip search for bites and quarantine for forty-eight hours. You will be given food and a change of clothes and you will be able to bathe. You will be expected to contribute and earn your keep in our facility, but you will be safe there. All weapons must be declared, but you will be allowed to keep them and will be expected to be armed at all times. Do you have any questions?"

One of the men gasped and pointed behind Rick. The dead teenage girl sat up, the silver space blanket falling off her face. Chris pulled the knife out of the sheath on the front of his armor and jammed the blade deep into the girl's temple. The girl fell over, dead for good. Chris retrieved his knife, stood, and stomped off towards the cockpit, cursing loudly. Evan pulled the blanket over the girl's head again. Blood seeped out from under the blanket across the non-skid floor

CHAPTER 35

Fort Bliss, Texas
February 16, Year 1

The diesel fuel from the Humvee's tank now filled the tank of the Land Rover, and the dozen gallon-sized milk jugs tied to the roof rack were also full of diesel. Apollo, Chivo, and Lindsey wasted no time in packing their new vehicle. Besides siphoning the fuel, all they had for supplies was the radio and what they had found the night before. Chivo took the first turn at driving, Apollo sitting in the passenger seat with the handwritten directions. Lindsey sat sideways in the fold-down seat in the back.

They all believed that getting out of El Paso would be the hardest part of their eastbound journey to Pyote. After their harrowing drive through the middle of El Paso to reach Fort Bliss and then escaping the middle of the Army post and the horde of walking corpses, none of them had any desire to travel back into El Paso ever again. The sun hung low against the western horizon by the time they drove the Land Rover past the ranges and down the gravel drive to the chain-link fence separating them from the Purple Heart Memorial Highway. Apollo exited the truck, bolt cutters in hand, and made quick work of cutting the fence before holding the section of chain-link back for the Land Rover to pass through.

A safety wire separated the travel lanes of the highway, so for now they were trapped on the wrong side for the way they were traveling—not that it really mattered anymore. Chivo drove slowly, trying to keep the speedometer near thirty miles per hour while navigating around the disabled and abandoned vehicles. All of them were happy to be in an enclosed vehicle for their journey. The open bed of the pickup truck was a major factor in Odin's death, and none of them wished his fate upon themselves. Chivo and Apollo just hoped they'd made the right choice in switching vehicles to the old Land Rover and that it wouldn't break down or get worse gas mileage than the abandoned Humvee.

Traveling eastbound, the number of undead on the roadway wasn't too heavy, and they were easily avoided by the quick reactions of Chivo behind the wheel. Some of their bony fingers dragged down the side of the truck, clawing at the flesh inside. Some bounced off the front fenders as they passed. None of the walking corpses fell off the overpasses as they cleared the last of the base's major buildings. They drove down the on-ramp to turn onto Montana Avenue and passed a Super Walmart. The parking lot teemed with undead swarming through the cars like ants. Chivo guessed that there were close to two thousand dead bouncing around the mass of cars left forever in the large parking lot. Apollo thought that number was low. Luck favors children, drunks, and soldiers on hopeless missions: the mass of undead didn't turn towards the passing SUV, nor did any of them follow out of the parking lot. If that horde had noticed their vehicle driving past and they got stuck, there would be no way to survive.

A tense twenty minutes passed before civilization began to spread out as they reached the edge of the city and started into the desert mountains. The further they drove away from El Paso, the sparser everything became. There were fewer vehicles on the roadway blocking their path and even fewer undead shambling across the road. Compared to their harrowing journey through El Paso, the open desert was a pleasant evening drive. Once clear of most of the signs of civilization, Chivo pushed the Land Rover to sixty miles per hour; the road was mostly empty and the sun sat low against their backs, pushing the three eastward.

The heater in the Land Rover worked well, and for the first time in a while the three of them felt warm and comfortable, finally protected from the cold winter air. Idle chat occupied their time and eventually Lindsey began to come out of her shell and open up about her life.

"I was studying journalism and photography at UTEP. I grew up in Van Horn, and after I ran out of food in my apartment, I really thought I could ride my scooter back to my parents' house. I figured they would know what to do."

"How far of a drive is that?"

"About two hours. It's just down I-10. I didn't know how bad it was out there. Before the electricity went out, there were warnings on Twitter and TV about an attack. So I locked the door to my apartment and hid inside until I just couldn't anymore. It wasn't bad around my apartment, and after the first couple of days, I didn't hear any more gunfire. So I thought it was getting safer and I left. What about you guys? Where did you come from?"

"Apollo here is from outside Denver, and when he left for boot camp after high school, his town was down to only one other black guy."

Apollo snorted loudly in response. "Chivo's family started in south L.A., but after jumping one fence, they kept going and ended up as the only Spanish-speaking family in North Dakota."

"Fuck you, mano, we were in *South* Dakota. That's where the real shit goes down."

Lindsey stared in horror at the two of them. "Do you guys really hate each other that much?"

"No way, Senorita. We've just been through a lot of shit together off and on over the last fifteen years. I'm actually from Laredo and Apollo really is from outside of Denver. We met when we were wet behind the ears baby-Rangers in the 75th from Ranger School. We were both selected for The Unit at about the same time and both left the Army at the same time for new adventures. Although we've been bounced around with different assignments here and there, this man is my brother from another mother."

"Yeah, same father though. You can see the resemblance."

Apollo and Chivo grinned wildly, both looking over their shoulders at Lindsey as she quickly looked back and forth at them, trying to see if there really was any resemblance—which there quite obviously was not. Chivo and Apollo laughed loudly at her reaction.

The Guadalupe Peak passed to their left, but the spilled ink darkness of the night enveloped the desert floor, and only the reflective green sign on the side of the highway gave them notice.

Lindsey pressed her face to the window. "There is nothing out here at all. We always stayed south along I-10; I've never been up this way."

"Nothing but a bunch of oil field workers, and that's just about it. Too bad the radio doesn't work; this drive might suck slightly less if we had some tunes."

"Sure, but then we would have to listen to fucking Tejano polka crap music and that would just add misery to the end of the world."

"Still beats your R&B gospel choir swaying and clapping while everyone sings a solo at the same time."

Lindsey stared at both of them. "You guys have serious problems."

Apollo turned around with a wink. "You have no idea, ma'am."

Terlingua, Texas

The whiskey bottle lay in a wet heap of shattered glass on the floor of the Starlight Theatre. A lone candle flickered in the dark room as Bexar stood uneasily and tripped over a chair trying to walk towards the bar. Staggering around the bar, Bexar grabbed a bottle of tequila off the shelf, pulled the pour spout out of the top, and took a long drink straight from the bottle. The clear alcohol burned down the back of his throat and for the first time in many years, Bexar's body betrayed him.

Vomit shot from his mouth, propelled by the sudden influx of the Mexican liquor on top of the bottle of whiskey he had already drunk. Bexar collapsed onto his hands and knees by the bar, dry heaving so hard that the muscles around his ribs and stomach started cramping. Snot and spit hung from his face while Bexar stayed on his hands and knees trying to catch his breath.

"Dammit."

Bexar climbed up the side of the bar and stood swaying, his shirt speckled with vomit, spit, and snot. He grabbed the tequila bottle and threw it across the room with a loud crash.

"Fucking bikers."

He grabbed the order ticket pad and a pen from beside the cash register and wrote slowly, trying to write legibly even though he was drunk.

Jessie,

I buried Keeley in the graveyard. I'm going to the park to kill every single biker and I hope I find you. If I don't make it, know that I loved you always and will love you forever.

~Bexar

Bexar tore the page from the pad, slung his rifle, shouldered his go-bag, and stepped onto the front porch. Night enveloped him, but the smell of burned wood still hung in the air. He clipped the ticket to the display for the restaurant's daily specials and stumbled to the trading post next door. Bexar needed water and more food, and he would need something for the headache he knew was coming soon, so he went into the general store next door.

Twenty minutes later Bexar stepped outside and off the porch towards the motorcycle, his go-bag heavier than before. The large spent casings from the machine gun twinkled beneath his feet as he staggered to the motorcycle, the green wool poncho over his body once again. Riding a motorcycle with a tire full of Fix-A-Flat, drunk, and with no helmet would have been well beyond what Bexar considered a safe and reasonable choice. But a few months ago, planning to ride through the desert night to kill every person associated with a biker gang would have been a crazy thought as well.

CHAPTER 38

Groom Lake, Nevada
February 16, Year 1

The C-130 banked and turned for final approach, the landing gear already down. The runway lights glowed against the dark desert floor and Arcuni brought the plane down gently, proud that with each flight his skill flying the big Herc was improving. It had been nearly sixty years since the Air Force allowed enlisted men to fly, and he'd always felt that if he could have graduated from college and earned a commission, he would have been a great pilot.

Cliff stood with a handful of airmen along with Major Wright on the surface just outside the hangar that housed the main entrance to the secret underground facility. The airmen, armed with M4s and facing outward, watched for any approaching undead, while Cliff and Wright watched the plane taxi to a stop. The ramp lowered and the engines slowed to a stop. The three PJs walked down the ramp towards Cliff. This time, the number of undead approaching the noise from the aircraft had increased compared to the previous flight. It took the airmen nearly half an hour to put down the shambling threat, but Cliff was happy to see that his tactics continued to work safely and efficiently. If the one-star general in Denver had listened to him in the first place, Cliff was sure he would be happily underground below the Denver International Airport with a better chance of restarting the government and country.

"Sitrep?"

"The Situation Report, Cliff, is no friendly killed. Just one civilian loss en route to the extraction point, but both groups opted to fly back instead of taking supplies and sheltering in place."

"Good. What changed the minds of the group from Colorado?"

"There is a rogue faction of aggressors in Cortez. That's how we had the civilian loss."

"OK. We need to address that. There was a project planned to take care of territorial warlord-type fiefdoms that would arise in the absence of a central government, but those plans were shot to hell with the rest of the project plans. Get secure and get below ground. We'll take care of the in-processing with our new guests and then come to terms with the problem in Cortez."

The PJs walked back to the plane and helped the airmen unload and escort the passengers to the hangar. The C-130 was refueled and tied down; Arcuni and Garcia joined the PJs and the new arrivals walking towards the hangar. Wright gathered the new arrivals in the hangar while the airmen pushed the doors closed and latched them into place. The painted floor shone, reflecting the electric lighting overhead, which caught the arriving refugees by surprise. None of them had seen a working electric light since the attacks in December.

Smiling, Wright addressed the crowd. "As you can see, we have electricity here. It is generated onsite and should continue to work for decades to come. We also have fresh clothing, beds, food, and water for everyone." He pointed to an open doorway in the floor of the hangar. "Down those stairs is an in-processing area. Our airmen are going to need you to cooperate. You are free to leave if you so choose, but to be given full access to the facility, you will have to submit to a strip search and examination for any bite marks and will further be quarantined for infection for forty-eight hours. Once we have determined that you won't be the start of an outbreak, you'll be brought into the main facility. You can dispose of your clothing in our incinerators, or we have laundry facilities and you're welcome to clean and keep them. We want you to keep any weapons you have, but we do need to inventory what you have."

Wright paused to see if there was any reaction from the people standing before him before continuing. "Is anyone related to the deceased?"

The teenage boy with the shaggy hair raised his hand. His face and eyes were red and puffy from crying. "I am. That is my wife."

"What's your name, son?"

"Jason."

"OK, Jason, we have no facilities to bury any bodies, so she will need to be cremated. You can join us for the task or we can bring you her ashes. You're welcome to keep them or come back topside to scatter them if you would like."

Jason looked at the floor and only slightly nodded in response.

"Once everyone is cleared to enter the main facility, we will have jobs and responsibilities for everyone. My staff is here to help you, but you will also be here to help us. We are in this together and if we are going to survive, it will take an incredible effort from us all. Over the next few days as you get settled in, we will be speaking with each of you to learn your talents and skills. Hopefully there will be many more following in your footsteps in the coming weeks. Our plan is to make Groom Lake the jump-off point for the survival of humanity and the rebuilding of our country."

Jason's head snapped up, and he raised his hand.

"Jason, we're not in school. Feel free to speak. What is on your mind?"

"Groom Lake, like Area 51?"

"Yes."

"So, aliens?"

Wright smiled. "Nope, no aliens. Just a secret base where flight testing used to be carried out. The aliens story was a complete fabrication of our government to hide the high-technology aircraft being tested."

Jason looked disappointed at the lack of aliens and turned to follow the airmen who had put his wife in a body bag and were carrying her into the facility.

Pecos, Texas

"Lindsey, get your skinny ass up here and take the wheel."

Apollo's left hand hung out the open window. The sound of a pistol echoed loudly inside the cab of the old Land Rover. Chivo hung halfway out of the window on the passenger's side, rifle barking loudly in the desert air. Lindsey climbed into the front seat and took hold of the steering wheel. Apollo holstered his pistol and, using both hands, leaned out of the open window with his rifle.

The moonlight helped to illuminate the scene around them only slightly more than their headlights. After East Third Street from Highway 285, the town appeared to be completely abandoned—not that Pecos, Texas was a large and well-populated town before the attacks, but the burned-out hulks of two oil field tanker trucks blocked the road by the Knights Inn, and when trying to turn to backtrack around the wreck, they were quickly overrun by over a hundred undead. The bodies trudged out of seemingly nowhere in the darkness and were a complete surprise to all three of them.

"Lindsey, drive slowly and smoothly. If we damage our ride and we're stuck in the middle of this, we might have a fight we can't win," Chivo yelled over the staccato sound of their rifle fire.

Chivo and Apollo fought hard to clear a way for their vehicle. After making a fast U-turn, the headlights showed what appeared to be a solid wall of approaching undead only fifty feet away.

"Take the parking lot," Apollo yelled, pointing left. Lindsey slid the truck in the small space between the fenced-off pool and the blue metal roof of the two-story hotel. Lindsey turned the wheel and sped into the parking lot, which was surprisingly clear of the shambling dead. The Land Rover bounced through the parking lot and onto the next street before turning left and paralleling its original direction. No more undead were visible in front of them, but movement still caught their eyes in the dark shadows just outside the reach of the Land Rover's headlights. Apollo and Chivo both slid back into the SUV; Apollo handed his rifle to Lindsey and took the steering wheel. She slid out of the front seat and returned to her spot in the back. A few minutes passed and the trio was on I-20, getting close to their destination.

"Jesus de Christo, that was close."

"Where did all of those bodies come from? I doubt there were that many people in that town before the attack."

"I don't know, buddy, but I hope they don't follow us for very long. And I say shit on traveling at night anymore."

The next twenty minutes passed in silence. I-20 was fairly clear, because the cars were pushed to the sides of the road and were heavily damaged, as if a bulldozer had cleared the road before them. Apollo slowed the Land Rover and drove across the desert scrub grass in the median to the frontage road before turning onto a small dirt road. He stopped at the metal gate under a white painted entry made out of welded pipe. Mesquite trees dotted the barren landscape in what little they could see in the light from the headlights. Chivo exited and made quick work of the padlock with the bolt cutters before pulling the chain off the gate. After Apollo drove through, Chivo closed the gate and wrapped the chain to hold it in place. A slow and bumpy drive across the desert ended on a worn concrete surface with grass growing through the cracks—the location of the supposed inland supply cache in the middle of nowhere Texas.

"What is this place?" Lindsey asked.

"Pecos Parachute School."

Both Apollo and Lindsey turned to Chivo, asking, "What?"

"Come on, haven't you guys seen the movie *Fandango*? It's where Truman Sparks has his parachute school."

"Chivo, dude, you're shitting me."

"No, really! This is where they filmed it."

Lindsey tried to ignore Chivo's answers. "Is it for real?"

"I don't know for sure. Cliff told us to drive here to resupply. I had a guess as to what it is, but I didn't realize we had any of these placed this far south."

Apollo drove in front of the skeletal remains of an old Army Air Base hangar and stopped by a small concrete building before turning the engine off. All three of them exited the Land Rover with a stretch and walked to the small abandoned building per Cliff's instructions. Chivo held the instructions in his hand and lifted the cover to what appeared to be a metal electrical box, but instead of fuses, in the box was a ten-key keypad under the lid. Chivo looked at his notes and punched in the twenty-four-digit long number before closing the metal lid and taking a few steps backwards. With a muffled hiss below their feet, the entire building rose before them, pushed upwards by a heavy ram. The building rose nearly twenty feet, revealing a dark ramp descending below ground. Lights flickered on and illuminated the ramp, which looked like the entrance to an underground parking garage. They climbed back into the Land Rover, started the engine, and drove down the ramp.

CHAPTER 37

Peyote, Texas
February 16, Year 1

The concrete ceiling stood at least fifteen feet above the floor of the underground area. Apollo parked the Land Rover in an area marked on the floor as a designated parking area. Like a scene from a low-budget TV movie, three long passageways stretched out before them, each cast in a yellow light from the sodium vapor lighting. The long passageways stretched beyond imagination. There were square concrete pillars every ten feet or so, each painted with a colored band and a letter followed by a number. Chivo walked to where a half-dozen flatbed electric carts sat in charging stations and found a map with a key for the different sections posted on a stand.

"Hey mano, it's like a map at the mall. It tells you where you should go shopping."

Apollo and Lindsey joined Chivo by the map. Surprised, Apollo saw that Chivo wasn't joking. The entire cache site had a key referencing the location of items by colored section, then by row and shelf number.

"Holy shit! It's like Christmas came early this year!" Apollo pulled a small notepad out of his shirt pocket and began jotting down notes on where to find the supplies he knew they needed before unplugging an electric cart.

"You two grab a cart for yourself and follow me. We have some shopping to do." Apollo drove off in a quiet whir of the electric cart.

"Hey Linds, think they sell Swedish meatballs at the concession stand?" Chivo drove after Apollo, laughing, followed by Lindsey in her own cart.

Two hours later, the three sat by their Land Rover with crates of gear. Apollo and Chivo both wore new Army-pattern ACUS and were packing their new packs with items from an incredible pile of supplies. After a quick test, they determined that the electronic gear stored below ground in the facility had survived the EMP attack. They agreed that a facility like this was hardened against just such an attack for that reason.

Lindsey gingerly opened box after box of new equipment, much of which she had never seen before, but her new friends insisted she needed. Chivo took care to assemble her new M4 rifle before driving to the end of one of the passageways to test fire her new rifle and sight-in the Acog combat sight-mounted on the top rail.

Apollo sat close to Lindsey and helped her assemble each piece of equipment, explaining how it all fit together and showing her how it worked. It was as if a film crew making a documentary about the equipment used by Special Forces Operators had decided to leave a pile of gear at her feet after wrapping principal photography.

"How in the world am I supposed to find all the things in all these little pouches, much less use them?" Lindsey was overwhelmed by it all, even with Apollo's help. He resisted the urge to explain how the MOLLE strap and gear system worked and how he liked it better than the old ALICE system he'd had when he was a young infantry soldier. "Don't worry. I'll show you and we'll practice enough to get you feeling comfortable before we leave."

Chivo walked back to the group and the pile of gear. He was done assembling his gear. His magazines were loaded, his pouches were full, and his kit was already being worn. The big Barrett fifty-caliber rifle lay on the ground, the bipod extended. The comically large suppressor already attached to the end of the barrel extended the length of the large rifle even further.

"Hey Apollo. If you wouldn't mind zipping it up, I could use a hand over here."

Apollo responded with an extended middle finger. Lindsey's fair skin glowed red. Apollo walked over to where Chivo lay behind the rifle and sat down behind the spotting scope attached to a tripod. Not wanting to risk verifying the accuracy of their optics and rifle sights above ground, Chivo had made an impromptu rifle range and walked it off, then stacked boxes four feet high nearly one thousand feet down the lit passageway. There was no way either of them would step foot beyond the wire and into this dangerous world without testing and sighting in their new rifles. Chivo slowed his breathing, taking deliberately metered breaths before pressing the trigger to the rear. The big rifle barked a four-foot long flame out of the end of the suppressor. The suppressed shot echoed loudly throughout the facility.

"Two down and three right," Apollo said, without looking away from the eyepiece of the spotting scope.

Chivo clicked the dials on the rifle's optic to make the adjustments, wrote some notes on a notepad, and reset his shooting position before repeating his breathing cadence and squeezing the trigger again.

"Hit."

Another series of deliberate breaths and another shot.

"I lit."

Seven more times, Chivo repeated the long distance shot, and seven more times he scored a hit. Chivo removed the empty magazine and promptly field-stripped the rifle to clean it. Four green metal ammo cans full of .50BMG sat next to Chivo's pile of gear.

Apollo and Chivo loaded the Land Rover with everything they decided they would need for their mission to South Texas, including some spares of their communications gear with earpieces and throat mics. If what Cliff told them was true, they might need to give some survivors a bit of gear so they could move and communicate effectively.

Lindsey looked at the old-style woodland BDUs that they'd found in her small size; the crisp clean fabric made her feel dirty. Her jeans were dark and greasy from the weeks of wear and days of surviving on the top of the highway sign. She was fairly sure she smelled horrible. The guys found some wet wipes and took an "astronaut bath," as they called it, before putting on clean underwear, shirts and ACUs. She took her sneakers and socks off before pulling her shirt over her head and stripping naked. Her panties looked disgusting and she was afraid to get too close to them for what they might smell like. They were quickly discarded into the throw-away pile. With a fresh box of wet wipes, she began with her face and worked her way down. The smell of the wet wipes brought a flood of memories rushing back. Memories of her family. They smelled just like baby wipes, and for the first time in weeks, she thought of her baby cousins and her sister's first child, a baby girl born two weeks before Christmas. She tried to finish wiping herself down, but ended up sitting naked on the cold concrete floor, crying.

Apollo walked around the side of the Land Rover and stopped in his tracks, caught off guard at the sight of Lindsey sitting completely nude on the ground, sobbing into her hands. Apollo's first and only marriage had lasted exactly ten months, just the amount of time it took for him to return from his first clandestine mission after being selected for The Unit. Not to say that Apollo wasn't experienced with women; he just wasn't very good at knowing what to say or do when someone he cared about was emotional. He resisted the urge to retreat back to the other side of the Land Rover, so he walked to Lindsey, sat beside her, and softly held her hand. Lindsey looked at him, her eyes puffy and red, her cheeks wet. "They're all gone, aren't they? My family is all gone and I'll never see them again."

He wanted to lie; Apollo wanted to say everything was all right, but he couldn't. He decided to tell the truth. "They probably are. I don't think many people survived this attack, but you have, and you have to live every day to honor their memory and their love. You know that is what they would want you to do."

Lindsey began sobbing again. This time Apollo wrapped his big arms around her, Lindsey burying her face in his strong chest. Apollo was scared to move, afraid that he'd told Lindsey the wrong thing, but eventually her crying slowed and her breathing came back to normal. She locked eyes with Apollo and whispered, "Thank you" before giving him a kiss on the cheek.

Lindsey stood and pulled the desert brown men's briefs to her waist. They'd been unable to find any women's underwear. The Under Armour shirt would have to serve as her bra until they could raid a Walmart or other store for her. Apollo sat there, stunned at what had happened. Strong-minded and of Type-A personality, Apollo simply couldn't comprehend Lindsey's emotional swing. Although he did smile upon noticing that her legs were hairy, which he guessed should be expected after the end of the world and all. Lindsey finished getting dressed, tied the laces of her new tactical boots, and looked down at Apollo still sitting on the floor.

"So are you going to sit there all day or are you going to teach me how to use my new rifle?"

Apollo smiled, stood, and looked at his new and also functioning watch. They had about seven hours until sunrise.

CHAPTER 30

The Basin
February 17, Year 1

Jessie didn't dare move a muscle or even open her eyes quickly. She couldn't remember what happened and didn't know where she was, but as consciousness crashed back into focus, some of her new nightmare started replaying in her mind. She had watched Keeley die; she had held her little girl in her arms as life drained from those little green eyes. After that, she remembered being beaten and dragged into a vehicle. The vehicle looked familiar, but Jessie couldn't recall the details.

Carefully and slowly Jessie wiggled her toes; they felt like they worked. She couldn't feel her arms and her shoulders burned harshly. Slowly she tried to open her eyes, the lids crusted heavily with dried blood and tears. The room was dark, but the moonlight filtered in through a small window. Her arms were tied tightly behind her and she was on the floor. Jessie realized she was naked and a wave of fear washed over her that she might have been raped.

Slowly more memories came back into focus and she remembered being beaten and spit on, but she didn't think anyone had raped her, yet. Jessie slowly turned her head and pain exploded from behind her eyes. The pain was so strong that it made her feel like the room was spinning even though she was lying on the floor. She felt like she was falling into a dark hole.

Jessie gasped awake. A flickering candle made shadows dance around the room. The room was familiar, and then she realized she was in a cabin in the park. Another woman sat down, her face blotched with dark purple patches, deep bruises visible in the dim light. She was also nude. The woman held a cup to

Jessie's lips and slowly poured water into her mouth. Then, she took a wet cloth and gently cleaned the dried blood, tears, and snot off Jessie's face. Jessie could smell urine and then remembered two men in leather vests pissing on her.

The unknown woman whispered into her ear. "Don't fight. Submit to them and they won't beat you as badly. If you're lucky, one of them will choose you to be his old lady, and then you'll be protected from the others."

Jessie couldn't believe what she was hearing. She had no intention on submitting to anyone except Bexar, and even then their relationship was built on trust and respect, not submission. The other woman untied Jessie's hands. Her hands, wrists, and arms throbbed in protest as blood flowed back into the muscles when she brought her hands from behind her back.

"Thank you," croaked Jessie.

"My name is Mary. If you do what I tell you to do, you might be able to survive. Otherwise, the men might kill you once they're done with you, or they might just keep beating you."

Jessie couldn't speak; she only nodded slightly, scared to move much more for the pain that held just on the edge of being unbearable. Mary gave her two white pills. "This will help with the pain." Jessie didn't know what the pills were, but she took them. She was barely able to swallow; the pills felt like they stuck in her throat.

"In a couple of hours, I'll try to sneak you in some more vikes, but those will have to do for now. I better get back to the female cabin before I'm caught. You'll start to feel better in about ten minutes."

Mary blew out the candle and quietly walked out of the cabin, leaving Jessie shivering in the dark. Jessie was scared to climb into the bed. She felt more vulnerable than she had ever felt in her life. A few moments later, she could feel the pain starting to fade. She crawled into the corner of the cabin on the other side of the bed, pulled the blanket off the bed and curled into a tight ball in the corner, hoping that her Bexar was still alive and that he could save her.

Terlingua, Texas

Bexar rode much faster than he should have been riding, the dark highway's curves appearing suddenly in the darkness. More than once, he had to swerve to dodge a walking corpse in the roadway. The eastern horizon faintly glowed with the approaching sunrise as he roared past the large Big Bend sign entering the park. For some reason, all Bexar could think about was Hannibal from the A-Team. He had no plan and he had no idea how it would all come together. There was only one thing Bexar was sure of—he was going to kill every single biker in the park. But to do that, he would have to sneak into The Basin from the trail going over The Window. He wasn't sure they would be in The Basin, but that's where the cabins were and that's where they'd attacked before; it was the most likely place and the first place to look. Bexar hoped they didn't know about the trail over The Window; he didn't think they would have discovered it in such a short time. Regardless, it was a better plan than riding up the main road.

Thirty minutes later, Bexar pulled off the Ross Maxwell onto the rocky road to the trailhead and where he had stashed the Wagoneer and RV before, hoping if the bikers heard the motorcycle, they would assume it was one of their own. That day seemed like it had happened years ago. Bexar stopped the motorcycle in the same spot the Wagoneer had been parked, pushed the side stand down, and stepped off the bike, which slid in the dirt and promptly fell over. Bexar shook his head. "Fuck this bike. I'm taking back my cabin."

Bexar removed the fireworks from a saddlebag, stuffed them in his go-bag, and took a step towards the trailhead. His right leg erupted in pain. The whiskey's ability to hold the pain of the gunshot wound at bay was quickly fading, and a hangover was approaching. Angry at himself, Bexar dug the other saddlebag out from under the motorcycle and pulled the zip-top bag full of drugs out. He took the bag of Vicodin out and stuffed it in his pocket, but not before washing two of them down with a bottle of water. The empty plastic bottle dropped to the ground. Bexar stepped gingerly to test his leg and then started limping slowly up the dark trail towards The Window.

CHAPTER 39

Groom Lake, Nevada
February 17, Year 1

Cliff and Wright sat in a conference room with the chosen leaders of the two civilian groups that had arrived at their facility just a few hours prior. The arrivals were still in quarantine, but after the SITREP from Rick, Cliff wanted to hear more about the group's survival and specifically about the militant aggressor group in Colorado.

Mike Rodriguez represented the Dumas, Texas group, and Jake Sills the group from Cortez. Both men wore new and clean BDUs and both bore the look of someone who'd had a full meal and a hot shower for the first time in a long time. Cliff knew that look well, having worn it himself many times after long missions. Still, both of the new men looked uneasy, unsure of their new positions in the government facility.

Cliff looked each man in the eyes and began. "Gentlemen. Welcome to your new home. You are welcome here as long as you choose and as long as you contribute to the group. I know you both have a lot of questions, but first let me cover some things, which may give you some of the answers you're looking for.

"My name is Cliff, and I'm in charge of the facility here. Many years ago, I was chosen by the United States Government to help facilitate the continuity of government, the survival of the United States, for a time that might come like what we have today. We, the intelligence community, knew this attack was coming, but the timetable caught us by surprise. We didn't expect the Chinese to achieve success in their development of the virus so quickly.

"You probably don't know this, but the Chinese, along with North Korea, initiated the surprise attack on the U.S. They detonated multiple nuclear warheads high in the atmosphere to generate an Electromagnetic Pulse, or EMP, which disabled just about every piece of technology on the continent. The reanimated corpses, zombies if you will, are also a result of the attack. The modified bombers they used were drones, either flown remotely or completely computer-controlled; we're not sure. Regardless, they sprayed the populated areas with the engineered virus that jump-started this whole mess. Obviously, you see the results of the infection."

Jake started to speak, but Cliff held up his hand.

"The Yama Strain is what we call it. It was first found by the Nazis in the Himalayas during one of their expeditions to research their idea of the master race. They tried to develop it, but couldn't; they ran out of time and technology. The Soviets tried as well and failed, taking the facilities researching the strain and the scientists during the end of the war behind the Iron Curtain. After the fall of the USSR, the Chinese ended up with it, and obviously they were successful. This facility we're at was on the cutting edge of finding a way to fight the virus, but the scientists and doctors working on that project were killed when the facility was overrun by reanimates. The last hope we had was killed when one of his research specimens broke containment and started another outbreak in the facility. Developing anything to fight the virus is thought to be impossible now. We are left only with survival.

"That brings us to our current mission—find as many survivors as we can, help them as much as we can, and get as many of them as possible back to the safety of Groom Lake. As we gain more numbers, we can start expanding from this facility, but we have to start here."

Jake spoke first. "So how many others are here?"

"Your two groups are the first civilians we've brought in. The major arrived with his handful of airmen from Colorado a few weeks ago. Rick and his group of special operators just arrived when we took command of the plane we used to evacuate you."

"Have you contacted many other survivors? What about our military? What about China?"

Wright nodded. "Jake, we've contacted a good number of survivors, but we believe there are many more that we can't contact due to the lack of communications gear that survived the EMP. As for the military, many of the bases and installations were completely overrun. Soldiers aren't typically armed or ready for an attack when garrisoned in CONUS. As for any overseas groups, we haven't been successful yet, but we're hoping in time our luck will change in that regard. Same with our naval vessels that are still at sea. Hopefully, as we speak, surviving vessels are sailing home as fast as they can. We're still trying to contact them. The only contact we've had outside of the U.S. are some spotty reports on the shortwave bands coming from the UK, and a transmission from the International Space Station that they were going to wait for their supplies to dwindle while attempting to convert a Dragon supply capsule to use for a return trip to Earth. After those initial transmissions with the ISS, we haven't been able to reestablish contact."

"Fine, but what about China? We're at war, right? Are we still under attack?"

Wright frowned. "We haven't been able to detect any transmissions from mainland China since the onset of the attack. Satellite imagery appears that the urban centers are completely overrun by the undead, just as we are here. They appear to be in the same state of emergency that we are. All we can assume at this point is that somehow they lost containment of the virus."

Jake shook his head. "But if they were planning an attack, wouldn't they have invasion forces? Do you think there are any Chinese troops here?"

Cliff raised his eyebrows. "Quite frankly, we haven't had the chance to consider that, because we've been so focused on trying to establish a survivable foothold and locating survivors. China's ability to move personnel and equipment has been quite limited historically, but a lot of the West Coast has been obscured by smoke for the past few weeks. But you're right, just because we didn't know about any troop transport ships of any significance doesn't mean they didn't build them. They did sneak the attack by us, after all. Major, would you put together some people to look into that?"

Wright jotted some notes on his notepad and nodded.

"Now, for our new guests: we should be able to release you from quarantine once you reach the forty-eight hour mark, but I have something for you to work on while you're in there. As your groups are the first civilian arrivals, you will be tasked with drafting the civilian rules, duties, rotation schedules for those duties, and leadership structure. We can meet tomorrow afternoon to discuss your starting thoughts, but please keep in mind that the Constitution is still the supreme law of the land. Our job is to uphold it; your job is to live it.

"Now Jake, I want you to tell me your group's survival story, and I want all the details you have about the aggressor group of survivors left in Cortez."

CHAPTER 40

Pyote, Texas
February 17, Year 1

Lindsey sat on the cold concrete floor, her new M4 field-stripped, while Apollo walked her through the process of inspecting and cleaning her new rifle. The past two hours had been spent teaching her how to operate and use the rifle, followed by a lot of live fire training. If someone came to the supply cache after them, they would be really upset if they needed spare tires for their Humvee.

Luckily the cache had numerous pallets of XM193 .556 ammo for their rifles. More than they could count. So they had no worries about using up their ammunition in training. In fact, their biggest worry with their ammo supply was that they'd loaded too much into the Land Rover and the weight would cause problems.

Even though at the beginning she was intimidated by the rifle and all the gear, by the end of her training, Lindsey was beginning to move and shoot like an old pro, pulling loaded magazines out of the mag pouches on her vest carrier, dumping the empty mags in a dump pouch, and even making smooth transitions from her rifle to her pistol. Although her accuracy still needed work, it was close enough that it could make a difference. It would take her more shots than Apollo or Chivo, but she would eventually get the job done and be a productive member of their fighting unit. Apollo was confident that if they had a month, he could turn Lindsey into someone who would be at home on any top-level SWAT team in the country.

"I didn't even think I would enjoy this kind of shooting this much. All I ever did was shoot skeet in high school."

"Well, times have changed, my friend. And I'm glad that now you have the skills to make sure you'll never be trapped on top of a highway sign again in your life."

Lindsey gave Apollo a long look with a gentle smile before Chivo interrupted, "If you're done holding hands with the senorita, come make a final inspection of our load out so we can get wheels up. We only have a few more hours until sunrise and then we need to get moving."

Apollo glanced at Lindsey. Instead of a face flushed with embarrassment, she gave him a sly smile as he walked off.

"Sorry to break up fun time in fantasy land, mano, but we're on mission; you need to get your shit squared."

"You're right. But this isn't like any mission we've ever run together over the past fifteen years. Besides, what's wrong with being friendly?"

"Nothing. Just remember your prayers."

Apollo bowed his head. "Dear Lord, please don't let me fuck up."

"Exactly."

Thirty minutes passed as Apollo and Chivo checked the load out in the Land Rover, checking equipment off the list each of them held. Lindsey joined them, M4 clean and reassembled, magazine inserted into the rifle and weapon on safe.

Chivo, satisfied with the inspection, unfolded a sleeping pad and lay down, pulling a poncho liner over his head. He quickly fell asleep. Apollo was always amazed at how quickly Chivo could fall asleep. The three had decided earlier that since the time was very short and the facility secure, they could all three sleep at the same time. Apollo walked to where Lindsey sat, laying out her sleeping pad.

"Lindsey, we only have a quick hour to sleep. Bag out while you can."

"How far do we need to travel today?"

"Chivo thinks it will be about three hours to reach the AO, Area of Operation, for the rescue attempt."

Apollo turned to walk around to the other side of the Land Rover.

"Please don't leave me alone. Why don't you lay down here next to me?"

Apollo looked over his shoulder to where Chivo lay sleeping and then back at Lindsey.

"OK, let me get my bed roll."

Apollo returned to find Lindsey lying on her sleep pad and laid his head a few feet away from her, pulling a poncho liner over himself. Lindsey stood and pushed her sleeping pad next to Apollo's and lay down again, draping her arm over his chest and resting her head on his shoulder.

"This is better," Lindsey said with another smile.

The Window

Bexar limped up the Oak Spring Trail to where it rejoined The Window Trail. He felt the intoxication of the whiskey fading, the strenuous hike on an injured leg having a strong sobering effect, and his mind was fuzzy from the Vicodin even though it helped take the edge off the pain. His thoughts were just out of reach. Bexar looked up the trail and towards the eastern horizon. The glowing approach of sunrise was his enemy. His only chance to get near the cabins to lay an ambush would be to get past the cabins on the Pinnacles Trail before fading into the woods, but to do that, he needed to get to the trail before daylight. The trail passed very close to the camping area, the hotels, the parking areas, and the cabins to give visitors easy access to the system of trails in The Basin. However, Bexar's immediate problem was that the rest of the morning's hike was all uphill.

The camping area passed on Bexar's left and he approached the back of The Basin Convenience Store before taking a fork in the trail to his right and passing behind the hotels. The rusty metal sign said the trail's name was Laguna Meadows, and as many times as Bexar had been in the park, he didn't recognize that name. He'd always thought it to be a part of The Window Trail from the cabins.

The sky was turning light gray as Bexar passed his old cabin. He smelled cigarette smoke, heard someone snoring loudly, and heard someone else coughing. Bexar could only hope they didn't notice him passing just below the back porch of the cabin. The trail widened out to a small rock-covered road that went to the large water tanks the entire Basin used. They were one of the sets of tanks at which Bexar had installed solar panels. Taking cover a few feet off the trail, Bexar stopped for a moment to catch his breath, drink some water, and listen to the surroundings while gathering his thoughts. The big green tanks loomed like dark shadows in the early morning light. Bexar jerked in excitement, realizing he could shut off the water supply to the cabins. He scanned the area around him to see if anyone had noticed and limped up the trail as quickly as he could.

Reaching the fenced area around the water tanks, Bexar opened the gate; the lock and chain had been removed the first time he visited the tank weeks ago. Sheltered under a lean-to with a metal roof were the main valves for the tanks. One controlled the water intake from a tank down near The Window; the other controlled the output to provide The Basin hotels, cabins, and restaurant with water. Using a large piece of angle iron lying next to the tank as a level, Bexar pushed hard against the valve. Slowly, it rotated closed. He had no idea how much water was in the pipes and how long that water would last before water stopped flowing out of the faucets, but he hoped it would be soon.

Closing the gate behind him, Bexar limped into the clump of trees and brush near the tanks, took cover, and waited.

CHAPTER 41

The Basin
February 17, Year 1

The water wasn't hot, but it flowed from the showerhead, which was more than Russell had enjoyed since the world stopped. He stood with his arms against the shower wall, water running over his head and down his back. Two naked women rubbed soapy washcloths on his body. He may not have hot water, but he was the king of the new world and now he didn't even have to bathe himself. Russell thought that was a fair trade.

The best part of the women bathing him was the last part. Both of them would spend extra time "cleaning" his dick. They had just started when the water cut off.

"What the fuck?"

Russell looked at the water knobs and turned them both off and on again with no result.

"God dammit." Russell pushed one of the women out of his way and stepped out of the shower. The back of her head bounced off the sink basin with a thud and she collapsed on the floor, a small trickle of blood starting to drip down her face. Russell stepped over his new bitch, whom he had found untied when he returned to the cabin the night before. This time her hands were tied tighter and also tied to the bed frame. One of her eyes looked like it was swollen shut, but Russell didn't care. He thought it was the start of teaching his new bitch her place. He pulled on his dirty jeans and a sweatshirt and, lighting a cigarette, stepped out of the cabin into the cold morning air.

"Buzzer, get over here!"

A prospect opened the door to a beat-up van with no windshield that was sitting in the middle of the parking area and jogged to Russell. "Buzzer's dead, President Russell."

"Shit, right. OK, you get someone to go with you and figure out why the fuck the water stopped."

The prospect turned and jogged back towards the other cabins behind him to find the only other prospect left besides himself.

Pyote, Texas

Apollo's eyes snapped open. Lindsey's arm was still on his chest and her head on his shoulder. Careful not to disturb her, he raised his free arm to look at his watch. 0500. *Shit, it's time to get wheels up.* At least he'd woken up before Chivo found them. He didn't know why he cared that Chivo cared. Chivo wasn't the team leader; there was no team leader. Hell, before being sheep dipped out of the Army, they both held the same rank. He and Lindsey were grown-ass people and it shouldn't matter. Apollo slowly extracted himself from under Lindsey's embrace, pulled the poncho liner off him, and began packing up his bedroll. He stuffed it in the Land Rover before shaking Chivo's shoulder. Waking his buddy resulted in a pistol being pointed at him while Chivo's eyes focused and his brain caught up with his surroundings. As quickly as the pistol had appeared, it disappeared back into his holster. After a quick breakfast of MREs, the unlikely trio was in the heavily laden Land Rover driving towards the ramp and the surface.

Chivo leaned out the driver's window and punched in the same sequence of numbers. The roof above the ramp raised with a muffled hiss as the hydraulics pushed the small concrete building up. After Chivo drove to the surface and onto the dark desert floor, Apollo exited the SUV and closed the entrance behind them. They weren't sure if they would need to stop back again to resupply, and it wouldn't do to have their bountiful supply cache looted or filled with undead.

The sky began to take a flat gray color as sunrise crept over the eastern horizon. Apollo had a notebook road atlas that had been found in the cache site. He flipped through the pages and compared the handwritten directions they had. "OK, back out to the frontage road, head east about two clicks to FM 1927, and turn south."

Chivo followed the directions and made the turn. The open expanse of the west Texas desert lay before them, and all they saw in the dim morning light was miles and miles of nothing dotted with pumper jacks. The six five-gallon cans of diesel fuel strapped to the roof from the supply cache and the refilled fuel tank of the Land Rover gave Chivo more confidence that they could reach wherever they needed to drive without too much concern with fuel economy. So, he took the opportunity with the open road to push the accelerator a little further towards the floor than he had yesterday. The desert blurred by beside them; they saw no cars, no people, nothing on the small Texas FM road. The morning grew lighter as they turned onto FM 1776 and continued south towards the AO, Big Bend National Park.

The sun continued its march into the sky and, without warning, the Land Rover approached the frontage road for I-10. Chivo stopped the SUV and over the sound of the engine they could hear it. All three of them climbed out of the Land Rover and onto the roof rack. Apollo raised a pair of field glasses and looked south towards I-10. An unfathomable mass of walking corpses was trudging eastbound on the highway. Cars groaned as they were pushed out of the way by the pressure of the sea of dead bodies. Like pebbles pushed to the beach by the rising tide, the cars slid to the side of the mob and onto the shoulder of the highway. Some of the zombies stumbled out into the low brush of the desert trees next to the highway, but most continued their mindless journey eastward like rats following the Pied Piper. Apollo scanned left and right with the field glasses.

"I don't see an end or a beginning. I couldn't even begin to guess how many there are."

"Un Chingo. I don't want to know; I don't want to wait to find out. How does the bridge look?"

Their road, thankfully, was not I-10, and it crossed over the Interstate instead of under it.

"Looks clear."

"Then we better get moving before those dead bodies figure out we're up here."

They climbed back into the Land Rover and quickly drove south. The far side of the bridge was clear, and now, on Highway 67 in the open desert, Chivo pushed the speedometer above seventy miles per hour, quickly leaving the horde of undead behind them. He had no desire to be anywhere near that many walking corpses, nor did the others.

CHAPTER 42

The Basin
February 17, Year 1

Bexar heard the grumbling voices and the heavy boots kicking rocks on the trail before he could see them. His rifle and go-bag lay hidden in the brush behind a nearby tree. Bexar gripped his heavy CM Forge knife in his hands and knelt in the shadows behind a tree near the gate to the water tanks, the green blanket poncho further breaking up his outline.

"I don't fucking know. All I know is that none of the cabins have water and these tanks might be the problem and I'm trying to get back on Russell's good side after that botched pharmacy raid."

"Seriously, what the fuck did you do with that?"

"I didn't do anything. The other assholes used too much C4 and blew the fuck out of the Walmart."

"It doesn't matter. We need water to get started cooking down all that gear or we're going to be in serious trouble when everyone runs out of the shit."

"No shit, brother."

The two bikers passed a few feet from Bexar; their cuts only had a curved patch on the back that labeled them as prospects, not full members of the club. He didn't care. They were part of the bike gang, and therefore, they would die.

Bexar's heart raced. He had used his knife to dispatch zombies, but he hadn't killed a living person with a knife before. His mind flashed with a series of memories of horrific stabbing deaths that he'd worked as a patrol officer in what felt like a lifetime ago. His right hand squeezed the knife handle; Bexar took a deep breath and as quietly as he could stepped out from the bushes. The two prospects stopped at the gate to open it. Bexar took three fast steps and plunged the knife deep into the side temple of the biker on the right. Bexar's knife stuck and was pulled out of his hand as the dead man fell to the ground in a crumpled heap. The second biker turned to face his dead buddy and stood with his mouth open, frozen in place from the surprise. Bexar's right hand fell to his pocket and his old Emerson folding knife opened in a flash. Bexar took a step forward and jammed the full length of the blade into the base of the biker's neck. This time Bexar was ready for the pull on the knife and kept a tight grip on the handle. The biker's hands grasped his own neck; a sickening gurgle rattled from his mouth and the severed artery in his neck sprayed Bexar in blood as the biker fell to the ground.

Reaching down, Bexar put his boot on the side of the first biker's face and pressed down while pulling his heavy knife out of the skull with a wet sucking sound. He cleaned the blood and small pieces of brain matter off his knives using one of the biker's shirts before putting the knives away. Bexar searched the dead bodies and found more meth, some marijuana, and a glass pipe for the meth, and each of them had a pistol stuck inside his motorcycle vest. Bexar had no use for the drugs, but the pistols were each made safe and put in his go-bag. He then dragged the dead bodies to the other side of the tree line, shouldered his go-bag, slung his rifle, and walked through the trees to the back of the southernmost cabins. The back roofline nearly reached the face of the hill, so Bexar was able to easily and quietly climb onto the back side of the cabin's roof. He took off his green wool blanket poncho and lay on the roof, covering himself with the poncho. The shingles were very cold against his body and Bexar hoped that the rising sun would help warm him up some more. Using the green blanket for warmth and as a blind, Bexar raised the cheap pair of binoculars he'd taken from the Terlingua store and surveyed the scene before him.

The cabins were the same, and Malachi's Scout sat in the parking lot further down the mountain by the motels and the store. A very beat-up white van with no glass in any of the windows sat in the middle of the parking area for the cabins. A man with long hair smoking a cigarette walked out of view and back into Bexar's old cabin, slamming the door shut. As much as Bexar wanted to bust into the biker camp like Chuck Norris in *Delta Force*, he knew better and decided to wait and observe. If he could figure out where Jessie was and pick off the bikers one by one in secret, he might actually succeed.

Marathon, Texas

Chivo stopped the Land Rover on the west side of town. The three of them stood on the roof rack of the SUV again; Apollo once again had his field glasses to his face, surveying the scene ahead of them.

"Looks like there are a couple of dozen walkers milling about in the street."

Chivo had the laminated map square out of the notebook and in his hand. "I don't really see a better way around the town. I think we would be better off driving through on the main road and dodge the walkers as we get near them."

The three of them stood quietly, each trying to think of alternate plans. Lindsey broke the silence. "Well, if we're going to do it, let's quit waiting around and go do it."

Apollo and Chivo looked at Lindsey with surprise and approval. It had only been a few days, but the woman in front of them was quickly changing to adapt to their new world.

They climbed back into the Land Rover, and Chivo drove them into town at a steady forty miles per hour, but slowed to thirty as they began nearing the first group of undead. Instead of trying to shoot clear a path, both of the side windows were closed and Chivo turned the steering wheel sharply left and right to dodge each new corpse in the town's welcoming committee. As quickly as they entered, they were leaving Marathon and turning south on Highway 385, the zombies behind them left reaching for the vehicle as it vanished into the distance. Back into the open desert, Chivo pushed the gas pedal and brought the SUV up to a steady seventy miles per hour again.

A bit over half an hour later, Chivo slowed to pass by the white guard shack where the park staff took money to enter the park. The ranger station and the guard shack appeared to be deserted, but they didn't stop to find out. Apollo dug out another laminated map and flipped through the pages before stopping on a topographical map of a mountainous area and tracing his finger along little gray lines, squinting to read the text next to them.

"According to Cliff, we need to check this area labeled the Chisos Basin. When the road T's, take a right, go about ten clicks and take a left."

A few minutes later, Chivo turned the Land Rover left and followed a sign with an arrow for the direction of the Chisos Basin.

"Pull over or drive past?" Chivo jerked his chin toward the road ahead.

Apollo squinted and looked ahead at the quickly approaching black speck in the distance.

"Drive past. We'll see what he does."

Chivo nodded and the black speck quickly grew in size until it roared by, traveling the opposite direction. It turned out to be a man on a motorcycle wearing blue jeans, black leather, and a vest with a bunch of patches sewn on it. Lindsey turned in her seat to look above all the gear and through the small piece of the back glass at the biker. Both Apollo and Chivo watched their side-view mirrors. The biker skidded to a stop before turning around and riding up on the Land Rover at a high rate of speed.

Apollo already had his seatbelt off and his pistol out, and he held it below the window where the rider wouldn't be able to see it. The biker caught up to the Land Rover and pulled alongside the driver's side. The rider reached under his vest with his left hand and drew a pistol, pointing it at Chivo. He yelled, "Pull over!"

Chivo smiled at the biker, who looked very confused at the man smiling at his pistol, before jamming on the Land Rover's brakes and yanking the steering wheel to the left. The biker shot, but the round skipped harmlessly off the hood of the Land Rover. The corner of the bumper hit the back of the motorcycle and knocked it sideways. The biker dropped the pistol and tried to grab the handlebars, but the motorcycle turned sharply and high sided, throwing the biker off. He slid on the asphalt. The hard surface ground the skin off the biker's left arm and the left side of his face. His right foot pointed at a ninety-degree angle away from his shin, but somehow the biker lived through the ordeal. Chivo stopped the Land Rover by the biker lying in the road. He and Apollo climbed out and walked over to him, finding him lying flat on his back in the middle of the road and yelling in pain.

"Hey guy, you should really be more kind to your arriving guests. I'm going to give your establishment a bad review on Yelp."

The biker spat bloodily at Apollo; he kicked the biker's broken ankle, resulting in another howl of pain. Chivo kicked the biker's hand away from the broken ankle and put his boot on it. While stepping on the biker's fingers, Chivo leaned over him. "So how many of you assholes are there up there?" he asked, pointing towards the Chisos Basin.

"Fuck you, wetback!"

Apollo raised his eyebrows at the racial slur the biker spat at Chivo, who replied by stomping his foot on the biker's hand. The crackling sound of breaking bones could be heard over the man's screams.

"OK *marica*, let's try this again. How many of you assholes are up there?"

Gasping for breath through the pain, the biker replied, "Only eleven of us left."

"Good. Now we're getting somewhere. What sort of weapons do you have?"

"M-16s and a fifty-cal machine gun."

Chivo looked at Apollo, and after years of working together, they exchanged their thoughts in a single glance. If the bikers had a machine gun emplacement deployed correctly, there was no way they could drive into the mountain basin without being ambushed.

"So those are what you have guarding the road?"

"No, no one is guarding the road," the biker replied through gritted teeth.

Apollo smirked, "You're a gang of idiots then."

"Fuck you nig—"

The biker's slur was interrupted by Chivo's pistol firing a single shot, erupting the biker's face and head in a geyser of blood.

"*No jodas, pendejo.* You can call me names, but you don't call my brother names."

Apollo grinned at Chivo. "Thanks buddy. Now what?"

"Statue of Liberty play, straight up the middle."

Apollo nodded, and they climbed back into the Land Rover.

CHAPTER 43

The Basin
February 17, Year 1

Bexar thought he heard a shot echoing off the mountains, but it was very faint and he wasn't completely sure. His head pounded and he felt nauseous; this was going to be a bad hangover. He snacked on a Snickers bar that he'd taken from the store in Terlingua, moving as slowly as he could to remain hidden. Bexar had never been in the military and never had any training as a sniper or in cover and concealment. All Bexar could rely upon was what he'd read in books like *American Sniper* to give him tips on what to do.

It was hard to keep count of the number of bikers in the basin; the binoculars just weren't powerful enough to see the details down by the motels very well. Bexar also didn't have anything to write on and was relying on his half-drunk encroaching hangover brain to keep track. There were the two he had already killed, but they didn't matter anymore. Another had left on his motorcycle towards the exit of the basin about twenty minutes ago. There was the one he saw enter his old cabin, and so far he had counted seven others milling about doing various things. Mainly, he saw them drinking beer and smoking dope in small glass pipes. Bexar wasn't sure what they were smoking, but from a distance it looked like either crack or meth.

Two mostly naked women went into his old cabin about thirty minutes ago, as best Bexar could tell, but they hadn't come back out yet. Bexar guessed that that was the leader's cabin since it was one of the nicest, and he hadn't seen any women entering any of the other cabins.

Movement caught the corner of his vision, and he panned his binoculars towards the road entering the basin to see an old Land Rover driving up the road. The vehicle drove slowly and turned off the road behind the basin store. Bexar assumed it was more bikers and they were too far away for him to engage. So he continued to watch the store until two people moving slowly around the far side of the building caught his eye. He glimpsed a man in BDUs moving west, using the buildings for cover, carrying the largest rifle Bexar had ever seen. That kept Bexar's attention until the man hit the low scrub of the desert floor and vanished like a ghost. Bexar held his breath and scanned with the binoculars, nearly convincing himself that the mix of alcohol, Vicodin, and the gunshot wound had him hallucinating. But he scanned back towards the store and saw the other two in BDUs moving up the road in a half jog before melting into the woods on the east side of the basin. He could have sworn that behind the black guy was someone with a blond ponytail, but it was hard to see with all the gear that guy had on.

Bexar was still trying to figure out who those new guys were and if they were a threat when he heard a woman scream. He panned his binoculars back towards his old cabin where the scream originated. One of the bikers he had killed with a knife had reanimated and was lumbering towards three women. Two of them were the ones that had gone into the cabin a while ago; the third one was completely nude and had her hands bound.

Bexar's heart nearly stopped when he realized that the nude woman was Jessie. She was badly beaten, but she was there and she was alive! Bexar dropped his binoculars and pulled his AR up from his side, took aim, and fired a single shot through the skull of the zombie biker. The woman nearest the re-killed biker was splattered with fragments of skull and diseased brain matter, which she responded to by freezing in her tracks and screaming again. The rifle's report echoed across the mountains. The biker with the ponytail erupted from the cabin and walked to the body of the biker, looked at the splatter of brain matter, and followed the path backwards and up the hill, seeing Bexar lying on top of the low cabin roof. The biker gang's president locked eyes with Bexar's before growing wide in surprise and then narrowing in anger.

The biker grabbed the first woman in reach and pulled her in front of his body, using her as a shield. He started backing up towards the cabin. Bexar looked at Jessie and at the retreating biker, and decided that if that woman led his nude wife into the parking lot bound by a rope, then she was a party to the gang's violation of his family and friends and deserved what she got. Bexar lined up the reticle of his ACOG and squeezed the trigger. The woman's head exploded in blood and brain matter. The biker fired his pistol wildly towards Bexar before Bexar could line up his follow-up shot. Four trigger pulls of the AR later, the biker with the pistol lay motionless on the asphalt. Jessie also lay on the ground, unable to move her hands. She rolled in pain on the ground, one of the biker's pistol rounds having nicked her in the calf. Blood began flowing from her wound onto the pavement.

The bikers smoking dope ran towards the two dead bodies. One drew his pistol and started towards Jessie; Bexar shot him a half-dozen times before he fell to the ground. Bexar threw the poncho aside, did a tactical reload of his rifle, and slid down the front of the roof to the patio to run down the walkway as quickly as he could, limping along the way. The adrenaline was so high that the hangover seemed to vanish instantly.

Breaking into view from between the next row of cabins, Bexar saw that the white van on the other side of the parking lot was smoking. The other biker must have shot it as well as Jessie by mistake. Bexar slowed and knelt, shouldering his AR now that he had more shots on the other bikers, when the head of the biker lined up in his reticle exploded in a red mist. Then another and another before Bexar realized that the guy with the big rifle was taking out the bikers. Bexar lowered his AR and scanned the pavement for other threats. The remaining two bikers ran down the hill to his right; Bexar began to turn to line up shots on the escaping bikers when he heard the staccato fire of an AR being fired rapidly.

"Well shit yeah," Bexar said out loud. He began to stand and noticed the white van had flames pouring out of the open holes where windows used to be. Suddenly, it felt like a giant punched him in the chest and knocked him off his feet onto the walkway behind the first row of cabins. Bexar's mind had just started to process the roaring sound of the explosion that rolled over him when he felt a blank curtain fall over his eyes and mind. Then, blackness.

CHAPTER 44

The Basin
February 17, Year 1

"What in the hell was that?" Lindsey yelled.

Both Lindsey and Apollo lay flat on the asphalt; Lindsey had no idea what had happened, just that Apollo had pushed her to the ground before he joined her.

"Fucking IED is what that sounded like."

"Like in Iraq?"

"Yes."

"What now?"

"You get the Land Rover and drive all the way up this road towards the cabins until you find me. If I think it's a trap, I'll come back down and meet you."

"But ..."

"No buts, go!"

Lindsey frowned at Apollo before hopping to her feet and running down the hill to where they'd left the Land Rover parked. Apollo climbed to his feet and jogged up the hill with his rifle ready. Before passing the two bodies of the bikers, Apollo fired a single shot into each one's skull to make sure they wouldn't get up again.

At the top of the hill, the destruction was incredible. The three stand-alone stone buildings to Apollo's right and in front of him were mostly destroyed and burning. The long row of cabins to his left were also catching fire. Chivo came from behind further west, jogging down the hill with the big Barrett fifty-caliber rifle over his shoulder.

"Our guy is on the other side of those cabins. You check here and I'll go after our guy."

Apollo flashed a quick thumbs-up and checked each of the bodies on the pavement. The bikers without any heads were obvious; Chivo did incredible work. There were two women on the pavement; both had burn marks on their bodies and one of them was nude. One of the women was very obviously dead; a large piece of shrapnel was lodged into her forehead and her eyes were open, focused on infinity in death. The other woman looked OK except for being nude and having what appeared to be a gunshot wound to the right calf. Apollo took out a pair of latex gloves, put them on and checked for a pulse, then took the stethoscope out of the MOLLE webbing on his chest carrier and checked for any signs of life. He couldn't find anything. Her eyes were closed, but Apollo was sure she was dead. Apollo stuffed the stethoscope back into his gear and moved on to the other bodies. Each body he checked, he found completely lifeless. If the biker they'd interrogated was correct, they were one body short. Apollo didn't know about the other two bikers Bexar had killed up the mountain by the water tanks.

Chivo returned with a limp body over his shoulders.

Apollo looked at Chivo and shrugged. Chivo nodded. "He's alive."

Apollo raised his eyebrows and before he could say anything, the Land Rover pulled up beside them. Chivo lay the unconscious man in the back of the Land Rover. "I'm going back for my rifle and this guy's bag. Prep for depart in five mikes," he said as he held up an open hand.

Apollo flashed another thumbs-up. This was like their year in Afghanistan and the terrain kind of looked like it too. Apollo pulled his stethoscope out again, along with a pair of EMS shears. He cut off the man's boots and all of his clothing before doing a blood check, rubbing the body to check for any blood that would signify an open wound. He found none except a gunshot wound to the right thigh that didn't look fresh and looked like it might be infected. Lindsey climbed into the front passenger's seat and Apollo handed her an IV bag. "Hold this up until I can rig something to hold it." Apollo started an IV as quickly and cleanly as any emergency room nurse. He'd trained and practiced as a combat medic in the Army Special Forces; that training was continued after he left to work for the CIA. Once the IV was taped down, Apollo unfolded a silver foil-like emergency blanket and wrapped the man in it followed by one of their poncho liners. Chivo returned just as Apollo ran a length of 550 cord from the roof rack through the door and across the ceiling to tie off on the other side of the vehicle. With a carabiner, he hung the IV on the line and gave a thumbs-up to Chivo, who handed Lindsey the man's bag and his big sniper rifle before climbing behind the wheel of the Land Rover.

Not waiting to see if the missing biker turned up with the fifty-caliber machine gun, Chivo drove quickly down the road and away from the basin. They needed to check in on the SATCOM with Cliff, but they also needed to get to a secure place.

CHAPTER 45

The Basin
February 17, Year 1

Jessie's mind slowly came into focus, and it took some time for her to figure out where she was and what had happened. Her eyelids opened to find a pale blue sky and trees, but she couldn't hear anything. Wait—she could hear a high-pitched ringing in her ears, but she knew that it wasn't a real sound; it was her ears protesting against an assault to her ear drums. But what happened to cause it? Jessie sat up and realized she was completely nude. She felt dizzy. Her hands were tied together with some rope. Turning her head, she saw that there were dead bodies on the asphalt and that the cabins were on fire. The cabins. She was in the park in the basin. The events before the explosion came back in a flood. She'd been kidnapped by the biker gang and had been savagely beaten. Jessie looked at her crotch and wasn't sure if she had been raped, but she could remember the beatings, the darkness, and being pissed on. Jessie was sure if she didn't flee, she would be violated sooner or later.

Jessie stood. Her right leg failed her and she fell to the road, painfully unable to catch herself with her hands tied. Tears welled up in her eyes and she wanted nothing more than to sit and cry, but Jessie knew that she had no time to feel sorry for herself. She had to get free; she had to get her mind right and she had to survive.

Bexar.

She remembered seeing a glimpse of Bexar with his AR, but the memory wasn't clear and Jessie wasn't completely sure she hadn't imagined her husband being there. Gingerly, Jessie stood again and very carefully hobbled to where the biker's leader lay dead on the pavement. His large KaBar knife was still on his belt. Jessie pulled the knife out, sat on the ground, and put the handle of the knife between her feet so she could rub the rope against the blade. A few moments of work and the rope fell away from her wrists, dark red abrasions burned into her skin. Jessie took the knife in her hand and stood. Carefully she checked the biker's vest and found a pistol. A press check told her that a round was in the chamber. Jessie pressed the magazine release and found that the Glock 21 had six rounds left in the magazine. With the round in the chamber, Jessie had seven rounds to her name.

Blood still poured from the wound in her calf, a chunk of meat missing where the bullet tore through her flesh as it passed by. Jessie limped to the next biker and found he was missing his head. She used the knife and cut off large strips of the dead biker's t-shirt, which she folded over her bleeding calf and then tied tightly into a makeshift bandage.

She limped to the last cabin, the cabin she and Bexar had lived in a few weeks earlier. The front wall was missing and the roof that had collapsed was smoldering in front of her eyes, but some of the structure and the back wall still stood. Jessie walked slowly towards what remained of the cabin and walked into the rubble. The dresser was broken beneath the fallen roof, but Jessie still found a pair of her pants and one of Bexar's t-shirts. Even without shoes or underwear, a pair of jeans and a t-shirt was better than nothing.

Limping out of the ruined cabin, Jessie looked at the bodies lying on the ground around her. The smallest biker was her choice; she walked to his body and pulled the leather boots off his feet. Square-toed with a strap across the front and a metal ring on the side, the boots were far from functional for anyone doing anything other than riding a motorcycle. They were two sizes too large, but boots too large are better than no boots at all, and Jessie put them on. Jessie looked at each of the bodies on the ground and didn't see Bexar. She walked to the walkway between the cabins and didn't see him or his body there either.

Maybe he was able to get away. Maybe he thought I was dead and left. Maybe he's chasing a biker that got away. Maybe he was never here at all. Maybe he's in Terlingua. Maybe he never came back from Lajitas. I need to get out of here.

Jessie limped back to the parking area, the boots clomping on the stone walkway. *Motorcycle boots, I never thought I would be wearing motorcycle boots. Motorcycle. The bikers had bikes nearby.* A handful of bikes lay in ruins from the blast, so Jessie gingerly limped down the hill towards the motels and the basin's store.

In the parking lot, she saw two more motorcycles, but even better yet she saw Malachi's International Scout. It was intact and looked to be just fine. She found the keys hanging from the ignition. The motor started effortlessly. She put the truck in gear and drove out of the parking lot, out of the basin and towards Terlingua with half a tank of gas and more questions than answers.

Big Bend National Park

The Land Rover turned north on Main Park Road and sped through the desert at seventy miles per hour in contempt of the marked forty-five miles per hour speed limit signs. Chivo drove as fast as he thought safe; Apollo continued to tend to the man they were sent to find; although Cliff had sent them in search of a group thought to be overrun by a biker gang, they only had one survivor. Apparently, they'd been overrun, but at least they were able to save one even if they left a dozen bodies on the pavement after the blast. Apollo still wasn't sure why the explosion happened. From the exploded remains of a vehicle, it appeared that it was a car bomb, but he couldn't figure out how or why there would be a car bomb. It didn't matter how or why. They'd gotten their high-value target and were rushing back to the underground cache site, hoping that the unconscious man would survive the effects from the blast ... and the infected leg. It was still too early to tell.

Chivo continued north, and twenty minutes later, the group drove through Marathon, but not after dodging a dozen zombies shambling across the main road in town. Apollo continued to check the man's vitals, which hadn't changed, and hoped that he would regain consciousness soon. The Land Rover turned right and pushed north on Highway 67. Apollo, with a lack of anything else to do, began teaching Lindsey what he was doing and why, although he didn't have a blood pressure cuff. He wished he did, but it didn't matter since he didn't have any medications to inject into the man if his blood pressure dropped. No, in this brave new world all Apollo could do was hope for the best.

Apollo reached behind the seat and brought the man's backpack to his lap, opened it, and began removing the contents. Pmags full of ammo, bottles of water, some snacks, a couple of broken-down MREs, and a good handful of firecrackers. It was like a teenager packed the bag, but it dawned on Apollo that it could be all the man was able to scavenge, and the most important thing to have is just about always ammo. Next, Apollo inspected the man's rifle and pistol. Both were well worn, but obviously maintained and recently cleaned. The cutoff remains of the man's clothing were next, and Apollo was surprised at the large heavy knife on the belt. The belt looked high-quality, except that it was forever ruined, cut clean through by Apollo's EMS sheers. Blood stained the blade of the big knife, and same with the Emerson folder clipped inside one of the pockets.

The sun blazed straight overhead as they approached I-10. Chivo, aware of what they'd encountered just hours before at I-10, stopped the Land Rover well short of the bridge. Apollo, Lindsey, and Chivo climbed out of the still-running SUV and stood on top of the big gear rack on the roof. Chivo held the field glasses to his eyes and scanned ahead of them.

"The bridge is gone."

"Gone?"

"Yeah, like demoed gone. I can see where it was. I can see where it is missing. It's fucking gone, mano."

Chivo handed the field glasses to Apollo, who scanned the bridge as well.

"Damn."

A dust cloud hung in the air near the Interstate.

"What do you think, Chivo?"

"Recon. Leave your *latiga* and we can check it out."

"You know what? Fuck you, man. Let it go."

Chivo shrugged, climbed off the roof of the Land Rover, and started walking up the roadway towards the Interstate.

"Lindsey, stay on the roof, stay cool, and keep your M4 ready. We'll be back in a few minutes. We're going to check this out."

Lindsey nodded and stood still on the roof of the SUV holding her M4 rifle.

Apollo climbed down and jogged to catch up with Chivo.

"Lay off me and Lindsey, man."

"Why?"

"You know what? If you haven't noticed, the world has gone to shit. If we find comfort in each other, then fuck it. It isn't like we're going to live very long in our new world. We might as well have a companion for it. It isn't like we're on a mission. Now we're just having to survive. This is worse than Panama."

"Fine, but you lose your edge and let my ass get bitten by those fucking things and I will fucking kill you."

Apollo smiled and punched his buddy in the shoulder.

"Besides, this isn't as bad as Panama, but it is much worse than fucking Bolivia. Fuck, that one sucked."

"Yeah, it did."

Both of the men stopped well short of the bridge, but could see what the dust cloud was from. The passing undead were like nothing they had seen; there were more than before. Many more.

"Holy shit. The fucking zombies knocked the bridge down. Unass it, dude. We've got to figure out a new plan."

The large herd of undead pushed up the embankment and some of the numbers reached the frontage road. The stream of walking dead was at least one hundred feet wide and stretched as far as they could see. The stench affronted them even from two hundred feet away.

"Looks like we have a fan club." Apollo pointed to the frontage road on their left. Close to three dozen undead ambled towards them.

"Shit on this. Time to haul ass."

Apollo and Chivo jogged back towards the Land Rover, Apollo circling his hand above his head. Lindsey didn't know what that meant, but correctly guessed it was time to go; she climbed down and into the still-running Land Rover. Chivo took the wheel, made a fast U-turn, and backtracked at a high rate of speed. After ten minutes of fleeing the approaching horde, Chivo turned off the highway and onto a dirt road to put a little distance between them and the highway before he stopped the SUV.

Apollo climbed out, pulled the Pelican case with the SATCOM out of the cargo area, and began setting up the antenna; they needed to check in with Groom Lake.

CHAPTER 46

Groom Lake, NV
February 17, Year 1

The two civilian leaders walked back to the quarantine under armed guard in case they somehow suddenly died and turned, which was a bit ridiculous, but so was everything else in the way of the new world. Cliff walked back to his office with the intention of drafting a plan to check for and defend against any Chinese assault forces. With everything that had happened, Cliff hadn't given serious thought to the possibility of invading parties already in CONUS before the civilians brought it up. Cliff frowned at the thought of his oversight before he was interrupted by his phone ringing. He pushed the speaker button. The extension showed to be from the radio hut.

"Cliff, you need to come in here. Someone asked for you by name and said he was a part of Lazarus."

For a fraction of a second, Cliff's eyes widened in surprise before he regained control of his emotions.

"Copy that, en route to you."

Cliff stood and walked briskly out of his door towards the radio hut.

Moments later, Cliff burst through the door and walked straight to the airman who had called him. Without speaking, Cliff took the headphones off the airman and put them on his own head. He turned to the airman and said, "Why don't you step out for a smoke?"

"I don't smoke."

"Why don't you step out and try picking up the habit?"

The rest of the men in the room looked at Cliff with puzzled expressions. In the past few weeks, they had never seen Cliff act so strangely or speak like that to anyone.

"In fact, why don't all of you step out and see about starting smoking."

With a number of raised eyebrows, the four other men stood and walked out of the room, shutting the door behind them. Cliff checked to make sure he was alone before he keyed the radio mic.

"Lazarus Four, go ahead with your traffic."

"Lazarus Six clear copy. Four status and package report, over?"

"Lazarus Four secure site three with zero package, one and two confirmed lost, all others presumed lost."

"Lazarus Six copy and secure in site seven with one package, package nine in hand."

Cliff's lips curved to a very slight smile. "Clint, open channel. We don't have time for this anymore."

"Cliff, why are you at three? You were assigned one."

"They didn't follow the plan and were overrun. Three was overrun too, but I was able to secure it. What is your current count?"

"Just the two of us, including package nine."

"I have zero copy from anyone else until you. I think nine is now promoted to one."

"I agree. My board shows green for sat link. Do you have anyone to witness?"

"Yeah, quite a few. Give me ten-mikes to get them set up. What freq?"

"Primary freq, channel one. We'll take the prime spot since it appears to be just us for now."

"Roger. Ten mikes from ... three, two, one, now."

"Copy, counting."

Cliff stood and walked out of the door to find the airmen near the door and very obvious about acting like they weren't trying to listen. Cliff ignored that transgression for now. "Get Wright, get the civilians out of quarantine, get everyone even if you have to wake them up, and come to auditorium two. You've got five minutes."

The airmen stood still for a moment and then quickly left down the hallway towards the rest of the facility. Cliff stood still for a moment, his hand resting on the butt of the pistol holstered on his right leg. *Guess I've got to get my shit together if we're going to swear in a new President of the United States.*

Bardwell Lake, Texas

Clint walked to the women's dormitory, where he and Amanda had been living together for the past few weeks. The computer system had experienced a serious malfunction, and it took Clint three weeks to break into the system and run the recovery diagnostic. Without computer access, Clint had no way of knowing which facilities were still in service. Even with a working radio and SATCOM systems, he didn't have the frequencies memorized and needed access to the system. Over the past three days, Clint had reviewed the SATINT imagery from the SeeMe system and what he found was devastating destruction across most of the United States. Worse yet, all the facilities except his and Groom Lake showed to be offline, most likely with no survivors. He didn't have the chance to investigate what happened to all the other facilities. That would have to wait. First, he had to complete the primary objective he began back in December.

"Amanda, I made contact with Groom Lake. They're setting up a satellite video link between our facilities. You need to come with me."

After gaining computer access, Clint was confident that Amanda was the last survivor in the Presidential line of succession, but he didn't tell her, because he wanted to make contact with the only other remaining facility that appeared to be operational first.

Both of them walked to the video room, which had video cameras pointing at three different walls with three different printed backgrounds. One was the background of a photo of the Capitol Building, another looked like the Oval Office, and the third was just an American flag. Clint chose the background of the American flag and stood Amanda in the middle of the background in front of the camera. Taking her hand, Clint faced Amanda, "I'm about to swear you in as the current President of the United States. I made contact with another from my team located at the bunker in Groom Lake. He was supposed to be at the bunker in Denver, but said they were overrun and both the President and the Vice President are dead. All others in the Presidential line of succession are missing and presumed dead."

Amanda laughed at Clint. "What about the President pro tempore or the Secretary of State or even the Attorney General? I'm really far down that list."

"You're number nine with the current administration. As of right now, my team believes you are the highest-ranking survivor. If we're going to succeed, we need someone to be the President. We need a leader to rally survivors and to take our country back from the dead."

"But I'm no President. I didn't have the first idea what to do or where to begin to run this country before the attack, much less now that society is all but lost."

"That's why you have me. Together we will succeed."

Amanda kissed Clint on the lips. "Well, if you're going to make the President, we better get started."

Clint looked at the digital clock on the wall before leaving Amanda standing in front of the wall print of the American flag so he could activate the cameras and start the broadcast.

"We have three minutes, so try to look Presidential."

Amanda looked down at the ACU pants and brown t-shirt she was wearing. She wasn't even wearing a bra and she felt like a fraud, like a child picked to be the class leader for the day before passing the duty on to someone else.

Clint opened a drawer and removed a laminated piece of paper. Long ago, he'd memorized the words printed on the paper, but since he had a little bit of time, he read through them three more times before returning the paper to the drawer and walking in front of the camera with his lover.

The light in the ceiling behind the camera turned from white to red, and the monitor next to the camera showed Clint and Amanda on one screen and a small auditorium full of people on the next.

Clint looked at the clock on the wall again before clearing his throat.

"Ladies and gentlemen, I present Amanda Lampton, the Secretary of Agriculture and the highest-ranking living member of the Presidential line of succession. If you would raise your right hand and repeat after me."

"I do solemnly swear. That I will faithfully execute the office of President of the United States, and to the best of my ability, preserve, protect, and defend the Constitution of the United States."

Clint shook Amanda's hand. "Ladies and gentlemen, Amanda Lampton, the President of the United States."

Amanda glanced at the monitor and at the people in the auditorium, who sat in stunned silence before erupting in applause. All the people on the other side of the satellite uplink stood and continued with eager applause. The applause slowly died down and the people in Groom Lake took their seats. Amanda was shocked and a little angry at Clint since she wasn't prepared to be sworn in as the President, much less give a speech.

"Thank you, Clint, and thanks to those of you on the other side of this uplink. We traveled from my home in Little Rock to this facility in Texas, fighting for our lives and losing Clint's teammate to the walking dead en route."

Amanda closed her eyes and took a deep breath, searching for the words to continue. Her knees felt weak and suddenly she felt a little dizzy. "To quote what Lincoln said in 1863: *It is for us, the living, rather, to be dedicated here to the unfinished work which they who fought here have thus far so nobly advanced. It is rather for us to be here dedicated to the great task remaining before us—that from these honored dead we take increased devotion to that cause for which they gave the last full measure of devotion—that we here highly resolve that these dead shall not have died in vain—that this nation, under God, shall have a new birth of freedom and that government of the people, by the people, for the people, shall not perish from the earth.* Thank you and God bless."

Amanda walked off camera and sat on the edge of a table, shaking. Once Clint shut down the video uplink, he walked to her and gave her a hug. Tears welled in her eyes and she cried into Clint's chest for a few moments before gaining her composure.

"Those people, they've survived, they're safe. We survived and we're safe. There have to be more people surviving for now. We have to help them. We have to do something. *I* have to do something. I just ... I mean, I have no idea what to do. It was bad enough being taken from my home by you and your partner to fight our way across Texas and to be safe, but alone in this huge bunker. What are we going to do?"

Clint gave her a rare smile. "Madam President, it is time that I brought you up to speed on a top secret project: Who I am, and what Cliff and I were tasked to accomplish."

Amanda sat in silence. The man she had taken as a lover and trusted had been lying to her—or at least keeping secrets.

"My name isn't really Clint. That name was assigned to me, just as my partner's name was. Who I was before is of no importance; I had no family before the attack and no personal history of note. However, in college I was approached by a secret taskforce headed under the banner of the CIA. I thought it was to be a superspy like what Tom Clancy wrote about. We began our training at the CIA's facility in Virginia commonly referred to as 'The Farm' then continued through an exceptional amount of special schools. There were originally thirty of us, each of us tasked with different priorities, missions, and objectives."

"We were all code named 'Lazarus,' and just like the man of the same name in the New Testament, we were supposed to rise from the dead. Well, not us, but we were supposed to help the United States rise from the dead. We've known about the Yama Strain for a number of years and have been working hard to find a way to protect ourselves against it. They attacked before we were ready. The unassuming man in charge in the uplink at Groom Lake is Cliff. We went through the training together, but we had different missions within the same project."

"Cliff was supposed to be in Denver with the Vice President and apparently he was; the facility under the Denver airport was overrun and the VP killed. Cliff verified that POTUS was also killed. He fled to Nevada and to Groom Lake."

"Wait, what exactly is Groom Lake? I know you said it was a base in Nevada, but it seems to be a bit more involved than that."

"In popular culture, it was always referred to as Area 51."

"*The* Area 51?"

"The same, but contrary to what some believe, there are no aliens. It started as a facility to test top-secret aircraft, but eventually a large underground bunker was constructed as a backup facility. As you saw on the monitor, Cliff has been successful in gathering a number of survivors. Normally, we would do the same here, except that I have a new mission objective."

"Which is?"

"To protect you against all threats foreign and domestic, living or undead. We are not going to actively seek survivors for our facility. It isn't safe to expose you to any outside threats until we can establish more containment and begin the process of repopulating the major open positions in the government. Besides, with only two of us, we can't manage any arriving persons. All of them would have to be searched, documented, and quarantined for signs of infection before being allowed into the main facility. If you die now, there is no one else in the line of succession. We would be outside the bounds of the Constitution."

"Cliff is trying to rally survivors at his facility in Nevada. If we are truly lucky, there are still enough citizens alive even to call ourselves a people and a country. Maybe someday we'll be able to fight back the dead and take our land out of their rotting grasp."

Amanda took a deep breath and put her hand on Clint's chest. "OK, but I think there are a lot of things you haven't told me that you should now. I'll order you to if I have to."

"Yes, Madam President," he said, and kissed her passionately.

CHAPTER 47

Cliff looked around the room of airmen and the civilians, all of whom were still cheering and giving each other high fives. It took weeks longer than anticipated, but now the Lazarus project was back on track and a new President of the United States was in place. Clint would direct the first female President in the next steps to help get things online, but for now Cliff had a new mission to accomplish. The debriefing that the civilian groups had given was chilling; the rogue militia group terrorizing the other survivors had to be stopped, and they had to be stopped immediately if any of the good people trapped outside the wire were to be helped.

If what Jake had spoken about in the debriefing were true, then there were some real nut jobs out there holding survivors hostage. There was no way that Cliff would stand by and let such atrocities continue; those survivors were the wives and families of the rescued survivors, and they needed to be reunited back in Groom Lake. It would be impossible to rally the survivors into a reconstituted nation if evil men continued their reign in the new world.

Cliff walked over to Arcuni and interrupted his excited conversation with Garcia. "Arcuni, is the Herc fueled and ready?"

"No, I'm waiting for our next destination to calculate the fuel load needed with a buffer; the less fuel we fly with, the more weight we can carry."

"OK. We're going back to Cortez, Colorado, a simple out and back. Get the PJs. Tell them we're doing a snatch and grab and to load out with my pickup in the cargo hold. Whoolo up in an hour."

Arcuni stood wide-eyed for a moment before nodding and leaving with Garcia trailing close behind.

Big Bend National Park

Jessie turned the steering wheel to leave the main road, pointing the old SUV towards Terlingua. An M4 rifle lay on the seat next to her and, to her surprise, there was a large machine gun in the back of the Scout. She'd never shot anything like it before, but she was confident Bexar could figure it out. It took all of her control to keep her speed at fifty miles per hour. As much as she wanted to drive as fast as the old Scout would go, she couldn't risk having a wreck or burning that much gas. She had to get to Terlingua, get Bexar, and get safe.

Some zombies walked aimlessly around the burnt-out wreckage of a motorcycle and turned to follow the Scout as Jessie turned onto Highway 1-70, but she didn't slow or care; she was a woman with a mission. Jessie was sure that the crashed and burned motorcycle wasn't Bexar's. Vaguely, she remembered seeing the wreck on the way back to the park after being taken by the bikers.

She barely heard the engine or the road noise, because the ringing in her ears filled her head with sound. At least the heater worked well in the Scout, and for once, she wasn't shivering. She was happy to have some clothing on her body. The previous night's memory was still coming in and out of focus, but the more she focused and tried to bring the memories to the surface, the more certain she was that no one had raped her.

Jessie drove past the turnoff for Terlingua and continued towards Lajitas. She wasn't sure that Bexar had ever made it back from his scavenger run for a vehicle, but if he was still there, then she should be able to find his motorcycle or his gear or him. Hopefully not his walking corpse. A couple of miles from the Lajitas Resort, the zombies shambling towards Terlingua on the road were growing in number. Each of them turned and followed the Scout. Jessie drove through the RV Park and found no sign of Bexar or his motorcycle. She had the same results driving through the parking lot of the resort hotel.

If the undead were walking towards Terlingua, then something caused them to walk that direction. It was probably Bexar leaving and they were trying to follow him.

Jessie slammed on the brakes and slid the old 4x4 to a screeching halt, made a U-turn in the middle of the highway and accelerated sharply to drive back towards Terlingua.

The Scout seemed to arrive back to the Starlight Theatre without any conscious control by the driver, who was lost in thought. Jessie turned the engine off and stepped out of the SUV into the parking lot that was still littered with the large spent brass from the machine gun attack the previous day. The cabin, their cabin, lay in a burned-out ruin, and dead zombies lay on the ground in the parking lot. It took her a moment, but she realized that a handful of undead had followed her up the hill. The M4 wasn't one of her and Bexar's AR-15s, but it worked the same, although she'd never had an AR-15 that had a selector switch that went past "fire." She thumbed the switch all the way around to the etched symbol of three bullets, shouldered the rifle, and looked through the ACOG at the mangled face of the walking corpse closest to her. Jessie took a deep breath and smoothly squeezed the trigger. The rifle fired three times in rapid succession and the zombie fell immediately, its rotting skull exploding in a black mist. Four more times, she took aim and fired at an approaching rotting corpse staggering up the hill and four more times, a skull exploded in a shower of black rotting tissue. The last shambling zombie looked like a little girl about six years old. Only part of a dirty pink dress hung in tatters on her broken body. Keeley's face flashed in Jessie's mind as she took aim and pulled the trigger. The rifle only fired once before the bolt locked back to the rear with deafening silence. All Jessie could hear was the ringing in her ears from the explosion.

Jessie tilted the rifle and looked at the ejection port to see that it was locked open on an empty chamber. She ejected the magazine and reached to her chest rig for a fresh one and found only the dirty t-shirt she was wearing. Realizing that she was now out of ammunition for her rifle, Jessie's eyes snapped open in fright before looking back to where the little girl lay on the ground, black fluid oozing out of her ruined skull. Jessie took a deep breath and climbed into the Scout to look for a fresh magazine. *I was stupid to waste so much ammo with the select fire* repeated again and again in her mind.

Jessie still had the Glock with seven rounds in it, but she didn't want to have to rely on a pistol or have to engage any more undead by waiting for them to get into pistol range. She opened the door to the Scout and dug around in the trash the bikers had left in the vehicle. One M4 magazine was found under the front seat. Jessie pressed down on the rounds and they barely moved. *Full, thank God!* She seated the magazine in the rifle and pressed the bolt release before thumbing the safety back to the safe position. Climbing out of the truck, Jessie scanned the area and didn't see any more threats approaching, so she went to the general store. Ten minutes later, Jessie exited sporting a green, white, and red Mexican blanket with a hole cut in the middle for her head, worn like a poncho. *If it is good enough for Bexar, it's good enough for me.*

Jessie walked down the porch towards the Starlight Theatre, her eye caught by a restaurant ticket tacked to the board out front with Bexar's handwriting. Finishing the note, Jessie fell to her knees with tears streaming down her face, not able to catch her breath. She felt like all of her hopes and dreams had turned against her. She had lost her daughter and she had lost her husband. She was all alone and there was no hope to survive.

Eventually, Jessie caught her breath, stood, and walked down the hill towards the ghost town graveyard; it felt like a dream. She found the new rock mound that held her daughter's body, leaned over, and kissed the top of the grave.

I have to go back. I have to find Bexar. If he is dead, I will bury him. If he is reanimated, I have to make sure that he isn't doomed to be a walking corpse. I have to make sure he has peace in death.

Jessie walked up the hill and back into the general store. Thirty minutes later, she had a dozen plastic bags full of water, beef jerky, shirts, blankets, and all the other supplies she could think of to survive. Jessie loaded the Scout, climbed in and started the old SUV, and then drove down the hill towards the highway for Big Bend.

CHAPTER 48

Groom Lake, NV
February 17, Year 1

Cliff stood on the ramp of the C-130. Arcuni, Garcia, and the three PJs stood on the ground looking up at him while he spoke. "There is a rogue element that is not only terrorizing other survivors, but according to our survivors, they also have a prison camp of women and children they are using for forced sexual reproduction and slave labor. We cannot let this stand; we have to destroy the rogue militia and we must save the innocents."

Cliff looked at each man. Their faces spoke of their solid resolve that they believed in the warrior's code to protect those who were in their charge with every ounce of their being until their last breath.

"Simple snatch and grab. We need one of those assholes and we need to get the information on their location, where the civilians are, and what their command structure is like. Wright is working on some SATINT for us, but we need HUMINT and we need it now. Arcuni and Garcia, you are responsible for maintaining security for the aircraft. Rick, Evan, and Chris, you are with me in the truck. The survivors gave me a rough idea on where we can find the outer edges of their Area of Operation. We have no comms, so we have to set a departure on a timed schedule. Once we land, we have two-five mikes, twenty-five minutes, to get our prisoner and be back on the Herc. Arcuni, I want you wheels up at thirty mikes if we're onboard or not. You are allowed to loiter on scene until bingo fuel for return if you have to take off without us. If we're broke dick, we'll return early, so be ready for an immediate departure. If we go Winchester on ammo and have to E&E, we'll return early. From the Intel that we have, we can expect semi-organized resistance using light arms. But the general idea is that the cult wackos do not have any formal military training or hardware. Are we clear?"

The five men all showed thumbs up.

"Great. Arcuni, light the fires; let's get this circus on the tracks."

Near Fort Stockton, Texas

"What the fuck do you mean he isn't there?"

"That's what the kid said. Ended up talking with someone calling himself Major Wright. He said that the route north is broke dick due to a high concentration of walkers and gave us coords to a secondary site."

Apollo handed Chivo the notepad with the coordinates. Chivo climbed into the Land Rover and dug through the map book until he had the right grid square.

"It looks like a camp site on a lake about five hundred miles from here, near Dallas."

"We can't go to Groom Lake because of a zombie horde, but we can go to Dallas? That's fucked up, man. That fucking mass of walking pus was headed towards Dallas when we went by before."

"Hey, fucking don't shoot me; it's not my clusterfuck. I'm just telling you what I've got, mano."

"What do you think? Do we trust Major Wrong or do we stick to our original plan?"

The two of them stood looking past the other and watching the surrounding area for threats, which Lindsey thought looked odd, two people having an argument and not even looking at each other.

Chivo shrugged. "Fuck it mano, let's go to the Big-D."

Lindsey didn't say anything, but thought that going towards a big city like Dallas was a bad idea. She didn't really care as long as she could be with Apollo. She felt safe with him and only wanted to be near him for as long as they lived, which she believed would probably not be very long at all.

The man they'd saved at the park was still unconscious and wrapped in the survival blanket. Apollo climbed behind the wheel, Lindsey took the front passenger seat, and Chivo climbed into the back to switch out the man's IV and keep tabs on him during the drive. Apollo turned the Land Rover around and bounced down the poorly made oil field road, back towards the small Texas highway, to find an alternate route across I-10 towards Dallas.

Cortez, CO

The C-130's nose pointed towards the numbers at the end of the runway. Once the wheels were on the ground and Arcuni pushed the props forward to stop the big lumbering cargo plane, Cliff and the PJs were out of their seats and going through their last gear checks. Magazines were touched in their pouches and weapons were press checked to make sure a round was in the chamber. Garcia began releasing the retraining straps holding the old pickup to the cargo floor, and by the time Arcuni turned the plane around at the other end of the runway, setting the plane for a rapid departure, the expedition crew were in the truck with the engine running. Garcia lowered the ramp and the truck began backing out of the plane. Rick was behind the wheel of the truck, Cliff sat in the cab with his window down, rifle ready, and the other two were in the bed of the truck, rifles pointed towards the cold open air outside the plane. Ramps in place, the truck backed down out of the plane before speeding off towards the open fence and the crashed semi-truck. Arcuni stayed in the cockpit with the engines running, ready to push the throttles wide open. Garcia stood at the end of the ramp, M4 ready and headset plugged into the intercom.

The truck drove north at a high rate of speed. According to Jake, the operating base of the aggressor group was probably at or near the middle school by Highway 491. They weren't ready to engage the full group, but they hoped to find a sentry on the edge of their area. Closing within a few miles of the middle school, Rick slowed the truck to a much more reasonable speed before turning off the highway and onto a side street. Cliff looked at his watch and the countdown timer running. They were ten minutes away from the plane; they had five more minutes to find someone to turn back and make the twenty-five-minute window. Rick slammed on the brakes, sliding the truck to a halt.

"There, a technical drove across on a street four blocks north."

Cliff nodded and climbed out of the truck. The other two PJs climbed out of the bed of the truck before Rick sped north towards the armed civilian vehicle he'd seen pass. The group's plan was to have Rick flush the target and have it follow in pursuit while the other three set a class "L" ambush. Although the destruction was apparent, the group was surprised at the lack of undead walking through the streets. Bodies lay on the street, rotting slowly in the cold winter air, but nothing appeared to be upright. A few moments later, they heard the truck's horn honk twice in the distance. Rick was signaling that he was en route to the ambush with the target following. A few moments later Rick and the truck flew through the intersection before sliding to a halt a block to the south. A rusty old Ford rambled down the road towards them, smoke billowing from the tailpipe. An M-2 fifty-caliber machine gun was mounted in the bed of the truck and the man standing in the bed behind the large weapon was firing a steady stream of rounds towards Rick. Cliff knelt on the sidewalk using a mailbox for concealment, raised his rifle, and fired a three-round burst. The machine gunner's head snapped back and he fell out of the bed of the truck to the road below with a wet thump.

The driver of the Ford slammed on the brakes and slid to a halt a block away from Rick, directly in the kill zone of the ambush. Cliff and the other two PJs opened fire, flattening the truck's tires and punching holes in the radiator while rushing forward towards the driver. The driver raised his hands in surrender. Cliff held cover while Evan ripped him out of the cab and onto the cold asphalt before using flex cuffs to secure his hands behind his back. Rick drove to the group and they tossed their prisoner into the bed of the Chevy before climbing in and driving south towards the waiting plane as fast as the truck would go.

Evan searched the prisoner and found a pistol, a pack of cigarettes, a lighter, a small glass pipe, and a baggy with small dirty crystals that looked like sand mixed with salt. Evan held up the baggy for Cliff. "Fucking meth, man." Cliff shook his head. Evan used EMS sheers and cut off the man's clothing, leaving him bound and completely nude in the cold winter air. A few minutes later, the truck drove up the ramps into the back of the C-130 while Garcia secured the truck to the cargo floor.

Cliff stopped Garcia from raising the ramp. "Leave it open for a little bit. I need to take care of something." Garcia shrugged and went forward in the plane. Cliff put on his headset and plugged into the intercom jack at the back of the plane. "Arcuni, I need you to do something special after taking off." He continued to explain his plan while Arcuni began running up power and released the brakes to begin rolling down the runway.

Moments later the plane launched airborne. Cliff, wearing a loadmaster's safety harness, pulled the naked man out of the bed of the truck and dragged him towards the half-open cargo ramp. Cliff clicked in his safety line and walked the prisoner to the edge of the ramp. Arcuni leveled the plane at about two hundred feet over the ground and banked the plane to fly over the town of Cortez. Cliff held the man by his cuffed arms behind his back, leaning the man over the edge of the ramp as the Colorado landscape sped beneath their feet. Urine trailed down the prisoner's leg.

"Where are the women and children being held?"

"F-f-fuck you."

Cliff slapped the man across the face with the side of his pistol. Blood erupted from the man's nose.

"Let's make something perfectly clear. You tell me what I want to know, or I'll push you off the ramp and you can rejoin your little group after trying your hand at learning to fly. Where are the women and children being held?"

The man shook his head back and forth violently. Cliff shot the man in the back of the shoulder. The prisoner screamed in pain. Blood poured down his naked body, the wind whipping the blood around the back of the plane.

"Where are the women and children being held?"

"T-t-t-the school."

The town of Cortez sped by below their feet. The plane banked hard to the right. Cliff looked over his shoulder, barely holding onto his prisoner, just in time to see a trail of smoke rocketing towards the plane. One of the engines on the left wing exploded in a ball of flame, pieces of wing, props, and engines falling off the wounded aircraft. The plane shuddered hard. Cliff fell on the ramp, remaining in the aircraft only because of the safety harness and tether. His prisoner fell off the cargo ramp into the wind, screaming as he fell into the cold abyss.

The truck slid against the tie-down straps and the pistol fell out of Cliff's hand and off the ramp to the earth below. Smoke trailed the plane, and the flames from the wing were visible behind the plane. The ground rushed towards the ramp while Cliff and the rest of the group held onto anything they could find. The plane hit the ground flat and the last thing Cliff saw was the dirt and sky alternating places as the fuselage tumbled violently across the ground.

CHAPTER 49

The Basin
February 17, Year 1

Jessie wheeled the Scout to what remained of the cabins. A handful of the previously killed bikers now wandered through the parking area, their burnt and broken bodies slowing their ability to move. This time Jessie was sure to thumb the safety to single fire to conserve ammo and quickly dispatch the undead. Jessie walked through the ruins of the three cabins destroyed by the blast. The fires were mostly burned out and the ruins just smoldered, smoke still rising into the cold desert air.

Grief and loss overwhelmed her as she looked at the destruction that was once their refuge. She couldn't fathom how a group of people could be so cruel. Her little girl, her princess, dead, and her family left in shambles. Jessie collapsed to the cold pavement, too tired even to cry, just looking at the macabre scene around her.

I can't sit like this. I have to survive. I have to focus and I have to take it all one step at a time.

Jessie stood unsteadily and walked towards the larger cabins. The cabin that had held Jessie and Bexar's supplies was in complete ruin, but it looked like some of the supplies might be salvageable, including a few boxes of .223 that Jessie saw at first glance.

Maybe I can check ammo off my must-have list.

She slowly checked each cabin in the rows of smaller cabins across the parking area. Using the technique that Jack and Bexar had developed the last time they'd cleared the Basin, Jessie opened a door and banged on it and then waited for a response. Every single cabin was found empty. Some had obviously been used by the bikers and their harem women, but some were untouched, clean, and had beds with blankets.

Now I can check shelter off my list.

The sun hung low in The Window, filling the cold desert sky with muted colors of purple, red, and pink—God's beauty overseeing unholy destruction and Jessie's profound loss. It was nearly dark by the time Jessie finished checking the cabins and the surrounding area in The Basin. There was no sign of Bexar.

If he was here, I would have found his body.

Before darkness fell, Jessie moved some of the supplies she'd found in the destroyed cabin to the Scout, including a case of MREs and two cases of ammo for her rifle. Jessie chose the cabin she and Bexar had stayed at over ten years before when they came to Big Bend for their honeymoon. She shut the curtains, locked the door, and collapsed on the bed, absolutely exhausted from the past two days, her ears still ringing from the blast that morning.

CHAPTER 50

Near Fort Stockton, TX
February 17, Year 1

Daylight was quickly fading by the time the group backtracked and made it to outside of Fort Stockton. The decision was made to drive through the night using NODs. Chivo would rest for the first half and he would switch with Apollo for the second half.

The drive through Fort Stockton and across I-10 was slow, but Apollo was able to drive around and evade the clusters of zombies, even with the Land Rover's headlights out, by using the flip-down night optic device. The discussion between Chivo and Apollo on which road to take north was settled for them when they found that Highway 18 crossed under I-10 and FM 1053 crossed over I-10. The number of shambling undead was still high on the Interstate and, after losing Odin, the thought of crossing under the Interstate and all of those zombies did not sit well with any of them.

The last hour of the trip was made in silence, each of the people in the Land Rover lost in their own thoughts. Lindsey held Apollo's hand while he drove. The open desert of West Texas between I-10 and I-20 was a heavy blanket of darkness, and with no lights, only Apollo could see anything past the hood of the Land Rover. A moan from the back of the Land Rover broke the peace. Apollo glanced in the rearview mirror at Chivo. "Did you let that fucker die and now he's going to bite your skinny ass?"

Chivo drew his pistol and pointed it at the man's head while searching for a pulse with his other hand. "No mano, he's got a pulse. Wait, do the zombies have pulses?"

"I seriously doubt it."

The man's eyes snapped open and blinked a few times very hard. Slowly his eyes came into focus and they found the muzzle of a pistol pointed at his face. "WHAT THE HELL?"

The man tried to sit up. Chivo held him down by his chest and holstered his pistol. "Hey man, I'm here to help. We saved your life today."

"What?"

"Cliff sent us to check on your group. We found you fighting that biker gang."

Bexar slowly looked around the inside of the Land Rover and caught a glimpse of long hair in the dark interior. "Jessie? Thank God, baby!"

Lindsey looked at Bexar, who sat up, not realizing that he had an IV in his arm. "My name is Lindsey."

Bexar looked at the woman and realized he didn't know her, then looked at the man next to him. "Where is my wife? Where is Jessie? She was there. The bikers had her, I saw her."

Chivo slowly shook his head. "I'm sorry, mano. You were the only one who survived the blast."

Bexar's shoulders slumped and the life seemed to dim out of his eyes, visible even in the semi-darkness. Lindsey took a deep breath, fighting back the urge to cry for the anguish plainly visible on the man's face.

Bexar realized that he was now completely alone. He'd failed, and his family was gone, all of them gone; the emptiness of that realization felt like a lead weight had pulled him to the bottom of the ocean. Chivo pumped up the pressure cuff on Bexar's arm and took his blood pressure before taking his pulse. Bexar felt the pressure cuff inflate and looked at it disinterestedly, seeing that there was an IV in his other arm. Immediately Bexar came to the realization that he was completely nude. "Where are my clothes? Who are you and where are you taking me?"

Chivo gave him a half smile. "First, what is your name, guy?"

"Bexar."

"OK Bexar, I'm Chivo, that's Apollo and Lindsey. The short version is that we work for a government organization. Another person in our organization made contact with you recently via HAM radio. He realized that you could be in danger and wanted us to come by and check on you since we were in the area."

"You were the sniper?"

"Yup."

"You set and blew the explosives?"

"No, I don't know how that happened. There was a van in the parking area; it caught fire and then exploded. It looked like a vehicle-borne IED, but I don't think those guys were stupid enough to do that."

"That was the bikers' van; they had a machine gun in it the first time they attacked us." Bexar drew in a sharp breath. "Don't you have anything for the pain?"

Chivo nodded, opened a red bag, dug out a small vial, and, with the hands of an experienced nurse, drew out the clear liquid before unscrewing the needle and inserting the syringe body onto the IV tube, administering the narcotic.

"There you go, mano. You know our story. What is yours?"

Slowly Bexar let his breath out as he felt warmth spread throughout his body from the shot. "I'm a Peace Officer, a cop, or at least I was one when this started. Jessie, my wife, and I, along with our daughter, fled our home to meet with our friends at our cache site ..."

It took Bexar about twenty minutes to give the Reader's Digest version of his journey, repeating himself and slurring some of his words as a result of the strong painkiller Chivo administered. A few minutes after finishing his story, Bexar succumbed to the warm comfort of the painkiller and fell asleep. Chivo checked his pulse and, satisfied that Bexar was probably going to be OK, rolled him to his side. It wasn't for a medical issue, but just because Bexar began snoring loudly.

CHAPTER 51

Cortez, CO
February 17, Year 1

Cliff's consciousness trickled slowly into his mind like a dripping faucet filling a sink; it took him a few moments to realize where he was and where he had been before everything filled with black. Cliff checked his body for injury, starting with wiggling his toes, and made a mental inventory of any major injuries. It took longer for Cliff to realize he was hanging upside down and outside of the aircraft. The sun barely peeked over the western horizon, giving Cliff a little light to investigate his surroundings.

I'm outside of the plane, but I feel the fuselage against me. I'm upside down and swinging. I'm in the safety harness. I think my rifle, my pistol, my gear, and my magazines are still on my body. The plane is nose down in a river or creek or canyon.

Cliff righted himself and felt like the world was spinning. A strong wave of pain rushed over him. He threw up, covering his chest with vomit, realizing that he must have a bad concussion. He gritted his teeth and determined that he might have cracked a couple of ribs, but everything else seemed intact. Cliff was finally able to figure out that he was dangling by the safety harness and lanyard outside of the open tail of the aircraft. Both of the wings appeared to be missing and the front of the plane was missing. Slowly, Cliff climbed up the side of the fuselage before cutting the lanyard and freeing himself from the plane. *At least my rifle is still slung across my body.* Using the light on his rifle, Cliff scanned the ruined interior of the

C-130. The pickup was still lashed to the cargo floor but was very badly damaged, and around the truck were the bodies of the PJs. All three of them were dead.

Damn.

Cliff climbed down the net seating to where the mangled bodies lay and was relieved to see that they did not and would not return as the undead. Cliff retrieved the loaded M4 magazines from their gear and did his best to secure them on his body. He didn't know exactly where he was, but Cliff knew from experience that he would need all the ammo he could find and carry. Cliff went through a mental checklist of gear that he should have on his body and, like a pilot pre-flighting an aircraft, touched each piece of kit to make sure he really had it.

No pistol.

It took a moment, but Cliff remembered holding the pistol and the prisoner on the ramp when the rocket struck. He realized the pistol had been lost and retrieved another one from Rick's body and placed it in his own holster. The fact that the prisoner had taken an impromptu skydiving lesson didn't bother Cliff in the least. He had the information he needed from that piece of trash, and had been planning on throwing him off the back of the aircraft regardless.

A few minutes later, Cliff climbed out of the upended fuselage and climbed down to the ground outside. He walked up the trail of ruined aircraft pieces. The remains of the engines still burned in the distance. A hundred yards away he found the nose of the aircraft, part of Garcia's body, and Arcuni still strapped into the pilot's seat. The instrument panel was crushed against the lower half of his body, but Arcuni's arms reached in the air towards Cliff while his teeth snapped towards the meal he so deeply wanted. Cliff raised his rifle and with a single shot released Arcuni to the peaceful death he deserved.

Shelter, water, and food. I need to get away from this clusterfuck and get shelter before every walking corpse in a hundred-mile radius comes to welcome me home.

Cliff walked stiffly up the road and away from the crashed aircraft, realizing that if he hadn't been *gently* asking his new friend questions at the back of the plane that he would probably be dead now. *There are worse things than death.* Cliff shook his head at the thought. He'd never given up before and he wouldn't start now.

Darkness filled the sky while Cliff walked into the outskirts of Cortez. Headlights bounced in the distance. They turned onto the street Cliff was walking on and headed towards him at a high rate of speed. Cliff melted into the darkness in an alley on his right, behind a dumpster. Barely peeking out from the edge of the dumpster with his rifle raised, he saw an old pickup truck, with three armed men in the bed, drive by quickly towards the crashed Hercules. Cliff edged around the dumpster and slowly walked in a crouch towards the edge of the buildings. His body began to ache from the beating it had received in the violent crash. He felt dizzy and his vision was blurry on the edges. He needed to rest. *Rest will come when I die … if I'm lucky.* Cliff took a shallow breath in deference to the pain from his ribs, gritted his teeth, and peeked out of the alley. No more vehicles appeared to follow the first and he didn't see any undead. He needed transportation like a toddler needs a cookie, so he took another shallow breath and unsteadily jogged back towards the wreckage and the militia's truck.

Groom Lake, NV

"Try again."

"Sir, no response, no radio contact."

"Jon, when will the next bird pass overhead Cortez?"

"Two hours, sir. Their comms could have failed."

"If that was true, Arcuni wouldn't have transmitted a mayday. Damnit. Damn this fucking new world." Wright threw his notepad across the room, "I'm going to check on our civilians. If I'm not back in thirty mikes, send someone to come kill my walking corpse." Wright stormed out of the radio hut.

The two airmen looked at each other. "What do you think?"

"I think they're dead or will be. No way they can survive on that side of the wire."

"Try raising SCC again to warn them of the arriving group. According to the memo that the major left, they should be arriving in about eight to ten hours."

"What the major needs to do is find a colony of hot female survivors in need of companions and bring them here."

"Hell yeah!"

The two young airmen high-fived.

Cortez, Co

Two men, dressed alike, both stood in awe of the incredible destruction found in the C-130's wreckage, while another climbed into the upended rear of the aircraft.

"Good shot, Brother James."

"Thank you, Brother Nick. I didn't think that the rocket would track that high."

"I wonder if this is the same plane that attacked our Brothers before?"

"How many other C-130s can there be flying around?"

Both of the men stood facing the furrow of destruction across the ground from the plane's crash, looking at the part of the fuselage sticking out of the creek bed. The third man climbed out of the tail of the aircraft, which stood twenty-five feet in the air.

Cliff slowly approached their old truck from behind, moving as quiet as a shadow, as fast as the wind. He knelt beside the truck and took aim at the man raising himself out of the destroyed fuselage and squeezed the trigger. The man's head snapped back and he fell into the plane's interior. The two other men stood with their backs to Cliff, both believing that their fellow militia member had slipped and fallen. Cliff took aim at the man on the right and pulled the trigger twice. The top of the man's head exploded in a red mist; the other man turned to face his falling friend with his mouth agape. Cliff fired once and struck the man in the right shoulder before standing and sprinting towards him. The man turned to face Cliff and tried to draw a pistol on his belt, but Cliff shot him in the left shoulder before closing the gap and stroking the man in the face with the butt of his rifle. The man's nose and mouth filled with blood and he fell to his knees, unable to raise either arm to hold his injured face.

Cliff kicked him to the ground, put his right boot on the man's throat, and held the muzzle of his rifle just inches away from the man's face.

"Who the fuck are you people?"

"The Chosen Tribe of Man." Blood spat from his mouth as he tried to talk.

"What is that?"

"The Prophet told of the end of the wicked, and we are now tasked with populating the Earth with the descendants of the Chosen Tribe to fill the New World with the righteous."

"The fuck you are." Cliff snapped the trigger of his M4 to the rear, punching a .223 hole in the man's forehead.

A damn cult. Well, that explains why they wanted the women and children.

Before leaving the bodies, Cliff checked their pockets for anything useful. Both men stunk as if they hadn't bathed in weeks, and they had only pocket Bibles in their back pockets.

Cliff checked the truck. It was old, but it started and ran; it would have to do. He needed a bus, something bulletproof like an old school bus, if he was going to be able to rescue the women being held prisoner. But this would have to do for now.

CHAPTER 52

Near Crane, TX
February 17, Year 1

Bexar didn't really fit in the spare pants and shirt that Apollo gave him, but it was significantly better than being completely nude on a road trip with three people he'd just met. However, he had no boots and no underwear, so they would stop if they found something they could raid. In this part of Texas, Bexar knew that people drove to Odessa or Fort Stockton to shop. He couldn't believe that he was traveling back towards the Metroplex, not after what it had taken to get to Big Bend in the first place. Now that his daughter and wife were dead, Bexar simply couldn't bear the thought of going back to The Basin. His best friend, his best friend's family, and his entire world had been killed there. Anger bubbled from deep in Bexar's being. He couldn't believe how stupid he had been to think they were safe anywhere. They should have stayed hidden and run instead of getting into a battle with the motorcycle tweakers.

Chivo sat behind the wheel of the Land Rover. The road to I-20 proved to be impassible, and calling on his experience driving from the Metroplex, Bexar suggested Highway 385 to bypass most of the major cities—although if they had made it to I-20, then they probably would have found him some underwear or at least some boots. Bexar touched the wound on his right leg through his pants and grimaced. The bullet wound was beginning to scab over, but the skin around the wound was becoming very tender and swollen; Bexar was worried that it was infected. An infection like that in the rotting hulk of modern society without modern medicine scared Bexar, who was sure that a major infection would be a slow and painful death sentence. Apollo injected his leg with what he claimed was a powerful antibiotic, but Bexar didn't recognize the name, not that he would have known what it was anyway.

Lindsey slept on the pile of bags beside him. On the surface, Bexar knew that she was attractive, but his mind ached in grief and even just riding in the SUV with this woman he'd just met caused sorrow to overwhelm him. Bexar really wished he could have a stiff drink.

The night was still dark and Bexar had no concept of what time it was or how long he had been asleep. The Land Rover lurched sharply to a stop, waking Lindsey with a gasp.

"There's something blocking the road ahead."

Apollo, blinking the sleep out of his eyes, flipped his NODs in front of his face. "Looks like a truck or a cargo box or something."

"Hey mano," Chivo called over his shoulder, "since you're still laid up, how about you drive, Lindsey holds security for you, and we'll recon whatever this is."

Bexar looked surprised that they were asking him to participate, even high on whatever painkiller they kept injecting him with. "Sure, you got it."

"OK, stay here, stay dark, and I'll flash twice with my tac-light when it's clear. If I flash rapidly, that means flip on the headlights and haul ass to get us for a hot extract."

Nodding, Bexar agreed and climbed over the front seat to take the driver's spot. Lindsey climbed into the passenger seat and held her M4 at the ready. Neither had the night vision devices that the other two had, but they could still see a little in each direction from the starlight.

Apollo and Chivo both walked into the desert perpendicular from the road and opposite from each other, neither of them needing to speak about their plan from the years of combat action they shared. Quickly, Lindsey and Bexar lost sight of the other two and could only wait patiently, hoping that the blockage ahead was nothing.

With no watch, no music, and no radio contact with the other two, time seemed to stand still in the inky black of the desert night. It felt like an absolute eternity, but in reality, only five minutes had elapsed from when Chivo and Apollo left the Land Rover to when the first muzzle flash and sharp staccato beat of an M4 being fired broke the desert peace.

The muted thumps of a pistol being fired also mixed into the symphony of war being played out on the other side of the windshield. The muzzle flashes slowed, and just as suddenly as they had begun, they stopped. Bexar stared at the darkness, wondering if something had happened to the other two, when a flashlight flashed twice in the distance. Bexar slowly drove forward, unable to see very far in front of the SUV. A half-mile later, Bexar saw Apollo and Chivo kneeling in the middle of the road facing opposite directions with their rifles raised. Bexar stopped and the two of them climbed into the back of the Land Rover, both smelling like cordite.

"All right, mano, flip on your headlights and drive. We need to move quickly, because I don't know if there are any more where that came from."

Bexar flipped on the headlights and toggled the high beams on. On the road ahead of him lay a half-dozen men, all shot in the head. Driving around the bodies, Bexar brought the Land Rover around the roadblock that turned out to be two semi-truck trailers offset to create a kill zone for ambush. Past the trailers were piles of clothes, shoes, and other items. Off the road to the right, a headlight beam lit a scene that Bexar recognized instantly. In the light, Bexar saw that a cattle pen had been erected and, standing in the pen, clawing at the SUV as it drove past, were two dozen completely nude zombies. Instantly Bexar realized what had happened at the roadblock. People were robbed of their belongings, then killed and discarded as walking corpses. It was more than Bexar could fathom.

Bexar slowly shook his head. "What the fuck is wrong with these people?"

Chivo stuck his head over the front seat. "I don't know, but when we saw that we decided we didn't want to find out. Oh, I got you these. I hope you like them."

Chivo handed up a pair of worn Red Wing work boots, sized twelve wide. They were a bit large for Bexar's feet, but shoes that were a little big were much better than no shoes at all, and he put them on while he drove. Apollo seemed to think that where they were going would have supply stores and that he might be able to be properly clothed and outfitted again, but until then this was still better than being naked.

The destruction in the town was staggering. Like a movie about a nuclear war, Bexar thought. Around them, even in the middle of the night, they could see that many of the homes and businesses lay in ruin. And here and there in the middle of all the destruction, they'd see a home standing like nothing had happened and the residents were only away on a vacation.

Apollo tapped Bexar's shoulder and pointed behind them. "We have a bunch of friends joining our parade. You might want to speed it up a little." Bexar looked in the side mirror and couldn't see any detail, but saw movement in the shadows. He focused on the road ahead and sped up.

"Chivo, how many more gas cans do you have?"

"Three. Five gallons each."

Bexar nodded. "After we lose our tail, we need to stop and top off."

As they left town, the eastern horizon faintly glowed orange with the impending sunrise.

CHAPTER 53

Cortez, CO
February 17, Year 1

Cliff drove into the outskirts of the town with the truck's headlights off. In the snow and the darkness, and with no hard intelligence of where The Tribe held its boundaries, he didn't want to chance being detected. Cliff turned off the main road and onto Empire Street, looking for a place to hide the truck from any roving patrols and to take shelter for the night. In his condition, Cliff wasn't sure he would be able to fight more than one or two people directly. He needed time to heal, he needed time to recon, he needed food, and he needed time to rest.

He took the next left and drove slowly, scanning the dark homes for one that would give him a place to hide the truck. At the end of the road, Cliff found a copse of trees that would have to do for now. He drove over the curb and through someone's yard, if that person was even still alive, and parked the truck behind the trees. Cliff climbed out and broke a branch off one of the smaller trees. He walked south back to the road and used the branch to brush the snow across the tire tracks and his foot tracks. There was nothing he could do about the light covering of snow on the road.

A single moan suddenly caught Cliff's attention. He spun in place to see an elderly corpse tripping through the snow to his left. More moans filled the cold air. Cliff turned and saw another half-dozen undead following the path he'd left driving to the end of the road.

I can't leave bodies out that would be too obvious for any patrols. I can't waste ammo. Damnit! I don't have time for this crap.

Cliff trotted towards the two-story house he was nearest, reached the side of the garage, climbed the wooden privacy fence, reached onto the roof, and painfully pulled himself up. On the roof he was safe, except that more undead would gather the longer he stayed visible. The second-story windows were over the garage. Cliff knocked on the first one loudly and waited for a response inside. Hearing nothing, Cliff broke the glass, punching the muzzle of his rifle through. He would have to gamble that a patrol wouldn't know if the glass was broken before.

The tactical light attached to Cliff's M4 illuminated the room, and dozens of lifeless eyes stared back at him. They were the dolls of a little girl whose bedroom he'd just entered, each dressed in a different outfit, but Cliff just thought they were creepy. The bedroom door stood open. Cliff walked to it and glanced into the hallway. No blood, no signs of death, and the house smelled normal. Cliff could only hope that meant the home was abandoned and no former residents still roamed the halls.

Twenty minutes later, Cliff verified the house was vacant; it appeared to have been hastily evacuated as all the dresser drawers were left open, clothes were thrown about, and some photos had been taken from the walls.

In the kitchen, Cliff found a fridge full of rotten leftovers and a can of stew and a can of tuna in the pantry. Luckily both cans had pull-tops, as he had no can opener. In the master bathroom, Cliff found a first-aid kit as well as an expired bottle of Tylenol. Expired or not, Cliff needed something to help take a little of the pain's edge off.

The garage was full of junk and a small gas grill. The propane bottle felt like it had a little left in it. Cliff returned to the kitchen, gathered the two largest pots he could find, and quietly opened the back door. Moments later, he returned with two pots full of snow. Back in the garage, Cliff pulled one of the small decorative windows off the garage door so he could vent the burning grill, turned on the propane tank, clicked the sparker, and was happy to see flames coming from the burners. Both pots went on the grill and Cliff only had to wait for the snow to melt and then boil.

With fresh water, Cliff knew he could survive; the rest just took time and planning. Tylenol swallowed as well as a full pot of water consumed, Cliff checked that all the doors were locked, lay on the master bed, and quickly fell asleep.

CHAPTER 54

Barnhart, TX
February 18, Year 1

"Look, I know you're all about going in straight lines, but I'm telling you that you don't want to go through San Angelo. It's the biggest town on this damn highway."

Chivo, who was driving, looked at Bexar riding in the passenger seat.

"Fine, mano, if that's what you say, but where else can we go?"

Bexar flipped through the map book. "Take a left on 163. We'll have to go out of our way, but it should be better. Much smaller towns."

In the back of the Land Rover, Apollo and Lindsey slept. The drive was taking much longer than Apollo had estimated. The fuel tank had been topped off about thirty minutes earlier, and only one jerry can of diesel fuel was left. All the detour sounded like to Chivo was a way to get stranded without fuel. Even though he'd grown up in Laredo, he'd left for the Army at eighteen and didn't really know this part of Texas very well.

After the last roadblock, Bexar told Chivo and Apollo the story about the roadblock in Comanche where he'd ambushed the townspeople, the same people who would have taken all they had and leave them to die. They had to be careful, but Chivo hoped that the darkness and using NODs to drive without headlights would help give them an element of surprise. It had already. Bexar's recounting also included the bikers herding zombies to overrun the town, or so he thought. Neither he nor Jack had been willing to investigate the town any further and risk a run-in with the bikers. Looking back, they probably should have forced a confrontation and killed every biker they saw. The Pistoleros had ruined his life.

Chivo scanned the road and surrounding area. This little Texas town looked more like an oilfield worker's camp than an actual town, but some of the greatest civilizations in history had started from humble beginnings.

The next three hours passed in silence, a handful of small towns passing in the darkness. Some looked devastated; others looked perfectly normal, but in no town did they see any signs of the living. Bexar and Chivo counted a total of seventy-four undead that they saw and avoided.

By the time they made the outskirts of Comanche, the sky was growing bright with the tip of the sun peeking over the horizon. Chivo stopped in the middle of Highway 377 and woke up Apollo and Lindsey.

"Bexar says he went through this town before and they had an ambush planned. He also said that the biker gang ran a herd of zombies through the town. To make things more fun, we need fuel. So all hands on deck, guns up, look alive back there."

Everyone took the opportunity to get out of the Land Rover, stretch, and answer nature's call. Bexar limped painfully around the back of the Land Rover and climbed into the rear compartment. Ten minutes later, the group drove through the middle of Comanche, Texas.

The street signs along the main road were all missing, the stoplights pushed to the ground and flattened. Windows were broken and the paint was stripped off the first floor of buildings along the roadway.

"Looks like the biker's herd of undead came through with such force that they destroyed everything in their path," said Apollo, in awe of the destruction. Across the parking area of the courthouse in the town square sat a white bus. Apollo pulled alongside the bus. "I bet that bus is a diesel. We should siphon while we have the chance."

"That's a chain bus."

Apollo looked in the rearview mirror at Bexar. "What's a chain bus?"

"See the windows? See how they're covered in steel mesh? It's a prisoner transport bus for the Texas Department of Corrections, the state prisons."

"So?"

"So it was probably full of prisoners at one point."

Chivo climbed out and retrieved the empty jerry cans from the roof rack. Apollo used the last full can to top off the Land Rover's tank before carrying it to the back of the bus, where Chivo pried open the fuel door and snaked a piece of garden hose into the filler spout. Moments later, Chivo spit fuel out of his mouth and cursed, but the diesel fuel was transferring to the first jerry can.

Lindsey and Apollo stood guard with Chivo. Bexar, not able to walk very well or very far, leaned against the hood of the Land Rover with his rifle. The sound of a chain scraping on the concrete broke the silence. Bexar turned and saw a large zombie shambling towards him in an off-white jumpsuit. The leg irons tripped the man every third step or so and he fell to the pavement, his hands still handcuffed and the handcuffs run through the metal loop on the leather control belt around his waist.

"Guys, we've got company! You might want to speed things up a bit!"

Bexar raised his rifle and fired a single shot, giving the prisoner the death penalty.

Apollo trotted around the front of the bus and began rapidly firing his rifle. "TIME TO LEAVE! WE'RE IN TROUBLE!"

Lindsey ran to Apollo and began firing her rifle. Chivo pulled the hose out of the bus, screwed on the lid of the half-full jerry can, and threw it on the Land Rover's roof rack. The other cans, still empty, were thrown on the roof. Bexar climbed into the passenger seat; Chivo dove behind the wheel and started the engine. At the sound of the engine, Apollo and Lindsey turned and ran as fast as they could to the open back hatch of the Land Rover and dove. Chivo accelerated sharply, causing two of the empty jerry cans to fall off, banging loudly on the roadway.

"Fuck it, man. Leave them! We're about to be overrun!"

As they passed the opposite side of the town square, a huge mass of undead bodies shuffled towards the SUV.

"Damn, looks like the herd of zombies the bikers used never left!"

Ten minutes later, the following herd of zombies were out of sight and Bexar was pointing out the gas station he had used as a shooting position and where the roadblock was.

"Hey guys, since we're going through Stephenville, would you like to stop and meet my friend Flo who runs a little convenience store?"

CHAPTER 55

The Basin
February 18, Year 1

Jessie woke as the cabin began to warm from the morning sun. Her entire body hurt, her ears were still ringing, and her swollen face was very tender to the touch. Jessie climbed out of bed and the room spun; she had to sit back down.

This is going to be tough.

Jessie slowly stood again, steadying herself against the cabin wall. She needed to eat, but couldn't stomach the thought of eating without getting some water first. She was dismayed to find that the water didn't work anymore. While Bexar restarted the water system, he'd explained how it worked, so Jessie held a little hope that she could figure it out. If not, then she would drive to Panther Junction and use the hand-pumped well water there.

Jessie put on her rifle, press checked the chamber to verify a round was ready to go, unlocked the door, and gingerly stepped out into the sun. The bodies from the previous day's battle still lay where they'd fallen. She was fairly sure that there weren't any walkers left, but she couldn't be sure. It took a few moments for her eyes to adjust to the bright morning light and she took the opportunity to scan the cabin area for any movement. All she saw were two mule deer grazing on the north end. Slowly, Jessie walked down to the parking area and continued to the north. Where the trail intersected with the cabin area was a service road and the first water tank. The fence gate stood open and after walking around the tank, Jessie found two dead bikers, each with a hole in his skull.

Maybe Bexar did this?

Jessie looked at the small shack that covered the plumbing for the tank. One of the valves looked scratched up and the scratches looked fresh and had no rust. There wasn't a wrench that Jessie could see, just a long scrap piece of metal. She tried to push on the valve with the scrap metal, but the valve wouldn't budge. Jessie slowly walked down to the Scout in the parking area and found that Malachi's canvas tool bag was still tucked under the passenger's seat. The only tool that looked like it might work was a big pair of vise grips. Jessie went back up the short service road and barely got the vise grips to lock closed on the valve. She pushed and the valve wouldn't budge. Jessie picked up the piece of metal and began swinging at the vise grips like a baseball bat, striking the back of the handle with each blow. Slowly the valve started to turn, and a few hits later, the valve turned ninety degrees. Jessie heard water rush into the pipes. A few taps on the tank with the vise grips and the tank sounded full.

If that didn't work, I don't know what will.

Jessie walked back to her cabin and tried the sink. After a few moments of sputtering air and gargling sounds, water rushed out of the faucet. Satisfied, Jessie locked the cabin door, propped her rifle against the toilet, and took a cold but very satisfying shower.

CHAPTER 56

Groom Lake, NV
February 18, Year 1

Major Wright sat in conference room D-1 once again, this time without Cliff, but attended by Jake from Colorado and Mike from Texas, the elected leaders of each group. The civilian rules were laid out in a simple single-page document. It contained basic rules like no theft and no assault, and the general needs for a civilized community. The second page showed a duty roster dividing the workload of the facility. Simply built, once again, but dividing the tasks of cooking, cleaning, and maintenance across a few teams of people rotated on a schedule. It was important that there were skilled people in each group, including one who was an experienced radio operator. Quickly the conversation turned to Cliff.

"Jake, the last transmission was a *mayday* transmitted only once by Arcuni. We've completely lost contact since then. We won't have another satellite pass over Cortez for three more hours. I don't know where they were when that call went out, but that's the place we're going to start."

"If something happened and the plane crashed, I hope my guys' wives and children weren't on it. I hope Sara wasn't on it. The Tribe was bad enough. I don't want to see what else could happen."

"Your group aren't the only survivors we've contacted who have had troubles with rogue groups trying to plunder like warlords. There's a group in Texas that was overrun by a motorcycle gang."

"Did you fly to them as well?"

"No, it's classified."

Mike slammed his hand on the table. "Classified my ass! There is no more classified. If you haven't noticed, we're in the goddamned Area 51. Everything has gone to hell. Who are you worried about, the fucking Soviets? It isn't 1980 anymore, guy."

Wright took a deep breath and sighed, shaking his head. "You're right. I know you're right. OK. A group of formal Special Forces who work for a joint CIA and DEA taskforce fought their way back to the United States from central Mexico. They intercepted the other group and eliminated the biker gang, but found and saved only a single survivor. They are en route to another facility similar to this one in Texas. Same one our new President is at."

"OK, what then?"

"Quite frankly, I don't know. Cliff had his own plan that fit his mission parameters. He didn't tell me what the entire plan was or even what all the assets were."

"Where in Texas?"

"Outside of Dallas."

"There's a secret base outside of Dallas? How did they ever build it?"

"I have no idea. Cliff didn't go into it. Besides, it doesn't matter."

Jake said, "Dallas to Cortez is only about a fifteen-hour drive. Could they go after our kidnapped members?"

Wright shook his head. "I have no idea. We've had no contact with them since yesterday, and I don't even know if they survived the trip to the other facility."

"So you're just going to give up?"

"No, we're going to be patient. First, we have to figure out where the plane is, if there are survivors, and if your people were on that plane. As of right now, we don't know enough to act."

"Well that's not good enough!" Jake stormed out of the room.

CHAPTER 57

Cortez, CO
February 18, Year 1

Cliff woke with the morning sun and considered the most pressing issue he had at the moment— where to pee. Figuring gravity would drain most of it away without any extra water, Cliff opted to pee in the master shower. He had blood in his urine. As violent as the plane crash had been, Cliff wasn't surprised. His kidneys had probably taken a beating with the rest of his body. That meant he needed to drink more water and he needed another day or two of rest. First, he needed to get a message to Wright that he had survived and where he was.

Glancing out the window, Cliff was glad to see his friends from last night had wandered off. He would still need to be quiet, because the last thing he needed was to attract any unwanted attention. Cliff was in no shape to fight and would try to avoid a fight until he could heal up some.

After drinking the second pot of melted water from the previous night, Cliff unlocked the back door and quietly walked into the cold winter's air. Across the road from the backyard was an open field. With the snow, he had a plan.

Twenty minutes later, Cliff went back into the house after stomping "CLIFF" into the snow in thirty-foot-tall letters. He went to the second story and climbed out of the broken window from the little girl's room. A few moments later he stood on the roof of the house and carefully kicked the snow off the roof to form a plus sign.

Once back in the house, Cliff filled the pots up with snow again and began replenishing his water supply while he ate the can of stew cold. He wasn't sure how long he was going to need to stay hidden and rest, but he was going to need more food very soon; even if Wright found his signal with a satellite pass, he had no idea how they could help him. Cliff was on his own to complete his mission. But first he was going to have to survive.

CHAPTER 58

The Basin
February 18, Year 1

It took an hour of being wrapped in every blanket in the cabin for Jessie to stop shivering from her cold shower, but at least she felt clean. Clean for now, at least. She still had a very long day ahead of her. Dressed in her scavenged clothes, Jessie pulled on her filthy scavenged blanket poncho.

Jessie retrieved a sheet from another cabin and cut a dozen long strips of cloth. For the next hour, she sat in the sunlight weaving a rope from the piece of cloth while trying to figure out what her next move should be. No matter how hard she thought, she couldn't fathom what might have happened to Bexar.

Two ropes completed, Jessie drove the Scout into the middle of the parking area and began dragging bodies to it. After a few were piled up, Jessie tied one of the sheet-ropes around the bodies and then tied the bodies to the hitch. Slowly, she used the Scout to drag the bodies to the tent camping area so they would be out of her sight and smell, and so any scavenging animals would stay away.

The gruesome task of moving the bodies took a few hours, and on the last return trip to the cabins, Jessie turned and stopped the Scout by the Basin's ranger station, climbed out, and looked around. The physical labor of moving the bodies caused her body to ache and she felt incredibly weak. She looked up at landscape, Emory Peak, and began to cry.

Eventually, the tears stopped and Jessie remembered that the radio was probably still in the cabinet on the mountaintop. Jessie was in no condition to make the long hike to the top—not yet—but she was confident she would be soon. First, she needed more supplies. She would drive back to Terlingua tomorrow to get all she could from the general store. That would be a start.

CHAPTER 59

I-20
February 18, Year 1

"I can't believe we're here. We're really close to my group's original cache site that was overrun in the beginning. That's why we fled to Big Bend. What is this place?"

Apollo shrugged. "Best I can guess is that it is a bunker or supply cache. Cliff sent us to another underground supply cache in the middle of nowhere west Texas en route to you. That place was something else. Completely underground, and you would have never known it was there. Absolutely cavernous, and it seemed like there was any kind of gear you could think of short of a tank."

"So if this is just a supply cache, are we going to stay here or what?"

Chivo shook his head, "I have no idea, mano. We tried to reach Cliff back before I-10, but someone else was handling comms and directed us here. Our plan was to go to Area 51."

"That's what we were planning until I crashed the Wagoneer. Fuck."

Bexar's emotional burden was obvious to the other three, and they had no idea what to do about it.

"Hey mano, nothing more now than to survive. As long as you make it, so do their memories. That's all we can hope for in our new world."

Bexar took a heavy breath. "I guess so."

The Land Rover slowed, turned into the broken gate, and passed a small guard shack with a sign that read "Waxahachie Creek Park."

CHAPTER 60

Big Bend National Park
March 1, Year 1

Jessie stood alone. The clear morning air betrayed the previous week's hard work, dragging the dead bodies out of the cabin area using the Scout and driving all over the park and area gathering enough supplies to survive. The work was slow and hard, given that she was completing it by herself, and the beating she'd taken at the hands of the bikers caused her whole body to throb in pain. The explosion surely hadn't helped her in that regard.

The previous two days, huge storms had passed through; Jessie never realized how violent the weather could be in the high desert. She had always visited the park during the winter months, never this late in the year. Leaves and branches covered the parking lot from the wind and the hail, and the lightning was incredible, but at least all the rain washed much of the blood off the pavement by the cabins.

The morning sun reached over the top of the desert mountains. In her scavenged motorcycle boots and clothes, and with her M4 slung across her chest, she leaned against a tree to dry heave again. Her scant breakfast of MRE crackers with peanut butter had already been vomited into the bushes next to her cabin. This morning, she'd waken up feeling nauseous, and her breasts were sore. The tears followed specks of puke on her jeans and boots as she began walking up the trail to Emory Peak again, still feeling a little dizzy and nauseated.

If it was a concussion, it would have been better by now. And why would my breasts hurt?

No, it can't be that. That couldn't happen, not now.

Jessie climbed on top of a small boulder that let her look over The Basin from the trail. She looked at the morning sunlight warming the air below, a soft yellow glow giving the appearance of peace, but Jessie knew no peace. Her dreams were punctuated by the horror of the day she watched her daughter die and by a vision of Bexar. She wasn't sure if the memory were real or not. Jessie walked back to the trail, starting her trek to Emory Peak and to the Yaesu HAM radio that she hoped would still be in the locker on the mountaintop.

If there's no body, he's not dead. He was here—I saw him—before the explosion. He has to be alive. I have to find him. I need help. I need to reach out to Cliff for help.

Acknowledgments

The people who make a single novel happen are numerous; it takes dedication and support from many facets of an author's life. For a second and more books in a series the support and dedication is tremendous. First and foremost my wife, Morgan. Without her love, support, and faith in me I could have never even started on this journey, much less made it to this point. Her willingness to not only say "go" but to be my first line beta reader, biggest fan, and my cheerleader when I needed it most wasn't exactly stated in our wedding vows, but she is my rock and my best friend and without her help the first step of this journey would never have been taken. My father lived long enough to know that I was writing a story and that I planned on publishing it, but he didn't live long enough to see what has happened since. I know he would be proud even if a single book more failed to sell. From the beginning he taught me that I can accomplish anything I choose, but expect to work very hard to make the accomplishment happen. He was right and is right today.

Winlock Press, the imprint of Permuted Press, plucked my story of three prepper families out of Texas from the indie-author world and gave me the push to get the whole Winchester Undead rolling like I never had thought it could. None of that would have happened without all of my friends, new friends, and readers getting behind a story with excitement, telling their friends about Winchester: Over and the start of a new zombie apocalypse prepper series.

Numerous friends have reached out and helped me chase down details and given advice. Thank all of you: Mark, Jerry, Jason, the other Mark, Freeflier, Kristi, DFA 1 and DFA 2 ... the list continues. Thank you, all of you.

Through the course of two releases in the series I have grown to know my characters, watching their journey unfold before me. Some of the twists and turns surprised me, but the characters told me it would be OK as long as I held on for the ride. So far they have been right. I hope as the series continues that the characters become as cherished to you as they have become to me. The foundation began twenty years ago, the project continues to be built, expanding through age and life's journeys ... DFA.

Keep your go-bags packed and be ready!

~Dave

About the Author

Dave Lund is a former Texas motorcycle cop with nearly a decade in active law enforcement. Previously he was a full-time skydiving instructor and competitor (in Canopy Piloting, aka swooping) with over 3,000 skydives. He also has a love for air-cooled VWs, including the 1973 Superbeetle that he built and drives.

Website: http://www.winchesterundead.com
Facebook: https://www.facebook.com/winchesterundead
Twitter: @WUzombies
Instagram: https://instagram.com/f8industries/
Tumblr: http://winchesterundead.tumblr.com/
Pinterest: https://www.pinterest.com/f8Industries/

The *Author Dave Lund Winchester Undead Newsletter*, the place for unique content, special contests and tales of adventure can be found here: http://winchesterundead. com/main/winchester-undead-newsletter/